Poetry by DEAD Men

MEGAN SHADE

This is a work of fiction. Names, characters, places, and incidents are products of the author's imagination or are used fictitiously and are not to be construed as real. Any resemblance to actual events, locales, organizations, or persons, living or dead, is entirely coincidental. Any products, companies, organizations, people, etc. are used fictitiously, and the author has no connection to the organizations, products, or companies in this book.

Copyright © 2025 by Megan Shade

All rights reserved.

No portion of this book may be reproduced in any form without written permission from the publisher or author, except as permitted by U.S. copyright law.

Published by: Shade Made Publishing LLC

First Edition

ISBN: 979-8-9878324-3-1

Editing by Sara Coombes: https://saracoombescom.wordpress.com/

Cover Art by Ink and Laurel: https://www.inkandlaurel.com/

Contents

For Michael

1991–2005

AUTHOR'S NOTE

This book includes physical, verbal, and emotional abuse from a romantic partner (not the main male character). For anyone this may resonate with, help is available, and you're not alone.
National Domestic Violence Hotline: https://www.thehotline.org/
1-800-799-7233

This story also contains a character whose younger brother has childhood cancer. Consider donating to pediatric cancer research here.
https://www.stjude.org/

It is highly encouraged that you enjoy this book with a lavender latte (yes, it's a real thing, and my favorite drink. May I suggest iced with sweet cream cold foam?) and while you're drinking it, make sure to raise your glass to the strength and resilience of women.

If you needed a reminder of how amazing you are today, this is it.

PROLOGUE

It's said by those who survive that time slows when you think you're going to die.

That's only partly true.

As our tires squeal and the metal frame of the car crunches in a deafening roar, I process *everything*.

Each second feels like thirty as pieces of glass fly around my head like glittering, lethal diamonds. I'm thrown back into my seat, all too aware of the searing agony of the bones in my nose snapping beneath the airbag. The sharp bite of pain when my seat belt catches, cutting into my skin as it tightens across my chest and collarbone.

My stomach lurches, and suddenly we're upside down, then upright again, then upside down. Rolling and rolling, orange and yellow sparks exploding in my periphery, brighter than fireworks on New Year's Eve.

The smell of gasoline and burning rubber makes my head swim, and the metallic tang of blood dripping from my nose into my mouth almost makes me vomit.

My whole life flashes before my eyes. My parents' disappointment. Molly's grief. Birthdays and graduations and late nights writing poetry beneath my covers. The sloping lines of the words gifted to me—the ones I've kept tucked close to my heart.

Harrison's poems.

Bobby's lyrics.

Someone cries out my name—a deep, desperate prayer.

An anguished, broken plea.

I'm aware of every miniscule detail as time slows to near stagnancy. And yet, I don't even have time to scream as my head smashes into the side window, and the world goes dark.

NOW

August 2024

Roses are red, writing poems takes a while
But for you, I will try it, to see your bright smile
I want to spend time learning all of your traits
Will you join me this Friday for dinner at eight?
—An attempt at poetry by Harrison Rouchester, requesting a first date with
Beth Winters

I glare at the stairs, certain if I try to go up and down them again, I'm going to break my neck. On cue, my ankles wobble, and I mentally curse myself for buying these absurdly tall heels. When I handed over my credit card in exchange for the gorgeous Jimmy Choo platforms, I did so with the expectation that, based on the price tag, they included some sort of technology that would keep me from teetering like a skyscraper in a storm.

"Harrison! Have you seen my bracelet?" My voice bounces down the marble steps like a rubber ball, pinging from wall to wall until it fades away. There's no answer, and I sigh, a pang of annoyance settling in my stomach. Even though we're due to leave for our engagement party in five minutes, I'd bet good money my fiancé is in his study answering emails or taking calls instead of getting ready.

"Harrison! Can you hear me?" I yell louder, leaning over the banister.

Nothing.

I start to head back to the bedroom, but my body turns back without permission.

"I want to go back to reporting!" I shout, the words escaping before I can stop them. My heart slams violently against my ribcage, and I suck in a sharp breath, my fingernails digging into my palms as I brace myself for the slam of a door or footsteps thundering up the stairs.

But they never come, and the silence is all the confirmation I need to know that Harrison is, in fact, in his study where he can't hear me.

Unclenching my fists, I force myself to exhale. It's the first time I've said those words out loud, and as the echo of my confession tapers away along with my moment of impulsive—or maybe reckless—bravery, I feel a confusing mixture of disappointment and relief pulsing behind my sternum.

While I *have* been wanting to get this particular conversation with Harrison over with, shouting the news from the top of the stairs certainly wouldn't be the best way to do it.

Out of habit, I reach to fidget with my bracelet—thirty-seven interlocking infinity signs—the gold tarnished from years of worrying at the delicate chain. For nearly half my adult life, it's been a permanent fixture on my wrist, but when my fingers touch my skin where the metal should be, it's bare.

Sighing, I wobble back to my nightstand, picking up my Morgan Harper Nichols book to make sure the bracelet isn't hiding underneath it, then peek behind the bed, the knots in my stomach twisting tighter with each passing second.

I've looked *everywhere*.

For the third time in the last hour, I crack open my jewelry chest, but this time, I let my fingers find the small divot on the edge of the plush satin bottom. A cold sweat breaks out on my neck as I hold my breath, listening for the squeak of a door or footfalls in the hallway.

There's still nothing but silence.

My heart races as I pop open the false bottom, and with quiet, efficient movements, swipe a hand across the thick stack of papers inside in case the bracelet somehow fell through, but all my fingers find is a half-written manuscript, a guitar pick, and some loose pages, all covered in cobwebs.

Metaphorical ones, but the sentiment is the same.

Popping the bottom back in place, I flip through the dozens of papers folded in with my jewelry: Harrison's poems. My chest warms as I pick one at random and open it.

You look so very pretty, in the bright lights of the city.
Yes, you certainly do. Oh, how I love you.

Despite being on edge about my missing bracelet, the poem makes me smile. I'm not sure Harrison's aware of how horrible his attempts at poetry are, and I'll never tell him. Each one is a little treasure, proof that he's willing to put in effort to make our relationship work.

The door creaks, and I jump when Harrison pops his head into our room. My heart slides into my throat as I realize how close he was to finding me digging in my box of secrets—the evidence of the girl I used to be—and for a second, I wonder if he heard my confession after all.

But no.

He's smiling, without even the slightest hint of disappointment in his perfectly groomed features, and I let out a sigh of relief.

"There you are," he says, eyes gleaming as he scans me from head to toe.

"Erhm…" I clear my throat. "I've been calling for you. Everything okay?" I ask, forcing a bright smile.

"Just catching up on work," he says, his mouth pinching in.

Not for the first time in the past few weeks, I consider asking if there's a problem at his firm. If there's more to the endless calls and constant emails than he's letting on. The words dance inside my cheeks and along my tongue, but I hold them back. Bringing up my concerns will only make him think I'm questioning his ability to handle things at work, and I don't want to fight tonight.

"You look beautiful," he says, changing the subject as he slides his arms loosely around my hips. "Is this what you're wearing?"

There's an undercurrent of something I can't quite place in his voice. Disappointment, maybe?

My smile falters, even as he bends down to brush a kiss across my neck. "Do you not like it?" I ask, trying to keep my voice light. Molly and I spent *hours* trying to find the perfect dress for tonight, and even though I'd preferred an ankle length champagne sheath, I'd specifically chosen this fitted navy one because it shows off my legs, Harrison's favorite feature.

"No, it's great." He nips at the skin above my collarbone. "I was just hoping you'd wear that purple one I like so much."

The navy dress I'd thought was perfect just a few hours ago suddenly feels too tight. Too short. Like I'm a child playing dress up.

I plaster on a smile. "I thought you'd like this one. I chose it for you."

Harrison takes a step back, tilting his head as he looks me up and down, and my cheeks sting with warmth. In a heartbeat, I'm fifteen again, my mother making me spin in a circle to judge if I'm presentable for the country club or one of Dad's political fundraisers.

"You know what, you're right. The purple one's my favorite, too." I say before he can answer, smiling so big my cheeks cramp. I head to my closet and grab the dress, pushing away the long-ago memories embedded into the fabric.

"By the way, have you seen my bracelet?" I call, grateful I can't see Harrison roll his eyes at my question. He *hates* my bracelet.

"Can't say I have," he says, his voice moving closer.

My shoulders fall, my mind reeling. *Where could it be?*

Harrison appears in the arched doorway. "You don't need it tonight, anyway."

"Why's that?" I ask, pulling the dress over my head.

"Well…" He pulls a long purple box out of his back pocket and lifts the lid. "I thought you could wear this." A glittering flash of silver hits the light where, nestled inside a bed of black velvet, sits a thin platinum chain, a single pea-sized pendant hanging from it with the letters HR carved into the polished metal.

"What do you think?" he asks, handing me the box and gesturing for me to turn around so he can zip me up.

I trail my fingers along the bracelet, impressed that Harrison picked this out himself. He usually opts for flashier jewelry. Gaudy, even. But this is understated and elegant, almost exactly the kind of thing I'd pick out for myself.

"I love it. It's beautiful," I say, pulling it out of the box.

Harrison finishes fastening the clip at the top of my zipper, and I turn back around, handing him the bracelet so he can clasp it for me.

He leans down, pressing a kiss to where my pulse beats in my wrist. "I like seeing my initials there. Especially that R, future Mrs. Rouchester," he says with a bright smile, his thumb caressing the pendant tenderly.

"I do, too. Finally moving up in the alphabet," I joke, letting him lead me out of the closet, but I pause when a hint of yellow gold catches my eye on one of the shelves. My heart leaps, and I reach for it, only for my excitement to shatter when I see it's the buckle of a strappy heel and not my other bracelet. The smile drops from my lips, my nostrils flaring as I let out a frustrated huff.

Harrison stops. "Something wrong?" he asks.

"No, sorry. I just thought I'd found my bracelet for a second—"

He drops my hand, his jaw ticking as he storms into our room.

"Wait, what's wrong?" I ask, fumbling behind him, nearly falling over my own feet.

Stupid shoes.

"What's wrong? What do you *think* is wrong, Elizabeth?" He whirls around to face me. "I spent a lot of time and money having something made special for you—and all you care about is that ugly piece of crap!"

"That's not true! I just thought I saw—"

"Right. You weren't hoping you'd found it so you could wear it tonight? Nevermind the new one!" Harrison's voice drops to a low rumble as he mumbles, "I should've thrown it away when I found it this morning."

"You wouldn't—" I pause, clenching my fists. "Wait. What do you *mean* when you found it?"

Harrison stomps to his sock drawer, shuffling through it until he pulls out a delicate gold bracelet—*my* bracelet—which he unceremoniously tosses on the vanity like loose change.

"There. Happy?" he snaps, staring at me for a long moment, his chest rising and falling in anger.

A car honks outside our brownstone, and Harrison turns on his heel. "If it means so much to you, go ahead. Wear it," he says, disappearing through the door without a second glance.

Heat flashes in my belly as I stare at the bracelet. Not only because Harrison hid it, but because of the careless way he threw it aside—like it was worthless. I snatch the gold chain from the polished wood and, using my teeth to hold one end in place, fasten it right next to my new one. It takes several deep breaths to relax my shoulders and force my feet to move, but I somehow manage it, shaking my head to squash down the anger making my body hot.

I *really* don't want to fight tonight.

I follow Harrison to the car, scooting to the far side of the bench seat, and his eyes flick to my wrist. He doesn't say a word, but his face falls, his lips tipping down into a frown.

I look away, ignoring the way his shoulders slump forward. I might not want to fight on the way to our engagement party, but I'm not ready to forgive him, either.

Harrison sighs, dropping his head back against the seat. "Hey," he says, taking my hand. "I'm sorry. I shouldn't have taken your bracelet. And I'd never throw it away. You know that. I just…" He sighs, rubbing a hand through his hair. "I'm really proud of the one I picked out for you, and I'd hoped you'd love it enough that you wouldn't care about the other one. But I shouldn't have gotten angry." He kisses my palm. "Forgive me?"

The rage I've managed to lower to a simmering anger turns to guilt, heavy and impossible to ignore. Of course, he wanted me to wear *his* bracelet tonight. It's our engagement party, after all. And even though he's been working so many hours he's barely sleeping, he somehow carved out enough time to pick it out for me. And not only that, he had it personalized.

I nod, and with a contrite smile, I unfasten the gold bracelet and slide it into my clutch. A silent apology, and a reminder to myself to be a little more understanding.

The change in his mood is instantaneous. "I have news."

"Tell me," I say, grateful we're moving on.

"I had a *huge* meeting today." His smile is so wide it crinkles his eyes, and the rest of my tension melts away. *This* is the man I fell in love with. *This* is my Harrison, happy and thoughtful. Driven and energetic.

"How big exactly?" I ask, running my fingers along the silky lapel of his fitted charcoal coat. He looks particularly handsome this evening, his blonde hair pushed back from his freshly shaved face.

"Big enough that if I bag this client, they'll *have* to make me partner," he says.

"Harrison! That's amazing!" I gush, twisting toward him. Hope and pride swell between my ribs. If Harrison makes partner, at least some of the pressure he's under at work will ease. He won't have to put in so many hours trying to prove himself, and he'll be happier.

We'll *both* be happier.

Our nights will no longer be full of incessant, soul-draining work obligations. He can go back to Thursday poker nights with his friends, and I'll have so much more time to make it to the symphonies and art exhibits I cover.

Used to cover.

This is it. My chance. The perfect opportunity to tell him I miss my job. That I'd like to focus on *my* career again for a while.

The best job a wife can have is to support her husband, Elizabeth. My mother's condescending voice slips into my mind, chiding me for oh-so-selfishly wanting a life different from the one she envisioned for me.

The life I've somehow slipped into over the past few years, even though it was never what I wanted.

The weight of the realization slides down my throat, settling like a ball of lead in my gut, but I shake my head, rattling the thought away.

I *haven't* slipped into that life, because this has all been temporary.

I don't regret taking a backseat for a bit to help Harrison. Our attendance at all the galas and fundraisers the past year and a half has allowed him to network himself into being one of the most highly requested entertainment lawyers at his firm, and I was more than willing to make a couple sacrifices to help him do it.

In the long run, it benefits both of us. I certainly can't pay our bills with only my freelance reporting, and even if I could, Harrison needed me. Making partner has been his dream since we met.

But now that he can see the finish line, it can be my turn. *He* can take the backseat for a while. Come along to my events. Proofread my reviews, just like he used to when we started dating.

That's what marriage is, right? Give and take. Harrison was so supportive of my career before I stepped away from it, and I'm sure he will be again, once he gets over the initial shock.

I clear my throat, digging for the courage to speak my thoughts into existence, but my tongue feels thick and sluggish.

"Harrison. I—"

His phone rings, "Eye of the Tiger" playing loud enough to make me jump, and he holds up a finger. "Harrison Rouchester."

My heart plummets, my resolve crumbling away like a sandcastle in the wind.

Tomorrow.

I'll tell him tomorrow, when we're not on the way to our engagement party. When he has more time to process the news. I wring my fingers together, still jittery, but Harrison doesn't seem to notice, his eyes lighting up.

"He's there? Perfect. Make sure he has whatever he needs. Yes, absolutely."

"Who?" I mouth, racking my brain for who on our guest list would warrant such VIP treatment.

"Great. Keep him happy till I get there." Harrison ends the call. "I have a surprise for you," he says with a guilty smile that looks more like a grimace.

"What? No! Why?" I whine like a petulant child. I *hate* surprises, and Harrison knows that. The intention is nice, and I appreciate the thought. Really, I do. But I *hate* having a room full of people watching my reactions. Having to master my facial expressions and mannerisms.

My fingers tap against my thighs in a nervous rhythm, and Harrison grabs my hands, forcing them to stop their drumming. "Elizabeth. This is a good surprise. There's no reason to be nervous. It's just a musician. One you love." He tucks a strand of auburn hair behind my ear, the piece I spent ten minutes styling trying to get the perfect face-framing flyaways. My fingers itch to fix it, but I squeeze my hands together to stop myself.

My forehead scrunches as I try to think of who it could be. "One I love?"

Harrison tilts his head in response. "Actually, now that I think about it, I'm not sure I've heard you listen to his music before. But even if you haven't, you'll love him after tonight. Everyone does."

"He's performing at the party?" I ask.

Harrison nods, his eyes sparkling with a mix of excitement and mischief.

"Ok, well… As far as surprises go, I guess this one's not too bad." I say, slightly less nervous now that I know it's not some sort of gift I'll have to open in front of a hundred and fifty people. "Will you tell me who it is?"

"You won't believe me," he teases, and my patience strains.

Harrison holds up his hands. "Okay, okay. Ready?" He wiggles his eyebrows. "It's Robert Beckett."

I stiffen as the air is sucked from my lungs, the name clanging around like shrapnel in my skull.

Robert.

Beckett.

My vision freckles with small black spots, and my mouth goes dry.

He's wrong. He has to be. Because I most definitely do *not* love Robert Beckett.

Not anymore.

Pride fills Harrison's brown eyes as he takes in my outright shock. My lungs struggle to expand, but the buzz of Harrison's phone pulls his attention away before he realizes that it's not excitement I'm feeling, but absolute dread.

"Isn't it great?" he continues, opening his email.

"*Robert Beckett* is playing at our party tonight?" I ask, like somehow the answer might change if I phrase the question a different way. It's hard to say his name out loud, and my voice sounds strained, even to my own ears.

"You're welcome," Harrison says with a grin.

"I don't understand. How did this happen?" I wipe my suddenly sweaty palms on the leather seats. All these years I've avoided him. Thoroughly and effectively. I blocked him on every social media platform possible. I listen to Spotify rather than the radio so I can make my own playlists, refuse to watch award shows, and I skip right past any news stories with his name in it.

Harrison looks at his phone again. "My big meeting was with him. He picked up the picture on my desk—the one from the night I proposed. He asked about you, and when I told him about the party tonight, the guy just *offered* to perform."

My mouth goes dry. So dry, I wouldn't be able to respond even if I could muddle through the chaos of my thoughts.

Harrison continues talking, completely unaware of the utter panic surging through my blood. "Really. I think I have this contract in the bag. Partner, here we come." He grabs my hand, squeezing, but his phone rings again, and he pulls away. "Harrison Rouchester," he answers. We're nearing the venue, but Harrison waves his hand in the air, indicating he'd like our driver to take a lap around the block. And thank God, because I need a minute.

My fingers itch to rub my bracelet. Not the one Harrison gave me moments before we left, but the one Bobby clasped around my wrist seven years ago when he promised me forever. The one in my clutch that now feels like a ticking bomb, somehow fragile and dangerous at the same time.

"Elizabeth?" Harrison's voice breaks through my haze of panic. The car has stopped moving, and I wonder how long we've been sitting here. I look up as Harrison shuffles through the open door, holding out his hand for me to join him. My stomach rolls, and for a moment, I think I'm going to be sick.

I fight through the nausea, keeping my face as neutral as possible, but my breaths are rapid and there's a fog clouding my brain that makes it hard to focus.

Swallowing it all down, I take Harrison's hand and follow him onto the sidewalk. Even after years of practice, it takes all my effort to school my features into a mask of calm. The debutante turned journalist turned devoted fiancée I'm expected to be.

But as we walk hand in hand toward the shiny doors of Nebula, I can't help but wonder if it's poor etiquette to call in sick to your own engagement party.

THEN

September 2016

A moment in time
Changing the fabric of who I am
A coffee cup
The smell of lavender, and suddenly, I understand
—An excerpt from "Almost There," written and performed by Robert Beckett

Taking the SATs is never enjoyable, but something about *retaking* them on a Saturday morning on the first bright, crisp day of fall is utterly suffocating. Even worse is knowing your mother is waiting to hear if you tested well enough to get into the school of *her* dreams.

I sigh, forcing myself to read the last question as the sun moves from behind a tree branch outside, taunting me as dappled light washes over my desk and test booklet.

I bubble in the final answer—C—and turn in my exam before making my way through the narrow hallway and heavy glass doors that lead outside, hoping the cool breeze will help me breathe a little easier, but it just makes me shiver as the knots in my empty stomach twist tighter.

Turning in the direction of my house only makes it worse, and dread creeps up my throat as I picture my mother pacing by the door with my father on speakerphone. I'd been instructed in no uncertain terms to come directly home after the test so we could discuss my performance.

That's what they'd called it, too.

A performance—like I'm an actress putting on a show.

They're not wrong.

I sigh, desperate for a latte. Preferably one made by my best friend, who just so happens to be manning the espresso machine at my favorite cafe a few blocks away.

My stomach rumbles, and before I can talk myself out of it, I'm speed-walking toward Joe's Place, squeezing my well-worn, dog-eared book of poetry tighter between my fingers. Adrenaline seeps into my bloodstream, and I pick up my pace to a near jog, wondering if my lack of caffeine combined with the stress of my forbidden coffee run is going to kill me.

The bell above the door dings as I push it open, and my mouth immediately waters, the aroma of espresso and caramel overtaking my senses. The shop isn't my usual cozy, girly vibe. With metal accents gleaming from every corner, the place looks as if it's been dreamed up by a man who loves camping. Or, I don't know, welding? But it's comfortable and welcoming and feels like home in a way I haven't found anywhere else.

Molly waves as I jiggle the door closed. She's clearly had a busy morning, her normally perfectly straight brunette hair pulled into a messy bun on top of her head and her apron stained with chocolate syrup.

I head straight to the counter, and Molly slides a drink in front of me, already made in a chipped mug as big as a bowl with a crooked square drawn into the foam. "Hot latte with 2 pumps lavender," she says with a broad smile.

My stomach growls as the sweet floral scent meets my nose. When Molly got the job here, we spent hours after the shop closed for the night making concoctions with different syrups and toppings. Most of them were awful, but the lavender stuck with me, and now I never order anything else. It's surprisingly sweet and slightly woodsy. It feels romantic somehow, and whenever I drink it, I can't help but think it's something Jane Austen would have loved.

I tilt my head, confused. "I thought I told you I wasn't coming by today."

"You did. But I know you better than that, and I wanted to practice my latte art. It's the SATs! See?" She points to her caffeinated rendition of my test booklet from this morning.

"Well, obviously!" I lie. It looks more like a slice of bread, but I'd never spoil her excitement. "You're the best. But can I get it to go?" I ask, my courage straining with every passing minute.

Molly shakes her head. "Nope. Go sit. Relax. You've earned it."

I rub the tense muscles between my eyebrows. "How can I relax when my parents are waiting to hear if I'll be getting into Harvard or if they need to renovate the attic to hide me in so they can pretend I died?"

"All the more reason to stay. Besides," she shoves a stack of disposable cups behind the milk steamer, "we're out of paper cups."

I reach around the counter to grab one from the towering, completely visible stack. "What are you talking about? I have to be home in less than eleven minutes," I argue, but she pushes them further out of my reach.

"Then drink fast. Enjoy!" she says, smiling sweetly and throwing me an exaggerated wink before turning away. I narrow my eyes, but Molly ignores me, moving on to the next customer. I reluctantly walk toward my seat, sniffing the drink I'm apparently about to chug. It smells the same as always, but that does nothing to make me feel better. She's up to something.

Several regulars are here, but they're not in their usual spots. It's unsettling, like falling asleep on the subway and waking up not knowing if you've missed your stop.

I twist toward my usual chair, hoping it wasn't taken in the weird shuffle, and freeze.

My breath rushes from my lungs, and my heart stutters. It's as if I've been dunked in freezing cold water and for a moment, I wonder if I'm *actually* dying.

But this time, it's not from the lack of caffeine or stress of the SATs.

A boy about my age with wavy brown hair sticking out from beneath a ball cap is relaxed in the oversized leather armchair.

My armchair.

There's a stack of notebooks practically falling off the table in front of him, and his book bag sits in the matching chair beside him—open as if he's been rustling through it.

Suddenly, it clicks. The reason for the wink. I mentally curse my best friend for her lack of an actual warning as I wonder what to do.

He's utterly handsome, with vibrant blue eyes beneath long, dark lashes. The angle of his jawline is strong, and the sleeves of his green henley are rolled to just below the elbow. He's writing something, and the sight of his muscular forearms flexing as the pen glides across the paper makes my stomach squeeze and my mouth go dry.

I start to turn away, but his head snaps up. The air crackles as he meets my gaze, and the electricity in his stare shocks me into taking a sudden step back. Coffee spills over the lip of my cup, the searing liquid burning my fingers and dripping onto the floor. I reach for some napkins, the redness in my cheeks spreading down my neck, but the boy beats me to them, grabbing a handful before dropping down and wiping up the drops of latte. The movement makes his shirt cling to his muscular back and biceps in the most delicious way, and it's as if there are a thousand butterflies tickling my stomach.

My phone rings, but I barely notice it as the boy smiles. A dimple appears in his cheek, and when we lock eyes again, his hand pauses and hovers over the floor. For a moment, neither of us moves a muscle. I'm not sure I'm even breathing.

The boy clears his throat as he stands and tosses the napkins into the trash, his eyebrows lowering as he looks at the pink patch of skin on my hand. "Are you okay?" he asks, and the movement of his full lips is so mesmerizing, I don't answer right away.

He raises his eyebrows at my silence, and I clear my throat, nodding as I stutter out a "Thank you."

Blue-eyes seems to notice my discomfort. Either that, or my impossibly red face gives me away, and mercifully, he breaks eye contact, nodding before returning to his seat and picking his notebook back up.

I feel his eyes on my back as I head to the counter to get a refill of my now half-full drink, but Molly's already waiting for me with a mug in hand.

"Here you go," she says with a wide grin, as if she anticipated me losing my cool completely and embarrassing myself with a spill. With another exaggerated wink, she hands me a fresh latte, the foam poured in the shape of what I think is supposed to be a baseball cap this time.

I openly glare at her, but it only makes her smile bigger, so I turn away, looking at the wrought iron clock by the door even though every fiber of my being is tugging me back toward the boy with the blue eyes and a dimple that makes my whole body feel fuzzy.

Seven minutes until I'm due home.

"This seat's open," a deep voice floats from next to the fireplace, brushing against my skin and sending a shiver down the length of my spine.

His voice.

The words are quiet, but smooth and confident, layered with something smoky that makes my toes tingle. "Oh—Uhh. Sorry," he continues, reaching over to remove his bag from the chair next to his. "I thought I'd moved this."

He smiles in apology, and no matter how much my nerves are begging me to leave my coffee and run home to do what's expected of me and avoid my probable punishment for being late, I *can't*. My feet pull me toward the boy with the voice like honey without permission, without hesitation. It's terrifying and thrilling, and goosebumps erupt along my skin as every facet of the moment comes into focus.

I'm suddenly all too aware of my body. *Have my steps always been this heavy and awkward? And why are my arms so stiff?*

I sit, pulling out my phone before my mother can call again, and turn it off. His smile spreads to his eyes, lighting up his entire face. The dimple in his right cheek deepens, and I forget all about the interrogation waiting for me at home. His smile is broad and white and a little crooked in a way that makes me strangely nauseous—like I'm plummeting through open air.

"Bobby." He offers his hand and I take it, my own disappearing in his warm grasp as a zing shoots up my arm. The calluses along the tips of his fingers are rough on my skin, and I imagine the gentle scrape of them trailing down my cheek.

"Do you play guitar?" I ask. I don't know where the words come from. They slip from between my lips without permission. But for some inexplicable reason, I *need* to know like I need my next breath.

"You're observant..." He raises his thick, dark eyebrows as he draws out the handshake, his voice lilting up in a question.

I stare at him for a second too long, my voice hiding somewhere in my uncooperative throat. "Beth. I'm Beth Winters. Sorry." I pull my hand away and twist my fingers together, thoroughly unsettled by how off kilter I feel.

"Beth Winters," he parrots back. My name sounds like it was made for his mouth, and it makes my heart pound so hard I almost throw up. "I do, yeah. Guitar, piano. Music's my thing."

"Is that what you're working on?" I try to look at the words in his notebook—scratchy, heavy-handed lines written in black ink, but he tips the pages out of my line of sight.

"Yeah. Um…songwriting, actually. It's also kind of my thing," he says, fidgeting in his seat.

I think my jaw drops, but I can't be sure. He's writing a *song*? Not ten-year plans or portfolios or embellished essays to try to get into Harvard or Yale? It's refreshing, like a summer storm, but instead of it cooling me off, my body only seems to get hotter.

"So, Beth," Bobby says my name again, this time as if it's the most important word in the lyrics of a song he's singing. He scoots forward like I'm a magnet, pulling him closer. "What's your thing?" He gestures to the book in my hands. "Poetry?" he asks, leaning closer to read the spine. "Written by dead men?"

I smile into my cup at his joke as I take a sip, considering my answer. He's not wrong. I do tend to live within the pages of my books and the lines of poems. I like stories with a predetermined ending. But for the first time, the idea of a blank page with endless possibilities excites me more than knowing what's coming next.

Bobby sits back in his chair as he waits for my answer, his smile dimpling his cheek again in a way that makes my toes curl.

"Poetry, dead or alive. Men or women," I say, writing out the first line of a story in the blank, imaginary book in my mind. One that begins with a blue-eyed boy with a kind smile and callused fingers.

When I look up, Bobby's on the edge of his seat, so close our knees are almost touching. *Almost.* So close that even through the small gap, I can somehow still feel him.

"What kind of poems do you like?" he asks, his lips tipping up at the side into a crooked smile that makes me dizzy.

I hand him my book, and when our fingers graze, tiny shocks erupt everywhere our skin meets. We both pause again, and as much as I want to hide behind my hair, I can't look away.

"Pretty ones," I say, finally pulling back. Bobby flips through the book, scanning random pages before he meets my eyes, and I blush at the way he seems to be searching inside me for something.

"Like you," he says. His eyes move from my eyes to my lips, and my cheeks grow so hot I wonder if they'll ever return to their pale, freckled state.

"Um... Do you go to school around here?" I ask, uncomfortable with the compliment. As soon as the words leave my mouth, I cringe. There's no way he's in high school. His shoulders are too broad, his eyes too knowing.

His answering smile is so warm, I have to shift away from the fire a bit.

"No, I graduated last year. I teach guitar and piano lessons around the city. Sometimes some handyman work here and there."

I can't help but glance down at his strong hands.

"I perform at night," he continues. "Bars. Restaurants. Anywhere I can, really."

Images of smoky bars with dim lighting fill my mind. I turned eighteen a few months ago, but I've never been anywhere like the places he probably plays. My normal haunts include this coffee shop and dinners with my family at establishments that require overcoats. No hats or shaggy hair allowed.

As if reading my mind, he pulls off his baseball cap, shaking his hair from his eyes before flipping the hat around and putting it on backward. My whole body screams in response. *Am I drooling?* My stomach clenches, and I try to pull my eyes away, but I *can't*. There's something about the confidence of his movements. The absolute aura of contentment and peace.

"You're happy," I say. It's an observation more than a question, and *another* embarrassing, random thing I blurt out without thinking.

He quirks an eyebrow at me. "Are you not?" His face creases in concern, and it makes my heart flutter.

"I'm…" The word won't come to me. I'm not *un*happy. I have good friends, and even if my family is overbearing, they love me. I've never wanted for anything, so how selfish and bratty would it be for me to admit that I feel like my life is missing something? "I'm almost there," I settle on.

He cocks his head at me, his eyes so focused on my face that the blood rushes back into my cheeks, and I'm forced to look away. Looking at him… It's too…intense? Like there's some sort of connection buzzing between us, and if I stare into it for too long, I'll be sucked in forever.

"Almost there, huh?" He leans back and flips the page in his notebook, scratching something out at the top. A title. "Let's see if we can get you all the way there, Beth."

His smile reaches his eyes again, and my name is a caress on his tongue. It's caring. Tender, somehow. And even though I'm rational to a fault, even though it's crazy and foolish, I know without a doubt that my name on his lips is the beginning of something life changing.

NOW

August 2024

The second I cross the threshold into the venue, I feel him. It's in the buzz of excitement thickening the air, making it hard to breathe. In the palpable electricity crackling along my skin.

Harrison sees a client he's been trying to contact, and with an apology and a kiss on the cheek, he beelines toward him, asking me to bring him over a scotch. Neat.

He says it in a rhyme, laughing as if it's the equivalent of a Shakespearean comedy.

I head toward the bar, not because he asked me to, but because *I* myself need a drink. Fortunately, I only make it six steps before Molly's there, pushing a crystal glass of champagne into my hand and leading me by the elbow to the linen-draped wall she designed in the back of the venue. Hundreds of white roses are attached to the fabric, a perfect backdrop for photos, and I take a deep inhale.

Maybe the sweet floral scent can push down the bitter taste of bile in my throat.

"I told you to stop turning your phone on silent. I called you like ten times!" She waves me off before I can answer. "Never mind. Listen, I need you to prepare yourself," Molly says, grabbing my shoulders. I lift the glass, swallowing the contents in two seamless gulps.

"May I?" I take the second glass from her hand and down it before she can answer.

"You *know*?" Her brown eyes go wide. "You know, and you walked through those doors? *Willingly*?"

"You look great. Is that a new dress?" I ask, wiping my mouth. I need to change the subject, think of *anything* else, before I throw up.

"Wha—Sorry. Am I having a stroke, or are you *actually* talking about my clothing choice when you should be freaking out?" Her voice turns into a whisper shout.

"I *am* freaking out. This is me freaking out." I look around for a server, hoping I can snag a third glass of champagne.

Molly narrows her eyes. "Nope. No more. You need a clear head tonight. Do I need to fake an emergency? It'll ruin the party, but if anything calls for ruining a party, this is it." Her eyes narrow as she thinks, then pop open wide. "I can pretend my appendix is bursting. It's foolproof. We can get you out of here without having to even see him." Molly clutches her side, her fingers digging into the soft pink fabric of her dress as if she's about to put on the performance of a lifetime, but I grab her hands.

"I love you." And oh, do I. She's the best friend I could ever ask for. Especially because she isn't kidding. She would collapse on the floor right here, right now, writhing in pain and begging for help if I asked her to. "But I'll be fine. He's just a man I used to know in another life."

Neither of us has said his name, yet, but we both know the exact *him* I'm referring to.

Molly gives me a look that says *nothing about this is fine,* but I hold my hands up.

"It's been six years. I'll be polite, and then I'll enjoy the night with my friends and my fiancé." It's a lie. Trying to enjoy tonight will be like trying to have fun during a root canal.

"Polite?" She's whisper shouting again. "This is *Bobby* we're talking about. He was your soulmate, Beth."

"*You're* my soulmate. But the love of my life," I say pointedly, "is right over…" I look around, finding Harrison speaking to his father. Harrison meets my eyes and holds up his empty hand, shaking it as if holding a glass. He wants that drink.

"Oh, stop it," Molly snaps at me, and I turn away from Harrison, pointing toward the bar. He can get it himself. And one for me, while he's at it.

But as I meet Molly's eyes again, I wish I'd gone to get him that scotch. She's leveling me with a look, one that causes shame to burn in my stomach.

She doesn't have to say what she's thinking. I already know. In no universe would she describe Harrison as the love of my life *or* my soulmate.

"I'm marrying him, Molly." I sigh.

"But you don't have to. You had a soulmate, once. Don't you want that again?"

I narrow my eyes, and Molly lifts her hands in mock surrender.

"Okay, a love of your life, then? What you have with Harrison isn't—"

"What I have with Harrison is perfect. In case you're somehow forgetting, that "soulmate" you're talking about *destroyed* me. Harrison is a good, stable man, and we're happy together. Why can't you just accept that?"

"I'm just saying, what if this is a sign? I mean, Bobby shows up here—"

I hold up a hand. "I appreciate your concern, but you've made how you feel very clear. I love Harrison. I'm marrying him," I repeat, keeping my voice gentle but firm.

This is what I want. The next rational step. I can have a good life with Harrison. A happy one. And here's the most important part. He's never walked away from me.

He actually wants me, and he's *never* faltered in that.

"Okay. I hear you," she says, then freezes, her mouth dropping open and her eyes widening, frantic.

A familiar snap of energy runs across my shoulders, and the air thickens with tension, buzzing and making the small hairs on my arms stand on end.

I don't need to turn around to know who's standing behind me.

I'd know that electricity anywhere.

"Beth." A deep, raspy voice sets my skin on fire—a voice that sounds as if it was made to say my name. I stiffen, plastering a practiced smile on my face. I refuse to let him rattle me. Or, at least, I refuse to let him see it.

Bobby's gaze skates down my dress as I turn, recognition flashing in his eyes. Warm, familiar blue eyes brimming with a hundred different emotions, and I'm still able to discern every single one of them. The room spins around us, like he's the sun and everything and everyone else is simply in his orbit. My chest cracks open, making me suck in a sharp breath at the pain spreading between my ribs.

A fool.

That's what I am.

A damn fucking fool to think six years of distance would change anything at all. My mouth goes dry, and Molly leans forward to speak in my ear.

"I'll grab you that third glass of champagne," she says, and I nod soundlessly before clearing my throat. I don't deserve her.

"Robert." I nod. *Polite. Be polite, and move on.* "It's nice to see you again," I say. But it's not. It's another lie.

Seeing him tonight just might be the worst thing that's ever happened to me.

"Listen, I—" he starts, but Harrison's at my side in an instant, wrapping his arm around my shoulders and tugging me to him so quickly, I stumble. Bobby reaches out a hand as if to steady me, but stops himself.

I barely notice as a vise of panic wraps around my lungs.

I meet Bobby's eyes, shaking my head almost imperceptibly, desperately hoping he'll understand what I'm trying to say. *Harrison doesn't know about you, and I don't want him to.*

A mask falls across Bobby's face as he nods, and in the blink of an eye, he becomes Robert Beckett. Not someone celebrating a friend's engagement. Not the boy I used to love, but a superstar who thrives on performing on stages for thousands of screaming, adoring fans decked out in t-shirts with his face and posters that say, "I'd make a great groupie."

"I see you've met my bride. Beautiful, isn't she?" Harrison asks, kissing me on the cheek.

"Stunning." Bobby's eyes dance across my face, bringing blood to the surface and making me blush like I'm eighteen again. "You're a lucky man," he continues, shaking Harrison's hand in greeting, then looking to mine.

He knows my hands well, and I bet that even after all these years, he could sketch out the lines across my palm and the small scar on my right pinky in perfect detail. Just as I could map out every callus and mark on his, but I don't want to test that theory.

Miraculously, Harrison saves me, and I feel a rush of gratitude for his old-boy mannerisms. "Thank you so much for offering to perform tonight, man." Harrison turns on the charm, slinging an arm around Bobby's shoulders. "Let's get you a drink, and then I'd like to introduce you to my father, Senator Rouchester."

Thank God for small mercies.

Harrison scans the crowd for his father, and I'm thankful I purposely chose a weekend for our party that my own parents were on the campaign trail, not wanting my mother's scrutiny on Molly's decor or my attire. Or even worse, tonight's entertainment.

Bobby gives me a tense smile before nodding to Harrison and walking with him to the bar, and I wonder if he'll opt for a beer over the hundred-dollar bottles of liquor. He never was much of a drinker, and he was certainly never pretentious about it. Then again, maybe I don't know him so well anymore.

They disappear into the throng, and I dash to the bathroom, needing a splash of cool water and a few minutes to gather my thoughts. I close the door firmly behind me, my perfectly practiced smile dropping the second I hear the *click* of the lock. It's a single stall, thank goodness, and I stand in front of the mirror, taking in my flushed face.

I'm not exactly sure why, but I expected myself to look different. I was sure experiencing such an earth-shattering moment would have left some sort of physical mark on my body—changed me in some visible way. But my hair is still red, my skin still smooth and pale, and my eyes still a vibrant green, despite the tears gathering there.

I'd thought I'd feel anger if I ever saw Bobby again, or maybe discomfort. I expected to want to slap him, or maybe to feel nothing at all. What I didn't expect was the raw, gaping wound in my heart that has apparently never closed. It was as if the sight of him caused the stitches holding it together to rip in half, turning the scarred muscle into a bloody mess, pumping that familiar pain throughout my entire body until it permeated the deepest marrow of my bones.

He's grown impossibly more handsome with age, his hair shorter than before, still slightly wavy but no longer shaggy around his ears, and his jaw is now thicker and shadowed in stubble, making him look impossibly masculine. Even more noticeable is that his muscles are… well… muscular. He'd been thinner before, not scrawny, but nowhere near as sculpted and powerful. But it's not even his handsome face or broad shoulders and defined arms causing my lungs to feel like they're breathing around shards of glass.

It's his eyes.

Blue. Tender. Familiar.

Regretful.

I splash cold water on my neck, then dab my face with a wet paper towel, careful not to smear my makeup as I try to replace my pain with anger. It's a more productive emotion, and it allows me to keep a healthier distance from the past and my memories. Plus, I *deserve* that anger.

He had no right to come here. No right to make me wonder what's causing that regret in his eyes.

I take several deep, steadying breaths, then pull the stray piece of hair from behind my ear and put it back into place. *I can do this. For myself and any semblance of dignity that Bobby didn't take from me, I have to do this.*

My fingers itch to find a pen and paper and purge my emotions onto a blank slate. It's a feeling I haven't experienced in a long time, and it makes my skin itch knowing *he's* the one who brought that urge back up inside me.

Minutes pass as I try to calm myself down. Too many of them. So with a final deep breath, I push my shoulders back and swing the door open, crashing directly into a broad, muscular chest.

"Shit, Beth. I'm sorry." Bobby catches me before I can fall, and his fingers on my skin feel like hot coals.

I stumble back as if he burned me. "What are you doing here, Robert?"

Hurt flashes in his eyes at the use of his full name, but he lets go, taking a tentative step back. "Look, I should have found a way to contact you before showing up here tonight. But I was in Harrison's office and there you were in that picture. And God, Beth. It was like I'd been stabbed in the chest. I just—" He rubs the back of his neck, shifting from foot to foot. "I needed to see you. See you happy, like you are in that picture."

"See me *happy*?" I must be in shock. Dreaming, because there is no way this man cares about my happiness. His words only stoke the anger burning in my blood. "Do you honestly feel like you have any right to know anything about my life anymore?"

He winces. "I know. I know what I did to you—to *us*—and I'm sorry. It wasn't—" Bobby runs a frustrated hand through his hair. "I'll leave. Right now, if that's what you want."

"You can't." I rub between my eyebrows, trying to get rid of the headache forming there. "Harrison already told everyone you're performing. If you leave…" I clear my throat, trying to ignore the sudden unwanted dread swirling in my stomach—the one begging me to not let him leave again. It must be ingrained within my muscle fibers, because as much as I want to put an ocean of distance between us, the thought of him walking away again is physically painful.

"Okay. You're right," he concedes, holding up his hands. "I just—I'm glad you're happy. Okay?" He smiles, but it doesn't reach his eyes, and there's no dimple in his cheek. "You *are* happy, right?"

My mouth opens, but nothing comes out but a shallow inhale. I don't know how to answer that. Am I as happy as I would have been with him?

Or am I happy enough?

I clear my throat. "Sure, Robert. I'm happy," I say, my voice cold and flat. He doesn't deserve anything more. I turn to leave, but he catches me by the elbow. With a clatter, my clutch falls, the clip popping open and its contents spilling onto the hardwood floor. I drop to the ground, shoving a lipstick back into the main compartment when strong, callused hands appear to help, pausing as they brush against cold metal.

My bracelet.

His bracelet.

Shit.

Bobby places his fingers beneath my chin, raising my face so I'm forced to meet his gaze. "Beth." His voice is rough, disbelieving, and I look away, humiliated and furious at what I see in his eyes. Not pity, but close enough to it that tears threaten to spill down my cheeks.

I grab the bracelet, shove it into my purse, and stand. "Excuse me," I say, walking away with my head held high. I'm not sure how I manage it, considering I feel like my soul was just ripped in half.

Molly finds me again, mercifully bringing me that third glass of champagne. I sip instead of chug this time, but the *pop* of a microphone makes me wish I'd downed it like the last two glasses. I turn as Harrison takes the stage. He's loving the attention, his cheeks flushed from the combination of applause and scotch, and he raises his hands to quiet the crowd.

"Thank you all for coming tonight," he starts, making eye contact with several people near the front. "If you know my Elizabeth—" he finds me in the crowd and places a hand over his heart. "You know she loves poetry. So I'd like to say a few words." He clears his throat and pulls out a piece of paper, and a blush immediately floods my cheeks as a spotlight finds me.

"My missing piece, it makes me whole, the way you fit into my life. Thank you, my dear, for loving me. I can't wait till you're my wife."

A woman I don't know next to me dabs at her cheeks, and it takes every bit of my control to keep smiling and not roll my eyes. Harrison waves for me to join him as the crowd politely applauds, and I oblige.

He wraps an arm around my waist and gives me a lingering kiss that borders on embarrassing, even for an engagement party, but our guests all cheer. "Thank you. Now, I'm not one for long speeches—"

"Unless you're in court!" someone yells from the back.

"Guilty," Harrison winks, and I force a laugh along with his coworkers. "Sorry. Legal humor. Anyway, I'll keep it short. I was lucky enough to trick Elizabeth here into marrying me, but even more lucky to snag some top tier entertainment for us tonight."

The room goes still, anticipation buzzing along with the microphone. "Honey, would you like to do the honors?" Harrison asks.

I look to the side where Robert waits. Not Bobby, but a superstar brimming with confidence and charisma, his guitar strapped to his back. Our eyes meet, and for just a second, his mask slips. My stomach twists, my smile faltering, but not enough for anyone to notice.

No one, at least, but him.

"Ladies and gentlemen." I look away, my heart pinching like it's cracking open as I smile broadly, big and fake, and sweep my arm toward the side of the stage. "Robert Beckett."

I stand with Harrison in the middle of the crowd as Bobby takes the stage, and Jesus, he looks even better standing in the spotlight. His plain black shirt is tight around his biceps, and the way his jeans fit him is *unholy*. He is pure, undiluted masculinity, and it pisses me off. I bet he was chopping wood before he came here tonight so he could cook some fish over an outdoor fire. Fish he caught with his bare hands. I'm not sure Harrison even knows how to *start* a fire.

"Evening, everyone," Bobby starts, his voice confident and dripping with sex-appeal. His stage voice. It's similar to his everyday tone, but somehow *more*. So intoxicating you fall under its spell instantly, and once it's gone, you crave it forever.

"I'm honored to be here this evening," he says, putting a hand over his heart in a gesture of humility, and the crowd cheers. Within the few seconds he's been on stage, tonight has turned from an engagement party to a full-on concert. The energy is vibrant, and I wonder if the women here are going to throw their bras at him, or if they somehow found a way to make those groupie posters.

"If there's anything I've learned in my twenty-eight years," Bobby continues, "it's that love is something that should be celebrated. Always. Especially when it's true and honest. I had a love like that once." Bobby's voice is as rough as sandpaper, and he stares not *at* me, but inside me, just like he used to do when we were younger. His lips turn down, just slightly. "Only once. And this is the song I wrote about it."

Bobby holds my stare until the lights dim, and the first strum of his guitar rings out, a chord I've heard before. Only then does he close his eyes and begin to play in earnest, a soulful sound that's a mix of rock and Americana.

When the moon wanes in a weary sky
When frost freezes roots, petals wither and die
You're gonna be ok, and I'll tell you why
You're safe in the arms of someone who loves you

Fuck. Him.

Of all the songs he could have chosen to perform tonight, why did it have to be *this* one?

He continues to sing, but I no longer hear the words. No longer feel my limbs. This is his biggest song. The one that won him both song *and* album of the year when he was just twenty-three years old. And it was written about me.

"I was listening to his most recent album earlier. He has a song called Dreamers and Poets," Harrison shouts in my ear, and my heart leaps into my throat. I force a smile. There's no way he's figured it out. It's not possible. "You speak the same language as this guy. I got the feeling he was going to walk away from our deal when we were talking with my dad. But I think I can save it. I think *you* can save it," he says, kissing me on the cheek before walking away to resume his mingling.

Normally, I'd be frustrated with him using our party to focus on networking. But tonight, I'm grateful. Because if he's focusing on clients, he won't notice I'm gone.

I take one last look at Robert, the ache in my chest growing so uncomfortable, I rub my sternum to ease it. Each word he sings is another stab in my heart. Another wound opening, threatening to bleed me dry. But Bobby's the only one who can see it.

His jaw clenches, and I shake my head, pressing my lips together and wrapping my arms around myself as if it will help hold me together. His eyes are pained as he takes in my expression, and he takes a step forward as if he wants to leap off the stage and make it better. But he can't. It's as impossible as me forgetting my favorite poem.

Or the lyrics of *this* song.

I turn on my heel and walk to the balcony, closing the door to muffle the solemn sound of guitar and loaded words. The pain of his melodic lies.

The air is crisp, and it shocks me back into reality. This is the man who destroyed me. And now, he's a stranger. Nothing good can come of me watching him perform, of allowing those memories space to sharpen. So instead, I wrap myself in armor, just like I've done every day for the past six years.

THEN

September 2016

What I've been searching for
Without even starting to look
A melody swimming straight into my blood
And the poems in an old dusty book
—*An excerpt from "Almost There," written and performed by Robert Beckett*

I'm not one to say meeting a boy is the best thing that's ever happened to me, but at a minimum, getting a latte after my SATs on Saturday feels like it was fate. I'm practically skipping as I rush to Joe's Place a few days later, somehow certain he'll be there.

With fake confidence, I walk straight to Molly behind the counter, not allowing my head to turn toward my usual spot *or* the chair next to it. But the way my skin buzzes tells me I was right. I can *feel* him.

"You're late." Molly plops a cup of coffee on the counter, full to the brim with foam. Today, she's attempted to draw a snowflake.

I think.

"I've been late before," I say, picking up the large, warm mug.

"Mhmm." Her eyes drift to my eyelashes and mouth. "Not wearing makeup, you haven't."

"It's just lip gloss." Blood rushes to my cheeks. "My lips were dry."

"Whatever you say, Beth," she sing-songs, turning away to clean the milk steamer. "Oh." Molly looks over her shoulder. "He's here, in case you were wondering."

"I wasn't—" I stop as her eyes flick back to my darkened eyelashes. "I hate you," I mumble, shoving a dollar into the tip jar.

Molly's laughter follows me as I turn and *carefully* carry my coffee toward my regular seat.

"Beth." His voice sets my skin on fire.

I finally allow my eyes to drift to where Bobby's sitting. He's slumped back in my chair with his ankle crossed over his knee as if he's settled in for the long haul. Maybe, as if he were waiting for me. A smile tugs at the corner of his mouth, and I can't help the blush that warms my cheeks again.

"You're here," I say, pointing out the obvious as I sit down and pull out my poetry book, opening it to one I've been working on since last night. Bobby's eyes drift across the page, but I don't pull it out of view.

"Fourth day in a row," he answers with a shy smile, rubbing the back of his neck as if suddenly nervous. "I wasn't sure if I'd see you again or not."

"I—" I have no words. My cheeks are on fire now, but I don't look away. I want to memorize every second of my time with him. Tuck them away so I can revisit them later.

Bobby leans forward in his chair and pulls out his phone, handing it to me. "How can I wait until you come to me? The once fleet mornings linger by the way. Their sunny smiles touched with malicious glee. At my unrest, they seem to pause, and play like truant children, while I sigh and say—"

"How can I wait..." my soft voice mixes with his rich tenor, almost breathless as I take the phone from his hand and stare at it. "Ella Wheeler Wilcox. But..." I trail off, understanding what he wants and finding myself confused at the same time. I feel like I'm in a movie, and I have the urge to pinch myself to see if it's actually possible this boy just quoted one of my favorite poets.

"I memorized it, in case you came back." Bobby stares into my eyes as if committing every fleck of color to memory.

"You did?" I breathe, even though he *just* told me that's exactly what happened. I'm frozen in place, my heart thundering so hard, I hear it roaring in my ears. He memorized the poem for *me*. It's so impossible I almost don't think it's true. And yet, he says it is, and I believe him.

"I'd like your number." He nods at the phone. "Um… If you'd like, of course. I have more poetry I can recite if that one didn't do the trick. Or maybe some *Romeo and Juliet*?"

"You memorized *Romeo and Juliet*? It's one of my favorites." My heart swells, but I tilt my head, not convinced he can recite an entire play.

His answering smile is cheeky. "'Romeo, Romeo. Wherefore art thou, Romeo? Thus, with a kiss, I die. To be, or not to be. That is the question.'"

I laugh. "That last one's *Hamlet*," I say, tapping my number into his phone and handing it back to him, a shockwave radiating through my skin when our fingers touch. "You're close, though."

"'Fair is foul, and foul is fair?'" He raises his eyebrows.

"*Macbeth*." I say, trying my best to look calm even though I'm absolutely giddy.

He presses his full lips together in a smile before looking down at his watch, and that beautiful smile disappears as his lips tip into a frown. I have the sudden urge to make a joke. A silly face. Anything to see his eyes twinkle and his cheek dimple.

"I have to go. I'm sorry, but I'm so glad you came back. Will you be here tomorrow?" he asks.

"And Friday," I blurt out, wincing at my inability to play it cool.

Bobby stands, grabbing his backpack. "Sweet, so would I. Yet I should kill thee with much cherishing. Good night, good night! Parting is such sweet sorrow. That I shall say good night till it be morrow,'" he says with an over-the-top flourish of his hand. He pulls a bright-pink, slightly wilted flower from his pocket and hands it to me. His fingers brush mine—only for a second—but it's enough to rip the air from my lungs.

It's a wild rose.

A summer bloom, just like from the Wilcox poem, and I have the urge to pinch myself to see if I'm dreaming. My cheeks ache from my smile and my head swims, but it isn't until he's walking out the door that I realize he quoted the play correctly, and as I trail my fingers along the flower's petals, I can't help but wonder if maybe he memorized it for me after all.

I tap on Molly's front door later that night with a few gentle kicks, my arms too full to use my hands. Twizzlers, Nerds, and Skittles for me, and mini Milky Ways and Hershey's Kisses for her. It's one of the first things we bonded over. I prefer fruity candy, and she prefers chocolate. It was an excellent arrangement growing up trick or treating, and probably the perfect recipe for becoming best friends.

Molly opens the door and pulls me inside, grabbing a bag.

"*What Lies Beneath* or *Rosemary's Baby*?" she asks, plopping down on the ridiculously comfortable couch in her family's home theater.

"I was thinking *The Shining*?" I say, settling in next to her and grabbing a blanket.

"Oooooh." She nudges my arm before continuing, "Stephen King. I like it." She searches her DVR and hits play without further discussion, and instantly, the room is plunged into pitch black as the opening credits roll.

My popcorn-filled hand is halfway to my mouth and two creepy little girls appear in the hallway of the Overlook Hotel when Molly suddenly pauses the movie.

"I need to tell you something," she says. Her voice is shaky, and I slowly lower my hand full of popcorn.

"What's wrong?" I ask, my stomach dropping.

"I don't even want to say it." She covers her face, and I sit up to grab her hand.

"Is Michael—I mean, is his cancer—" My stomach drops. Her little brother has normally wiggled his way into joining our movie nights by now, and I wonder if he's back in the hospital.

"No! No. Michael's okay. Or...he hasn't gotten any worse. Sorry, I should've..." She trails off. "It's about me, and I'm fine. But I've made a big decision."

"You're freaking me out. Just tell me," I beg, my whole body on edge.

"I'm not going to college." The words tumble from Molly's lips as if she's been struggling to hold in a mouth full of marbles for days.

I audibly exhale, the tension immediately easing from my shoulders. "Holy crap, Molly!" I throw a handful of popcorn at her. "You scared me!"

"You don't think that's bad news?" she breathes.

I shrug. "Not unless you're forgoing college to run off to Bali with some guy I don't know." I shove a Twizzler in my mouth.

"What? No. I just don't know what I want to do. I think I'm going to try for an internship somewhere in fashion, or interior design, maybe."

"You'd be amazing at either," I say. Molly's always the one I call for help when I need to pick out something to wear for an important event. And Lord knows you can make a living decorating rich people's houses. My mother alone has spent tens of thousands redecorating just our kitchen, and she's hardly even home to use it.

"Okay then," Molly says, sounding surprised.

"Okay. I'm not sure what you expected. Did you think I'd be mad?" I ask, placing a hand over my heart, pretending to be wounded.

"I don't know. I thought I'd at least get some pushback. Maybe I'm using you as a trial run before I talk to my parents. I mean, I spent all this time applying to schools with them, and their friends pulled strings to get me interviews. They're going to be pissed."

They're not. I'm certain of it. They're too busy taking her six-year-old brother, Michael, to treatments, watching their son fight for his life. "They're going to be proud of you, just like I am," I say. "I think it's brave."

Molly leans forward, grabbing my hands. "You can be brave, too," she says, and I know instantly what she's talking about. My mind shifts to the applications sitting filled out on the cluttered desk in my room: Harvard, Princeton, Stanford, Brown, Dartmouth, and... NYU. I wince as I think about what my mother's reaction would be if she learned I've been considering applying anywhere other than a university smothered in ivy. Without a doubt, she'd consider my betrayal to her plan a true tragedy. One worthy of a poem that would be immortalized for eternity in remembrance of the great disappointment that was Beth Winters.

I wish I was brave enough not to care.

My phone buzzes. *Hey Beth, it's Bobby*, the screen reads, and in the blink of an eye, there are *dozens* of butterflies in my stomach, flapping their wings so hard it makes me nauseous.

Molly squeals, her confession about bailing on college completely forgotten. She slaps my arm. "I didn't know you and Bobby text!"

Molly grabs the phone from my hand and unlocks it.

"We don't! Remind me to change my code when you give that back," I say sarcastically, but my annoyance trails off as a smile spreads across her face, and she turns the phone toward me.

Bobby: Hey Beth, it's Bobby. I wanted to let you know that I won't be at Joe's tomorrow. I'm teaching a last-minute guitar lesson. I tried to reschedule it, but you know… bills.

The text is simple, but at the same time, loaded with meaning.

"He's so into you," Molly says with another squeal, and I swat at her, my cheeks turning red.

"He's just being polite," I say.

"Okay. No offense, but that's the dumbest thing you've ever said. He *likes* you."

"He does not." I blush, typing back a very lame, *Thanks for letting me know*. But it's all I can think of with Molly hovering over my shoulder. Three little dots appear almost immediately, as if he was waiting for my reply, and the thought makes my chest tighten.

Bobby: Was that a new poem you were working on today? Did you finish it?

Molly throws herself back into the cushions dramatically. "Riiiiiight. He doesn't like you."

"Play the movie, and leave me alone," I say, trying to hide my smile as I curl up in the corner of the couch to type out my reply.

Me: Yes! I'll need to tweak it some. But it's getting there.
Bobby: I'm sure it's amazing

Me: You're amazing. I type, then promptly delete my confession, wishing once again I was brave like Molly.

Me: So who's the lesson for tomorrow? Is it a beginner? Or a college student?
Bobby: Both. He's never picked up a guitar before, but he wants to impress a girl at school.
Me: I mean, I get it. Guitar players are super hot.

I hit send before I can think too much about it, then instantly regret it.

My cheeks heat as the three little dots appear, then disappear. Then appear again. A few seconds later, his reply comes through.

Bobby: Is that the general population speaking, or is that what you think?
Me: Both.
Bobby: Good to know.

Our conversation continues as he asks about my weekend plans, flowing so easily, I don't even realize that the movie has ended and Molly is snoring next to me. We text back-and-forth about nothing and everything, sending messages nearly until the sun comes up.

It's not until I'm bleary eyed with exhaustion that we say goodnight.

Bobby: I'll see you Thursday. I'll have a latte waiting to make it up to you.
Beth: With lavender?

I lie down and pull a blanket around me.

Bobby: For you? Always with lavender.

NOW

August 2024

Roses are still red,
They also are thorny.
When you wear that dress,
I get really (redacted)
—A poem by Harrison Rouchester, stolen from a grocery store greeting card

My tongue feels like sandpaper, and my head is throbbing. I squeeze my eyes tighter against the bright sun filtering in through the slatted window shades, wishing we'd picked a different townhome. One that doesn't greet the sunrise at the butt-crack of dawn every morning.

It's never bothered you before, my subconscious says.

"Shut up," I mumble, very much aware that I'm arguing with myself. I blame the alcohol—my third glass of champagne turning into several more before we'd finally gone home.

The door creaks open, and I pull down the covers a bit and crack open an eye. Harrison walks in, already showered and in his golf attire. I almost tell him to leave me alone, but then I see the cup in his hands.

Coffee.

Blessed caffeine.

I might have changed a lot since the last time I saw Bobby, but one thing that *hasn't* changed is my insatiable need for strong, liquid sludge.

Harrison sits gently on the bed, handing me the cup. Black. I groan inwardly but sit up and take the warm mug from his hands. It's not that Harrison doesn't know how I like my coffee. He just flat out refuses to indulge me.

Serious people drink black coffee, he always teases. It's become a sort of joke between us, and whenever I get the chance around him, I order my normal concoction with a broad, shit-eating grin. It doesn't normally bother me that he doesn't make my morning cup the way I'd prefer it, but just this once, I wish he'd made at least a *little* effort. I don't even need the lavender, but couldn't he dump in some milk, at the very least?

"Serious people drink black coffee," he says, smiling as if reading my mind.

I smile and nod. "So you've said," I answer, taking a large gulp.

Instantly, I feel like a new person. My mouth is less gritty, and my eyes finally open fully. "You're golfing today?" I ask, leaning back into the pillows.

"*We're* going to the club," he says, and I groan again, outwardly this time as I set the coffee down and try to pull the covers over my head.

"I know." He pulls me back up and presses a kiss to my forehead. "I'm sorry. But you don't have to come right away. Sleep a little longer. Have another coffee. I'll even make you one of those dumb ones, if it'll help."

Ouch. I wasn't aware a coffee could be dumb. I exhale slowly, pushing away my hurt feelings. Harrison's just teasing me. It's not his fault my over-consumption last night has me on edge.

"I'm on duty today, huh?" I ask after I take another gulp. Somehow, over the past few years, I ended up with a part-time job with Harrison's law firm. Head of Client Acquisition and Retention. It's not a paid position, or even a real position. Actually, I made up the title myself, but I'm good at it. I've helped Harrison sign almost forty clients to his firm.

But it's not as fulfilling as writing. Not even close.

I was a journalist for various magazines before I got the "job" with Harrison. Freelance *and* covering the arts, much to my parents' ire. And I was *really* good at it.

"You can take your time. I only need you for lunch. Let's say 2:00?" He checks his watch.

"I'll be there at 1:45," I mumble, cocooning myself back under the covers so I can continue to pretend last night didn't happen.

"Elizabeth!" Harrison calls from the bar. I turn around to find him nursing a scotch, and I freeze when I see Bobby next to him with a beer that appears untouched by his elbow.

My stomach plummets and sweat beads on my neck, and I kick myself for not asking who Harrison's client was before agreeing to come here.

Somehow, I convince my body to move forward, keeping a neutral expression on my face. Harrison still doesn't know anything about my past with Bobby, and I certainly don't want him asking questions about why I'm acting weird with the guy who could be his most important client.

Seeing Bobby and Harrison side by side in the light of day is startling. Both are exceptionally handsome, but while Harrison is all meticulous grooming and expertly chiseled muscle, Bobby is pure masculine ener-gy. While his hair isn't perfectly in place like Harrison's, the relaxed style suits him and complements his thick, strong jaw. Taking him in makes my traitorous body heat, but as my eyes drift down from his handsome face, I feel a bit more confident.

Because he looks utterly ridiculous.

If there was ever a man *not* meant for golf attire, it's Robert Beckett. It looks as if he googled "what to wear golfing" and sent his personal assistant to pick up the exact clothes that came up on google images. His polo is too tight in the arms, and even though it accentuates his muscles perfectly, the robin's egg blue color makes him look more like a college frat boy than a world famous musician. His shorts are the same length as Harrison's, but on Robert, they look hilarious. Too short. Too tight around his thick thighs.

I press my lips together to hide my smile as I make my way toward my fiancé and my… what? Ex? That word feels too insignificant, but I can't think of a better one.

"Robert," I nod, walking into Harrison's outstretched arm. "You look… colorful."

Robert licks his teeth, suppressing a laugh. The spark in his eye tells me he has a retort locked and loaded, but is holding back. Dangerous.

"Elizabeth!" Harrison hisses in my ear, and he squeezes my arm, turning me toward him. His grip is tight. I don't allow myself to wince, but it hurts, and I pull my arm out of his grasp as discreetly as possible.

It doesn't matter. Bobby's gaze is locked on my elbow, his jaw clenched and his forearms bunching as if he's physically holding himself back. The jovial glint in his eyes is gone, replaced with a mixture of concern and an unmistakable fury Harrison doesn't appear to notice.

"She's joking, of course." Harrison straightens, finishing his scotch in one large gulp and picking up his phone from the polished wood countertop.

Bobby lifts his chin. "She's not. And she's right. I look ridiculous." He gestures to his ensemble as if we're all in on a joke together, but his voice is like gravel. And not in the sexy, I played for a sold-out crowd last night so I'm a little hoarse, kind of way. No. It sounds like he's pushing out words he doesn't mean so he can hold the ones he does at bay. "Maybe I wouldn't if you'd given me more notice about today."

His words are curt, and Harrison blanches. "Next time, I promise. A whole week's notice." He tries to move on, dialing up the charm with a dazzling smile as he looks at his watch. "Speaking of little notice, my next meeting starts in ten, but Beth here will take excellent care of you at lunch, Robert."

"I'm sure she will…" Bobby's voice deepens, the rough quality smoothing over. It reminds me of aged whiskey, intoxicating and warm when it hits my stomach.

"But, if I could trouble you for a few more minutes, I have something I'd like to discuss with you both." Bobby smiles, but his cheek doesn't dimple, and his eyes remain hard.

The panic on Harrison's face is almost comical. He's used to being in charge. It's a rare occurrence that anyone questions him about anything, and he doesn't seem to know how to react. He looks at his watch, then back at Robert. "I can spare a few minutes," he says as if his eyes hadn't just bugged out of his head. "Shall we?" He grabs my elbow again, gently this time, and leads us toward our reserved table.

I don't miss the way Bobby watches his every move, his eyes never leaving Harrison's fingers on my skin. A server scrambles for another chair as Harrison pulls out mine, gesturing for Bobby to sit across from me. "Well. What is it you would like to talk about?" Harrison asks, standing over the table.

"Let's wait until you get comfortable," Robert replies, picking up his menu and flipping it over. I see the move for exactly what it is—he's showing Harrison who has the power here.

I don't look, pretending to be interested in what I'm going to order, but I would bet good money that the vein above Harrison's eyebrow is pulsing right now.

A third chair is brought to the table, and only once Harrison sits does Robert look back up, finally giving him the attention he so desperately wants. "Let's cut to the chase here. You want me as a client." Bobby tents his fingers together, leaning forward.

"I do. I think that as far as your needs for legal representation go, my firm is perfect—"

"Respectfully," Bobby cuts him off, "I think as far as my legal needs go, pretty much any firm would suffice. It's basic copyright law. I just need someone to look over my contracts and protect my assets."

He's right. I might not have followed Bobby's career, but I do know his reputation is spotless. He doesn't appear to party like most rock stars do—has never gotten himself into trouble or had any negative press at all, really.

"If it's a matter of cost..." Harrison sputters. He looks utterly panicked. This was clearly not how he expected this meeting to go, and nerves bubble in my stomach. If he doesn't want to work with Harrison, then why does he want *me* here?

"It's not." Bobby shakes his head. "It's more that I want to ensure that my legal counsel has my back in maintaining the image I've worked so hard to grow. I want to work with a firm that is behind me completely. A partnership."

"Absolutely," Harrison nods eagerly. "And we can provide that by—"

"That's where Beth comes in," Bobby interrupts again, and I sit up straighter in my chair. Harrison must be fuming at being interrupted a third time, but I don't dare look at him to confirm my suspicions, too anxious about where Bobby's going with this.

"I'm not a lawyer," I say, but he knows that already.

"She's not," Harrison echoes, seeming personally affronted by the idea that Bobby would potentially want to work with me rather than him. "But I assure you—"

"I know," he cuts Harrison off again, and even without looking at him, I sense the switch flip. I glance out of the corner of my eye and watch as Harrison's demeanor changes, his jaw going tight and his eyes narrowing. It's a look I've only seen twice before. Once, when he was losing his fifth game of poker and ended up breaking his friend's nose when he laid down a full house, only to be beaten by a royal flush. The second time... Well. It's in the past.

"I take care to thoroughly research everyone I'm considering hiring," Bobby continues. "Background checks, personal references. I have someone who finds out everything they can about my potential employee's family, close friends."

"Sounds like you don't trust people," Harrison says tightly, and he waves over our server, Ella, barking at her to get him a scotch. Neat. I wince. Normally, he's extremely polite to servers, but at the moment, he's no longer my sweet, charming fiancé. I scoot my chair a few inches away from him, making a mental note to apologize to Ella once Harrison leaves.

"I trust the people who've earned it. You can never be too careful in my position. I'm sure you understand," Bobby says with a smile, and Harrison lifts his chin, as if having family money causes the same amount of public scrutiny as being a billionaire musician.

"Of course I do," he says, defensive. Not a single thing Bobby has said was outright insulting or rude, but Harrison's on edge.

I want to chime in and force them to get to the point, but I'm nothing but a spectator in their pissing match, my voice trapped in my throat.

"My manager has been on me for years to allow *Rolling Stone* an all access feature about my life. The real Robert Beckett. I like my privacy, but with my upcoming album release," Ella brings Harrison's scotch, and Bobby pauses. "Excuse me, I'd love a coffee, please. Beth?"

I clear my throat. "Yes, same. Um, black please, Ella."

Bobby narrows his eyes. They have a full coffee bar here, and apparently, he knows it. I look at the menu in front of him, flipped to the side featuring the many beverages available here, including lattes. My body practically begs me to order one, but Harrison is already testy. The last thing I need is for him to snap at me about ordering a silly, embarrassing drink in front of a potential client.

Bobby sighs, shaking his head slightly before leaning back in his chair, and I relax, grateful he's decided to let my coffee order go. "Anyway. Back to where Beth comes in."

"It's Elizabeth. And I'm not sure I understand." Harrison is snappy, quickly losing his patience.

"Funny. That's not how she introduced herself to me." Bobby's focus shifts to me completely, making blood roar in my ears. "*Beth*, I understand you're a writer."

Harrison scoffs. "Not a real one," he says, and Robert freezes. I feel like I've been punched in the stomach, my breath whooshing out of me as his words twist like a knife in my gut.

"I'm sorry," Bobby says, his words made of white-hot fire. "I'm confused." He pulls out his phone. "Beth Winters. Twenty-six. Graduated with honors from NYU with a degree in English Lit. Has published dozens of articles in several major publications. Am I missing something?"

From the angle I'm sitting at, I can see the screen of his phone.

It's blank.

"Oh, I didn't mean it like that. I'm sorry," Harrison says, patting my hand. "Yes, Elizabeth has done some freelance writing in the past. But I'm still not sure what that has to do with signing on with my firm."

"I've run out of excuses for not doing the *Rolling Stone* story. Except, I don't want just any reporter poking their nose into my business. I would feel far more…" he trails off, his finger tapping on the table, "protected"—he finally settles on the word—"if the person writing the story had my best interest at heart. Who better than the wife-to-be of my future lawyer?"

The coffee arrives, and Bobby hands me mine before accepting his own. He thanks Ella by name, and she looks as if she might faint before scurrying away.

Harrison's phone rings. "I really am sorry, but this is my next meeting. I have to run. But I want to make sure I understand correctly. Elizabeth writes the story for *Rolling Stone*, spins it to make sure you look good, and you'll sign with Prodding and Smith?"

"Yes. Beth will come on the next leg of my tour. Two months. Everything will be provided, of course. Lodging, food. You'll be paid, Beth. I get final approval of the story. Those are my terms. Assuming you both agree, I'll sign the papers this evening."

"Excellent," Harrison pops up from his chair, not even looking at me before shaking Robert's hand. "It's a deal. I'll have my assistant send you the contract, and of course, let me know if you have any questions." He kisses the top of my head. "Keep him happy," he whispers in my ear and there's an intensity in his words that sets my whole body on edge. I nod, and Harrison squeezes my shoulder tightly before answering his phone and walking away.

"Well? Looks like your fiancé agrees. Not that he bothered asking you." Bobby doesn't hide the look of disgust on his face.

"He's just late for his meeting," I counter, feeling the need to defend him despite the fact that I wholeheartedly agree. I'm his fiancée. Not his employee. He can't just order me away on a tour bus for two months with my ex-whatever. *Not that he knows he was ever anything to you at all*, that annoying voice in my head says.

"Well, *I'm* asking, Beth." His voice is honey and gravel, still rough with anger at Harrison, but softer now that we're alone. I wish it was all gravel, because the honey makes my thoughts go fuzzy and my traitorous body buzz. "Two months on the road. Come on tour with me. Write the story. Get Harrison the contract he so desperately wants." His fingers resume drumming on the table as his eyes burrow beneath my skin. "What do you say?"

NOW

AUGUST 2024

Your sad eyes tell me you're lying
When you say you're almost happy
What other lies would I find beneath that hair so red?
—An excerpt from "Almost There," written and performed by Robert Beckett

"What's this really about, Robert?" I ask, politely waving Ella over to order. "Whatever entrée takes the least time to make, please. Two of them."

Bobby narrows his eyes at me, but he doesn't argue. "This is about me needing someone I trust to write this article."

"That's bullshit, and we both know it. You could find a hundred people to write the article. Did you already know I was engaged to Harrison when you met with him?" The Bobby I knew would never be so calculated, but I don't know this man.

"What? No!" He leans back as if I just slapped him. "You think I'm stalking you? Do you know how hard it's been for me to *not* look you up all these years? To not hire a damn private investigator to tell me everything about your life? This is *exactly* what I said it was. I met with Harrison, and there you were, staring at me like a ghost from a picture on his desk."

I examine his words, his posture, trying to decide if I believe him.

"Once I saw that picture, I needed to talk to you. Because, If I'm being honest—"

"Please," I breathe, needing the truth. I squeeze my hands together to keep them from shaking.

"I don't like him," Bobby says flatly. "He's not right for you, Beth. Not even close."

My mouth opens and closes as if forming words, but I don't know how to respond. "That's not for you to decide. You don't even know Harrison. Or *me,* for that matter." I look away, unable to hold eye contact as I say it.

"Look, I can't get out of doing this article. Not unless I want to do months' worth of talk show appearances and interviews, and I don't have time for that shit. Marissa said if I agree to an all-access, in-depth snapshot into my life, she'll keep the appearances to a minimum. Harrison wants to represent me, and you're the best writer I know. Please, let's do each other this favor."

"Marissa's still your manager?" I ask, and he nods.

I chew on my lip, considering his offer. Harrison signing Bobby as a client would be incredible for his career, and I *have* been thinking about going back to writing. What better way to make my comeback than an exclusive feature in the biggest music publication out there?

"If I agree, what are the terms? Where will I stay?"

"All access, Beth," he says, leaning back in his chair and crossing his arms. His biceps bunch, and despite the ridiculous blue polo he's wearing, he's annoyingly attractive. My cheeks heat. "That means you'll stay on the bus with me."

"Nope." I press my palms on the table, the blush creeping all the way down my throat. "We're done."

"It's the only way we'll have time to do the article. You'll be by yourself most of the time. You can write. Or plan your wedding. I have studio hours booked in every city we go to, songwriting sessions whenever I'm not recording, and then my shows at night. You'll have your own space. Complete privacy."

I rub my forehead where my headache is starting to thrum again. "I don't get it Bobby. I haven't seen you in six years. Why do you think me writing this article will be different from anyone else writing it? Hire Harrison, or don't. But leave me out of it." I stand. I can eat at home.

"Beth. I haven't told you the best part. Half the proceeds from the sale of this edition will be donated. It's already been negotiated. Childhood cancer research."

I freeze, slowly sitting back down. "You *actually* expect me to believe this wasn't pre-planned?" He has to know that if anything could get me to say yes, it's this. Raising money and awareness for childhood cancer. He looks at me with sad eyes, knowing where my mind has gone.

"I started my own charity two years ago, and the contract with *Rolling Stone* was signed before I met with Harrison. I can show you the paperwork. It had nothing to do with you."

I think of Michael, and how he should be alive right now. How maybe he would be, if science had caught up with his horrific, nasty disease. "I want my own space," I say, pausing. "And if at any point it gets to be too..." I don't know how to phrase what I'm thinking. Or maybe I just don't want to admit out loud that being around him already feels like digging a shard of glass into an open wound.

"If it's too much, I'll get you a hotel room," he finishes for me. "Do this with me, Beth."

I exhale. "No women on the tour bus." I guess I'm listing my conditions now, and while that one isn't fair for me to ask, it's necessary. I've seen the way women fall over him and have no interest seeing him partake in that particular benefit of being a rockstar.

Bobby clears his throat, clearly uncomfortable. "Agreed. No men for you either."

"I'm engaged," I spit, but he holds up a hand.

"I'm talking about Harrison."

I consider this for a moment. I was the wronged party in our relationship, but it doesn't change the fact that, at least for a while, Bobby and I really were in love. I'm sure he doesn't want to hear me having sex with my fiancé any more than I want to hear him hooking up with some random groupie. So, I nod. If Harrison wants to come see me, we'll book a hotel for the night.

"Anything else?" he asks.

"Do I have to go to your shows?"

"That's part of it, yes. You'll have backstage access, of course."

"Then I have one more condition," I say.

"Name it," he meets my eyes, and there's a glint of victory there. He knows he's won.

"If I come on tour with you," I say, enunciating every word carefully so there's no mistaking what I'm saying, "and that's still a *big* if, then you're taking that damn song out of your set list."

THEN

OCTOBER 2016

There's someone else sitting in my seat today—Molly's little brother, and by extension, mine—Michael.

"Hey kiddo!" I ruffle his hair, but he doesn't look up from the notebook Bobby's holding open between them.

"Bobby needs a word that rhymes with application," Michael says, his eyes scrunched in concentration as he stares at Bobby's notebook like it's the most important task he's ever been given.

"You're writing a song about applications?" I say, narrowing my eyes at Bobby and grabbing the coffee waiting for me on the table.

Bobby nods. "Not about *any* application. About a girl who won't send in her NYU application."

"It's a *very* sad song," Michael adds.

"He's right. Very sad. I think it'll be my first big hit."

I snatch the paper from Bobby's hands, ready to call his bluff, but the song is there—line after line of black ink.

"Wait. You're *actually* writing a song called The Application?"

He snatches the page back from me. "You're missing the subtext. It's not about the piece of paper. The girl in the song is amazing. Talented and smart and beautiful," Bobby says, looking up at me—looking *through* me—and I wonder if that's really how he feels. "But she's afraid to go after what she wants."

Bobby's searching my face, and I somehow both love and hate how he seems to see straight into the deepest parts of me. The ones I try my best to hide. "I'm going to send it. Tomorrow. I think," I say, trying to convince the blood to stop rushing to my cheeks.

"Station! That rhymes!" Michael bounces up and down.

Bobby nods, chewing on his lip. "That *is* a good one. I think you might be a songwriter one day. But I don't think it's quite right..." Bobby snaps his fingers, then blatantly meets my eyes. "Deprivation," he says, scribbling the word down.

"That's perfect." Michael nods emphatically, and even though I want to groan at Bobby's persistence about my NYU application, I can't stop myself from laughing at how seriously Michael is taking this assignment.

"Do you even know what that word means?" I ask, crossing my arms. Michael just shrugs.

"I'm six. I know it rhymes," he says, his little brow furrowing.

"Sure does," Bobby says, giving Michael a high five. "Thanks for the help, Bud."

Michael nods, mission complete. "I'm gonna go see if Molly will make me a hot chocolate," he says, scurrying toward the counter.

"Why are you doing this?" I groan, plopping into the empty chair. "I probably wouldn't even get in."

Bobby's eyes almost bug out of his head, and he tosses his notebook to the side. "Tell me, Miss Captain of the Debate Team, 5.36 GPA, Model UN ambassador, and editor of the school newspaper. Why in the actual world do you think they wouldn't accept you?"

"Because," I gesture to my uniform: an oxford shirt, plaid kilt, and knee-high socks. "It's a liberal arts school. Do I look liberal artsy? Does that resumé you just listed off sound liberal or artsy to you?" This time, I don't back away from his stare. I hold it, because I know the truth.

I wasn't bred for an art university *or* a creative career. I was bred to be a lawyer. Until the time comes to become a wife and a mother, retire my lawyer's hat, and shift my career to managing the household for my politician husband.

Bobby shrugs, but I can tell he's more frustrated than he's letting on. "You have the soul of an artist."

"Even if I get in, my parents—"

"It's *your* life, Beth," Bobby says gently. "Do you think my mom was thrilled when I didn't go to college? When I told her I was going to be a handyman and teach guitar lessons and play shows six nights a week at dive bars?"

"But can you even make a living as a poet?" I ask.

Bobby takes my hand in his, and suddenly my skin feels like it's covered in warm glitter. *Has his hand always been this big?* I think about how it would feel cupping the back of my neck, pulling me in for a kiss.

"Do what makes you happy, then fill in the blanks. Work here on the side. Or the library." His brow scrunches as if he's thinking deeply about my future, and it's secretly thrilling.

"What if it's still not enough?" my voice goes soft.

"You find a way," he says. "I'll help you. But it doesn't matter what I think, and it doesn't matter what anyone else thinks. Live your life for *yourself*, Beth. There will be a time when you'll have to sacrifice for other people. But that time isn't now. You're eighteen. Now's the time you're supposed to be out there chasing your dreams, running toward them as fast as you possibly can with your arms outstretched. I don't want to look back in ten years and only feel content with the life I've lived. Do you? I want to be able to say that I grabbed what I wanted by the throat and squeezed with everything I had."

"Wouldn't that be killing your dreams?" I ask, cracking a smile.

Bobby tries not to laugh, but he's unsuccessful, and his cheek dimples.

"You know what I mean," he says. "My mom was a musician, you know. Piano. She studied at Julliard. Played with famous symphonies. And then she met my dad. When he got a job opportunity in Nebraska, far away from any sort of classical music scene, she went with him. Every time I play a new song for her, there's a hidden glint of sadness in her eyes. She made a decision for someone else and has spent the rest of her life wondering if she made the right choice."

"That can't be true. No one could possibly regret anything that led them to having you in their life." My neck warms at my confession. He squeezes my hand this time, and I almost faint. My heart thumps rapidly, and I hope he can't feel my pulse through my skin.

"I know she doesn't. But when we look back at our life someday, it's going to be the culmination of a bunch of small decisions that didn't seem like that big of a deal at the time. But they *are* a big deal. And the decisions are yours to make alone. Ignore the doubts. Why are you giving them valuable space in your brain? Space I know is already full of words and emotions and feelings." He taps my forehead.

He's not wrong. Even though I'd rather run into traffic than let go of his hand, ideas *are* swirling in my mind, and my fingers itch to find a pen and write them down before they disappear. "I hear you," I say. It's all I can give him right now. I need to make a plan. Do some research and find a clear path forward, not just follow some dream of *maybe* becoming successful as a writer.

As if he knows I'm considering his words, Bobby relaxes in his chair, grabbing his notebook and flipping to a brand-new page. I feel the loss of his touch all the way to my toes, and I wonder, as he looks at my hands once more, if he feels it, too.

"Embrace the chaos, Beth." He smiles at me, and I uncap my pen, opening to a poem I've worked on for months that has every line written. By all measures, it's finished, and yet it still doesn't feel quite right. Maybe it never will.

Maybe perfect is an idea I'm chasing in my mind, the line always moving no matter how good my work gets. Maybe just writing down my words is enough.

Enough for what? I'm not sure. But if one person wants to read them, that feels like success. And that one person seems to be sitting across from me, believing in me unconditionally as he writes his own words, searching for one that rhymes with application.

My heart flutters as my decision solidifies, as I dive off the edge of the cliff I've been standing on for months. "Validation," I say as I rip out the poem and hand it to him to read, then turn the page to a fresh, unblemished one. "Thank you… For believing in me." A new idea churns through my mind. Emotions I need to purge onto paper.

"You'll submit your NYU application, then?" His voice is bursting with hope and maybe a little bit of pride. His eyes scan my work, sparkling as if he's reading a masterpiece, and my entire body warms.

"I'll submit it," I confirm as I drag my purple ink pen across the stark white of my journal, my heart rate slowing as I confess my planned familial betrayal to the page.

Three months later, I sprint to the coffee shop after school, flashing *the* envelope from NYU at Molly and inclining my head toward our seats. At precisely 3:07 p.m., I'm standing in front of Bobby, severely out of breath, with my sweaty bangs sticking to my forehead.

Once again, I wave the envelope frantically at Molly, but she's running back and forth as a sour-faced twenty-something impatiently taps her foot by the counter.

Bobby shoots upright in his seat when he sees the envelope, his notebook clattering to the ground as he takes it from my hand. "It's here?" he asks, flipping the letter over and staring at the ink as if making sure it's my name printed on the outside.

"Got here this morning. I couldn't open it. You do it," I blurt out, squeezing my eyes shut and swallowing down bile.

Bobby doesn't hesitate, sliding his thumb beneath the corner and peeling apart the seal.

"Wait!" I lurch toward him, placing my hands on his. Even through the panic, my skin ignites. "Maybe we should wait. I don't want to know. Not for a few more days." *Maybe this weekend,* I think, so if I don't get in, I can crawl into bed and wallow away this little nugget of a dream, one I'm still not even sure I'll follow through with. But if it's a rejection, that's it. Off to law school I go. No more dreaming.

The thought almost makes me vomit.

"Beth," he flips my hand over and interlaces his fingers with mine, and suddenly I'm not sure I care so much if I get into NYU. I'm floating, tethered to this boy, the rhythm of my pulse matching his, and I want to stay here in this moment for the rest of my life, my fingers buzzing and my heart fluttering.

He squeezes and I take a sharp inhale. "This *is* an acceptance letter," he says confidently, as if the idea that I wouldn't be accepted is completely out of the realm of possibilities.

"How do you know?" I ask. My lip trembles, and I pull it between my teeth.

"Because not letting you in would be the biggest mistake they ever made," he says, but his attempt at reassurance bounces off my anxiety like it's an impenetrable iron shield.

"I can't watch." I cover my face, and Bobby laughs.

"Go get your drink. Molly's been working on your latte art for at least ten minutes. I think it's a butterfly. Or maybe an apple. The stem could be an antenna—"

"Focus, Bobby!" I smooth down my impeccably ironed uniform skirt, needing to busy my hands.

"Sorry. Go." He waves me toward the counter. "I'll open it, and then we can celebrate with coffee in hand."

I nod. *Coffee. Yes.* I know it makes no sense, but the caffeine will calm my nerves. Robotically, as if the guy I have a massive crush on isn't either opening or closing the door to my future just a few feet away, I go get my drink.

"It came?" Molly quirks an eyebrow, and I nod, pushing down the urge to vomit.

"What if they rejected me?" I catch myself biting my nails, a habit I kicked years ago. Molly understands why I'm so nervous. She's the only one who knows, *really* knows, what a risk it was for me to even send the application in. How bare and exposed it made me feel.

"Stop worrying," she says with a smile so big, the apples of her cheeks turn pink, "and go let Bobby tell you that you got in."

"But seriously, what if I didn't—"

"Beth. Turn around." It's a rare order from a usually not-at-all-bossy Molly, so I oblige.

The floor falls out from beneath my feet when I see the huge grin on Bobby's face.

"I'm in?" I'm frozen. Can't move. Can't breathe.

"You're in. Beth, you're in!" He jumps up from the chair and rushes toward me, wrapping his arms around my waist and lifting me into the air. He spins me around as Molly runs around the counter, squealing.

"You're in!" She joins our hug.

"I'm in!" I shout, so unlike myself. I blush as the other patrons politely clap, still squeezing my arms around Bobby's neck until he sets me back down and pulls back to look at me. I feel the loss of his body heat like the sun disappearing behind a storm cloud, but his hands slide from my waist up my arms, burning me as they graze my skin.

"I never doubted it. Not for one second." He tucks my hair back behind my ears, and I stare into his eyes, unable to look away. With a smile so full of pride you'd think he was the one who just got accepted into his dream school, Bobby hugs me again, and I take a second to memorize it all.

The way he believes in me.

The way he celebrates me.

And maybe most importantly, the way he made me feel strong enough to choose something for myself for the first time ever.

NOW

AUGUST 2024

What I wouldn't do for you,
To hear your laugh, or see you grin.
Do you feel the same, my love?
Am I underneath your skin?
—A poem by Harrison Rouchester to Beth Winters

The smell of vodka sauce hits my nose the moment I open the front door, and my stomach growls. It's been hours since the lunch I barely touched, and I'm starving.

Harrison's at the stove when I enter the kitchen, changed out of his golf clothes into sweatpants and a white T-shirt, a towel slung over his shoulder. He looks hot, and my shoulders relax as I take in his casual attire. Something about seeing him domestic and dressed down makes some of my annoyance about him agreeing to Bobby's deal dissipate.

"You made dinner?"

He jumps, but I'm not surprised he didn't hear me over the bass almost vibrating the skin off my bones. He switches off the music, but my ears continue to buzz. "Sure did." He turns back to the stove, stirring constantly. "I called you a couple times. I was worried it'd be cold by the time you got home," he says, not looking at me.

The oven timer goes off, and I open the door to find a steaming loaf of bread.

I take a second to think of how to respond, taking out the bread and sliding out of my heels. My arches ache as my feet stretch out on the cold tile floor.

"Why would you worry?" I ask, keeping my tone light. I knew Harrison would be concerned when I didn't answer my phone earlier, but I hadn't been ready to talk to him after he'd agreed to Bobby's terms without asking me. "I was just at the club."

"I know. I checked your location. You were there for *hours*." The muscles in his jaw bunch. "Long lunch?" he asks, the wooden spatula making a *scritch* sound as it aggressively scrapes the bottom of the pan.

Is that jealousy I hear in his voice?

I have to stop myself from rolling my eyes as I lean against the counter. He's the one insisting I live on a bus with a rockstar for the next two months. "They had a last-minute opening for a massage, and then I went to the sauna for a bit," I say, not mentioning I'd done those things to give me time to think. To consider how I could get out of this tour without making Harrison question why.

He nods, the tension in his posture easing as he turns back to the sauce, and I exhale slowly.

"How about I go change, and then I can make the salad?" I suggest.

"Take your time," he says, offering me a smile before grabbing some basil from my tiny herb garden by the window. I rush upstairs to change into sweatpants and a tank, throwing my hair up in a loose bun.

By the time I get back, there's two steaming bowls of sausage pasta on the table along with the warm bread and a green salad, already made.

"This looks phenomenal," I say, sitting down. My mouth waters when Harrison brings me a glass of red wine, sliding it into my hand and kissing the top of my head.

"You deserve it. I haven't cooked for you in a while. I thought it was past due." He winks, sitting down and taking a sip of his scotch.

I wave him off. "You're busy at work. I get it," I say, stabbing the pasta with my fork and taking a bite. "Ohhmmygossshh," I say through a mouth full of food. It's amazing. Creamy with plenty of garlic and parmesan, and I take another bite, ripping off a piece of bread and dipping it in the sauce. "How'd your other meeting go?" I ask.

"Great." Harrison leans forward, his eyes lighting up with excitement. "Don't tell anyone, but Shane Brown got a DUI," he digs into his own pasta, nodding his head in appreciation as he talks.

"The guy from News 6?" I try to picture what he looks like, but all I can see in my mind is dirty blonde hair and jowls.

"The one and only. They coerced him into the breathalyzer without explaining his other options. Rookie move. He'll get off on a technicality."

"Interesting," I respond, trying to sound happy for Harrison's win, even though I hate the idea of anyone getting off without consequences after driving drunk.

"We meet with the judge tomorrow afternoon at four, but I thought afterward maybe you and I could go grab drinks at Copper's. A special night out, just the two of us. I'll even leave my phone at home."

My chest warms at the gesture, and I laugh, stabbing my fork toward him. "No, you won't. You'd have to have it surgically removed."

"Okay. But I'll leave it in my pocket unless it's an absolute emergency. I swear." He gets up to top off my wine, and I take another bite of pasta, my stomach warming.

"If it's emergency only phone use, I think I can pencil you in," I say with a smile, curling up in the chair to sit cross-legged. "What's gotten into you? Date nights? Dinner? Is this what I have to look forward to in married life?"

God, I hope it is. If Harrison could just be a little more present sometimes—like he's being right now—it would be so much easier to communicate with him and get on the same page again.

"Once I make partner, I'll cook for you at least once a week. Like I used to. You really do deserve it. Tonight, especially. Seriously, I couldn't have closed the deal with Robert without you." He takes a sip of his scotch. "I have no clue why he wants *you* to write the feature so badly, but I have to admit, I think it's the reason he agreed to sign."

Suddenly, there's a rock the size of a grapefruit in my stomach.

"Listen," I say, ignoring his not-so-subtle jab and taking a mouthful of wine for courage. "About the tour. I need a few days to think about it."

There. I pulled off the band aid.

Harrison and I might have fallen into a pattern of me helping him with work obligations without question, but I'm not his employee. I'm going to be his wife, so the best way through this is with honesty.

At least, partial honesty.

Harrison freezes mid bite, the vein in his forehead becoming visible. "What do you *mean*, you need a few days to think about it?"

Shit.

THEN

JANUARY 2017

I knew Bobby lived in a shoebox apartment in Brooklyn, but it's not until I make it to his front door and press the button for 4B that I realize just how far he travels every day to meet me at Joe's.

Bobby immediately answers. "Coming!" he says, buzzing the door open for me. I slide inside and wait at the bottom of the stairs, nervously fidgeting with my class ring. I feel vulnerable here, like I don't know what to do with my body. This is the first time that I've hung out with Bobby somewhere other than the coffee shop. The first time I'm entering his personal space, and it sets me on edge in a swirling mess of anxiety.

There's a shuffling of feet rushing down the stairs, and I turn.

"Beth!" Bobby says with a huge grin, wrapping me in a tight, but all-too-brief, hug. "Come on, I'm up here." He grabs my hand and tugs me up the stairs, his warmth spreading up my arm and into my chest.

"It's not a lot," he says, taking off his ball cap, bending the bill as if nervous, before flipping it backward. "I mean, obviously. But my roommate's family owns it, and they don't charge me much for rent." He rocks onto his heels, still not opening the door.

"It can't be that bad. Step aside." I try to shoo him away, but he plants his feet and leans against the door.

"Maybe we should go somewhere else. There's a great coffee shop up the street." He raises his eyebrows like he just made a brilliant suggestion.

"It can't be that great if you hike forty minutes to get to Joe's every day. Why don't you want to go in? You got dead bodies in there or something?" I ask, reaching toward the doorknob.

He steps in front of me. "Nine of them. All decomposing. It's disgusting."

I narrow my eyes. "What's this about?" Suddenly, I'm stressed in a different way. What if his apartment is revolting and this clean, put together guy I've been spending all this time with is actually a slob who leaves empty pizza boxes everywhere and dirty plates on the floor? Or worse, what if he has some weird hobby, like he collects those creepy Victorian-era porcelain dolls or his fingernail clippings or something?

"It's just not as nice as where you live," he says with a shrug, averting his eyes.

"You've never been to my house. I could live in a one-room studio with four other families and no plumbing for all you know."

"Yeah, no. I looked up your address on Zillow. It's a legit mansion. You could fit nineteen of my apartments in that house," he says, not an ounce of shame in his expression.

"What?" my mouth drops open with mock outrage. "I can't believe you did that. You cyber-stalked me!"

"You actually can. Fit nineteen of my apartments in there, I mean. I did the math. And I was just doing some basic reconnaissance. Making sure you weren't some weirdo before I slogged all the way across town to see you every day."

His admission makes my stomach dip and my cheeks warm. "Let me in the apartment." I cross my arms.

"Okay, but prepare to be disappointed," he relents, stepping to the side.

"Oh my God, I'm not going to be disappointed." I roll my eyes and open the door to a surprisingly bright and clean apartment. The room is small, but they've used the space well, and the only mess I see is a pile of papers on the floor between a leather couch and a black armchair.

I turn around to tell him I love it, but stop when I find Bobby still standing in the doorway, shifting from foot to foot.

"What in the world are you worried about?" I plop down on the couch, reaching around the coffee table to grab the song on the top of the pile. "And where are the bodies?"

"They're in the back. You really like it?" he asks, his dimple appearing, and I have the sudden urge to grab a pen and write out every facet of it in lyrical stanzas I know still won't do it justice.

"It's perfect," I say honestly. "Comfortable."

I think Bobby blushes, but he hides it by gesturing toward the hallway. "Anyway. We share a bathroom. It doesn't lock, but I already told Johnny to knock before he goes in. My room's to the left, and his is in the very back."

"Got it." My stomach flips at the thought of being so close to his bedroom, but I keep my butt firmly planted on the couch. "What does Johnny do? Is he in school?"

"He's studying music production, but he plays guitar as well." Bobby gestures to the six guitars hanging on the wall near the kitchen.

As if saying his name summoned him, the front door swings open, and a tall, dark-haired boy around our age walks in.

"Well, if it isn't the famous Beth," he swings his arms wide and smiles broadly, and I warm to him immediately.

"I thought you were working today," Bobby stabs a finger at him, his brows narrowing as if accusing him of something sinister.

"And I thought you weren't doing anything fun today. Thank God I looked at your phone and saw a text from your girl here about coming over so I could drop in. He's been trying to hide you from me, Beth." Johnny crosses his arms and sticks his lip out in a pout.

Bobby's jaw drops, his mouth gaping open as if he's trying to figure out how to reply.

"Not his girl." I save him, standing up to shake Johnny's hand. I don't like the way the words taste coming out of my mouth, but I swallow down the bitterness.

"Interesting… that's what he keeps saying, too," Johnny says, and something wilts inside me, but I force a smile as he steps past my outstretched hand and wraps me in a bear hug. "Semantics. Either way, I'm glad to meet you. You sure seem to inspire Bobby. He's written some of the best music I've ever heard in the past couple months." He pulls back but keeps his hands on my arms.

Bobby's gaze locks on Johnny's fingers, his eyes narrowed. I've been under the impression they're friends, but based on how tense Bobby is, I'm wondering if they're more roommates who tolerate one another.

"Do you guys play together?" I ignore his absurd insinuation that I am the reason Bobby's been writing great songs and take a step back, hoping to break the tension.

"Sometimes." He shrugs. "But I'll play for anyone who will hire me. You don't need any backup guitar by chance, do you?" he jokes.

"Considering that I sound like a drowning cat when I sing, that would be a firm no." I hold my hands up in front of me.

"I can't imagine you're bad at anything," Johnny says. "Not with the way Bobby talks about you. Does everything you touch turn to gold?"

"Oh my God. Leave her alone. Don't you have somewhere to be, Johnny?" Bobby wipes his hands on his jeans.

"Unfortunately," he sighs dramatically, "I do."

"Great!" Bobby stands up straighter. "I mean… Oh no, don't go," he says, his voice flat.

"I'm sure I'll see you around, Beth," Johnny says with a wink.

"Only come home if you decide to be less annoying," Bobby says, leading him to the door.

Johnny smiles and flips Bobby off, then turns and starts singing a song I've never heard before, his voice disappearing down the hallway.

I'm not the man I was this morning,
The one who wore the ground down pacing…

"Sorry about him," Bobby says, pouring a mug full of coffee from what's clearly a hand-me-down coffee pot, then dumping in some milk and a three second pour from a bottle of lavender syrup he must have bought just for me. I can't help but smile at his thoughtfulness, even if it feels like he's avoiding looking at me as he ambles around, never quite turning in my direction.

"It's not your normal fancy latte, but—"

"It's perfect," I say genuinely as I snuggle into the corner of the couch. And I mean it. Really, I do. It's perfect. *He's* perfect. Except… Johnny's words twist tighter in my stomach. *That's what he keeps saying, too…* I shake the thought away. "So, um, I have a favor to ask you," I say, twisting my fingers together.

"Anything," he replies, pouring himself a cup of black coffee and coming to sit next to me. He positions himself on the other end of the couch, too far for our legs to touch, and I'm glad. I'm not sure I'd have the courage to ask him this if he was touching me.

"I have an assignment for school; for English class. We had to write something in a medium we've never tried before."

"Interesting… So, what did you choose? Slam poetry?" He finally looks at me. Apparently, all he needed was the opportunity to tease me to banish whatever tension Johnny caused.

"Actually, I did that last month," I say. "It was terrible. This time, I um… Well, I chose to write a song."

A dimple appears in Bobby's cheek and my heart shoots into my throat as he leans back to study me. "You, Beth Winters, self-proclaimed drowning cat, have written a song?"

"I have." I ignore his ribbing. "It's umm…" Blood warms my cheeks, and I let my hair fall in front of my eyes. "It's a love song. I thought maybe you could look at it for me. Tell me if it's any good? We have to read it to the class, and you know how I feel about having a bunch of eyes on me. I *really* don't want to get up there if it's terrible."

"You're not going to sing it?" he teases.

I lower my voice. "I want to get a good grade on this. Not fail."

"Fail? I'd never let that happen," he crinkles his brow as if offended. "*Or* let you write a terrible song. Hand it over."

"You can't laugh, okay? I need you to promise." I think I might actually throw up.

"Beth, there is no way anything you wrote in any medium is bad, and if by some miracle it is, it'll just make me like you more. Make you seem a bit more… on my level."

Like me *more*. He shifts closer to me as he says it, and I panic. How much *does* he like me? And is it as a friend, or more? But it can't be more, right? Because if that were the case, wouldn't he have said so by now?

Bobby must mistake my spinning thoughts for nerves as his expression turns serious. "Beth, I promise I won't laugh."

I take a deep breath, then pull the folded piece of paper from my jacket pocket. It's creased and worn, a little tattered on the corner from how many times I've opened and closed it. I've been working on it all week, carrying it with me for when inspiration struck.

"Be nice." I hand it to Bobby, and he unfolds it carefully, like he already thinks it's special.

He quirks an eyebrow. "You titled the song 'Poetry?' Why am I not surprised?" His eyes shine as he settles back, picking up his coffee.

"You said you wouldn't laugh."

"Have I laughed? Now shh," he teases, his eyes scanning the paper, and my mouth goes dry. It's unreasonable how handsome he looks right now, his ankle casually slung over his knee, settled in on his leather couch with his guitars hanging above his head. My belly warms as he shifts, and I watch his lips move, silently reading the words I've written and rewritten at least a dozen times.

"You actually wrote this?" he asks, raising an eyebrow. "This isn't from some old album somewhere and you plagiarized the lyrics, trying to convince me you're a better songwriter than I am?"

"Every word is mine." My skin buzzes, and I smile so wide, my cheeks hurt. "You're not full of crap? Really? You like it?"

"Amazing," he says again, setting his coffee cup down and lifting the page to reread it. "Just amazing," his voice is rough as he repeats the word he always seems to use to describe anything I write.

"Don't you lie to me, Bobby Beckett. I don't want you trying to make me feel good here."

He lowers the page and looks at me. Looks *into* me in the way only he can.

"Is this about anyone in particular?" he asks, searching my face. His eyes move from mine to my nose, my lips, then my hands.

My entire body heats as I blush again, and I wonder if there's some sort of surgery I can have that will make my blood vessels stop betraying me. "Nope. Just a song." My throat squeezes uncomfortably around the lie. I'm falling back into my old patterns, not brave enough to go after what I want, and I hope that he can't see right through me. Bobby's expression shifts, a flash of something akin to disappointment flickering in his eyes before he goes back to read the song again.

"Do you have another copy of it?" he finally asks.

"It's typed on my computer. I have to submit it tonight."

"Don't change a word," he says, reading it one more time, his eyes sparkling. Bobby folds it back up almost reverently and takes his wallet out of his back pocket, sliding my song in next to his driver's license.

"What are you doing?" I ask, grabbing at his arm, but he pulls the wallet out of my reach.

"No way. I'm keeping it," he says, as if the matter is decided.

And it is.

Because Bobby could ask me to do just about anything, and I think I'd have no choice but to agree.

I don't ask how Bobby got me a fake ID, or let myself look nervous as the enormous, tattooed bouncer checks it. With barely a glance, he hands it back to me, and I walk into Baby's All Right, looking for a place to hang out until Bobby's set starts. I've never been anywhere like this before, and even without using my ID to order a drink, I feel intoxicated.

There's something bluesy playing, a rhythm that makes me want to sway my hips. Instead, I lean against the stage, watching as the room starts to fill up.

"Do you think he'll sing "Save You for Last?" the girl next to me asks. At first, I think she's talking to me, but when I turn around, I'm met with a group of girls, all dressed nearly identical in tight black dresses and heels.

The tallest one, a stunner with long blonde hair and bright pink lipstick pulls out her phone. "You can send him a message on Instagram and request it if you want. I already requested 'Captive.' He played it last show, and I swear he looked right at me when he sang it."

A shorter, but equally beautiful brunette sighs. "I'm not sure he reads the requests. He never responds," she says.

"Kelly. He must get a hundred requests before every show. You think he's going to respond to them all?" the blonde snaps.

"I'm sorry," I interrupt, not knowing the songs they're talking about. "Is someone playing tonight other than Bobby?"

"Bobby?" The girl called Kelly laughs but stops, her eyes bugging out when she realizes I'm not joking. "Wait, do you *know* Robert Beckett?"

"There's no way she knows Robert," a different girl says, her red lips tipping into a smirk as her eyes drag up my jeans and black t-shirt. Suddenly, I'm self-conscious. I felt good when I left the house this evening. A little sexy even, with jeans that hug my legs like a second skin and a slightly cropped shirt. My hair is half up, the ends curled into loose waves.

"Excuse me," I force a smile and turn around, ignoring them as I try not to let their jab bother me. I *do* know Bobby. And so far, I haven't needed a skintight black mini dress to get his attention.

Except, you are firmly in the friend zone, that annoying little voice in my head reminds me.

The lights dim, and I take a final look around. This place is packed. To-the-brim packed, mostly with women.

Bobby talks about his songwriting a lot. About his music. But he doesn't talk about his performances very often. Sometimes, he'll tell me about changing a word on the fly, or when he feels like he made a mistake. I *know* he can sing, because sometimes, when our heads are hovering over his notebook dissecting a lyric, he quietly sings the melody along with the words to give me a better picture of what the song is like.

But this? This is *insane.* So much bigger and more thrilling than anything I've ever pictured.

The house music quiets, and the lights dim. An older man with obviously dyed hair saunters across the stage. There's no preamble, no long-winded introduction.

"Robert Beckett, everybody," he says, and the audience goes wild. It's exhilarating, and I can't help but join in.

Bobby walks out on stage and beams at me. Actually *beams* at me, and I know my expression is an echo of his. Pride swells in my chest as he grabs the microphone stand. The crowd cheers again, and he waves confidently. Bobby has found himself quite the following here in New York, and I am so happy for him I feel like I could explode.

"Good evening!" It's Bobby's voice coming through the speakers, the same voice as the boy I share coffee with every day, but *more.* It's commanding, vibrant, and so incredibly sexy, it makes my toes tingle. My core clenches, and I feel myself morphing into another fan-girl. But tonight, I'm okay with it. I *am* fan-girling.

"Thank you all for being here." He strums a chord on his guitar——then quickly adjusts the second to last knob, tuning it before continuing. It's easily the sexiest thing I've ever seen. I squeeze my legs together, unable to look away from his strong, callused fingers.

"We're gonna start with a new song tonight." The crowd quiets down, their anticipation palpable. "This one's called 'The Application.'"

My jaw drops as Bobby winks at me, then strums the first note. The four girls who taunted me earlier turn as one to look in my direction, but I can't pry my gaze from Bobby's face. He owns the stage, commands it in a way I've never seen before. It's like it was built specifically for him, and even if I wasn't already nursing this major crush on him, I surely would be after watching him perform.

He looks at me several times during the song, and every time, I almost black out, blood rushing to my head and sweat breaking out on my neck. His voice is intoxicating, and with every word I fall a little harder until I'm certain, as the last note rings out and his vibrato trails off, that regardless of if he feels the same, I am completely and hopelessly in love with Bobby Beckett.

NOW

AUGUST 2024

Would you just fucking listen to what I'm asking you to do?
You don't even care what I want. Don't argue with me, Elizabeth. You know
it's the truth.
—An unintentional poem by Harrison Rouchester during an argument with
Beth Winters

Harrison's voice drops an octave, his spine straightening. "What do you *mean,* you need a few days to think about it?" The fork in his hand falls to his plate with a clatter, pinkish-red vodka sauce splattering across the white linen tablecloth like drops of blood.

"I just..." I take another sip of wine, stalling for time. Even after hours at the club racking my brain for a believable reason why I wouldn't want to do the article, I couldn't come up with a good excuse. There's no explanation that makes sense.

At least, not without telling Harrison about my history with Bobby—something I still have no intention of doing.

How could I at this point? My lie of omission is too woven into the fabric that makes up Elizabeth Winters—the woman Harrison fell in love with. A woman so very different from Beth—the free spirited girl with the heart of a poet who trusted the entirety of her heart in her rockstar boyfriend's callused fingers.

Harrison wouldn't recognize that version of me, because after Bobby, being that girl hurt too much. I couldn't take it, and so I'd slipped back into the skin I'd worn before him, my pain easing another degree every day as I settled deeper into my predetermined path.

"You just *what*?" Harrison practically hisses.

I put my wine glass down. "I'm just not sure the assignment is a great fit for my style of work. I don't normally cover rock shows."

"Your style of work," Harrison scoffs, rolling his eyes and taking a sip of scotch. "I already told him we had a deal, Elizabeth. We shook on it."

"I know, but you didn't exactly ask me. I mean, we didn't even have a conversation before—"

Harrison slams his palms on the table. The candles flicker and the silverware rattles, and I suck in a sharp breath, every cell in my body on alert.

"Would you just fucking listen to what I'm asking you to do? You don't even care what I want!" He throws back another gulp of scotch. I crack open my mouth to tell him that's not true, but Harrison stabs a finger in my direction as he stands, his chair flying back into the wall with a crash. His voice drops, his vein throbbing now. "Don't argue with me, Elizabeth. You know it's the truth."

The hair on my neck stands on end, my hands gripping the armrests as Harrison waits for me to say something, but I'm frozen in place.

I don't know what to say, because *this* is not my Harrison.

He takes several deep breaths, his nostrils flaring, and I curl my shoulders in, trying to make myself small.

"I know you want to write," he continues. "You fucking yelled it from the top of the stairs before we left for the party."

My heart slams against my ribcage, my muscles tensing.

He heard me.

My shock must show on my face, because Harrison smiles. "I'm not an idiot, Elizabeth. It's right there on our security footage. I watched it to see how much time you wasted looking for that fucking bracelet." He leans forward, holding eye contact. "So you want to write, just not if it benefits someone other than yourself? Like, I don't know. Your fiancé?" he accuses, beating an open palm on his chest.

"This has nothing to do with you," I say, careful to keep my voice gentle.

"So, you're just a selfish bitch, then?" he spits, picking up his rocks glass and throwing it at the wall behind me, missing me by less than a foot. The pain of his words is almost as sharp as the piece of glass that pierces the back of my arm.

Almost.

Tears fill my eyes, but I refuse to let them fall. Harrison preys on weakness. I've seen it before in court, and I can sense his hunger for it now. For me to cower so he can make the killing blow.

I clear my throat. "I'm sorry. I didn't realize it was this important to you," I say calmly, like this is just another cordial conversation over dinner.

Except it's obviously not. I'm far too aware of the uncharacteristic darkness in Harrison's eyes and the way his fingers are clenching the table so firmly, I fear it will crack.

For the first time in almost two years, I'm afraid of Harrison.

"You're doing this, Beth." He stands, stabbing a finger at me as he throws his napkin on the floor.

"Of course. You're right," I say, my tone as placating as possible. "Forgive me. I was just worried about managing my time. With the wedding planning. I just…" I swallow. "I want the day to be perfect."

Harrison grips the back of his chair, his posture easing enough to let me breathe again, but the sharp rage in his eyes remains. "Of course it's about the wedding," he says, rubbing a hand down his face. "I'll hire you the best planner money can buy. God knows we'll have enough of it after Robert signs his contract."

"Okay, then. A wedding planner will help. I'll start packing after we finish eating," I say, hoping a full belly will slow the effects of the alcohol in his bloodstream.

"You eat," he says, storming toward his study. "I'm not hungry anymore."

He slams the door so hard the pictures on the wall shake, and the relief I feel when he's gone is overwhelming.

Not only that, it's wildly unsettling. I shouldn't feel this way.

Not about my fiancé.

Not when I thought we were past this. Firmly on the other side of his anger.

One moment of weakness, years ago. A fist through the wall. A shattered chair. That's all he's ever shown to make me worry what he's capable of. But he went to therapy. Did the work and swore he was sorry. That he would never lash out in anger again.

Tears burn my eyes as I wipe away the trail of blood running down the back of my arm with my napkin, holding pressure.

Only once I'm certain the bleeding has stopped do I pull out my phone.

I stare at it for what feels like hours. Until my glass is dry and my food has long gone cold.

Nausea works its way up my throat as I sit there, doubt creeping onto my shoulders and pressing down until my body threatens to buckle under its weight. I'm not sure I'm capable of spending two months on the road with Bobby. I'm afraid that having him in my life again will reopen every scar in my heart, turning them into gaping wounds that will bleed me dry.

A shiver flits down my spine, and the back of my arm throbs—the spot where real blood stains my skin.

Even if I don't want to go, I can't stay here.

Not after what just happened.

I need some distance. Space from Harrison to figure out what I want and what I can live with. Because it's certainly not this—being afraid of what my husband-to-be might do when I don't play subservient wife. When I question him.

With trembling fingers, I dial the number written on the napkin Bobby handed me, expecting to need to leave a message, but he answers on the first ring.

"Hello?"

"Hi. Um…it's Beth?" I say it like a question, my voice shaking. I haven't spoken since Harrison stormed from the room, but maybe I should have said a few words or recited a poem to even out the nerves his reaction caused. I clear my throat, forcing myself to take even breaths.

"Beth. What's wrong?" Bobby's voice is sharp, and I picture him sitting up straight and putting his guitar down, as if holding it would keep him from listening intently enough.

"Nothing. I think I'm coming down with a cold. Um—" I continue on, not giving him time to question me.

"I'm coming to get you," he says, and I hear the jingle of car keys in the background.

"No, stop it. Listen, I'm fine. Really. I'm just calling to tell you that you wore me down. I'll do it."

There's a long pause. A heavy, loaded silence from the other end of the phone.

"Bobby?"

"Swear you're okay, Beth. And don't lie to me." His honey and gravel voice is firm, but gentle.

It takes every ounce of self-control I have to hold back the tears rising up my throat at his concern. It's comforting, and I *hate* it. That my marriage might be falling apart before it's even started, and *he's* the one trying to take care of me. "I swear it," I say, and even I'm impressed at how convincing I sound.

There's a heavy, tense sigh, and I picture Bobby taking off his ball cap and nervously flipping it backward. "Fine. I'll pick you up tomorrow morning. We're leaving a couple days earlier than expected."

My heart is thundering, but I keep my voice steady as I reply. "I'll take a cab. Text me the address."

There's a long silence, and I wonder what Bobby's thinking. "Tomorrow," he says, and before the concern I feel from him through the phone can make me cry, I hang up.

I place my head in my hands, forcing myself to take deep breaths. *What have I done?*

THEN

FEBRUARY 2017

I'm not the man I was a week ago
My head down, numb in the hustle
My days lost among the bustle
—An excerpt from "Dreamers and Poets" written and performed by Robert
Beckett

"Read this one," I tell Bobby, thrusting my open book at him.

"*Another* poem?" he groans, but I don't miss his crooked smile as he shifts in what I now consider *his* seat at Joe's Place. I know he loves reading poetry as we sip our coffee. Sometimes, he even asks for my book so he can read it out loud to me.

"Yes. It's my favorite. I can't believe I haven't shown it to you before."

"Well, if it's your favorite, hand it over." His cheek dimples as he holds out his hand and clears his throat dramatically. "It was many and many a year ago, in a kingdom by the sea, that a maiden there lived whom you may know by the name of Annabel Lee. And this maiden she lived with no other thought than to love and be loved by me." Bobby narrows his eyes. "So sweet… Not your usual jam."

"Keep going," I swat at him, and he holds up a hand in surrender, continuing on. His tenor is perfect for this poem, and I imagine Edgar

Allen Poe sitting in Charleston, overlooking Annabel Lee's buttercup yellow home and missing her so desperately he wrote these words.

"That the wind came out of the cloud by night, chilling and killing my Annabel Lee." He pauses for a moment, rubbing a hand across the back of his neck. "There it is. Jeez, this poem is depressing," Bobby tries to close the book, but I stop him. He's not wrong about my tastes. I do enjoy poetry layered with grief and sorrow. It somehow makes the love feel bigger—eternal.

"Please keep reading." I roll my eyes. He does, and as he reaches the final lines, chills break out along my arms.

"In her sepulchre there by the sea. In her tomb by the sounding sea."

I'm quiet for a moment as I let the immensity of the emotions of the poem sink in. Bobby leans forward, slowly, his eyebrows lowered as he rubs the back of his neck. He takes a deep breath, and I smile at the way the beauty of Poe's words seem to be affecting him.

He meets my eyes. "No really, Beth. Are you okay? That is a very, very sad poem."

"What? Are you *kidding* me? It's the greatest love poem of all time!" I say, ripping the book from his hands. "Their love is so great, not even the angels can keep them apart. It's beautiful."

"It's *tragic*," he says. "To love someone so much you'd rather die than live without them? It's so… vulnerable."

I gasp. It's dramatic. I know that, but I can't help it. "It's *beautiful*," I repeat. "I want a love like that."

Bobby studies me for a moment, but I can't tell what he's thinking. I know what I *hope* he's thinking. Maybe this is it.

Maybe he's thinking about me.

About what loving me would be like.

My stomach sinks as, instead of professing his love for me, he picks up his notebook and begins to write on a new page. "If that's what you want, I'm sure you'll find it," he finally says.

To my disappointment, he doesn't add "with me" to the end of his sentence, and even though it's unfair, it makes me angry.

"Noah asked me on a date," I blurt, unable to stop myself. Bobby's hand freezes over the paper, and he shifts in his seat.

"Noah?" he asks, resuming his song.

"My biology partner. I've told you about him," I say.

"Have you?" He flips his ball cap backward.

I debated bringing it up with Bobby—the fact that Noah suggested we go to dinner this weekend. But I tell Bobby everything, and he's continued to make no moves toward being anything other than friends.

I pretend to be just as flippant. "Sure have." I turn the page.

"Is that what you want, then?" His voice is sharper than before, and he avoids my eyes.

"Is something wrong?" I ask, not understanding why he's acting this way. I might be totally in love with him, but he doesn't seem to feel the same, so why should I wait around hoping for something that might never happen? He's had hundreds of opportunities to ask me out. He *has* to know that. But he hasn't.

My chest aches at the reminder.

"Nope," Bobby writes a comma, the tip of his pen ripping into the paper.

"Hey." I lean forward, snatching the pen from his hand. "What's your problem?"

Bobby sighs, clearly exasperated, then looks up at me. "If what you want is to go on a date with Noah, then I think you should go on a date with Noah. In fact, bring him to my show tonight."

"Really?" I'm baffled. Utterly astounded. And a little sick to my stomach. I thought maybe Bobby was unsure about dating me because I'm still in high school. I'm a few months away from nineteen and he just turned twenty, after all. Or... I don't know, maybe he has some other reason he's not telling me, like he just wants to focus on his music. What I *didn't* expect was for him to suggest I go on my date right in front of him.

"That's what *you* want?" I ask.

"That's not what I said." Bobby grabs his pen back, hovering the tip over the paper, but he can't seem to figure out what words to write anymore.

"Then why are you acting like this? You haven't asked me out!" I snap.

There.

I said it.

My heart slams against my ribcage as Bobby freezes, and I wish I could take my words back. I don't want to know what thoughts are causing Bobby's eyebrows to pinch in and his jaw to clench as he slowly puts down his paper and pen. His expression is guarded, difficult to read, but his shoulders are rigid as he leans forward.

"Where are you going to college, Beth?" he says. His voice is soft, but the intensity in his eyes makes me feel exposed.

"I don't know, yet. What does that have to do with anything?" I ask.

He doesn't break eye contact, and despite how vulnerable it makes me feel, I do the same.

"Where do you *want* to go?" he insists.

"That's not fair." Immediately, my guard is up, and I cross my arms as if I can protect myself from whatever he's getting at.

He sighs, placing a hand on my knee. This time, I don't want his touch, but I don't pull away. "That's what I'm saying. You don't know what you want. This is the *rest of your life*. You are so talented. Your words, they inspire me. Influence my own."

"What does that have to do with me going out with Noah?"

"Why are you focusing on dating when you should be deciding what you want to do with your future? You have, what, two weeks before you lose your spot at NYU? Which is fine if that's not where you want to go, but otherwise—"

"It's none of your business what I choose." The pitch of my voice rises.

"That's my entire point, Beth! It's *your* life." He sighs, rubbing a hand behind his neck before meeting my eyes. "Look, I have to go. We can talk about this later. I'm going to be late." He collects his things in a rush and disappears through the doorway, leaving me burning with shame and embarrassment.

I know it's my life, I think as I pack up, desperate to get out of here. But it's not that easy. I want to be successful. I want to write. I want to go to NYU, but I don't want to disappoint my parents, and I want to know I can support myself. I want to go on dates, and I want them to be with Bobby, but he doesn't ask.

So what am I supposed to do when all the things I want simply don't go together? When they're not possible?

I grab my backpack, waving goodbye to Molly as I unlock my phone and scroll through my saved contacts. My thumb hovers over one for just a second before I build up the courage to click it.

"Hey, Noah?" My voice comes out squeaky, but I continue. "What are you doing tonight?"

As Noah is paying for our cab, I wish I'd chosen a different night and a different place for our date. I don't want him and Bobby to meet, especially when Bobby has been nearly radio silent all day.

Normally, we text back and forth almost constantly, but I haven't heard from him since our... Was it a fight? At a minimum, it was an uneasy conversation loaded with things neither of us were willing to say. He sent one single text:

Bobby: I have two backstage passes waiting for you at will call. Find me before the show.

I stand by my decision to go out with Noah. If Bobby has feelings for me, he's not *acting* on them, and he can't expect me to wait around while he figures out whatever it is that's holding him back. If he's not going to pursue me, and a perfectly nice guy does, why shouldn't I give that guy a chance?

"Did I tell you how amazing you look tonight?" Noah says, taking my hand and leading me toward the venue. He looks handsome, his blonde hair pushed to the side and dressed nicely in a charcoal coat and slacks. He walks on the side of the sidewalk with traffic, ever the gentleman. I'm not surprised. He's one of the kindest, most popular guys at school. No one has a bad word to say about him, so even if it's awkward, I'm certain that Bobby will have to like him, too.

Not that it matters. It's about what *I* want. Right? Isn't that what Bobby said?

"Thank you," I say. I *feel* pretty tonight. It's very rare that I wear an open-toed shoe, but my brown peep-toe booties make me feel confident, as does the new purple dress I'm wearing. It's fitted, but not skin tight. With billowing sleeves cuffed at my wrist, the dress is cinched at the waist, then falls loosely to a hem that swishes around my knees. It makes me feel mature, womanly, and I'm flattered he actually noticed.

I'm also a little ashamed that I hope Bobby notices, too.

"This is incredible," Noah says as he holds open the door to the massive venue for me. It's the biggest one Bobby's ever played and is already standing room only, so we have to squeeze between bodies to make our way inside.

"Let's go find Bobby." I pull Noah by the hand toward the back of the venue beneath a glowing red exit sign, just as the woman at will-call instructed us to. With a flash of our lanyards, we're backstage. It's nothing like what I expected it to be. There's equipment everywhere, wires and lighting setups, plus so many people. A few I recognize, like Kelly and her gang of mean girls that seem to follow Bobby from show to show. I feel a twinge of jealousy. Did Bobby give them backstage passes tonight, too?

I brush it off. It shouldn't matter, because I'm here with Noah.

"What now?" Noah asks, and I shrug, my head swiveling around. I don't see Bobby anywhere, but as if I conjured him out of thin air, I hear my name from the very back of the room.

"Beth!"

I stand on my tiptoes to see Bobby waving us over as someone adjusts an earpiece and wire, tucking it through the collar of his black t-shirt and attaching it to a pack clipped to his jeans.

I pull Noah through the crowd toward Bobby, the pack for his in-ear monitors firmly in place by the time we get to him.

"I'm so glad you could come," Bobby says, giving me a giant hug. I feel the tension drain from his body as I return the embrace, and he kisses me on the cheek.

I freeze, my skin igniting. Never once has he kissed me. Sure, it's just the cheek. But still, why *now*?

"Robert," Bobby sticks out his hand to shake Noah's, and I realize he already has his stage persona on. He seems bigger, oozing confidence as he puffs his chest out and lifts his chin.

"Noah," my date says graciously as he returns the handshake, either ignoring or not noticing that it appears Bobby's trying to intimidate him. "This is incredible, man! Thanks so much for the passes."

"Beth deserves the best," Bobby replies, and I *feel* the heat of his gaze on me.

"She does," Noah agrees, wrapping an arm around my shoulders. "She tells me you guys met at a coffee shop?"

"We did. Meet there most days, actually." Bobby smiles broadly at Noah. "What about you? Math class or something?" He sounds dismissive, and I bristle.

"Biology lab, but yeah, at school," Noah says, winking at me.

"Great. Speaking of school, what are your plans for college? Are you staying in New York?"

"No, actually. Boston," Noah says, and I smile at his accomplishment.

"So, Harvard then?" Bobby turns to me. "Why do people never just say Harvard?"

"Boston college." Noah corrects him before I have the chance to. "I have a scholarship for biological sciences, but I didn't even try for the Ivy's. I'm not quite as smart as our girl here."

Our girl.

I don't miss the way Bobby's eyes flash at the words. Once again, Noah doesn't seem to notice. Either that or he's too confident to care.

"I mean seriously. Can you believe all the places she got into? Yale *and* Harvard? It's pretty impressive."

"It is. Very impressive," Bobby agrees, staring at me so intensely my arms break out in goosebumps. "So many schools she could go to. So many options. What if she chooses Brown? How do you feel about long-distance relationships?" Bobby stands a few inches taller than Noah and looks down at him, his eyes assessing.

"Stop it, Bobby," I try to keep my tone light, but I hope he hears the bite in my words. This is my first date with Noah. We're not in a relationship, let alone a long-distance one. *Why are you being such an asshole,* I ask with my eyes.

"What?" he counters. "It's an important question. Graduation's coming up. Then you'll have the summer, and then you'll be in school. It's a practical thing to think about. Right, Noah?"

For the first time, Noah looks vaguely uncomfortable as he taps his fingers against his thighs. "I guess you do what you have to do for the people you care about. Right?" He crosses his arms. "What about you? Are you planning on staying here?"

"I'll find out soon." Bobby's mood shifts. He flips his hat backward, clearly nervous, and even though I want to stay angry for how he's treating Noah, I feel an overwhelming urge to hug him instead.

"What do you mean?" I ask, taking a subconscious step toward him.

"There's a representative from Columbia Records here tonight. Denver Varnes is going on tour soon and needs an opening act." Bobby messes with his earpiece. "They came to see if I'm a good fit."

"Three minutes," a tall man with a headset says, switching on Bobby's in-ears.

"We'll let you get ready," Noah says politely. "Break a leg out there," he says, shaking Bobby's hand again before turning and walking to the side of the stage next to the thick black velvet curtains.

"Hey." I grab Bobby's arm, forcing him to meet my eyes. "Why didn't you tell me?"

"I didn't know until this afternoon." He shakes out his hands. "That's why I left your tickets at will call. I wanted you backstage. For luck."

"You don't need luck, Bobby." My hand slides down his arm until my fingers are locked with his, and I squeeze tight. Bobby lets his Robert mask slip, and I see his nerves clearly in the lines around his eyes and the way he fidgets with the mic wire. "You're going to do amazing. You *always* do amazing. And I'll be right there the whole time." I point to my spot next to the curtains.

He leans down and gives me a hug, and I can feel his heart thundering under his shirt. "Don't go anywhere," he says in my ear.

"I won't. Break a leg," I echo Noah's sentiment, reaching up on my tiptoes and kissing his cheek. Just for luck. Just to give him something to think about other than this life-changing opportunity that all depends on the next thirty minutes.

"Robert Beckett!" the announcer shouts, and Bobby's mask slips back on.

"Wait for me after the show," he says, then strides on stage, his guitar slung around his back and his steps unfaltering, as if this is just another night at a small bar instead of a show for thousands of people and a record executive.

My heart pounds as I force myself to return to Noah, only to find him putting on his jacket.

"I'm going to head out," he says, buttoning the top button, "but I'll see you in class on Monday."

"Wait." My stomach twists into knots. "Did I do something wrong?"

"Nothing's wrong. But I'm not interested in—excuse my music pun—playing second fiddle."

He's leaving because of *Bobby*? "What are you talking about?" I ask. Maybe if I play dumb, I can convince both myself and Noah that I wasn't a horrible person inviting him here tonight when there's clearly some sort of tension between Bobby and me.

"I'm not exactly sure what's going on between you two, but it's *something*. I know when to bow out." He smiles at his second music pun, but it doesn't ease the sting of his rejection.

Tears prick in the back of my eyes, even though I know it's my own fault. "We're just friends," I say, because it's the truth. "Nothing's ever happened between us."

"But that doesn't mean you don't want something to."

I open my mouth to speak, but Noah smiles, leaning down to give me a hug. "It's fine. I promise. Enjoy the show. Can you make it home okay?"

I nod. "I'll grab a cab. I'm really sorry, Noah," I say, my voice cracking. The guilt is overwhelming, because he's right. I don't feel even a sliver of the same pull to him as I do with Bobby. It wasn't intentional. But it doesn't change reality.

He pulls away and gives me a kind smile before sliding out the door, leaving me standing alone as Robert Beckett strums his first chord. His eyes find mine, and his shoulders relax, so I stay there, smiling back to show my support.

He starts his first song, and his energy is unmatched. It's as if he's feeding off the audience's cheers, and as his voice rings out confident and clear, I know without a doubt that he's getting this spot on tour, as well as the record deal that likely comes with it.

As he sings the last note of "Roots," he meets my eyes, tapping his pocket where my song sits in his wallet. Any hint of nerves or doubt is gone as he beams at me, turning back at the audience to introduce "The Application."

Even with a slower song, the vibe doesn't shift. It's electrifying, each minute more thrilling than the last, and when Bobby finishes his set and walks off the stage, he's practically vibrating.

"You were incredible!" I shout, throwing my arms around his neck.

"It felt incredible!" he says, lifting me and swinging me in a circle. He's sweaty from his performance, and I shiver as he presses his warm face against my neck. "Thank you for being here," he says into my skin.

"Robert!" Marissa, Bobby's manager, calls to him, waving him over. She's small with dark hair and is all New York. Somehow, Marissa looks like she can simultaneously kick your ass and be your best friend, and without a doubt, she would have the perfect playlist for both occasions. Her girlfriend, Kate, stands next to her—a petite redhead with an infectious smile and kind eyes.

There's a third woman I don't know with them. She's a bit older and is wearing jeans that look like they cost more than Bobby's guitar, paired with a fitted white shirt and leather jacket. She has an aura of importance about her, and I'm confident this is the representative from Columbia Records.

"I have to—"

"Go!" I urge, pushing him forward. "I want to watch No Rest's set, anyway. Good luck," I say with a smile so big my cheeks hurt as he gives me one last look and strides over to where his future awaits.

Bobby, Marissa, and the woman holding Bobby's music career in her hands disappear into his dressing room, and I resume standing side-stage as they set up for the headliner.

After opening with their current single and singing a couple more songs I know, No Rest starts to get into material from their upcoming album. Songs I don't know and can't sing along to, and suddenly, I feel strange standing here by myself. I look around for Bobby, but he must still be in his dressing room.

I hope it's a good sign. That they're signing contracts and planning what Bobby will need to get ready to join Denver Varnes on tour.

Except, *there's* Marissa and Kate watching No Rest from the other side of the stage. My stomach drops. Surely if Bobby was making arrangements for a tour, his manager would be with him, making sure everyone was acting in his best interest.

I walk back to Bobby's dressing room and put my ear to the door, not wanting to interrupt if he's still meeting with the record executive, but something feels off. Voices vibrate through the wood—Bobby's deep tenor and then a high-pitched giggle. I can't imagine that noise coming from the serious, businesslike woman I saw.

So who's in there with him?

The door handle turns, and I jump backward, ducking around the corner and out of sight. Bobby walks through the door, his arm around Kelly. He says something I can't hear, and she giggles again, putting her hand on his arm and looking up at him with adoring eyes. They slip out the back door, and I feel like I've been punched repeatedly in the stomach.

My feet follow, even though I'm not sure my eyes want to see what's happening. As soon as the door opens, that giggle hits my ears again, and I think I'm going to throw up. Bobby and Kelly stand on the street, his hand outstretched as he hails a cab. It doesn't take long before one pulls over, and he opens the door for her.

Kelly slides in, scooting to the side before reaching forward, grabbing Bobby's hand. He leans down and ducks his head inside, and I've seen enough. I let the door close quietly as I turn my back on them and sneak around to the front of the building, where I hail a cab for myself.

I don't particularly want to be playing second fiddle tonight, either.

Tears prick my eyes, and I squeeze my hands into fists, the bite of my fingernails digging into my skin keeping me from falling apart completely.

Bobby's voice echoes in my mind. *What do you want, Beth?*

You.

I want *you.*

I can't hold back the tears any longer. They spill over my lashes, my throat closing around the sob trying to work its way out.

I have wanted Bobby from the moment I saw him, when the earth stopped spinning and my perfectly curated life cracked into two identities. Elizabeth, the senator's daughter, and Beth, the poet with a wild heart and a hunger for exploring the beauty of the world.

Bobby helped me find my bravery when he convinced me to send in my application to NYU, but I'd faltered.

It wasn't the only risk I should have taken. And now it might be too late.

THEN

Then I heard her, then I felt her
And suddenly I know it
I'm falling in love, me a dreamer, with a poet
—An excerpt from "Dreamers and Poets," written and performed by Robert
Beckett

I'm not home for an hour before there's banging at my door.

My parents are in Paris. Or maybe it's Spain. It's hard to remember where they are when they seem to be somewhere different every week, but regardless, it's just me here. I freeze in fear. I can't remember if I locked the door, even though I *always* lock it without fail. I'm almost overly conscious of safety, of securing the deadbolt and double checking the oven after I finish using it to make sure it's turned off. But in the chaos of tonight, I can't remember.

Closing my eyes, I walk through exactly what I did when I got home. I got to the front door, unlocked it, and came inside. I remember leaning down to pet Scout, our Scottish Terrier. But I can't recall turning the lock.

The banging gets even louder, and I scramble for my phone. I turned it off on the cab ride home after speaking with my parents, not wanting to listen to Bobby's excuses when he remembered that he left me alone at the concert venue.

Now, I regret it. It feels like time wasted.

What if I need to call the police before it fully powers back on? I creep down the stairs, trying to peek through the small window next to my front door without being seen, but it's so dark outside I can't make anything out.

The door handle wiggles, and I stumble, my hair standing on end.

"Beth!" I hear my name, and I exhale, almost dizzy from relief.

Not a burglar then. Just the *so-called* friend I'm trying to avoid.

I scramble down the stairs, flipping on the porch light and yanking open the front door before he can wake up the entire neighborhood. The relief on his face is instant, and he pulls me into a bone-crushing hug, his arms enveloping me so completely that I'm cocooned in his warmth.

"Oh, thank God," he says, pulling back to look at me. "What the hell happened? You were just *gone*, and I couldn't get a hold of you. I was so worried that—" he pauses. "Have you been crying?" His thumbs rub the swollen skin beneath my eyes, and I pull away, once again uncomfortable with his scrutiny.

He wasn't supposed to come here.

Not *now* at least.

Not during the designated hours I was taught it was suitable to cry—at night, when no one was around to see it.

It's an invasion of my privacy, but guilt gnaws at my belly. I should've known he'd worry at some point—once he remembered that I'd been there and he left me alone.

"I should've told you I was leaving. I'm sorry," I say, sniffling as I cross my arms, ignoring his question about crying.

"What happened? I called Noah and—"

"You did *what?*" I groan, covering my face with my hands. "No. Why? How did you even get his phone number?"

"I asked Molly to send it to me. He said he left before my set started. I didn't even realize—"

"You shouldn't have called him," I scold. My stomach flips as I think about what Noah might have told him. That he had a headache and needed to go home? Or that he could tell I was in love with Bobby, and so he left?

"I can't believe he just left you there alone. I told him to stay away from you, that you deserved better, and that I'd kill him if I ever saw him again. I mean, you were on a date! And he seriously just left—"

"*He* didn't leave me there! *You* did!" I shout, unable to take it anymore.

"What?" Bobby freezes, his eyes blinking rapidly as if he was just completely blindsided by my accusation. He shakes his head, the movement almost frantic. "What are you talking about? I was meeting with the label executive."

"Right. And then you were alone in your dressing room with that girl, Kelly." I fold my arms around myself. "Which is fine. You're allowed to be with whoever you want."

Bobby opens his mouth to speak, but I can't seem to stop talking.

"But maybe don't choose *her*," I continue. "She's not even nice. She's rude to me at every show. And she just follows you around like some groupie. It's gross, and you can do better."

"Kelly?" He says her name like he's describing a disease. "Are you upset because I was helping *Kelly* get a cab?"

"I'm not upset." I say, raising my chin. It's a lie.

"But—" He reaches for my face again, my swollen eyes, but I take a step back, "You've been crying. Are you telling me this isn't about Noah? Are you saying you're crying because of *me*?"

He looks nauseous, his face pale and eyes wide with panic. He flexes his fingers as if he's having to hold himself back from pulling me closer.

"I'm crying because I came to see your show, and was waiting for you backstage, and then I saw you come out of your dressing room with your arm around another girl as she giggled and fawned over you like you were some famous rockstar. And *then* I watched you get in a cab with her, leaving me behind at said show."

"Beth, that girl is at most of my shows. She's a friend of my cousin. I've only met her in passing, but tonight she came to my dressing room before I had the chance to find you again, and she was so drunk. It didn't feel right just sending her back out into the crowd."

"Don't lie to me, Bobby." I take another step back, my spine pressing against the scratchy bricks of the porch wall. "I *watched* you get into that cab."

Bobby runs a hand through his hair. "I sat in the cab to try to get her address so she could get home safe. If you'd kept spying on me for thirty more seconds, you would've seen me climb back out and come inside to find *you*. And then you could have watched me panic and embarrass myself because you were just *gone*. I thought something had happened to you! God, Beth! I thought you'd been hurt." He throws his arms out to the side, his jaw ticking.

My cheeks turn red, and suddenly I'm not feeling so self-righteous. Was it possible I'd really misread the situation that badly? Bobby's *never* lied to me. Not once. But his story doesn't explain everything.

Like telling me to invite Noah tonight. And the way Kelly giggled and touched him. Was she really so brazen she'd act that way with a stranger? His arm had been around her, and he'd smiled down at her like they'd been sharing an inside joke.

"I'm not upset about you wanting another girl, Bobby. But you just left me there. Or—I thought you just left me there." I'm not so sure anymore.

"You th—You think I want another girl?" Bobby stutters. He blinks repeatedly, shaking his head as his hands drop to his sides. He looks defeated, or maybe it's shock I'm seeing in his hunched shoulders and wide eyes. "You think I have any interest, at all, in *anyone* else?"

I press my lips together. "I don't know," I finally say, confused. He treats me like I'm his best friend, like I'm more than that, but then again, he's never expressed how he feels. Not explicitly. Not with words.

Bobby's voice turns rough as he steps closer to me, taking my hand. He leans into me as if pulled by a magnet, his calloused fingers grazing my skin as the other hand comes up to cup my cheek.

"Beth, you're *all* I think about. I didn't even notice your date had left tonight, because even though it was maybe the most important night of my career, every time I looked to the side of the stage, all I could see was *you*." Bobby's chest rises and falls with shallow breaths that mirror my own.

My stomach churns with nerves as his gaze flicks between my eyes, and my heart pounds so hard there's no room for my lungs to expand. I can't tell if I'm leaning into his touch, or if the world is actually tilting sideways.

"But I—" My thoughts spin too fast to keep up with. "You've never said anything. I— I thought—" I stutter, unable to form coherent thoughts.

"I was waiting for you," Bobby steps back and starts to pace, rubbing the back of his neck. "I didn't want to influence your decisions. You took this huge risk applying to NYU, but honestly, I don't know if you even want to go there. You've been accepted into all these amazing schools, and the whole world is open before you, and I didn't want to make your decision even harder for you."

"*That's* what this is about? Where I'm going to *college*?" I throw my arms out. I'm yelling, too overwhelmed with my emotions to control my volume, and my neighbors are probably all listening through their open windows, but I can't bring myself to care.

"It's about letting you take control of your life!" He paces faster, his footsteps heavy and rhythmic. "I don't want you to choose something because you think it's what I would want. Just like I don't want you to choose something because it's what your parents want." Bobby takes a deep breath, his voice softening. "I don't think you realize how special you are. How much you have to offer the world, and I just wanted you to make this decision for yourself before I told you how I feel. I was trying to do the right thing, Beth." Bobby finally stops pacing, closing the distance between us. "But then you look at me, and I watch poetry come from your perfect lips and— And it makes doing the right thing so damn hard."

"How *do* you feel?" I ask. I need to hear him say it before I can believe this is happening. I need to hear the *words*. Because that's how I seem to understand emotion—carefully chosen letters put together so intentionally, you have to understand their meaning. My mouth is dry and my skin buzzing as he threads his fingers through my hair, tilting my head back to stare directly into his eyes.

I feel vulnerable, but I don't want him to look away this time. This moment, it's intense and terrifying and he's holding me so close, but I somehow still need him even closer.

"I feel like I saw you that day in the cafe and a spotlight was turned on, aimed right at you. It was like I suddenly realized I'd always been missing this huge piece of myself and never knew it. I feel like you're so beautiful I can hardly breathe. That I can't think or write about anything other than *you*, and I feel like, even though I've never tasted your lips, I know every curve and crease of them, because the feeling I get watching them as you read me a poem or one of my songs is a high I will spend the rest of my life chasing."

He leans closer. So close, I can feel his breath mixing with the intense energy that always seems to crackle between us. My stomach flutters, and my body feels like it's on fire.

"I feel like from the moment I saw you, you've been *mine*. And I've been yours, and this thing between us is one of those once in a lifetime love stories your poets write about. Except I don't want you to stay in New York for me. Because we're bigger than that. And I know that no matter where you go, or what you do, there *will* be a time for us. But I want you to chase your dreams first, because that's what you deserve."

"I'm going to NYU," I say breathlessly.

"No, Beth." He shakes his head, his lips tilting down and his forehead creasing. "This is exactly what I don't want you to do—choose a school so we can be together."

"Bobby," I put a hand on his arm, and he freezes, his fingers tangling deeper into my hair as he tilts my head back further, like he doesn't know whether to pull me close or push me away. "I called my parents on my way home from the show. I told them I applied and got accepted to NYU. That I want to be a writer."

"You—" Bobby swallows, his throat bobbing. "How did they take it?" His body is taut, so still I'm worried he might fall over with the slightest breeze.

I shrug. "They disowned me," I joke. "I've been packing my things to move into the poorhouse."

"I won't let you live in the poorhouse." Bobby's voice comes out like a prayer, rough and begging for some sort of salvation as he takes a step closer to me.

"They're disappointed," I say, truthfully this time. "Mom started crying and had to give the phone to dad. But he didn't yell. So that's a start, I guess."

"You're staying in New York?" he asks, pressing his body against mine, pinning me to the porch wall.

"I'm staying in New York," I say, my heart thundering.

"Because *you* want to?" He leans forward, his lips only a breath away, and I can barely breathe.

"Because I want to. I chose this for myself." My voice is nothing but a whisper.

Bobby exhales slowly, tracing his thumb along my cheekbone. "I love you, Beth Winters," he says, but before I can process his confession, his arms are around me and his lips are against mine.

The world detonates into an explosion of fireworks that make the black behind my eyelids erupt in a magical, glittering display of color. The firm, confident pressure of his soft lips against mine is life-altering, earth-shattering in a way that makes something deep inside me shift, and I know from this moment forward I will never be the same. My hands slide around his waist and up his back as he pulls me closer, a groan leaving the back of his throat.

I gasp as he tugs my hair backward to deepen the kiss, his tongue swirling with mine and his hands so bound in my hair it's almost as if we become one. Bobby whispers my name against my mouth, his body pressing against mine so firmly, I don't know where I end and he begins.

My heart thunders in my chest, and my knees go weak. Bobby devours me like a starving man, tasting every part of my mouth until I'm breathless, until I can barely stand. When he finally breaks away, his smile lights up the night, his dimple deeper than I've ever seen it.

"I love you," he says again, this time pressing a soft kiss to my lips, then my neck.

I'm speechless. I'm in a million tiny pieces and somehow more whole than I've ever been. I'm not sure I'm even physically in my body anymore, but I have to be, because I can feel *everything*.

"You mean to tell me," I say breathlessly, my chest heaving with shallow breaths, "we could've been doing that all along, but you've been holding yourself back because you were afraid I would choose my *college* for you?"

"It sounds dumb when you say it like that," Bobby laughs against my throat. "Turns out, you could have gone anywhere. We'd have to figure out how to see each other next year, no matter where you chose."

I freeze. "You got it?"

Bobby leans back to look at me, his smile growing impossibly wider. "I got it."

I squeal, so excited for him, I feel like I could burst.

"I got the tour!" he shouts, most definitely waking up my neighbors as he picks me up and spins me around. It reminds me of when I got into NYU, the way he celebrated me and my achievements as if they were his own.

I don't ask him to be quiet. If there was ever a time to shout something from the rooftops, it's now.

"Congratulations! This is amazing!" He got the tour, *and* he loves me. Bobby sets me down, my body sliding against his as he lowers me to my feet. I reach up and cup his cheek, rising on my tiptoes to brush my lips against his.

"I'm so proud of you. And I love you, too," I whisper, and Bobby freezes, his mouth dropping open as he looks down at me like I'm the sun after days of storms.

"You don't have to say it just because I did," he breathes, searching my eyes.

"I *want* to. It's the truth," I say.

"You love me," his rough voice scrapes down my spine, and my body arches into him. "Of everything that's happened tonight, *this* is what I'm going to remember forever," he whispers, kissing me again. Harder and deeper until my lips are swollen, and the sun is rising, and our lungs are full of the same air.

And when the kiss ends, I don't feel the loss of it. Because Bobby loves me, and we're not really done. We have forever.

NOW

August 2024

I'm sorry if I hurt you,
For my anger. It wasn't right.
I just love you so very much
My emotions won last night.
You're my world and my obsession,
My sun, bright for all to see.
So once again, my love, I'm sorry.
Will you please forgive me?
—A poem by Harrison Rouchester, asking forgiveness after a fight with Beth
Winters

There's a cup of coffee on my nightstand the next morning when I get out of the shower—a latte with lavender from the café down the street—along with a little poem printed out on stark white paper. Harrison was gone when I woke up, out running like he does every morning, I'd assumed, but he must be feeling guilty if he skipped his workout to write out an apology and get me my *dumb* drink.

I ignore it, not wanting to give him credit for doing what is honestly the bare minimum after how he behaved last night.

I spent a few hours packing after getting off the phone with Bobby, so there's not much to grab other than my phone charger and toothbrush.

I throw them in and zip up my bag, then pause. Walking to my jewelry chest, I slide off the silver bracelet with Harrison's initials and drop it inside next to the gold infinity bracelet that's remained unworn since the night of our engagement party. My fingers trail along the delicate links, and my heart aches, but I push it to the side.

I feel naked with my wrist bare, but it's far too easy to lose things on a moving tour bus, and I'm not risking either bracelet getting lost.

My pulse kicks up in rhythm as I open the false bottom of the chest and thumb through my half-finished manuscript. The one I'd been writing about mine and Bobby's love story until it exploded. Before I can overthink it, I grab the stack of papers and shove them into the bottom of my bag. I don't know why I do it, but for some reason I *have* to, and even though my luggage feels twenty pounds heavier with the pages inside, I can't convince myself to take them out.

I carry everything downstairs, dressed casually for a day on the road—jeans and a black t-shirt, my hair up in a messy ponytail with gold music note earrings. I'm not trying to look good for Bobby, but I feel pretty this morning, and it gives me the confidence I need to face Harrison.

He hangs up the phone as I enter the kitchen. "Good morning, beautiful," he says, leaning in and kissing my cheek. I flinch at the sudden movement, and Harrison pulls back, his face crumbling.

"Hey." He wraps his arms around my waist, but I don't melt into them like I normally would. "I'm really sorry about last night. I was out of line. You know I love you, right?"

He leans his head on top of mine.

"I know," I say, sighing. "But that anger—"

"I know, and I'm sorry. There's no excuse for it. And I swear to you, it won't happen again. Work has been stressful, and I don't think I've been handling it well. I…" His voice drops, shame creeping into his normally confident tone. "I lost a big account a few weeks ago, and I've been killing myself trying to make up for it. I let everything going on at the office get the best of me, but I booked a session with Phil for later this week."

I relax, the weight of what happened last night infinitely lighter as he tells me about going for a check in with his therapist. Not only that, but he's letting me in—admitting he's having a tough time at work—which he *never* does.

"I'm really, really sorry. Can you forgive me?" he asks, pressing a kiss to the crown of my head.

I turn in his arms, pressing my cheek against his chest and nodding. "Thank you. I'm sorry work's been hard."

"It's okay, especially now that I'm bringing Bobby in. Thank you again for doing this for me." He squeezes my arms, then pulls back to grab something from the counter.

"I got this for you. As a thank you," he says, handing me a large flat box with a pink ribbon.

"You didn't need to get me anything," I say, undoing the bow. When I open the box, there's a shiny new laptop inside, infinitely fancier than the one in my bag.

"I remembered you saying yours was running slow."

I pull the computer out and turn it on. "This is amazing. How in the world did you get it so fast?"

"Dad's social media manager pulled a few strings, and my secretary picked it up this morning. It's all set up for you to use. Everything you could possibly need is on there, ready to go," he says, nodding at the screen.

"Thank you," I say, closing the computer and reaching up on tiptoes to give him a kiss.

"Are you ready? Is there anything you need help with?" Harrison asks, tucking my flyways behind my ears.

I shake my head, once again forcing myself to not pull them back out. "All packed. But do you want to drop me off on your way to work?" I ask.

"Oh, honey, I'd love to." He takes a bite of his bagel. "I absolutely would, but I have a meeting this morning over breakfast, and I won't be going anywhere near the office. How about you take my car? I can call a cab for myself."

I rub my forehead, considering. "No, I'll take a cab. I'm not leaving for a bit. Your driver would just be waiting around for me."

Harrison nods, taking another bite of his bagel. "Thank you for doing this, Elizabeth. Really. Robert sent over the signed contracts late last night. I can't wait to see everyone's faces when I submit them," he says through a mouthful of bread.

"Congratulations," I say. I might be frustrated with the circumstances of how this deal came to be, but today will be a big one for Harrison at the office, and I want him to enjoy it.

"I need to run, but I love you." He presses his forehead against mine, then leans in for a long, lingering kiss, and another thick layer of my anger melts. "Oh! I booked a massage for you next week when you're in Texas. I'll send you the details. Text me when you're on the road, okay?" he says, grabbing his suitcase and giving me one last peck.

"Thank you!" I call out after him as he disappears through the door.

I finally take a sip of my latte, and the heightened emotions from last night ease further, the lavender chasing away my worries like they were only a nightmare. Harrison can be thoughtful—*is* thoughtful most of the time. In the light of day, I feel a little silly for being afraid of him. He never even left his side of the table, never got close to me. He was angry, and that's a side I knew he had. Work is the most important thing to him.

Maybe he really *was* just upset he might lose Bobby as a client.

And after him admitting he lost a big contract recently, I can even kind of understand why he was so frustrated last night.

It doesn't excuse him throwing a glass at the wall, but he was right. I *do* want to write again. I used to talk about it all the time. Harrison's always dissuaded me, saying we don't need the money, and it's a waste of time and energy, but now he's encouraging me to do it, and suddenly I don't want to write anymore? Even if it would help him? I can see why that would be confusing.

I sigh, not allowing my fingers to trail along the small line of sliced skin on the back of my arm.

It was an accident, I remind myself. He'd never *actually* hurt me.

Right?

I rub at the headache forming between my eyes.

I glance at the clock, not sure what time the bus is leaving or how long the cab will take, so I grab my things. My arms are overflowing, but I don't want to take two trips to the curb. I open the door, hoping to see a long line of cabs just waiting on the street and a very nice driver who might help me with my luggage, but instead, there's Bobby, leaning against a black Explorer.

His arms are crossed, and his sunglasses and hat hide most of his face, but it's definitely him. His muscular arms and strong jaw are unmistakable, as is the buzz of electricity tingling across my skin and the way my stomach squeezes when I see him.

Somehow, we match.

Well, almost.

His jeans aren't as tight as mine, and his black T-shirt isn't cropped, but it definitely looks as if we coordinated. Apparently, Bobby notices as well, because his lips tip up into a wry smile as he takes in my appearance.

"You look great. Ready to go?" He walks straight to me and takes the luggage teetering in my arms as if they're a couple grocery bags.

"Sure," I say, slightly confused and annoyingly impressed. "I could've taken a cab, you know."

He mumbles something I can't hear—some sort of grunt combined with what sounds vaguely like words before dropping my bags in and doubling back to open the passenger door for me. I don't miss the way he examines my face, then my arms, and I know that he's searching for the reason my voice was so shaky last night.

I ignore his concern, *and* the nerves pinging through my chest as I press my arm against my side so he won't see the cut.

I overreacted.

We all do it from time to time.

"Thank you," I say with forced cheeriness, climbing in and closing the door myself. He walks around to get in the driver's side, then hands me a coffee. I pull down the cardboard sleeve, smiling when I see the familiar Joe's logo on the side.

"Hot latte with lavender," he says. "Two of them, actually." He dips his chin and looks at me pointedly, and I realize he's making a point. *Does anything escape his notice?*

I ignore him and take a sip, holding back a groan as the familiar flavors dance along my tongue. Nothing beats Joe's. It's the best coffee I've had in months, but I'll be damned if I let Bobby know that.

It takes about forty-five minutes to get to where the tour bus is parked. Actually, tour *buses*. There are three of them, and so many freight trucks, I can't even begin to count them all.

Bobby parks the car and opens my door for me, then walks toward the blue bus at the front of the line. He's friendly with everyone we pass, hugging and shaking hands, calling each person by name, and I get the sense that his crew members are more like family to him than employees.

My stomach twists. Maybe this was a mistake. I've only been with him for an hour, and already I'm dissecting how great he is.

If Bobby notices my change in demeanor, he doesn't say anything. He opens the door to the bus, then gestures for me to walk inside. I climb the steps, and my lungs squeeze, my breaths becoming shallow and my head swimming.

It's like I've traveled back in time, the bus decorated nearly identical to how it was six years ago, with a large seating area as well as a dining table and kitchenette. Bobby's leather jacket is tossed lazily over the back of a chair, and his Taylor guitar leans up against the wall—still the color of honey with a blue-speckled mother-of-pearl rosette that reminds me of his eyes. But now the edge of the sound hole is worn down, as if the strums of Bobby's pick against it over the years were so full of pain, they had no choice but to etch themselves into the wood.

There are stacks of papers on the floor near the couch, and I have a feeling he was up late last night writing. My fingers itch to pick one up and read it, and I close my hands into fists to stop myself.

It even smells the same: guitar polish and leather.

My throat burns as I walk further into the living area, and I feel like I'm slipping into a memory of the last time I was here, except there's one key difference.

This time, my heart isn't shattering into a million pieces.

THEN

MAY 2017

I think I prayed for you
Without speaking the words
I think I listened for you
In the songs of the birds
A melody calling to the rhythm of my heart
So hang on tight, my love
It's only the start
—An excerpt from "Someone Who Loves You," written and performed by
Robert Beckett

It's the day after graduation, and as I walk hand-in-hand with Bobby leading me blindfolded to an unknown location, all I can think about is how happy I am to have that particular life event behind me.

My parents still aren't thrilled with my choice of school—possibly even less thrilled with my choice of boyfriend—but I'm finding I care a little less every day about their disappointment in me.

The idea of him being a musician instead of a lawyer or doctor is absurd to them, and I'm fairly certain they think I'll get Bobby out of my system and come around to their way of life.

"He's a nice boy, but don't you want someone who can provide you with the life you've become accustomed to?" my mother had asked, her mouth pinching in like she was sucking on something sour.

But what they don't understand is I will *never* get Bobby out of my system. I'd rather risk everything for a love that makes my heart sing than settle for a comfortable life without passion.

"There's a little step here," Bobby says, interrupting my thoughts as he slows us down to let me find my footing.

From the warmth of the sun on my face and the slight breeze tickling my hair, I can tell we're still outside. But besides that, I have no idea where we are *or* where my insane boyfriend is leading me.

"You know surprises make me nervous," I remind him, but really, I'm not worried.

"This one shouldn't," he says as he puts his hands on my shoulders and stops me. "We're here," he says. I hear a click and then Bobby is helping me up some stairs. "Ta-da!" He pulls off my blindfold.

We're on a tour bus.

A freaking tour bus.

"No way!" I say, moving deeper inside, trying to take in every inch. It's spotless and smells like a new car, but the scent is stronger. There's a large seating area with a couch that I think pulls out into a bed and two chairs, plus a sturdy wooden coffee table. In the kitchen, there's a dining table and a stove with two burners, a microwave, and a coffee pot.

"This is *yours*?" I ask, completely awestruck.

"Well, mine and the bands. Welcome to Big Blue." Bobby's smile is so broad his dimple makes an appearance, and my heart soars at his excitement. That's what we're calling her. We're renting it for the tour. Look." He pulls me toward the back where the living space opens up to a hallway with six bunk beds. "The guys are going to sleep here. This one's Johnny's," he says, pulling back the bottom right curtain to a bunk that's already decorated with blue bedding, a reading light, and a phone charger.

"Is one of these mine?" I joke, wiggling my eyebrows.

"Absolutely not," he says, pulling me even further to the back of the bus. "When you visit, you'll stay with me." He opens the door at the end of the hallway, revealing a queen size bed and small nightstand. Windows flank either side, and I imagine laying under the covers after a big show, falling asleep as we watch the road fly past.

I jump onto the bed, spreading my arms wide. "So, this is how rockstars live, huh?"

Bobby crawls over me, dragging his nose up my neck until his lips reach just behind my ear.

"Hearing that come out of your mouth sounds absolutely"—he nips at my ear—"ridiculous," he says, pressing a kiss to my forehead before flopping next to me and pulling me close to rest against his chest.

"What do you mean, it sounds *ridiculous*?" I ask, my heart beating faster as I look around the room. "We're on a freaking tour bus! You're going on freaking tour, your name is going to be on freaking tickets, and do you have merch? Oh my gosh, I hadn't even thought about that. Bobby merch. Is it weird to hang a poster of your boyfriend on the wall?"

"Marissa is in charge of the *freaking* merch, but I'll be sure to get you a T-shirt with my face on it."

"I'll wear it proudly," I say. "Can I get two? One a little bit bigger to sleep in and one I can wear to your shows?"

"You can have fifty if it'll make you happy," he says into my hair.

"I think two will be good, maybe an extra one to keep here for when I'm able to visit."

"I wanted to talk to you about that." Bobby sits up, leaning over to the nightstand and opening the drawer. There's a photo of us in a frame next to a lamp that I missed before. Both of us are beaming at the camera after one of his shows, Bobby holding his guitar in one arm and me in the other. He pulls out a notebook, flipping it open. I expect a new song, but instead, it's a list of venues.

"This is when we'll get into each city, and when we leave. A lot of them are within a couple of hours' drive from New York, or less by train. I don't expect you to follow me around all summer, but I thought we could figure out all the easiest places for you to come watch the show and maybe stay with me for a couple days. I know it'll be harder once classes start."

"Are you kidding? I want to come to as many shows as I can. And Molly will want to come with me sometimes. Maybe on the longer trips she can tag along? You don't have an extra bunk, do you?"

"Actually, I do." He smiles. "I can't believe it's all happening," Bobby says, setting the notebook down and trailing his fingers across the long list of cities he'll be performing in over the next several months.

"I can," I say, squeezing his hand, and I mean it. If anyone deserves this, it's Bobby. But it's not just his talent. It's his kindness, his drive, his hard work. "You deserve all this, and more."

He tilts my head up, pressing a long, lingering kiss to my lips. "I have something for you," he says, pulling me off the bed and back toward the leather couch. It's soft and plush, and I scoot to the corner and curl my legs under me.

Bobby sits on the table and picks up his guitar. "I wrote this for you," he says, taking his ball cap off and bending the bill before flipping it backwards, as if suddenly nervous. "I've been working on it for a while, actually, but it finally feels finished."

"Is this the one you wouldn't let me read?" I ask, even though I'm sure it has to be. He always lets me read his songs, every single one of them, except for the one mysterious page in his notebook he made me promise not to look at months ago.

"I hadn't told you how I felt yet, when I started it." He leans forward and kisses me, soft and sweet, and my body warms all the way to my toes.

"Go on then," I urge when he pulls back, my heart so light I wonder if I'm levitating off the couch.

Bobby closes his eyes and starts to play. A soft, sweet, slow melody that makes me feel like asking him to dance. But then he'd have to stop singing, and that is the last thing on earth I want.

When the moon wanes in a weary sky

When frost freezes roots, petals wither and die
You're gonna be okay, and I'll tell you why
You're safe in the arms of someone who loves you

You won't feel alone and you won't be afraid
When the sun starts to set at the end of the day
Come hell or high water, come whatever may
You're safe in the arms of someone who loves you

I think I prayed for you without speaking the words
I think I listened for you in the songs of the birds
A melody calling to the rhythm of my heart
So hang on tight, my love.
It's just the start.

When your body's tired and heavy are your eyes
When the world tries to break you with believable lies
I'll be right there with you through your lows and your highs
You're safe in the arms of someone who loves you.

Oh I prayed for you without speaking the words
And I listened for you in the songs of the birds
A melody calling to the rhythm of my heart
So hang on tight, my love
It's only the start

Bobby finally meets my eyes, and they're so full of love and devotion it makes me almost dizzy.

If your words stop flowing, I'll be your rhyme
And if the clock stops ticking, I'll find you time
Because I am yours, and you darling, are mine
And you're safe in the arms of someone who loves you.

I can barely see him through the tears now, and while I'm not quite sure when I started crying, I can't seem to stop them. The song is beautiful. Utterly perfect. I'm speechless and overwhelmed and a little sad, because part of me wishes this song could just be mine and Bobby's.

But I could never ask that of him. Could never ask him to keep it private and not play this for an audience or record it for an album.

It's too amazing.

Too perfect.

The song itself might be about me, but it will never be only mine. It'll belong to a bride and groom as they sway back and forth for their first dance, or a mother singing it to her first child. It'll belong to anyone and everyone who will ever love another, will be the soundtrack to humid, magical summers when the sun stays out late and people fall in love.

The last chord rings out, and I shift closer.

"You really wrote that for me?" I ask. Just like my favorite poems, his words have given me chills, have caused me to feel a longing deep in a hidden part of me. I want to hang them on my wall and tattoo them on my skin.

He nods, reaching forward to cup my cheek, callused fingers caressing my skin. "I love you, Beth," he answers. "*Every* song is for you." Bobby moves to sit beside me, then pulls me gently on top of him until I'm straddling his thighs.

Strong hands weave through my unbound hair, and I know there are no words I could find to express how much I love him, too. So, I simply lean down, brushing my lips against his.

"Thank you," I whisper.

Bobby's only answer is a groan as I deepen the kiss, his lips parting as my tongue sweeps inside, exploring the mouth that sang such beautiful, soul-moving lyrics.

My body takes over, and even with his hands roaming beneath the hem of my shirt, even as I rock against him, rolling my hips where he's grown thick and hard beneath me, I need to be even closer.

Bobby protests with a strangled gasp as I pull back, but his disappointment doesn't last. I meet his eyes, slowly pulling my shirt over my head and dropping it next to his guitar. Chest heaving, Bobby watches me with the intensity of a lion, his eyes hungry and his mouth slightly open.

I reach behind my back and undo my bra, my breasts springing free as the cups slide down.

"Beth." My name is a prayer on his lips. "You're so beautiful," he says, drinking in every curve and hollow. I lean down to kiss him again, allowing him to explore my body in a way he never has before. His thumb rolls over my nipple, and I gasp against his mouth, but he swallows the sound as he uses his other thumb to graze the other side.

"More…" I don't know if I say the word out loud, or if it's only in my mind, but Bobby agrees as he flips me to my back on the couch and crawls over me. He starts at my belly button, trailing kisses upward until he reaches my breasts. His tongue swirls across my skin and I groan, reaching for his shirt.

I need to feel him.

Need his skin against mine more than I need my next breath.

Bobby's eyes are hungry as he sits up and pulls his shirt off in one fluid motion, but I barely even get a glance before he's on top of me again, our chests pressed together and electricity cracking between our skin as his attention returns to my mouth. His hand grazes the side of my breast, and mine trace the hard planes of his shoulders and back.

"Do you have a condom?" I ask him breathlessly, and Bobby freezes.

We've never gone this far before. We're always at my house, or the coffee shop, or Bobby's apartment with Johnny only a *very* thin wall away.

"I— Are you sure?" Bobby pulls back to look into my eyes, as if just hearing me say yes isn't enough for him.

"I love you," I say with a nod.

"I love you, too," he breathes.

"Then show me." I lean up to kiss him, running my hands across the planes of his abs.

Bobby devours me, his tongue dancing with mine until he has to break away. He kicks off his shoes as he grabs a condom from his wallet, then pulls off the rest of his clothes and puts it on. His breaths are ragged as his fingers dip beneath my waistband and pull my pants and underwear down my legs, so slowly it's almost painful.

"So beautiful," he whispers, tracing the line of my hip bone to dip between my legs, and I ache for him like I never have before.

He presses a finger inside me, and I moan, but it's not enough. The song and the kissing and the feel of his skin has me ready for him.

"I need you, Bobby. Please," I beg, squirming.

Bobby kisses me deeply, then pulls back to look into my eyes. "I love you, Beth," he says, lining himself up and pressing inside me inch by inch. His eyes never leave mine, his hands still roaming as if worshipping me.

There's a pinch of pain, and I must show it on my face because Bobby stops, pulling back a fraction.

"Am I hurting you?" he asks, a line of worry appearing between his eyebrows.

"No. I'm okay," I whisper, needing to feel him in the deepest parts of me more than I've ever needed anything before. "I'm more than okay." I lift my hips, urging him to continue, the need building inside me almost unbearable. "Please," I beg, and Bobby groans, finding my lips again as he pushes deeper, stretching and claiming my body until I have nothing left to give him. Until we are so physically and emotionally connected to one another that I'm certain nothing will ever be able to pull us apart.

He pauses as he reaches the end of me, pressing his forehead against mine and exhaling as if he's finally whole. His fingers thread through my hair as he begins to move, and my body ignites, my heart pounding and my skin tingling. I gasp, my back arching off the couch at the pleasure building inside me. Because it's too much and not enough. He's thick and hard, branding me from within until I am his, irrevocably tied to him in a way I can't explain.

But he feels it, too.

It's in every stroke of his tongue.

Each caress of his fingers and whisper of affection.

And as I tighten around him, my body filling with an ecstasy so intense I cry out, Bobby finds his release, my name tumbling from his lips like a promise of forever.

NOW

AUGUST 2024

I fill up my lungs and try to run
But my feet are stuck to the ground
And if you're not moving forward
The only place to go is down
Feels like I'm running round in circles
Lord, can you set me right
I'm singing the prayer of a lost man tonight
—An excerpt from "Prayer of the Lost," written and performed by Robert
Beckett

I shake my head against the onslaught of memories. "Is this the *same* bus?" I ask, not sure how that would even be possible. The number of miles on this thing would be insane. And things don't look *exactly* the same. There are subtle differences in the layout. The coffee table is different, for instance, and what looks like an extremely expensive espresso machine sits on the counter where a simple coffee pot used to be.

I spin in a circle as I wait for his answer, robotically moving toward the living room. My eyes snag on a vase full of bright flowers on an end table—wild roses. Summer blooms that pluck the ghost of Bobby's voice quoting a Wilcox poem to me so many years ago from the depths of my mind. I close my eyes for a moment, willing the sound—and the wave of sorrow it brings along with it—away.

"Parts of it," Bobby answers. "Got a new engine last year, and I've done some renovations. But the bones are all the same."

Seeing it all makes me dizzy, and I sit down in the corner of the couch.

"You always liked that spot," Bobby says as he inclines his head to where I'm sitting. His eyes are sad, regretful, and he leans against the doorframe, staring intently as if using all his energy to commit this moment to memory.

I glance down at the brown leather under me, and my palms start to sweat. "There is no way this is the same couch," I say, even though the soft, buttery fabric feels so familiar to me, I think my energy is embedded into it.

Bobby gets a mischievous glint in his eye, and his serious mouth tilts up into a smirk. "Trust me," he says. "I will never, for as long as I live, get rid of this couch."

I shift uncomfortably, memories of a night several years ago flooding my mind. Blood warms my cheeks, and I duck my chin to hide my face from his scrutiny.

Bobby pushes off the doorframe and walks to the kitchen counter, pulling out a light-purple coffee cup I recognize and placing it beneath the espresso machine. My jaw drops as I look at the small crack in the handle of *my* cup, the one I'd kept as my designated mug while Bobby was on tour.

An unexpected pang of grief shoots through my chest at the memories of the porcelain warming my hands on cold winter nights. Of Bobby making me countless cups of coffee with lavender in the mornings.

The only thing more painful than the memories is the fact that he's kept it all these years.

"What?" he asks, as if we're talking about the weather. "It's a really comfortable couch. Me keeping it has absolutely nothing to do with—"

"Stop. I remember." I say, standing abruptly, suddenly very uncomfortable with sitting on *the* couch.

Bobby's eyes flash to mine, and I swear the heat in them could set the world aflame. *Don't play with fire, Beth,* I remind myself.

"What time do we hit the road?" I ask, desperate to change the subject.

He pauses as he reaches to grab the espresso beans but recovers quickly. "My first show isn't for three days. We'll pull out around four."

The coffee maker kicks into gear, and I take the final swig of my cooled coffee from Joe's, ready for my third cup of the day.

"Wait—" His words catch up to me. "We're not leaving till four?"

"Yep." Bobby spoons some espresso into the handle, the aroma mixing with the earthy scent of leather and giving me a sense of déjà vu.

"Right." I shake my head, trying to clear the memories muddying my thoughts. "And why is it then that you told me we were leaving early this morning?"

Bobby's jaw tightens as the espresso starts to drip. He grabs some milk from the fridge and begins steaming it, avoiding my question.

"Bobby," I say again, my cheeks heating. "Why did you tell me we were leaving early?"

His jaw hardens. "What was wrong when you called me last night?" he asks without turning to face me, his voice tight.

I stiffen. Bobby had always been able to read me like I read my poems, but I'd hoped that years of distance would have changed that. I clear my throat.

"Nothing was wrong. I told you I was coming down with a cold," I say, attempting to keep the defensiveness from my voice.

"You sound fine today," he says under his breath. On the outside, Bobby seems calm as he casually prepares our coffees, but I can *feel* the tension bubbling under the surface. He's not the only one of us who was good at reading the other.

"Tell me why you lied about leaving early," I demand, a flash of anger filling my chest. I lift my chin, not backing down. I already know the answer, but dammit, I want him to admit it.

Bobby places his hands flat on the counter and takes a deep breath, appearing to try to fight off his frustration, but he loses, shaking his head and turning to face me. He points a finger in my direction. "Because no matter what you say now, you were afraid last night. Your voice was *shaking*, Beth. Fuck!" He pulls his hat off and flips it backward, taking two long steps toward me. "I mean…it took everything in me to not get in my car right then and drag you onto this bus to make sure you were safe."

My mouth cracks open, and the air from my lungs escapes in a *whoosh*. "What— What did you think was happening? Look at me! I'm perfectly fine." I gesture up and down my body, but wince at the small stab of guilt that nestles between my ribs. I *had* been afraid last night. Even if I'd overreacted.

"What happened to your arm?" his eyes turn stormy as he closes the distance between us and gently twists my arm to look at the cut.

I can't meet his gaze. "Molly's cat scratched me. Let go."

Bobby drops his hands immediately, but he narrows his eyes, his jaw bunching and his hands clenching into fists.

"I don't believe you." He shakes his head. "I've met too many men like Harrison before."

"What exactly do you mean by *men like Harrison?*" I take a step back. It's too hard to think when he's so close. When I can feel that familiar electricity against my skin.

Bobby crosses his arms. "Men who are used to getting what they want without pushback. Men who get a little too angry when they hear anything other than 'Yes, sir.'"

I turn away, busying myself with straightening my top. Anything to make it so I don't have to look at him, because his words water the seed of doubt in my mind about Harrison's character. The same one Harrison planted last night during his outburst. That'd I'd stepped on like a weed this morning in the light of day, certain I'd been overreacting. "I'm not having this conversation with you," I say.

He moves to the side, right back into my line of vision. "So, you're saying there's a conversation to be had?"

"God! You're as infuriating as ever!" I throw up my hands. "Harrison surprised me with dinner last night. We talked, and I decided to take this job."

Bobby scoffs as he takes a step closer. "And you were trembling with excitement at the opportunity to spend time with me? You expect me to believe that was it?"

"Harrison has *never* hurt me." I stand my ground, refusing to break eye contact as I lie. No. It's not a lie, because it was an *accident*.

"I guess I have to take you at your word then," he says, raising his chin.

He sees right through me, just like he always has.

"I'm done," I say, walking over to where Bobby dropped my bags by the door. "This was a mistake."

"No, Beth, wait." He sighs, running his palm down his face. His sleeves bunch around his muscles with the movement, and my stomach squeezes, despite my anger. I look away. "I was worried about you," Bobby says, his arms falling to his sides as if it's all the explanation he needs.

I twist my engagement ring around my finger nervously.

"I'm not yours to worry about anymore."

He nods several times, but it looks forced. "I understand that." He holds his hands out. "But I will *always* protect you. You can't expect anything less. It's in my DNA. Please. One more chance."

I chew on the side of my cheek, my emotions swirling together, so dense, I can hardly puzzle out how I'm feeling. Last night, I felt like I needed space from Harrison. Time to figure out if I could be who he wants me to be, if I even *want* to be the kind of partner he wants me to be. But he's meeting with his therapist this week, and he's under so much pressure at work. This is just a bump in the road.

Right?

The back of my arm stings as if in warning, and my stomach drops, a warning bell ringing in the back of my mind.

"One more chance. But if I stay, Harrison's off limits. You've made how you feel about him very clear. I understand, and there's nothing more to say. Got it?"

"Got it," Bobby agrees, but the pained expression on his face tells a different story.

I drop my bags, and he opens the cabinet above the espresso machine, grabbing a purple bottle. He pours some lavender syrup in and stirs, then sets it on the table in front of the couch, and the gesture makes my already aching heart throb.

"Take a seat. Why don't you ask me some questions to get you started on the article?" He tilts his head side to side, stretching the tension out of his neck as he's forced to move the conversation forward, but he keeps his promise and holds back whatever he's thinking.

I pick up my coffee, curling my legs back underneath me as I sit back on the couch. Bobby watches me for a second, his eyes going glassy as if he's seen a ghost, but he quickly composes himself, shaking his head as he moves to sit in the chair across from me.

We sit in silence for a moment as I drink my latte and try to come up with a few questions, cursing myself for not taking at least a couple minutes last night to prepare. I glance around as I think, noticing some new touches since the last time I was here. There are a few pictures on the wall with Bobby and other celebrities. The TV is in a different spot and far more modern. Not to mention *way* bigger, and the hallway looks different. There are only two bunks.

"Does your band still stay with you?" I ask. Bobby's shoulders lower, apparently deciding that my asking a question means I'm no longer at risk of backing out before the bus can even pull away.

"Sometimes Johnny stays over if we're working on a song or watching a game. But the guys have a different bus."

"Oh." I hate the way that makes me feel, as if a poem I thought I had memorized suddenly changed. Is there a reason he needs his own bus? A girlfriend who stays with him? Or a rotating door of women to warm his bed? It isn't any of my business, but the thought still makes me feel like I drank sour milk.

But that's not the only thing making me uneasy. The fact that the band staying elsewhere means Bobby and I will be *alone* for two whole months on this bus. When I agreed to this assignment, I thought I'd have the padding of several other people at all times.

"So, it'll be just you and me, then?"

"Yep. Well…and Patrick, when he's driving." Bobby takes a slow sip of his own coffee, crossing one ankle over his knee as he relaxes back into the chair, and suddenly, I'm eighteen again, sitting across from him having a coffee at Joe's Place. His mannerisms are so similar, he almost looks like the same exact boy I fell in love with so long ago. Except now he's a man, with a confidence in his movements that hadn't been there before and six years of life experiences that have shaped him into someone I no longer know.

His eyes look tired, as if he didn't get much sleep last night, and he has a bit of scruff on his face and neck that always used to be clean and smooth.

"Erm…" I clear my throat. "Should we start the interview?" I ask.

"Go ahead," Bobby nods. "What do you want to know?"

I rack my brain for where to start. I could ask what he owes his success to, but I already know it's an unmatched work ethic, natural talent, and a charm that permeates the stage and sinks into your blood. I already know his history. Every detail of how he got his record deal and his first tour.

I was there, after all.

"Patrick's still your driver?" I ask, my heart warming at the memories of sitting next to him in the front, talking about his wife and singing along to the radio.

Bobby nods. "You'll find a lot of my team is the same. We're a family," he says.

My heart aches.

A family.

One I used to be part of.

"Tell me about her," I say, not sure where the courage to bring up the reason I'm no longer part of that family came from. "I assume you two aren't together anymore?"

Bobby freezes, lowering his coffee cup in slow motion, swallowing as he uncrosses his legs and sets it on the table. He leans forward, bracing his forearms on his knees as he meets my eyes, the intensity of his blue stare refusing to let me look away.

"Are you ready to go there, Beth? The reason we broke up? Because I assure you, it's nowhere near what you think." His voice is thick with emotion, deep and scratchy and pained.

"We'd already broken up. You were free to do whatever you wanted." I feel sick, the nausea only making the memories of that night more vivid.

Bobby's eyes are deep blue wells, begging me to listen. To hear him out. "It was only ever you for me. *Only* you. You knew that."

"It didn't look like it—"

"I don't care what it looked like." He shakes his head, still holding my stare. "I called you a thousand times. I texted, and I showed up at your house, at Molly's house, at your dorm. I wrote a whole damn album to try to explain what happened. You just disappeared!" Bobby stands up, and it's as if he can't contain what he's feeling within his body anymore. His shoulders are tight and his hands fidgety, going into his pockets and then across the scruff of his face.

"You're angry at *me*? You cheated on me!" It's the first time I've said the words, and they feel like shards of glass in my throat. "There was nothing to explain!"

Bobby's jaw clenches, and he lowers his chin. His voice deepens, a mix of fury over my accusation and sorrow over love lost. "I *never* would have cheated on you. *Never*. The fact that you've believed that all these years—" Bobby's nostrils flare as he takes a deep breath. "You were *everything* to me, Beth." His voice cracks.

"No. You know what? Never mind. I can't talk about this." There are tears in my eyes, dancing on my eyelashes and begging me to let them fall. But I will not cry over him.

Not again.

I *know* what I saw that night.

"We're going to have to, Beth. You've ignored me for six years." Bobby says, sitting back down, this time on the coffee table in front of me. "You owe me a chance to explain. To make things right." His fingers twitch as if he wants to reach for me, but he squeezes them into a fist.

"No. Not today." My bottom lip trembles. *I will not cry. I will not cry.* "Please," I whisper, a soft breeze away from shattering completely, and his eyes soften.

Bobby presses his lips together, then sighs, his face falling. "For now, we can table this." He doesn't break eye contact for several seconds, so I do. Because looking at him makes me feel like a peeled orange, my insides exposed and vulnerable.

Bobby stands, grabbing my bags. "I have a few things to work out with my tour manager, anyway. And I have a feeling you were up late last night. You should rest."

My shoulders relax. In less than a second, without the impending conversation hanging over my head, the tears are easier to hold at bay.

"But, Beth?" Bobby pauses, searching my eyes. "We *are* going to have to talk about this," he says gently, and I wish I didn't know him so well. His mannerisms, and tendencies. Because beneath that voice of honey is the same pain I'm feeling trying to bubble up to the surface.

"I know." I can't look at him, because he's right. Neither of us can handle two months of unspoken history and tension. But if he keeps talking, I *will* fall apart. I'm too tired from my fight with Harrison. Too raw being around him. And seeing him here, on *this* bus, makes everything feel too fresh.

Bobby nods at me, the lines on his face betraying the extent of how much this must weigh on him. He leads me to the back of the bus, but surprises me when he walks right past the bunks and into the main bedroom.

"There's not a chance in hell—"

"Calm down," Bobby says, dropping my bags. "I'll take a bunk. You need your own space, and you know I can sleep anywhere."

I do.

I've seen the man sleep standing up, but it doesn't feel right to take his bed. He's the one performing for sold out stadiums in between recording sessions and writing and God knows whatever else rockstars do. But his arms are crossed, and his jaw is set, and as much as I wish it weren't the case, I can read this man well enough to see that I won't be changing his mind.

"Thank you," I say, and I mean it.

"I'll be around, but call me if you need me. Welcome back, Beth." Bobby turns and leaves before I can answer, leaving me standing there speechless.

I collapse backward on the bed, needing a moment to calm my racing heart. Maybe a nap will clear my head, give me enough strength and resolve to face the next two months. Not to mention it will shut off my brain, give me a reprieve from the blade of doubt trying to carve through my memories.

I waste no time and roll over, reaching to turn off the lamp bolted to the nightstand, but freeze when I see what sits next to it—a photo of Bobby and me from *before*. It's the same one that sat there six years ago, his smile so genuine and broad that it makes my heart hurt. We were so young, so full of joy in a way that feels foreign and unattainable to me now.

I reach for the picture, some deep part of me needing to inspect it closer, but when I pull on the frame, it doesn't move. It's bolted to the nightstand. A permanent fixture. Just like I was supposed to be.

NOW

AUGUST 2024

Your futures wrapped in paper
Full of ink and sweat and tears
You say you'll do it later
I can't watch later turn to years
—An excerpt from "The Application," written and performed by Robert
Beckett

Bobby's gone for the next several hours, and I'm excessively grateful. It gives me time to rest and collect my thoughts—something I desperately need after anxiously tossing and turning all night. It also gives me some time to break the news of where I am to Molly, whose calls and texts I've been avoiding for the last twenty-four hours.

Molly: If you don't answer in ten minutes, I'm calling the police.

I sigh, taking a deep breath as I type out a message I know is going to send her into a tailspin.

Me: I need you to not freak out. I believe in you. I'm going to tell you what I'm doing, and you're going to stay calm.
Molly: What have you done, Beth?

I rip off the metaphorical band aid.

Me: Bobby needed a writer for an article with Rolling Stone. He asked me to do it. And before you try to talk me out of it, I agreed. In exchange, he's going to sign with Harrison's firm. This is a good thing.

Three little dots appear on the screen, then disappear. This happens about three times before the phone rings.

"This is a horrible idea," Molly says with no preamble or greeting.

"You promised you'd stay calm," I remind her.

She half laughs, but it's tense. "I didn't promise anything. Beth, have you lost your mind? Do you not remember me having to literally drag you into the shower after weeks of you lying in bed in the same clothes after what happened?"

Even though she can't see me, I roll my eyes. "That's a little dramatic. It was four days. And I've moved on."

The bus door hisses as it opens, and a familiar voice from long ago meets my ears. "What's the surprise, dude?"

"Listen, Molly. I have to go. But I *am* okay. And I will *stay* okay. I love you, and I'll call you later," I say, hanging up before she can argue.

A text from Harrison pops up before I put my phone away: *Did Robert pick you up this morning?*

I bristle. *You made me take this job and then were too busy to take me.* I want to say.

Nerves churn in my stomach. *No. One of his drivers,* I text back.

It's a lie, but what's one more on top of everything else? I don't want to argue with Harrison again, and our doorbell camera is grainy, at best. There's no way he'd be able to tell for sure it was Bobby with him disguised in a hat and sunglasses.

"You'll see," Bobby answers as I put my phone down, his voice full of mischief.

"It's quite the surprise," another voice I recognize as Patrick chimes in, and my chest warms. Losing Bobby meant losing a lot of other people I cared about, Patrick and Johnny included. It wasn't fair, but are breakups ever?

The bus door closes with a hiss, and there's a thud of a guitar case being set on the floor.

"Well?" Johnny asks.

I stand from the chair next to Bobby's bed and run to the bathroom to find a hairbrush, then quickly wipe a streak of mascara from beneath my eye. With one last look in the mirror, I straighten my shirt and walk to the door.

Footsteps approach from the other side, but I don't wait for whoever it is to get here as I step out into the hallway.

"I'm guessing I'm the surprise?" I say, coming face-to-chest with Bobby. He smells like soap and leather and coffee, and my head swims.

"Holy shit! Is that Bethy?" Johnny shouts from the front lounge, and the use of his nickname for me makes me grin. There's a thundering of feet and suddenly Johnny's there, shoving Bobby out of the way. He grabs my shoulders and holds me at arm's length, his eyes narrowing.

"You found a clone of your girl. Bobby. This is creepy, dude. Did you *actually* clone her?"

"Shut up, Johnny," Bobby snaps, and I choke on my laugh at the way they still seem to be arguing, even after six years.

"Not his girl," I say. "And not a clone."

"Reunion!" Johnny pulls me into a hug, and I return his embrace, realizing how much I've missed him as his warmth envelopes me.

"This is amazing! The best surprise ever. I mean, really. I can't believe you guys are back together." Johnny says, bouncing on his toes.

I look at Bobby over Johnny's shoulder, but he's avoiding my gaze. Instead, he's staring at my ring finger, his posture strained.

"Back together for *work* purposes," I say, stepping away. "I'm writing the Rolling Stone article about the famous Robert Beckett. Would you like to go on the record and tell me all his deepest, darkest secrets?"

"You know the guy's spotless. I guess I could make some stuff up. Just to add a little bit of spice," Johnny jokes, and Bobby rolls his eyes.

"You think on that. I'll be around for the next couple months, so enjoy having me here while you can," I say, not wanting to egg Johnny on about making up stories. I don't doubt that he'd do it, and then I'll have to wade between the truth and lies to figure out what I can actually include in my tell-all.

"I'll have you anytime," Johnny says with a smirk, and I roll my eyes.

"You haven't changed a bit, have you?" I ask.

"He hasn't, unfortunately," Bobby agrees, grabbing Johnny's arm and pulling him away from me. "Beth, you remember Patrick?"

I turn to the bus driver, but instead of waiting for him to approach me, I rush forward and give him a big hug. I feel like an eighteen-year-old kid again, and hugging him feels like reuniting with a long-lost family member. "Of course, I remember Patrick. How are you? How's Lily?"

"She's just fine, Beth, dear," Patrick gives me a tight squeeze, then grabs a circular tin out of his bag. "She baked these special for you. Said to give you her best."

"Wait, you told Patrick she was coming and not me? What the fu—Ouch!"

Bobby punches Johnny in the arm, interrupting him. "Can you be normal for five minutes?"

I ignore their bickering, opening the tin to find at least two dozen chocolate chip cookies, my absolute favorite treat from the old days. I'm not sure what Lily puts in them, but they're perfectly gooey and salty and sweet with a bit of a crunch at the edges. "Feed me like this, Patrick, and I might have to stay for a lot longer than two months," I joke.

"We wouldn't mind that at all," Patrick says, giving me another bone-crushing hug and a kiss on the cheek. "We've missed you," he says in my ear before walking to the front of the bus and disappearing behind the wall into the driver's seat.

I turn around and Bobby and Johnny snap to attention, Johnny grinning like a fool and Bobby scowling at him.

"So..." I don't know what to say or how to break through the awkwardness. It's been so long since the three of us were together that now these men who I used to call family are virtually strangers. I know nothing about them anymore. Not really.

"I think we need alcohol," Johnny says, clapping Bobby on the back before wrapping an arm around my shoulders and leading me to the couch. "Alcohol makes everything better."

"It definitely does not. And stay away from the good stuff, Johnny," Bobby says as Johnny opens a cabinet to reveal several shelves of wine and liquor.

"Are you saying that our dear, sweet Beth here doesn't deserve the absolute best?" Johnny swings his head to look at Bobby, mock horror and disgust on his face.

"Of course she does," Bobby's gaze snaps to me again, and I squirm uncomfortably. My cheeks heat, because I know exactly what he's saying. He's talking about Harrison and his *gut feeling.*

"But *you* mooch off my liquor cabinet too much, and then when I want a drink, I never have what I'm looking for."

"Oh, whatever. You wouldn't drink at all if I wasn't here making you do it," Johnny argues. "What'll it be, Bethy?"

"Red wine?" Bobby asks, grabbing a glass.

"Yes, please. That sounds great," I answer, but I hate that he still knows what I want. I didn't even drink wine when we were together, so how could he possibly know that what I'm craving right now is a heavy pour of Merlot to dull the sharp edges of the memories flooding my brain?

"I'll get hers," Bobby tells Johnny. "Help yourself," he concedes, nodding toward the liquor cabinet, and Johnny grabs an expensive-looking bottle of bourbon like a kid grabbing candy.

"One for you?" Johnny asks as he pours two fingers into his glass, then hovers the bottle over the second.

"Maybe later," Bobby says, pouring several glugs of wine. "I need to talk to Patrick about our schedule. I'll let you two catch up." Bobby hands me my glass, and his fingers brush against mine, causing an electric current to run up to my elbow. It's a shock to the system. Intoxicating. Without having taken a single sip of alcohol, I feel buzzed.

Bobby stares at my fingers, that muscle in his jaw ticking as he forces himself to turn away. The second he disappears, Johnny plops down next to me.

"I see nothing's changed," he says, taking a sip of his bourbon.

"Are you kidding? *Everything* has changed," I say into my wine glass.

"Okay yeah…say that to the busload of sexual tension." He waves his hands as if trying to get smoke out of his face. "I mean, it's even turning me on a little bit, feeling the energy between the two of you."

"Stop it." I try to keep my voice light, but I feel anything but. "There's nothing between us anymore. You know that."

He narrows his eyes. "You two have always been so good at lying to yourselves," Johnny says, and suddenly the lack of filter I used to see as refreshing and endearing seems more annoying and interfering.

"And you're still not great at minding your own business," I say back, taking a large swig of wine.

"That, my friend, is absolutely the truth," he says, holding his glass up to cheers mine. "So, what is the great Beth Winters up to these days?" he asks. "Sounds like you're still writing."

I don't have the courage to tell him that this is the first thing I've written in a very long time, so I just nod. "Are you still living in New York?"

Johnny's eyes are suddenly sad, haunted. "I do. But a little outside the city. I wanted my daughter to have some space to run."

My jaw drops, and a lump forms in my throat. "You have a daughter?" My voice comes out shaky.

Johnny pulls out his phone and unlocks it, showing me a picture of a tiny blonde girl, maybe two years old. "Ella," he says, and the look of grief fades, just a little.

"You're a *dad*? Are you married?" There are tears in my eyes. Happy ones, but also sad ones. I've missed so much.

Johnny looks out the window. "I was. She died. Car accident."

He says it without emotion, and I wonder if he's had to lock it away so he can take care of that beautiful little girl on his phone.

"I'm so sorry." I place a hand on his arm, but Johnny leans back, absently rubbing his thumb on his naked ring finger.

"Anyway. Ella comes on tour with me a lot. She's with her grand-parents right now, but she'll be here in a couple weeks."

"I can't believe I didn't know you have a daughter," I say, choosing to focus on Ella. I don't press about his wife, but I can tell her memory is in the room with us now, the shadows in his eyes thick and hazy.

"How would you? You haven't exactly kept in touch," he says, and the words cut deeper than they should. I knew it would hurt him to cut all contact between us, but it'd been necessary at the time. I can't take it back, even if I wanted to, so why is guilt sitting so heavy in my stomach?

"I'm sorry," I say, and I *do* mean it, even if I wouldn't change it. "It was just too much. Bobby—"

"I'm not Bobby," he interrupts me, his voice teetering on angry.

"I know." We fall into silence, and for the second time today, I wonder if never looking back *had* been a mistake. It was as if I'd excised the damaged piece of my heart so thoroughly, I'd cut away healthy tissue to make sure the pain couldn't fester and spread, instead of trying to find a way to heal the injured bits. Instead of fighting to become whole again.

I couldn't take the pain, so I'd simply cut that bleeding piece out and continued on with life.

A little bit less me, but also less broken—less damaged.

Johnny takes another sip of his bourbon, his eyes taking me in as if he's considering the sincerity of my apology. "I forgive you," he finally says. He smiles at me, but it doesn't quite reach his eyes. Not the way it used to. "But, Beth? When you leave this time, don't just disappear."

I exhale in relief.

That is something I can agree to.

"Deal," I say, picking my wine back up and clinking his glass again.

Someone clears their throat behind me, and I turn around to find Bobby leaning against the doorframe, his arms crossed and his expres-sion guarded. "Promise?" he asks. His voice is as tight as a guitar string and rough as the growl of a harmonica, and the gravity of what he's asking pulls at my lungs, making it hard to breathe. I take a second to consider my answer. He says there are things I don't know. That my version of events isn't the whole truth of what happened that night, and that I never gave him a chance to explain.

When I left that day, I vowed to never see or speak to Bobby again, but now that I'm here with him? Now that I've felt his touch and heard his voice. I don't think I have the strength to walk away again. Maybe all those years of history don't have to be a waste. Maybe a friendship can form out of this strange situation we've found ourselves in.

I nod.

It's all I can do.

"Tell me about your daughter," I say to Johnny, needing to move on from the heaviness of the moment. Johnny's joy is instant and contagious, and as he flips through photos on his phone, I feel more at ease.

Until the bus whines as Patrick shifts it into gear, and we pull away.

The abrupt departure sends nerves skittering down my spine, and I realize how little control I have of this situation. I have no idea what's going to happen, or what the next two months will bring, and it scares me.

I willingly walked onto this bus, and now I'm stuck here.

Along for the ride, wherever it takes me.

THEN

July 2017

I can't watch your words wither away in your mind
While mine ring out clear and loud
I'd rather let my own words die
Than let yours disappear into the clouds
—An excerpt from "Little Bird," written and performed by Robert Beckett

"Holy shit! Holy shit, holy shit, holy shit!" Molly seems to have malfunctioned, because that's essentially all she's been saying for the past hour. "Holy—"

"Shit?" I tilt my head and grin, and Molly bites her tongue.

"Mom says that's a bad word," Michael's little voice pipes in. I peer around Molly to look at him for the hundredth time since dinner. He's wearing *all* the freaking merch, and it's oddly hilarious to see my boyfriend's face on his way-too-big shirt.

It took quite a bit of convincing for Molly's parents to let him tag along tonight, and his mom's picking him up as soon as Bobby's set is over, but she couldn't say no.

Not when Michael is officially a Robert Beckett super fan.

"Sorry. You're right, buddy. It's just so cool, right?" Molly says, patting his head.

"Right! Holy shit!" He jumps up, his eyes darting between Molly and me. "Don't tell Mom."

"I'd never," I say, ruffling his hair.

We're standing in the very front of the arena. There's a suite somewhere above us with some of Bobby's friends and his mom, and while I got an invitation to watch the show with them, I immediately, and politely, declined. There's no way in hell I'm going to watch Bobby's first show on tour from anywhere other than the front row.

I bounce on my toes, so nervous I feel like I could throw up. Bobby's been practicing around the clock for the past few weeks with a full band. Most of the guys played with him in New York, but they've added a few more to fill out the sound. He has roadies and a bus driver and even a guy, Wes, who's entire job is to hand him different guitars throughout his set. It's incredible, and it's well-deserved.

I look at my phone—6:55. Five minutes until Bobby is officially a touring musician. And not just a touring musician, but one opening arena shows.

Giant arenas, with thousands of full seats.

My stomach flips again.

"I think I'm going to vomit," I say, sitting down and putting my head in my hands.

"Don't do that. They'll kick us out," Michael says.

"No one's kicking us out." Molly rolls her eyes. "Excuse me. Can I have this?" Molly asks the girl next to her, grabbing the beer out of her hand without waiting for a reply.

"Hey!" The girl protests, but Molly stops her.

"This is Robert Beckett's girlfriend, and she's about to have a panic attack. Here." Molly hands me the beer, then pulls a twenty out of her purse. "Thank you so much," she says to the girl as she smiles broadly and hands her the cash, her voice as sweet as sugar.

Molly's good at that. At getting what she wants with confidence. I take a sip of the frothy beer. It's disgusting, but it makes my belly warm and distracts me from my nerves, so I tilt my head back and take a few deep gulps.

Molly blocks me from Michael's view so he doesn't see.

"He's going to crush it, okay? Your job isn't to worry about him. Your job is to be his biggest fan," Molly reminds me.

"Right. Got it. Biggest fan." It shouldn't be a problem, because I genuinely *am* his biggest fan. In every way possible.

Well, maybe other than Michael.

The lights dim, and I take another gulp, my heart fluttering in anticipation, and I stand back up. A soulful note rings out—a guitar solo by Johnny. I'd heard all about it on the bus last night—that he was getting the opening notes of the show, so technically, it was his show, too. Bobby had laughed his good-natured laugh and reminded him that there were two other guitar players he could give the solo to if it was going to inflate his ego.

The band walks on stage, beginning to play alongside Johnny. It's one of Bobby's older songs, "Roots," but it's one of my favorites. A guitar-heavy banger about where he came from and where he plans to go—the perfect introduction song. Bobby finally walks into the spotlight, his guitar slung around his shoulder and an enormous grin plastered on his face. My whole body heats, just like it does every time he takes the stage.

The bass drum pounds and Johnny shreds on the guitar, and then Bobby opens his mouth to sing.

Anchor me down in the cold, dark dirt—

His voice sounds like butter, with hints of gritty sugar mixed in now and then. I can't even focus on the words as I watch the spotlight grow brighter, the stage lights rising and flashing in shades of red and white.

I knew this was a legitimate tour with an actual production budget, but actually seeing it? Seeing him up on that stage with all the equipment and the lights and the crowd—it's the most incredible thing I've ever been lucky enough to witness. Bobby walks forward, his eyes scanning the audience. He has that way about him that makes people feel special, and I can tell that as he meets his fans' eyes, they all think he's singing to them.

But I know the truth.

As his gaze meets mine, he beams at me, throwing his arm up in the air. He points toward me, winks, then pats his pocket where my song is tucked for luck.

My smile feels like it might split my face in half, my cheeks nearly cramping as I blow him a kiss.

Bobby finishes the song, and the crowd devours it. Their roars are near deafening as he thanks them and switches out guitars. Wes is doing an excellent job already. "Good evening, Albany!" Bobby shouts, his voice booming through the speakers. Anyone watching him now would never believe he'd been so anxious only twenty minutes ago.

"Thank you all for being here tonight. For giving me this opportunity." His words come across humble and grateful, and I know it's sincere. He takes a moment to scan the room, from the front row to the last. "This has been a dream of mine for as long as I can remember." I swear the floor vibrates with the cheers, and Bobby laughs as someone behind me yells out, "I love you, Robert!"

"I love you all. Truly." He places a hand on his heart. "Settle in for a few songs. I hope you hear something you like!"

And boy, do they. I'm not sure I've ever seen a crowd as interested in an opening act before. Nobody's chatting with friends or using that time to go to the bathroom. They're singing along, or for the ones who've never heard of Bobby before, they're swaying on their feet and holding up drinks. A couple girls next to me are searching his name on Spotify and Instagram, following him and swiping through his photos.

After the initial shock and pride of seeing him on stage wears off, I scream every word, along with Molly and Michael, and by the time his set ends, we're all hoarse. Bobby thanks the crowd and throws a handful of guitar pics into the front row, making sure Molly and Michael both get one, then walks to me and puts the one he played with in my hand.

"A good luck charm for you. I love you," he says, only to me, before standing and waving as he walks off the stage.

To anyone else, it would look like just an interaction with a fan, but for me, it's the best moment of my life.

NOW

August 2024: Rogers, AR

The stadium is *actually* vibrating. If I was anywhere other than backstage, I think I'd be terrified that the whole place is going to tumble down around me. The rumble of footsteps and roar of applause is exhilarating, growing with every song Bobby plays.

I don't recognize them all, but even the new ones pluck the strings of my memories. They're all built from pieces of our past. Each and every one of them.

It's painful, but despite it all, I'm proud of Bobby. Of everything he's accomplished. Of the beautifully poetic words he's written, and the absolutely intoxicating way he performs them.

Bobby sings the final note of his encore and still, the crowd demands more, even after playing for almost three straight hours.

I never forgot how attractive Bobby is on stage, all sweaty and vibrant and full of life. But something about seeing him here, older and more confident, makes my body react in a way that feels like a betrayal.

Harrison. You're engaged to Harrison.

Despite my rational mind and weighted ring finger, my body heats. I try to find shame, but I can't. It's not my fault. Being around Bobby has always made me feel this way, ever since the first time I saw his shaggy hair and blue eyes. It was like we were two halves of the same soul, and while I know in my head that it isn't true, the rest of me didn't seem to get the memo.

Because he went and messed everything up, I remind myself, hoping it will douse the fire in my belly.

It doesn't.

Just as agreed, Bobby left *the* song out of his set list and held strong to his promise, despite the chant from the crowd to sing it. They chanted several times, actually, but he'd distracted them with his blinding smile and perky butt.

Or *maybe* that's just how he'd distracted me.

Bobby waves to the crowd as he exits the stage and strides straight over to me. Someone hands him a towel, and he dabs at his neck. The way his biceps ripple with the movement makes my mouth go dry. This is getting ridiculous.

"What'd you think?" he asks with a smile that almost looks nervous, so out of place from his confident stage demeanor. "Have I lost my touch?"

"As much as I hate to admit it, you're better than ever." I smile back at him, tucking my notebook under my arm.

"Bobby!" someone shouts from the side of the stage. "We have some VIPs here to meet you."

Bobby hesitates, as if questioning whether he wants to leave me alone or not. "Go ahead," I say, wanting a bit of space from the super hot rockstar I used to be in love with. Seeing him back in his element is heady—dangerous—and I need a cold shower and a glass of wine to come down from the experience.

Maybe I'll see if Harrison is still up. When we'd spoken this morning, he told me about a big day in court for a case he's been working on for *months*, and I don't even know how it went, other than it ran late and he had to reschedule his therapy appointment.

"I'll meet you back on the bus," I nod to where Big Blue is parked behind the stadium.

"Are you sure?" He quirks an eyebrow, grabbing a bottle of water and taking a deep swig. His throat bobs and some water drips onto his shirt, and suddenly I'm wishing he'd take it off. Except I'm not. Because Harrison.

"Yep, I'm very, *very* sure," I hold back a groan, and his forehead scrunches.

"Are you okay?" he asks, confused by my answer. "I don't have to go."

"Yes, Bobby. I think I can make it a hundred steps back to the bus. Go do your thing. I should type this up before I forget what I was thinking, anyway," I say, tapping my notebook.

"Okay then. I'll see you in fifteen." He disappears around the corner, and I'm about to leave when I'm stopped by a hand on my arm.

"If it isn't Beth fucking Winters," Bobby's manager, Marissa, says. "Or am I seeing things in my old age?"

"Aren't you like thirty-eight, Marissa?" I ask, leaning to give her a big hug.

"Which is almost forty, which is almost fifty, which is almost dead," she says, returning the hug. "You know, I didn't believe Bobby when he told me you were coming on tour. After what happened. I mean, I can't help but feel a bit responsible—"

I raise my hands in the air and cut her off, not wanting to go there. "Water under the bridge," I say, even though that's not exactly the truth.

"I also hear you're the one writing the article. I need to buy you a drink to thank you. Hell, you deserve a whole case of champagne for getting him to finally do this interview. I've been hounding him about it for almost two years."

"Well, you know how Bobby feels about doing press," I say with a shrug.

"Oh, I'm aware. Make him look good, will you? I'm hoping this album makes us enough that I can buy a boat for Kate."

"Don't you hate the water?" I question, remembering a time when Bobby was on tour in Florida that Marissa flat out refused to set foot on the pontoon boat we'd rented for a day on the ocean.

"I do, but Kate doesn't. Plus, successful people own boats," she says, her mouth tilting up in a smirk. I laugh. Marissa seems to be as ridiculous as ever, but I'm grateful she's still with Bobby—that he's had someone tough and loyal like her by his side.

"I will do my absolute best to present him in a way that increases record sales so you can buy your wife a boat," I say, nudging her with my elbow.

"I always liked you." Marissa elbows me back as if we're in on an inside joke together. "I'll see you at the show tomorrow," she says, walking away without so much as a goodbye.

The backstage area has cleared out, and dozens of men are taking apart the stage. That was one thing that always amazed me after a show, how quickly everything's taken down and packed up, leaving only the ghost of the music present in the space.

I walk toward the exit, eager for that wine, but freeze when I hear Bobby's voice. It's almost a shout, and uncharacteristically angry, which makes me uneasy. I can count on one hand how many times I've heard Bobby raise his voice, and that's including right now.

"It's none of your business what I'm doing!" he shouts, and I shrink back, certain I'm not supposed to be hearing this.

There's a humorless laugh—Johnny's. "Are you fucking kidding me? It's *absolutely* my business. I'm the one who had to watch you after she left last time. The one who had to pick you up off the floor and convince you to get out of bed in the morning."

"She's writing a story about me, and then she's leaving, and I'll probably never see her again."

"And you *actually* think you can handle that? You think you can let the love of your life walk away a second time and go marry some rich prick who doesn't respect her?"

I wince at his directness.

"I know you better than that. This is going to wreck you." Johnny's voice is strained.

There's a long, loaded silence. I wait for Bobby to deny it, to argue that he doesn't love me. That he was fine after we broke up, but it never comes.

"It's *Beth*," Johnny says, as if my name is all the explanation he needs to convince Bobby that it's crazy and irresponsible to have me here.

Finally, Bobby speaks. He's no longer shouting, but the anger is still there, vibrating within his words. "I learned my lesson six years ago. It's not my job to make decisions for her. She's a grown woman, and she can do what she wants. Now if you'll excuse me, I just played a three-hour show, and I haven't exactly been sleeping well. I'm going to go before I say something I regret. Come by the bus later if you feel like minding your own business."

My throat is dry, and my stomach is in knots. Had Bobby really felt that way when I left? How could that be possible, when he's the one who ended things?

The back door slams, and I exhale as I creep toward the bus, but stop short when Johnny walks around the corner. He doesn't see me at first, and his face is red. He looks pissed, his hair messy as if he's been running his hands through it repeatedly. His eyes pop open wide when he sees me, and at least he has the decency to look sheepish.

"Oh, hey there Bethy." He shuffles his feet. "Did you uh..." he hesitates, and I know what he's asking. *Did you hear what I just said? Did you hear me telling my best friend that having you around is a ridiculous, horrible idea?*

"Hey!" I force a big smile despite the pit in my stomach and lump in my throat. "I was just catching up with Marissa. She's as feisty as ever, right?" I laugh, but it doesn't sound convincing. Johnny doesn't seem to notice, and he visibly relaxes.

"That's an understatement. I think she's only gotten feistier. Anyway, Bobby just left. I'm going to call and check in on Ella," he says, and the sudden sparkle in his eye reminds me he's not a bad guy, and he doesn't hate me. He loves hard, and he's worried about his friend. I can't fault him for that, even if my feelings have been put in a blender and turned on high.

"Have a nice chat with her," I say, turning to leave. "Great job tonight, by the way."

He nods in thanks and gives me a small wave before he turns and leaves, and once again I'm overwhelmed by the possibility that what I think happened that night six years ago might not be the entire truth. The pit in my stomach grows into a massive cave.

It's a conversation I'm going to have to have with Bobby.

But not tonight.

A few more days, and I'll be ready, I tell myself. But if I'm being honest, I don't think that's true. I don't think I will ever, in a million years, be ready to learn if it's my fault that I lost Bobby Beckett.

THEN

AUGUST 2017

When my words fall short, yours soar among the stars
When my hopes feel distant, I just go where you are
And what I thought I wanted, it just doesn't feel so new
Because when the lights rise, darling, well… all I see is you
I may be a dreamer and have nothing to show it
But I'm falling in love
Yes I'm falling in love
I'm falling in love with a poet
—An excerpt from "Dreamers and Poets," written and performed by Robert
Beckett

My body is still buzzing with excitement as I sit on the bus waiting for Bobby to get through his meet and greet. Tonight was the last show of Bobby's tour—at least, the last one I'm going to be able to go to for a while since classes start Wednesday.

It was incredible, one of his best yet. Over the last month and a half, he's honed his performance into a perfectly choreographed thirty minutes, but even so, I never get bored with it. And clearly the fans don't either.

Bobby's initial contract was for the first twenty shows of the tour, but it's been extended for him to finish out the rest of the dates as well, and he's even been booked for some late-night television performances in the upcoming weeks. Between starting classes, getting into the swing of college life, and Bobby's hectic schedule, it's going to be a bit before we can spend time together again.

My stomach churns uncomfortably as I think about it.

It's not that I'm *worried*.

It's more that Bobby's become a part of me—another limb or an organ that I've always had but never really paid attention to. I never think about my lungs, but if suddenly I was facing the possibility of them being taken away for an extended period of time, I'd be pretty uneasy about it.

The bus doors open, and Bobby jumps up the steps, clearly still amped from the show. He collapses on the couch, grabbing me and wrapping me in a big sweaty hug.

"Gross!" I cringe as his damp hair tickles my neck. "Go shower! You're going to ruin the couch."

"*Nothing* could ruin this couch," Bobby's eyes twinkle as he leans in for a long kiss, and suddenly I really don't care about how sweaty he is. "You're only here for," he looks at his watch, "seven more hours before I have to take you to the airport. I don't want to waste a second of it showering."

"Well, maybe I'll join you." I climb into his lap, straddling him. "Two birds, one stone."

Bobby threads his fingers through my hair and pulls me down to kiss him again. He tastes like *life*. Like fresh air and new experiences and somehow, at the same time, home.

"I feel awful I can't be there to help you move in," Bobby says when he pulls back, his eyes crinkled with worry at the edges.

"We've already talked about this. You kind of have bigger things going on," I remind him, gesturing around the bus.

Bobby sighs, leaning his head back against the couch. "I know, but I feel like I'm missing out on *your* big life experiences while you follow me around to live mine with me."

"Well, I have four more years, so we will just schedule your next tour around move-in day, if it's concerning you that much."

"Perfect." He kisses me, then tilts my head back to meet my eyes. "I have news."

"Tell me," I say, suddenly nervous, but in an excited way.

"'Gray' hit number one today on the billboard charts. The label is already picking my next single, and I think it's going to be 'Someone Who Loves You.'"

My lips tilt up in a genuine smile as my stomach flips. "So, you're saying that *I* am the reason you might have a second hit single?"

Bobby throws his head back, laughing in the way I love so much, his dimple growing deeper. "That's exactly what I'm saying. I'm adding it into my set next week. We practiced it today, and it sounds amazing with the full band."

The anticipation fills my stomach with butterflies. "I can't wait to see you play it on a stage for thousands of fans. How many people do you think will use that song to propose during your shows?"

"Probably at least a few a night," he jokes, then presses his forehead to mine. "I'm happy that's what they're picking. It'll be like I have a little piece of you with me at every show, even though you'll be back in New York writing the next great American novel or dissecting Shakespeare."

His unwavering belief in me sends warmth through my chest. "I mean, more likely I'll be sitting in History or English 101, but I get what you're saying."

"Whatever you're studying, you'll be amazing at it." He's looking at me as if I'm a sunset over the ocean, beautiful and bursting with color. Since the day I met him, he has never failed to make me feel special. But I don't think I'm the special one. It's *us* that's so special.

"I'm going to miss you," I admit.

"I know. I'll miss you, too." Bobby's thumbs caress across my cheeks. "But we'll see each other in a month or so. And we'll be so busy, it's gonna fly by. Time doesn't matter for us, Beth. It's just days passing until we're together again. Plus, we'll spend all winter break together, and then who knows what will be happening next summer? I might not be touring at all."

The idea is absurd. "No way. I'm sure you'll be playing throughout Europe or something," I say.

"Well, if that's the case, maybe you can come along," Bobby says, and my pulse kicks up in rhythm. Bobby leans over me to reach the end table. "Here. I have something for you."

I don't know how I missed the box, seeing as it's bright purple with an enormous, shiny bow on top.

"I was going to get you a ring," he says, handing the box to me. "Kind of like a promise ring, you know? Just something to remind you what you are to me when we're apart. But then I saw this, and I had to buy it instead."

"You didn't need to buy me anything," I say, taking the box. "I know how much you love me." The word 'ring' circles in my mind. Sure, he hadn't planned on buying an engagement ring. I know we're not quite there yet. Even if I'm sure I'm going to spend the rest of my life with Bobby, I just turned nineteen a few weeks ago, and I'm starting college, and he's a twenty-one-year-old chasing his dreams of superstardom without abandon.

I crack open the box, and before I can even take it in, Bobby asks, "Do you like it?" He shifts closer to me, peering behind the lid with a shy smile. I nod, tears welling in my eyes. I can barely speak.

"It's beautiful," I whisper. The box holds a bracelet, a gold chain made up of tiny infinity signs, all connecting until they meet back together at the delicate clasp. "Just... perfect," I whisper as I hand it to him to put on my wrist, all thoughts of a ring completely disappearing from my mind.

"I think of it kind of like pieces of our lives, the things that pull us apart for a little while. You go off to school here," he touches an infinity sign, "and I go on tour here, but they're still linked together, never breaking until they meet right back around where they started. No matter where our lives take us, Beth, you're it for me." He lifts my chin, meeting my eyes and swiping a tear away with his thumb.

"I love you so much," I say, and my voice cracks. "I wish I had something for you."

"I have your song," he says, patting his pocket. "I read it before every show, and it reminds me that some things are just meant to be." Bobby leans closer, his hand sliding through my hair, tilting my head back and brushing his lips against mine. "We're one of those things," Bobby whispers against my lips before claiming them wholly and desperately.

And while I love the bracelet and never want to take it off, this, what Bobby and I have together, is the only gift I really need.

NOW

August 2024: Arlington, TX

Don't hide behind your pretty words
Pretend your heart's not black and blue
But may the jealous weep, if they try to keep
All those pretty words inside you
—An excerpt from "The Application," written and performed by Robert
Beckett

"How's the article coming?" Harrison asks on FaceTime a couple days later. He's working as we chat, looking at his computer screen rather than the phone. Even so, he's been making an effort to call me every morning since I left. He should be, considering I'm here writing the article that's solidifying his career.

"Great. It's fun writing again—being creative."

"Have you figured out why he wanted *you* to write it?" His voice is playful, but I hear the meaning between his words loud and clear.

"Besides the reason he already told you?" I sigh and rub my forehead. "Because I'm a talented writer, Harrison." I say, feeling brave. I should, seeing as there's several states of distance between us.

"Of course you are, babe! I'm just kidding…" he trails off, typing for a few seconds. "You know that's not what I meant."

"Isn't it?" I ask.

Harrison stops and finally looks at the screen. "What are you mad about now? I'm just saying he could have chosen anyone," he says, as if *I'm* the problem here.

I sigh. "I'm not mad," I say, because I don't want to get into it. Not because I'm afraid of what Harrison will say, but because I'm starting to think I could tell him how I feel until I'm blue in the face, and he won't care. It's exhausting. "I need to get to soundcheck."

"Right. Wouldn't want to miss time with *Robert*." He says his name like an insult. "You can't miss one soundcheck with the guy to talk to your fiancé?" he says, and I roll my eyes.

"No. This is my job. One *you* insisted I take, if you'll remember. I'll call you later," I say, hanging up before he can argue with me further. I turn my phone on vibrate, sliding it into my pocket as I walk out into the sweltering Texas heat.

It feels like I'm swimming in the air, the humidity so thick, I swear water droplets are sticking to my hair and making it damp. I pull my shirt away from my sweaty stomach as I walk around the stage, wondering how it seems like we're *always* in stadiums in the hottest cities.

I walk around the corner toward the front of the stage, pulling my sunglasses down from on top of my head and my notebook from my back pocket, and pick a random seat in the front row. Bobby's singing one of his new songs. One that he wrote *after,* and it's quickly becoming one of my favorites. It's slow and sensual, full of emotion and hope, with about twenty seconds right in the middle for one of Johnny's signature guitar solos—which is what I'm listening to right now.

The solo ends and Bobby's voice bounces across the empty stadium seats, the echo somehow rough and smooth at the same time. It makes heat bloom in my stomach, and I grit my teeth in annoyance.

You're a professional, I remind myself. *This is just a job.*

But then I look up, and I desperately wish I'd been a little less professional and skipped this particular soundcheck. Bobby hasn't noticed me yet, his back toward me as he sings facing his band. But that's not what makes me regret my decision to be a committed journalist.

It's the fact that apparently, even Bobby isn't immune to the Texas heat. He's shirtless on the stage, as is much of the band. But they don't make my knees feel like rubber or my breath come in short spurts.

Get a grip. I chide myself, but I'm not sure it's possible. Not with how this man looks shirtless.

His back is nothing but stone-hard, muscular perfection, his tan shoulders broad and strong, tapering into a thin, but perfectly honed waist. It's absurd how fit he is, and completely unfair—something I should have been made aware of so I could add *no taking your shirt off* to my list of demands.

The song ends, and Bobby fist pumps into the air on the last beat of the drum. There's a flash of pink on the inside of his arm—a tattoo—and I squint to see what it is, but it's too small to make out the details. His smile is enthralling as he turns toward the front of the stage, taking off his cap and putting it on backward.

Fuck. Me.

My mouth goes dry and my skin ignites. The heat of the sun is nothing compared to the heat coiling in my stomach. Bobby's steps falter as he notices me in the front row, his eyebrows raising in surprise. His throat bobs as his bright blue eyes slide down my body, which, if I'm being honest, isn't much more covered than his. With the heat index of a hundred and twelve, I'm wearing the shortest shorts I own and a top that's more sports bra than tank.

My hair's up in a messy bun to get it off my shoulders, which shows off my neck and collarbones. Bobby recovers quickly, coming to squat down in front of me. He tips up his bottle of water, taking several glugs so deep the plastic crinkles, before dumping the rest on the back of his neck. Water trickles down his chest, and suddenly the heat index feels closer to two hundred degrees.

I know that Bobby did it because it's truly *that* hot out here, that it has nothing to do with turning me on, but it feels like a dirty move. I look down, pretending to take some notes, when really, I'm just writing my favorite colors in order. But even looking away, I'm pretty sure his physique is burned into my vision. I close my eyes for a moment, willing the image away, but all I can see are his perfectly toned pecs with a sprinkling of chest hair between them and many, *many* abs.

Ones I could certainly wash clothes on.

Or eat dinner off of.

"Jesus Christ," I say under my breath, suddenly hating myself. Am I really this weak?

"I thought you were going to skip this one," Bobby says, plopping on the edge of the stage and swinging his legs over the side.

"Got a job to do, remember?" I still don't look at him.

"It's the same soundcheck every show," he answers, grabbing another bottle of water from the front of the stage and tossing it to me. "Except this one is hotter than Satan's sauna."

I can't help but laugh. "I think that makes it pretty different, don't you?" I joke, but in truth that's not the only reason this soundcheck is significantly hotter. "Plus, it shows off your dedication and professionalism and your..." I clear my throat again. *Get it together, and whatever you do, do* not *say abs.* "Ab...ility to withstand extreme temperatures."

Shit.

Bobby must notice my eyes avoiding looking anywhere near his tan, glistening skin. He twists the cap off another bottle and grins. "I can go get a shirt, if you'd like," he says, teasing me.

"It's not you. It's Johnny," I reply. "He's aged like fine wine." I wiggle my fingers at Johnny, who's standing not too far away from us, clearly eavesdropping.

He throws his head back and laughs. "I *have* aged well, thank you. Does this mean you're finally agreeing to a date with me after all these years, Bethy?" Johnny asks, raising his eyebrows. "I think there's an Applebee's down the road."

"Applebee's?" I ask, my forehead wrinkling in confusion.

"I don't know, they're always getting it as a reward on Survivor. And they seem so excited. Must be amazing," Johnny shrugs. "Plus, I don't need fancy dinners. I have *game*, you know."

"Actually, Beth's busy this afternoon," Bobby interrupts, hopping back up to his feet.

"I am?" I ask.

"You are," Bobby confirms. "And you," Bobby points his water bottle toward Johnny, "messed up your solo. Again."

"Creative liberties, man." Johnny throws his arms out as if insulted.

"They're only creative liberties if they're played in the right key," Bobby responds, crossing his arms. "Maybe some practice before the show would be good?"

"I was born with a guitar in my hands. Maybe *you* need to practice that key change. Sounded a little pitchy to me."

Bobby picks up his water bottle and throws it at Johnny, and I settle back to watch them.

It's just like old times, their playful energy, the constant ribbing. It makes my stomach sink to witness the way their lives have continued on together so seamlessly when I was so crudely cut out.

Bobby slings an arm around Johnny's shoulder, and the flash of pink appears again, but now that he's closer, I can make out the shape.

It's a single flower, roughly the size of a baseball, tattooed on the inside of his left arm.

A wild rose.

I suck in a breath, and a wave of dizziness passes over me, almost knocking me sideways.

The tattoo is for me. I know it the way I know my own name.

I close my eyes, but the memory of Bobby handing me a slightly-wilted rose as he quoted Shakespeare at Joe's Place circles through my mind. *Parting is such sweet sorrow…* he'd said, his fingers brushing mine, setting my body on fire.

My phone vibrates, a welcome distraction, and I pull it from my pocket.

Harrison: *I'm coming to visit this weekend.*

The image vanishes, a feeling of dread replacing it.

It's not a question or a request. Harrison is coming, no matter what I want.

And having him here is going to make everything worse.

NOW

August 2024: Austin, TX

Blame it all on me
Guess it's still my fault
But I wanted you to fly
Yeah I made mistakes
Sure I have regrets
It wasn't meant to be goodbye
—An excerpt from "Please," written and performed by Robert Beckett

Harrison doesn't wave to me as he exits the terminal, already on his phone and scrolling through Lord knows how many emails he's gotten since he got on the flight.

"Harrison!" I shout his name, and he finally looks up, a broad smile spreading across his clean-shaven face. He pockets his phone and hurries toward me, setting down his bag so he can pick me up and hug me properly.

The smell of scotch is unmistakable as he wraps his arms around me, and I stiffen, my skin going itchy.

"I've missed you," he says into my ear, and even though I'm still struggling with where I stand, not to mention frustrated he decided to partake in the airport bar before his flight, it feels nice to have something from my life back home here with me. I've been confronted with too many memories and emotions since I stepped foot on the tour bus, and that doesn't even include those regarding *the* talk I've been avoiding with Bobby.

"Man, it's good to see you," Harrison says as he puts me down. "I don't think I like this whole you being a writer thing." He says it like a joke, but there's an obvious truth threaded into his words, and I wonder how much he had to drink on the plane.

To my disappointment, I realize I expected nothing less, on both counts.

Maybe this time away was *good* for us. For our relationship. Since I've been gone, I'm more certain than ever that I'm not content with just being a wife and socialite. It's not enough for me to pretend I have a job by helping Harrison hook clients. And maybe Harrison being on his own for a little while will help him see how much I do for him that goes unnoticed and make him appreciate it more.

Appreciate *me* more.

Harrison slings an arm around my shoulders as we walk toward the front of the airport.

"What do you want to do?" I ask. "We could explore Austin. I've never been here before."

My suggestion is met with Harrison's nose scrunching up as if he's just smelled something rotten. "Texas has nothing but rednecks, cattle, and cornfields. Why don't we go back to the tour bus? I feel like I should check in on my client, anyway."

My throat burns as if I've swallowed a hot coal. "Why don't we just go back to the hotel? Bobby will be in soundcheck, anyway—"

He waves a hand. "Nonsense. I canceled the hotel."

My stomach drops.

I made a deal with Bobby, and he's kept his word. No one outside of his band and Marissa has set foot on his tour bus since I got here. But what do I tell Harrison? How could I possibly explain that he's technically not allowed on the bus without making him want to go there even more?

"I don't think that's a good idea. You wouldn't be comfortable. There's not enough space to spread out. Maybe we can still get a room somewhere?"

"Not comfortable? Isn't that where you sleep every night? You certainly look well rested." Harrison's voice has a bite to it that I'm not comfortable with. If I know Harrison at all, he thinks he deserves this—a VIP, all-access backstage pass. A peek behind the curtain so he can go home and brag to his co-workers.

"I do, but it's still Bobby's space. He doesn't really like having people on the bus." Maybe if I make it a general rule, instead of just about him, he won't get so offended.

"*Bobby*, huh? Seems like you two have gotten close." That lump of coal grows hotter, and I feel like I'm choking, but I push it down and force myself to swallow.

"Not really." I keep my voice light. "But that's what everyone calls him. I must've picked it up."

"Hmph…" Our car arrives, and Harrison tosses his bag into the trunk while the driver opens the door for me.

"Tell him the address to the bus, Beth," Harrison orders as he climbs in beside me. There's tension in his voice, and before I know what I'm doing, I'm shifting away from him a bit. He looks at me expectantly, and I know there's no changing his mind.

"I think I should see where my girl has been spending all her time. Don't you?" And though he smiles, it sounds like an accusation—but what is he accusing me of?

My blood heats. I didn't want to come here, but Harrison forced my hand. *He's* the one who made me take this assignment. And now, what? He's questioning what I've been doing with Bobby for the past couple weeks?

I reluctantly give the driver the address, somehow keeping my tone casual.

"See? Was that so hard?" Harrison grumbles, opening his phone and returning to his emails, so I pull up Bobby's number on my own phone.

Me: I'm so sorry, but I have to bring Harrison by the bus. I type, then press send.
   Bobby: We made a deal, Beth. His reply is instant.
   Me: I know. And I'm sorry.

I don't know what else to say. If I tell him Harrison's just trying to mark his territory, it will only make Bobby hate him more.

Me: Just this once. It won't happen again.

Bobby doesn't answer for several minutes, but as we're pulling in, I finally get a reply.

Bobby: Just this once. But if he's an ass, he's gone. Got it?

I exhale in relief.

Me: He'll be on his best behavior, I promise.

I press send on the text and slide my phone back into my pocket as we pull up next to the bus.
   "Home Sweet Home," I say brightly, climbing out of the car. I might be all smiles and cheeriness on the outside, but inside, my stomach is churning, and I have to swallow down wave after wave of nausea. Harrison's possessive hand on my lower back and the way he's studying me makes me think he doesn't plan on being on his best behavior at all.

Bobby's the perfect gentleman as Harrison makes himself at home. After Harrison introduces himself to Johnny, who has his feet kicked up on the coffee table in a way I'm certain Bobby hates, he promptly asks if there's anything to drink on board.

"Of course," Bobby says, grabbing him a scotch and settling into the chair across from us on the couch.

"So, Robert," Harrison says after taking a swig of his drink. "Is Elizabeth here doing her job up to your standards?"

Bobby smiles broadly. "I have no complaints," he says. "Thanks for letting me borrow her. I'm sure you've missed her since she's been gone."

"Boy, have I. You know, I never realized how much I detested going to all those functions alone." Harrison takes another long sip.

"I'm sure," Bobby says under his breath, appearing to fight against rolling his eyes, but Harrison doesn't seem to catch it.

He takes another swig. "Nice bus, man." Harrison looks around. "Little dated, though."

"Harrison!" I scold, bristling.

"No, it's okay." Bobby laughs good-naturedly. "He's right. But I have a lot of good memories on this particular bus," Bobby says directly to me. "It seems I just can't let it go."

I'm blushing, and this time Harrison *does* notice. "Oh, don't look so scandalized. He said he knows the bus is dated."

Johnny's eyes remind me of a ping-pong ball as they bounce back and forth between Harrison and Bobby. "It's our original bus. We could never get rid of her," he says with an exaggerated shrug.

Bobby nods. "She's an old girl, but she gets us from here to there. How was your flight in?" Bobby asks, and I'm grateful he's trying to change the subject.

"Just great." Harrison says, his words clipped.

"Beth gave me a glimpse of her piece for Rolling Stone. It's coming along nicely. She's quite the writer, isn't she?" Bobby continues, trying to keep the mood light.

Harrison's eyes narrow at the use of my nickname. "If you like fluff pieces about symphonies and dreary art exhibits, absolutely." Harrison says, smiling like a snake watching a mouse stumble straight into its path. I stiffen, sweat beading on my neck as he impatiently taps his fingers on the chair arm.

Bobby's eyes flash with white-hot anger, and I silently beg for him to let it go, but I know him better than that. Johnny sits up, scooting to the edge of his seat and watching Bobby as if preparing himself to step in if his friend loses it.

"I'm sorry, but don't you think that's extremely disrespectful?" Bobby says. His tone is harsh and his voice tight, but honestly, I'm just grateful he chose words instead of standing up, punching Harrison in the face, and telling him to get lost.

Harrison stiffens, his jaw cracking open as if he's in complete shock and disbelief that someone dared to call him out.

"I *think*," the word crackles as he hits the consonant hard enough to make me wince, "if *Elizabeth* had truly been a gifted, phenomenal writer, she'd still be doing it today. Don't get me wrong," he raises his hands and smiles. "I'm grateful that her writing this article for you allowed us to sign our deal. But she knows her time is better spent doing other things. Right?"

Harrison's eyes meet mine, and there's no mistaking the demand there.

Agree with him.

Admit it's all been a waste of my time.

Admit I belong at home with him.

I don't answer, and Harrison's vein begins to pulse above his eyebrow. "Thanks for your concern, though, *Bobby*." He says the nickname pointedly, and I know he's doing it to get to me. "What do you think, Johnny?"

"I think you're out of line," Johnny answers, then stands. "Actually, no. I think you're an asshole."

Harrison tips his head back and laughs, and the menace in it sends a shiver down my spine. "Takes one to know one, eh?" he says, taking another gulp of scotch.

I don't understand what's happening. Sure, we had a fight before I left, and he might've said roughly the same things to me before about how he thinks my time could better be used elsewhere than writing, but he's never been so harsh about it.

So blatantly cruel.

"I don't see anyone else here glugging scotch and berating their fiancée." Bobby's fists are clenched, his shoulders tight and his breaths deep and slow as if he's counting the length of his inhales and exhales in an attempt to keep calm.

"Well, if my fiancée is as good with words as you say, I'm sure she'll have no trouble telling me how she feels herself." Harrison's no longer making an effort to make it seem as if this is just a jovial conversation.

He's trying to prove a point.

Bobby looks at me expectantly, waiting for me to chime in, but I'm frozen.

"See? She agrees." Harrison finishes his drink in what I think might be record time. "Or have you spent so much time with *my* fiancée that you know her better than I do?" He spits the word, as if it's a shackle tying me to him.

As if he owns me.

"After all, you're the greatest performer of our generation. One that makes women question why they bothered to settle down with that boring accountant. The one who allows those same women to feel loved vicariously through the..." Harrison pretends to think. "What was it you said, Beth? The soulful sounds and tender words of the songs he writes."

My article.

"How did you get that?" I ask, a shiver running down my spine.

Harrison's eyes flash. "You think I'd give you a new laptop without making sure I have access to everything on it?"

I stiffen. "You had no right to do that."

"Why? Hiding something, Elizabeth?" Harrison asks, cocking his head.

"Of course not!" I throw my arms out, no longer caring that Bobby's sitting in the room with us. "That's what this is about? My article?"

"What what's about?" Harrison feigns innocence. "I'm not sure I understand what you mean. We're just sitting here hanging out. Having a drink." He stands and goes to the bar to pour himself another, and the embarrassment of his behavior makes my teeth hurt.

"*You're* having a drink," Johnny says. "Several, it seems."

"Well Johnny boy, you're welcome to join me." Harrison rattles the ice in his glass.

I've never seen this version of Harrison before. This rude, combative man with no regard for manners or decorum, and in front of a client, no less.

Bobby's jaw clenches so hard I think his teeth might crack. Anger has deepened the lines of his face, and his knuckles are white on the armrest.

"Listen," Bobby stands up, and Johnny tenses. "I don't know if this is how you normally speak to Beth, but you're certainly not going to do it in front of me. I suggest you put that bottle down, and apologize."

Harrison laughs, but it's humorless. "Come on, man. I'm not insulting—"

"Actually, you are," I say, finally finding my voice, even if it comes out soft and shaky. I lift my chin. I've had enough of this. How dare he embarrass me and give Bobby even more ammunition to hate him, all because he's angry about what I wrote in my article. The article *he* made me agree to in the first place. I've never known Harrison to be insecure or vindictive, but there's no other way to describe how he's behaving right now.

"Is that right?" he asks, slamming the liquor bottle on the counter. "So, what, a couple weeks on the road and you think you're better than me now?"

"Harrison!" I stand up, but Bobby steps forward, putting himself between Harrison and me. "What on earth are you talking about?" I ask around his shoulder.

"It's time for you to leave," Bobby says. "Go cool off. Sober up. I need Beth for soundcheck, anyway. You know, part of our *deal*." Johnny moves toward Harrison, and he straightens, tilting his head back as the fakest smile I've ever seen spreads across his face.

"Of course," Harrison says, raising his hands before Johnny can force him off the bus. "Wouldn't want to get in the middle of your *work*." He uses his fingers to put quotations around the word, then grabs the liquor bottle, sneering at me before storming off the bus.

Bobby turns to me as Johnny excuses himself, likely to make sure Harrison isn't going to cause trouble somewhere else, but I can't look at him. This isn't the Harrison I know, and I'm not sure how to explain that to Bobby. Usually, he's funny and charming and kind, if not a little distracted.

Sure, he has a temper, but it's so rare, and never, ever in public or over something so petty. This side of him scares me, and if I have to unpack it and figure out what the hell is going on with him, I can't do it with Bobby staring at me with pity in his eyes.

"Beth—" he says, taking a step forward, but I hold my hands up.

"I'm gonna grab my notebook." I clear my throat as I scramble toward the back of the bus as fast as I can. "I'll see you at soundcheck," I say. But I never go.

Instead, I curl up in a ball on Bobby's bed and cry, wondering how I'm going to make it through the next three days with Harrison here.

That is, if Bobby even lets him stay.

There's only an hour until Bobby's opening act goes on, and Harrison hasn't come back.

I've called him at least a dozen times over the past several hours, but every call has gone straight to voicemail, and I wonder if he packed up and went back home. My stomach's been in knots since he stormed out, but not really over the argument.

What has me so on edge is what that argument represents. It's blatantly obvious how he feels about me having things in my life I enjoy other than him, about my writing, so how am I supposed to tie myself to him forever?

Bobby was kind enough to not question me on why I missed sound-check, though it's likely because he didn't have to ask. My hundred-dollar eye cream and Tom Ford concealer did nothing to hide the puffiness around my eyes or my red nose.

I don't have to ask how Bobby's feeling, either. The tension in his shoulders, clenched jaw, and constant fidgeting tells me he's livid. Furious. Another, more elegant, word for angry that my poet mind can't seem to think of.

Because you're so out of practice.

I don't think I can even call myself a poet anymore, not when I haven't written a poem in years.

There's a tentative knock at the bus door, and I pause, putting down my notebook where I'm jotting down ideas for the rest of the article. Harrison pops his head in, waving his handkerchief above him with a sheepish smile on his face. He means to break the tension, but all it does is infuriate me further.

Who carries around a white handkerchief in their pocket to use as a prop?

He's certainly never offered it to me when I've had a sniffly nose.

He climbs the stairs. "Are we ready for the show, rockstar?" Harrison asks, walking to put an arm around my shoulders as if nothing ever happened. Bobby makes a noncommittal kind of grunting noise in the back of his throat, but his eyes are locked on Harrison touching me.

"Hey man, I need to apologize for earlier," Harrison says. "Had a few drinks on the plane ride over. You know how it is." He pulls out his phone, swiping the screen to unlock it.

"Can't say I do," Bobby answers, walking to the coffeemaker. He grabs the lavender from the cabinet, and a bit of my anxiety eases. A latte is *exactly* what I need right now.

"Elizabeth knows what I meant," Harrison continues. "Of course she's a writer. She went to NYU for it, after all. And she wrote for several different magazines."

"Premier magazines. An internship in Europe. Top of her class. There's a reason I chose her," Bobby says, each word a sharp dagger aimed directly at Harrison as he pours steamed milk into my cup.

My stomach squeezes uncomfortably, my heart jolting out of rhythm.

"What internship in Europe? Elizabeth's never even been to Europe." Harrison meets my eyes and holds his thumb and index fingers to his lips, as if saying, *what's this guy smoking?* Bobby freezes at the counter, his knuckles going white around the mug, and I wonder if it's about to shatter, but he recovers quickly, pouring some syrup into the mug.

"My mistake. I thought I read in my file that Beth spent a year in an elite study abroad opportunity for literature."

"I got accepted. It's probably on my transcripts, but… I didn't go," I add softly. This feels like a conversation that should be had in private, but I can't stop myself from sharing this little nugget of information.

Bobby stays by the coffeemaker for a few more moments, pretending to be busy. But my cup sits there, steaming and finished, fragrant with lavender and ready for me to drink.

He can't even look at me, and for some reason, that breaks my heart more thoroughly than Harrison's recent behavior.

"Anyway," Harrison continues, scrunching his eyebrows and once again looking at Bobby like he's lost his mind. "Beth's a great writer. I shouldn't have insinuated otherwise. It was a bad joke. I just miss having her home with me. You can understand that, can't you, man?"

Bobby finally turns around, and his piercing blue eyes meet mine. I expect to see anger there, maybe some annoyance that I'd turned down the internship he'd pushed so hard for me to take. But instead, all I see is grief swirling within the blue, so thick and heavy, it takes my breath away. I don't think I've seen him look this sad since the day Michael died.

"Here," he says, but his voice is flat. He hands me my coffee and goes to sit on the couch.

"Seriously?" Harrison says, his voice tight. "Have you been drinking those dumb coffees the whole time you've been here?" Harrison rolls his eyes. "I always tell her serious people drink black coffee."

Bobby opens his mouth, the grief in his expression replaced by pure, fiery rage.

I hold up my hands. "You know what, Harrison? I need to finish getting ready for the show. Maybe you should grab us a room at a hotel. I really don't think there's enough space here." I don't even try to hide the exhaustion from my voice.

That's all I feel.

Exhaustion.

I'm tired from how he's acted today. No, I'm tired from how he's been acting for *weeks*, and now I can't even enjoy my cup of comfort in peace without him poking and picking at me.

"Are you sure, babe? I think there's plenty of room," he says, gesturing around.

"Actually, I threw out my back and had to take my bed back. Doctor's orders," Bobby chimes in. "Beth's just got a bunk in the hallway. Plus, the band normally comes over after the show, and they'll act like idiots till the sun comes up."

It's a lie. The band *never* comes to the bus after the show, but I'm grateful he's covering for me. Because I have no intention of spending the next three days on this bus here with Bobby and Harrison in a one sided pissing match.

I need to call Molly to get her advice on how to handle this situation.

I'm engaged to be married to this man in less than a year. Deposits have been paid, an announcement posted in the papers. I wanted to marry Harrison, but I don't want this—to be spoken down to. Belittled until I'm left raw, only a shell of who I used to be.

But for some reason, the idea of calling it all off makes me paralyzed with terror. Because as embarrassing as it is to admit, I'm not sure who I am without Harrison anymore. Our lives are so intertwined that I don't know how I could even begin untangling them.

Harrison makes a face that looks like he's just been offered uncooked brussel sprouts for breakfast. "Maybe a hotel will be better for us after all. How about I go sort out the details, and I'll pick you up after the show?" he asks.

"Sounds great," I say, forcing a smile as he walks over and gives me a kiss on the cheek before sliding his phone from his pocket, completely unaware of how shattered I'm feeling.

By his words.

His actions.

The way he truly feels about me.

The bus doors closing triggers something in me I don't understand, and as much as I wish I could make it to the back room before the tears start falling, I can't. They burst out of me in a sob, and I cover my mouth, trying to muffle the sound.

My shoulders shake as I turn away, but a strong hand catches me gently by the elbow.

Without a word, Bobby pulls me into his arms, wrapping himself around me as if he can hold my broken pieces together. It's the first time we've hugged in six years, and it feels different. But despite the time and the pain and the distance, one thing hasn't changed.

Holding him still feels like coming home.

"You don't deserve this. None of it." Bobby's voice has a fervor to it that makes me shiver.

"I know," I say into his shirt. "But I don't know what to do. This isn't Harrison. He's not like this."

"Beth." I can tell Bobby's forcing himself to soften his tone, but sharp edges of anger still cut through. "You don't write poetry anymore. You can't even drink your damn coffee without criticism."

"Harrison's not the reason I don't write poems anymore." I pull away, forcing myself to look into Bobby's eyes. Eyes filled with so many unspoken emotions, it makes my head spin.

"Are you ready to have that conversation now?" he asks, but I don't even take time to consider. The tears start to fall again, tracks of sorrow that run down my cheeks and spill onto my shirt.

I can't even speak.

I'm afraid if I do, I'll never stop crying.

I shake my head, because it's all too much. I'm not strong enough right now. And if I find out something else that demolishes a piece of the world I've built in my mind, the series of events I've lived through that have created the picture of who I am, I will fall apart so completely that I don't think anyone, not even Bobby, will be able to put me back together.

"Not now. Please," I say finally, my voice almost a whisper. Bobby nods solemnly, and I know he understands.

"Okay, Beth," he says, wrapping his arms back around me and squeezing me tight. "Okay."

We stand there together until he's called to the stage to perform, tears silently streaming from my eyes as Bobby rubs my back, my hair, telling me he's sorry. And while I know he's talking about what's happening with Harrison, I can feel in my bones that the events of today aren't the entirety of what he's apologizing for.

After he leaves, I call Molly, who stays on the phone and listens to me cry until I have no more tears.

"Go wash your face," she finally says when my sobs have turned to sniffles. "Put on some lip gloss and straighten your spine. You are beautiful. You are strong. And you are my best friend. Not a doormat or a sad puppy to be kicked around." The anger in her voice is unmistakable, but it softens as she adds, "And Beth? You don't have to go through with this."

My eyes are filling with tears again as I hang up the phone, because I know she's right—I could end things with Harrison right now, and the world would keep spinning. The problem is, I don't know *how* to walk away, or if I truly want to.

I chose this life.

I chose Harrison, and we were happy. At least, until Robert showed back up and everything changed.

Until being around him reminded me that a long time ago, I made a different choice.

I chose myself. And somewhere deep down, beneath the pieces of perfect daughter and fiancée and friend, hidden under broken bits of who I used to be, is the girl who didn't let other people's actions turn her into someone she never wanted to be. The girl who writes what she feels and drinks her stupid coffee without shame.

I just need to see if I can find her again.

THEN

DECEMBER 2017

The shiny, silver doors to Mount Sinai Kravis Children's Hospital loom in front of us as Bobby tries to calm himself down enough to enter. Molly and I have walked through those doors a hundred times to see Michael over the years, so often that I know exactly where to get the best cup of coffee and how to get to the nurses' station to get extra ice chips or peanut butter crackers.

Bobby, on the other hand, hasn't been to a hospital since his dad passed away. His knuckles are white on his guitar case, his breathing slightly shallow.

"Ready?" I ask, grabbing his hand.

Bobby looks at me, and I feel him pulling strength from my skin into his own. He flips the switch, and in the blink of an eye he becomes Robert. Charming. Confident. And completely unfazed by walking through those doors.

"Lead the way," he says, motioning for me to go ahead. Molly's waiting inside, standing with her mom, Stephanie, Bobby's new assistant, Carol, and a squat, older woman with rosy cheeks. I go to give Stephanie a hug, pulling Bobby behind me.

"Oh good! You're here!" the older woman says, immediately recognizing Bobby and introducing herself. "It's so nice to meet you. I'm Rita. The kids are all ready for you. The ones allowed to leave their rooms are in the playroom."

"And the kids who can't?" Bobby asks.

"Well, they're too immunocompromised to be around all the other children."

"Can I go to them? Is that…" he trails off, seemingly nervous about saying the right thing.

Rita smiles gently. "If you're willing to gown and glove up, that would be just fine. I'm sure they would love that."

"Great. Okay. Well. Is there anything else I need to know?" Bobby's forehead is creased as he takes off his ball cap, flipping it backward.

"Well…you should know that you have a lot of little fans in there who are thrilled to meet you. You're making a bad day infinitely brighter. So just have fun with them. That's what they need."

Bobby visibly relaxes, a broad smile growing on his face. "Fun. I can do fun." He nods, taking my hand again as we follow Rita to the playroom.

As we walk up to the door, Bobby pulls Molly aside. "Could you go get Michael for me?" Molly nods, tears already forming in her eyes. Molly slips into the room, returning seconds later with Michael, who is bouncing on his toes as if he can't contain his big excitement in his tiny body.

"Hey, Big Man!" Bobby says, kneeling in front of him. Michael's brown eyes sparkle, and he smiles his enormous, gap-toothed grin.

"You're really here!" Michael says, jumping up and down, then launching himself into Bobby's arms.

"Of course I am! *You're* here. I obviously had to come say hi." He gives Michael a tight squeeze, holding on until he starts to giggle and squirm. "I have something special for you, seeing as you're my number one fan and all, but I wanted to give it to you out here, so the other kids don't get jealous."

There's a mischievous twinkle in Bobby's eyes as he pulls back, grabbing the enormous box from Carol. It's wrapped in blue paper, and Michael wastes no time ripping into it. Inside is a child-sized guitar, a new Robert Beckett t-shirt, a ball cap that matches the one Bobby's currently wearing, and two Nerf guns.

"Woah! This is all for me?" Michael says, grabbing the hat and putting it on.

"Sure is, Buddy. But don't worry, Carol here has another box in the car full of merch for the other kids. But this guitar and Nerf gun?" He picks up the toy. "They're only for you," he says as he pulls the trigger, the foam dart hitting Michael in the belly.

Michael's jaw drops. "You're toast!" he says, grabbing the other gun as he runs to hide behind the nurses' desk.

"Michael!" Molly's mom, Stephanie, scolds, but there's no bite to it. "Manners!"

Molly grabs Michael from where he's hiding. "I'll play with you later, munchkin," she says as Michael giggles. "Let's let Robert get in there with all your friends. He has a concert to put on, after all."

Bobby stands up, pulling his guitar back over his shoulder. "She's right, Mike." Bobby winks at him, and I swear Michael's smile is bright enough to power the entire hospital. "We have a show to do. Why don't you go tell your friends to gather up, and I'll be there in a second," Bobby suggests.

"You got it!" Michael beams as he scrambles toward the door, pulling his hat off and flipping it backward like Bobby's. Michael disappears through the door, but not before Bobby pulls his Nerf gun from behind him, hitting Michael square between the shoulder blades and pushing the Nerf gun into my hands.

"Hey!" Michael spins around, narrowing his eyes. "Not fair, Beth!"

I push the gun back to Bobby, but he raises his hands in the air, refusing to take it.

"Woah, cheap move. We'll have to get her back later, right Mikey?" Bobby says conspiratorially.

Michael points two fingers at his eyes, then at me as if saying, *I'm watching you,* before running in the playroom.

"He's here!" Michael screams as the door clicks shut.

Bobby turns around to talk to Carol about getting the merch for the other kids from the car now that her arms aren't full with Michael's enormous present, then strides into the room with the confidence of a rockstar.

He waves to the kids, sitting down on a stool in the front of the open room.

"Any requests?" he asks, and thirty hands shoot up in the air.

"Woah! Okay, well, let's start with Michael, then we'll make our way through."

"You know which one I want," Michael says, bouncing up and down on his knees, and Bobby laughs, strumming the first chord of "Roots."

There's no amplifier. No microphone or band or fancy lights, but it's full of joy, and easily my favorite show I've seen him play yet.

"Roots" turns into "Love Story" by Taylor Swift, which I was shocked to find Bobby knew every word to, and then a song he made up on the spot when a little boy around the age of five requested a song called "Green Race Cars and Boogers".

Bobby doesn't stop until every request has been played to the best of his ability, including the made-up ones, and when we finally leave the room, my cheeks hurt from smiling.

What a gift he's given them—not only to these kids, but to their parents, who got to see their children laughing and singing and dancing in the midst of what will likely be the biggest trial of their lives.

We spend the next few hours visiting the kids in isolation. Room after room, I wait outside as he gowns and gloves and then de-gowns and de-gloves and gowns and gloves again, a new set of protective clothing, mask, and gloves for each room.

Bobby keeps his Robert mask on the entire time, only slipping when he leaves the room of a little girl with sarcoma and has to stop for a moment to wipe the tears from his eyes. I don't ask what caused his armor to crack, just hug him as he takes deep breaths for several minutes, then moves on to the next room.

After every kid has been met, and every shirt has been signed, and every song has been sung, we return to Michael's room, where Molly and her family are watching a movie.

"Hey there, Mikey," Bobby says, inclining his head at Stephanie who's sitting with Michael on his bed. She kisses his head, then stands. "I'm going to get a coffee. You girls want to come with?" she asks as Bobby kicks his shoes off and climbs onto the bed next to Michael.

"What are we watching?" he asks, scooting down and putting his hands behind his head.

Michael pauses the movie. "Cars 2!" he says excitedly as he fills Bobby in on the parts he's missed already.

"Yes, please." I try to stifle a yawn, exhausted despite the fact that I've done nothing but watch Bobby do all the work today. We've been here since ten this morning, and it's nearing sunset.

It's a short walk to the café, where we each grab a cup and a lemonade for Michael.

"I can't tell you how much I appreciate today," Stephanie says as we walk back to Michael's room. "How much all of us do."

I shake my head. "It was all Bobby," I say, uncomfortable with taking any credit.

"Well, I still want to thank you for asking him. I haven't seen Michael this happy in a long time. You've got a good one, Beth," Stephanie says as she holds the door open for me.

"Yes, I do," I say with a smile as I walk through the door.

A rubber dart hits me directly between the eyes, while another one brushes my shoulder.

"Gotcha!" Michael dissolves in a fit of laughter as Bobby blows on the top of his Nerf gun.

I really do, I think, making a mental note to get them back.

NOW

September 2024: New Orleans, LA

There's been an emergency at work, so I'm already on my way to the airport.
I'm sorry for earlier. I'll make it up to you, I swear.
—"Excuses," a free verse poem by Harrison Rouchester

A week later, Molly's laying on Bobby's bed with me, having flown out to spend a few days back on Big Blue. She's painting my nails, just like we used to do as teenagers, except this time the color isn't electric blue or neon green.

"I have a confession to make," Molly says, never taking her eyes off the soft pink polish she's coating on my thumbnail.

"Okay… I'm nervous," I say, because if Molly has been holding something in for the last two days that she's been with me, then it's something big.

"You know the work emergency that called Harrison away last weekend?"

"You mean the universe *finally* doing something kind and merciful for me?" I ask. Of course I know, because it had been a miracle. I'd been dreading meeting up with Harrison after the show, unsure what to say or how to act like the events of the previous twelve hours hadn't happened, but Harrison never came. He'd texted me about halfway through Bobby's set, saying he'd been called back to the office for some sort of work emergency.

And I've all but avoided thinking about our fight ever since. I'm living in denial. I'm fully aware of it, but I'm tired of trying to be someone else all the time. Especially with Harrison.

Being back on the bus allows me to just be *Beth* again, and I'm holding on to that feeling for as long as I can, even if it means burying my head in the sand.

"Hi, Beth." Molly finally looks up from my nails and gives me a wide grin. "I'm the universe."

"What? Molly, you didn't!" I scramble into a sitting position, careful to not get polish on the black, buttery-soft comforter.

Molly puts her hand to her ear as if it's a phone and raises the pitch of her voice, putting a slight Boston accent into it.

"Yes, hello? This is Lucy Wilcox's personal assistant. Yes, the movie star, who else? She needs a meeting with you tonight. Yes, I'm aware, but it's an emergency. No, I'm afraid it can't be discussed over the phone. She'll need you to meet her at the Manhattan Detention Complex. Yes, I understand it will be late. Just get on the first flight out." She pretends to hang up the phone.

A bubble of laughter tries to work its way up my throat, but my anxiety pops it. "Oh my God. You're insane! What were you thinking?"

Molly shrugs. "I was *thinking* that you called me crying because Harrison was insulting you and being even more of a dick than usual."

"He's not usually a dick," I argue, but my words don't sound convincing.

"If he's not an outright dick, he's dick-adjacent. And he's certainly no Bobby."

"What do you mean he's no Bobby?" I ask. "You've been around him for two days and now you're team Bobby again? You know what happened between us."

"Yeah…about that." Molly has the decency to look sheepish. "Last night after we fell asleep, or actually, after *you* fell asleep, I may have gone back out for one more drink."

I throw a pillow at her. "You are such a sneak! I said you didn't have to come to bed just because I was tired."

"I know, but I wanted to speak to Bobby alone. And I knew you wouldn't let me." She pulls my hand back out and puts one more coat of Tickle Me Pink on my pinky, which I apparently smudged on Bobby's pillow, and screws the cap back on. "I never got to really rip into him over what he did to you." She grins. "This seemed like the perfect opportunity."

"Oh, Molly," I rub between my eyebrows to soothe away the tension, careful not to smear my nails again. "You didn't."

"Of course I did. Actually, I'm a bit offended that you'd invite me here and think I'd spend three days with the guy and never scold him for breaking your heart," she says, lowering her eyebrows.

I swing my legs over the bed, needing to move. I have too much nervous energy to sit still. "That was years ago. We've moved past it."

"Well, I'll tell you one thing," Molly grabs a different color, Stiletto Red, and hands it to me, patting the bed in front of her. "He certainly hasn't. And I'm not so sure you have either."

I oblige her, sitting down and unscrewing the cap to start on her nails. "That's ridiculous. Absolutely absurd."

"Mhm... Did you know Bobby hasn't had a relationship last more than a month since you? He rarely even dates anymore."

I fight the temptation to paint red all over her cuticles. "Of course I don't. You think we've spent our time talking about his dating history?"

Molly ignores me. "The girls he dates are great. Nice girls, beautiful, smart, and talented. But they're not *you*."

I narrow my eyes at her.

"Those were his words, just in case you were wondering," she says pointedly, and my cheeks heat.

"I got that, thanks," I say, moving on to her other hand. I keep my eyes down, afraid of what I'll find in hers if I meet them.

She sees right through me and pulls her arm back, forcing me to look at her. "You need to hear him out, Beth."

"I know." It's the truth. I *do* know it. Not just because I owe it to our newfound friendship or for the integrity of the article, but because Bobby was the love of my life, and that deserves a conversation and some closure, for both of us.

"Did he tell you his version of what happened that night?" I ask. Maybe if I hear it from Molly, it'll be easier to chew. Maybe it'll hurt less, or if nothing else, give me some time to process it and decide my response before I talk to Bobby.

Molly shakes her head. "He wouldn't tell me. He said you deserve to hear it first, and you deserve to hear it from him. Jesus, that man's a saint. I forgot guys like him existed."

"He practically cheated on me, Molly. No matter what else happened, no matter what his excuse is, I know what I saw."

Molly sighs, giving me back her hand. "I know what you think you saw. But there has to be an explanation. I never knew Bobby to be a liar. He was always such a good guy. Remember what he did for Michael?"

The memory stings.

"He was honest, to a fault, even. And completely in love with you. He always put you first. *Always.*"

That's the part that's never added up. Molly's right. Bobby *did* always put me first. My feelings, my safety, my happiness. He wanted the world for me. And I wanted him. He was my world. And then he took it away, leaving me to create a new one for myself without him in it.

The bus is quiet when I wake far too early, the sun just beginning to peek out above the horizon.

My mind hasn't stopped spinning since talking to Molly last night. I can't seem to work out how I feel. Is it possible I have everything wrong?

It shouldn't be, and yet, the thought refuses to release its hold on me.

As quietly as I can so I don't wake Molly, I shuffle through my bag until I find my old manuscript—the story based on Bobby and me from *before.*

I'm not sure what I'll write for the ending.

I'm not even sure I *will* write an ending, but maybe reading through it again will give me some clarity. Not just about where Bobby and I could have gone wrong, but about the girl I used to be—full of life and hope and words that mattered.

I creep past the bunks where Bobby's still asleep, but they're empty, and I wonder where he is.

No women on the bus. That was my rule. But there was no rule about him not sleeping elsewhere.

A pinch of something ugly settles beneath my ribs, but I work to push the feeling away. Bobby can do whatever he wants, because even though there's no use denying our history or the emotions that come along with it, pulling out this old manuscript isn't about him.

It's about finding myself again.

Flicking on the lamp, I settle into my spot on the couch and pick up a pen. It takes several moments to gather enough courage to flip past the first page—Untitled, by Beth Winters—and when I do, my heart skips a beat.

I fight through the tightness in my chest, and by the time I've read through the first chapter, I'm calmer. The writing is choppy, but there's a story in there full of heart. Full of life, and a flicker of brightness catches behind my sternum, burning away some of the restraints I've put on my creativity over the last several years.

Or did Harrison put them there?

I can't seem to parse out if he forced me into the box he wanted me to fit in, or if I folded myself in willingly. But as I continue to read, I know I can't go back inside it.

I adjusted for him. If he wants this to work—if that's even possible—he'll have to do some adjusting, too.

An hour passes as I make notes, and I'm so engrossed in revisions that I jump when the bus door opens.

I stiffen. An image of Bobby with sex-mussed hair flicks through my mind, making me nauseous, but that's not the Bobby that walks onto the bus.

He's sweaty and shirtless, with tennis shoes on and headphones still in his ears. He freezes when he sees me, his forehead creasing in concern.

"Early morning jog?" I ask with a smile, relieved to see he wasn't with another woman.

The frown lines in his forehead relax as he takes out his headphones, moving to the coffee maker to grab a bag of espresso.

"Wanted to get it in before it got too hot out. Everything okay?" he asks, keeping his voice casual, but the remaining tension in his shoulders tells me he's unsettled by my being awake. Worried something happened.

"Yeah, I'm fine. I just—" I hesitate, chewing on the side of my mouth. Saying it out loud feels like a monumental step. Like once the words escape my mouth, they'll fly away into the universe and I'll have no choice but to follow through. I twist my fingers together. "I'm working on my book again."

Bobby turns, crossing his arms and leaning against the counter, his eyes bright. "Yeah?"

I nod, my cheeks warming.

His lips twist in a smile, his dimple appearing, but he doesn't make a big deal out of it. I'm grateful when he turns back to the coffee maker, giving me space to process what my admission means.

My phone rings, and I flip it over, Harrison's picture flashing on the screen, and the joy of the moment dims.

"Good morning," I answer, closing the manuscript.

"Hey." He sounds surprised. "I wanted to call before work, but I didn't think I'd actually catch you. You're up early."

"I had an idea," I say, digging for my bravery again. I've already said it out loud once. I can do it again. "Um, for a book. I'm working on a book," I say, leaving out the part about the book being largely written already *and* about Bobby.

"A book?" Harrison laughs, but it's not a good-natured sound. "Elizabeth. What's with all this nonsense? You're writing one article. That's it."

"Yeah, well…" I turn away from where Bobby stands steaming some milk, his knuckles white. "I'm going to do more freelance work after this article. I like writing."

"But why?" Harrison sounds utterly perplexed. "You don't *need* to work. I make plenty of money. More than enough for both of us."

"That's not what it's about. I'm *good* at writing," I say, but a sliver of doubt slides down my throat.

"It's a fine hobby," he says, and the dismissiveness in his tone makes me bristle. "But don't be ridiculous—"

Tears burn my eyes, and I hang up before he can insult me any more. I knew Harrison wouldn't be excited about me wanting to pursue writing again, but I thought that maybe, with time, he'd come around.

But I'm beginning to realize the man who once wrote me love poems doesn't see the value of words if they're not being written to get him what he wants.

My phone rings again, but I ignore it, turning it on silent as Bobby hands me my coffee.

"Extra lavender?" he asks, shaking the container. His eyes are a mix of fury and sorrow, but he doesn't ask what Harrison said to make me cry.

I rub my forehead and sigh. "Please," I say, wishing Bobby hadn't been here to witness another crack spreading in the foundation of my relationship.

THEN

AUGUST 2018

Lord forgive me for my sins
I never meant to lie
Oh I may have lost my love
But God I never let that love die
—An excerpt from "Prayer of the Lost," written and performed by Robert
Beckett

Even though the door is firmly shut, I know the moment Bobby arrives at my dorm. Maybe it's the electricity in the air, or maybe it's the sound of footsteps combined with hushed whispers and giggling in the hallway. I swing open the door before Bobby can even knock and pull him inside, saving him from the paparazzi, aka my hall-mates.

We're used to it by now, how the phones automatically come out and people start whispering as soon as they see Bobby in public. It's rare we go *out* on dates anymore. Other than a few of our safe spots, Joe's included, being in public just means photos and autographs and girls falling over Bobby while I sit there awkwardly, his fans completely ignoring me.

"You're early!" I throw my arms around his neck. It's my first week of classes for the fall semester, and Bobby kept his promise of scheduling his performances around move in day this year.

"I just couldn't wait to see you." He squeezes me back, kissing my hair.

"You must have made poor Patrick drive all night," I say, lowering my chin as if scolding him.

He waves a hand in the air. "Patrick loves driving at night. He'd prefer to be the only one on the road," he says, handing me a bouquet of pink wild roses.

I take a deep inhale of the sweet floral scent. "Thank you. How was Maine?? I press a kiss to his cheek before turning back to the box I'm unpacking, pulling out some fresh notebooks. "Any proposals?" I ask. It's become our new joke, because when I anticipated 'Someone Who Loves You' becoming the song to use for weddings and proposals, I was spot on.

Bobby grabs a box off the floor and rips the tape off to help unpack it. "Actually, two different couples got engaged last night. They didn't necessarily seem thrilled to be sharing the spotlight."

"Then they should come up with a more original idea," I joke.

Bobby's jaw drops open in mock outrage. "What? But that's how I planned on proposing to you!" He grabs my arm and pulls me against him, leaning down to kiss me again. "It's *your* song, after all."

Bobby could propose to me in a McDonald's parking lot with a french fry ring, and I would be thrilled. This isn't the first time he's mentioned wanting to marry me, but that doesn't lessen the effect of his words. My heart starts to flutter and my stomach twists into knots. I know we're still way off from an actual proposal, but it's fun to think about forever with him.

When he pulls away, I'm breathless. "Back to the drawing board, I guess," he says as he returns to the box.

"I'll say yes, no matter how you ask me, Bobby Beckett," I say. "Hand me those pens, will you?"

He digs through the box until he finds the bag of pens I'm talking about, tossing them to me to put into my desk. "Hey, what's this?" he asks, pulling out a thick navy-blue packet. Flipping it over, Bobby trails his finger across the return address. "London, England?"

I snatch the packet from his hands. "Nosy much?" I ask, shoving the papers underneath a textbook. "It's nothing."

Bobby turns and faces me, crossing his arms. "The London Institute of Literature and Creative Writing? That doesn't exactly sound like nothing."

Shit.

There's a reason I didn't tell Bobby about the study abroad opportunity, and it mostly has to do with the fact that I didn't think there was a chance in hell I'd get it. But part of it is also that now that I've been accepted, I don't want to go.

"What's with the secrecy? We don't keep things from each other." Bobby's forehead creases.

I sit down on the bed. "It's really not a big deal. My Lit 101 professor had me apply. It was a long shot that I'd get accepted and didn't seem all that important."

"Are you kidding me?" Bobby comes to sit next to me, abandoning the box he was unpacking.

I sigh, grabbing the acceptance letter from under the textbook and handing it to him. I am proud I was accepted into the program, even if I don't plan on taking the spot.

Bobby's eyes scan the page, bright and excited. "This is amazing, Beth. And you get class credit for this? I'm so proud of you. When does it start?"

I press my lips together. "After Christmas break. But I'm not taking it," I say in one breath.

"Are you kidding me? Look at this—England, Italy, Austria. You'll get to travel all over Europe." He points to a line in the packet. "This sounds like your absolute dream."

"It's an entire year," I say, as if that's the only explanation I need.

Bobby turns us so that I'm now leaning against the headboard. "What's this really about, Beth? This is an incredible opportunity."

"I know it is, but a year? We said we'd do Europe together once your tour takes you there. I can still see all those places. Just... later. Plus, I don't want to leave Molly right now, or school. I'm finally finding my place here."

Bobby chews on the side of his lip, taking his hat off and flipping it backward. "I want you to be honest with me. Please," he says, bending down to look directly in my eyes, and I know what's coming.

My stomach falls. I can't lie to him. I never have, and I don't plan on starting today.

"Does this have to do with me? About being so far away?"

I sigh, rubbing the space between my eyebrows. "Maybe a little, but it's not the entire reason. Look, you're starting your own tour in February. Headlining. Bobby, I'm *not* going to miss that. There will be time for me to travel to Europe. Maybe I can even apply again next year," I say, even though I know I won't get it again. This is a prestigious program with very limited spots. If I turn it down now, I'll lose my chance. But I can live with that, because watching the love of my life headline his first tour is also a once in a lifetime opportunity.

And I wasn't lying about my other reasons. I've found a solid group of friends here and gotten into a good routine with classes. Molly's been having a tough time figuring out the career thing, not to mention the stress over Michael, and I can't imagine being an ocean away from her right now.

Bobby's silent, his lips pressed together.

"Talk to me, please. It's not like I'm dropping out of school. I still can write and learn about books and poems just as well here as I can in England."

He sighs. "I just can't help but feel like you're giving up this amazing opportunity for me while I travel the country to follow my dreams and leave you behind. Don't you see how fucked up that is? You're too talented to sit around in your dorm waiting for weekends to watch me perform my songs for the world. *Your* words are important too, Beth."

I grab Bobby's hands, hoping touching him will remind him of what's important. "I know my words are important. I will continue to write them. But I love you. *You* are my future. Europe will always be there. Poems will *always* be there."

"Beth, I think—" He's interrupted by my phone ringing.

I flip it over on the bed. "It's Molly. Give me a second," I say, answering before I can miss her. We've played phone tag the past week or so, and I want to hear her voice.

"Hello?"

"Beth?" Molly's crying, her breaths shuddering so violently I can barely understand her. I jump to my feet, the air rushing from my lungs.

"What's wrong? Molly, slow down." I can hear the panic in my voice, but there's nothing I can do to stop it. Because I know what she's going to say. I can feel it with a certainty that makes my head swim and the room spin. My knees buckle, but Bobby's instantly at my side, holding me up.

"It's Michael," Molly finally says through her sobs. "He's gone, Beth. My brother is gone."

I don't remember much of the next few hours other than Bobby taking the phone from me as the tears stream from my eyes. I'm rambling. "I'm sorry, Molly. I'm so, so sorry." It's all I can say, over and over and over again.

Somewhere in my haze of grief, I register Bobby talking to Molly. "What do you need?"

And then we're driving, and the tears still won't stop, and I fear they're going to drown me.

Not Michael.

This can't be happening.

But it *is* happening.

Another wave crashes over me, and I struggle to stay at the surface. I can't breathe, but somehow, I do.

Bobby leads me to Molly's door and then she's in my arms and I'm in hers and we're collapsing to our knees, and it's not fucking fair.

"What happened? I don't understand," I finally say after we've cried together for what feels like hours. Bobby's on the phone, and I hear something about canceling shows, but my focus is on Molly.

"He got a fever on Thursday, and we took him to the hospital. He's had fevers before, but it was an infection, and his little body just couldn't fight it. Why *Michael*?" she sobs.

"I know," I say. "I'm so sorry. I'm so, so sorry." I'm a broken record, and I don't think I'll ever say anything else ever again. "I'm so sorry."

Bobby finally helps us off the floor and moves us to the couch, but Molly never lets go of me. We cry until we fall asleep, and I dream of a world with Michael still in it. Of dancing in the kitchen to "Gray," and Nerf gun wars and big, gap-toothed smiles.

But when I wake up, my eyes are still swollen, and Molly's breaths still shudder.

"Bobby?" I whisper, looking around in a panic. Molly might need me, and I will be here for her as long as she does, but I need him.

He's kneeling in front of me in an instant, his calloused fingers cupping my face. "I'm here, Beth. I'm not going anywhere." His eyes and nose are red, and I realize he's been crying, too. I fall apart all over again, my face pressed into his shirt to muffle my sobs so I don't wake Molly.

Because she's going to wake up soon enough. And just like I did, she's going to be confronted with the horrific, unfair reality that her brother is gone, and he won't be coming back.

Every day for the rest of her life, she will wake up and have to remember what she lost.

And I know it's selfish, but all I can think about is that I never want to feel the pain of a broken heart ever again.

NOW

September 2024: Nashville, TN

I let you let me in
Then I let you walk away
Now I don't know who I am
I think I lost myself that day
—*An excerpt from "Prayer of the Lost," written and performed by Robert*
Beckett

"What about this one by Yeats?" Bobby asks, a stack of poetry books in front of him. He's gotten the idea that a song inspired by a famous poem would be a hit, similar to the one I wrote for my class assignment so long ago, and he's been obsessed with the idea for days. So much so that he forced us to stop at Parnassus Books this morning to browse for inspiration on our way out of Nashville.

"How many loved your moments of glad grace, and loved your beauty with love false or true? But one man loved the pilgrim soul in you, and loved the sorrows of your changing face."

A lump forms in my throat. "I don't think that one's right," I say, even though it's a favorite of mine.

Because you had a pilgrim soul once, too, my subconscious says. *Before Harrison.* The thought makes my stomach twist into knots, but I swallow past it.

As if I summoned him, my phone rings, his face popping up on the screen, but I send it to voicemail.

"It's too heavy for radio," I continue.

"Hmmm." Robert flips through several pages. "What about Sylvia Plath?"

"Absolutely not. Too sad." I crinkle my nose. "What's the vibe you're going for?" I ask, trying to pretend I'm less interested than I am. I don't want Bobby to know how excited thinking about this song has me. How it's inspired parts of my manuscript.

I've stayed up late the past two nights reading through books of poetry, the words not only soothing my soul and softening the jagged pieces of my wounded self-esteem, but sparking my creativity.

Bobby stretches, and it takes every bit of my self-control to not examine the way his muscles ripple with the movement so I can immortalize the sheer masculine beauty of it in a poem.

He leans forward, tenting his fingers. "I'm going for a feeling." His voice is soft, almost wistful, as he looks out the window. He's still for a moment, and I can tell his mind has wandered somewhere far away. He shakes his head. "I don't know how to describe it... It's this all-consuming, wholly encompassing love. Not lust or infatuation or passion. I'm talking about loving someone to their very core."

His words rip out one of the stitches in my heart, and a wave of sorrow gushes out, so strong, it feels like I might bleed out.

Isn't that what *every* love story should be like?

It's certainly not with Harrison.

Maybe that kind of love only lives in poetry and fairytales. In fiction. Maybe it doesn't exist in real life.

Bobby meets my gaze, his eyes filling with a heavy sorrow just as intense as the grief weeping from my own heart.

When he speaks again, his voice is gritty. "I'm looking for poems that feel the same as the way we felt about each other. Before, you know? *That* kind of love."

I press my lips together, forcing down the anguish trying to drown me. I know *exactly* what he means.

"I've never read a poem like that," I say, almost a whisper.

"I have," he says, taking out his wallet and putting it on the table between us. "Your song."

My heart clenches, and I look away. I don't want to think about my song.

I don't want the glaring reminder that a love like Bobby's describing *does* exist.

Or…it did.

"It's still in there, you know. The song," he says, nodding at the wallet. "It's traveled the world with me. I haven't performed a single show without it. I'm not sure I even could at this point."

Another stitch rips away, and the stab of pain in my chest makes it hard to breathe. "Maybe you should just put that to music," I say, standing up. My body begs me to flee—to get out of this conversation before I'm pulled too deeply back into my memories, but Bobby stops me.

"Wait. Would you really consider… Would you let me do that? Put your words to music?" he asks, but I don't have an answer.

Not for the question he's asking, or the ones I'm asking myself. So I just give him a sad smile and walk away.

NOW

September 2024: Birmingham, Alabama

I'm standing to the side of the meet and greet while Bobby signs hats and t-shirts and takes pictures with smiling fans. It's going to be a great addition to my story, a human element, because every type of person is here. Old, young, preppy, hipster, black, white, brown, tattooed and ink-free. The people making up the line wrapping nearly to the entrance of the building are as different as grains of sand, and I take advantage of their time waiting to snag some interviews.

There's an older man, probably seventy, who brought his teenage granddaughter. He tells a sweet story about them bonding over Bobby's music, and that tonight will be their third show together. They try to make it an annual tradition to find a show within driving distance and make a whole day out of it.

I find a couple in their mid-twenties, just a little younger than I am. When the girlfriend sneaks away to the restroom, the guy pulls out a ring and tells me how he plans to propose during "Someone Who Loves

You" tonight, and asks if I can pass it along to Bobby to help make the moment extra special.

My chest aches at his request, my heart throbbing, but I smile and tell him I'd be happy to.

The line has maybe fifteen people left when Bobby waves me over.

"Beth. I want you to meet Mrs. Mendez. She was my high school music teacher, and a big reason why I get to be up on stage every night." Bobby says, pulling me close to him as a tiny woman with curly, graying hair and glasses shakes my hand.

"Beth," she says, her eyebrows raising. "Am I right to assume—"

"That's the one." Bobby doesn't let her finish her question, clearing his throat as if uncomfortable. "I thought she might make a good interview for the article?" Bobby turns his attention to me, his blue eyes questioning. "That is, if you have time, Mrs. Mendez."

"Anything for you, Bobby. And it's Patsy. Stop calling me Mrs. Mendez." She turns to me. "I'm afraid I'm late for my grandson's basketball game. Could we do a phone interview?"

"Absolutely," I say. "Why don't we step to the side, and I'll get you my contact information. Then you can call me when it's convenient for you."

"Thank you," I mouth to Bobby, but he doesn't notice, his eyes brightening as he looks at the next person in line.

"Aaron, buddy! I didn't know you were coming today!" Bobby says, picking up a little boy who appears to be around the age of six.

Bobby takes the boy's hat off and flips it around so it's backward, matching the way Bobby prefers to wear his. My heart squeezes as a wave of déjà vu passes over me.

There's no hair on Aaron's head, nor where his eyebrows or eyelashes should be. He reminds me of Michael so much that I feel like there's a shard of glass in my chest, ripping into my lungs with every breath. It's physically painful, but I can't pull my eyes away.

Bobby spins in a circle, then turns to Aaron's mom. "You guys should've told someone you were here. I wouldn't have made you wait in line."

"Oh, don't be ridiculous. We've had fun waiting, haven't we, Aaron?"

"We played what's that song!" Aaron says.

Bobby taps his chin with a finger. "How do you play?" he asks.

"You start humming and see how long it takes the other person to figure out what song it is," Aaron tells him, his face flushed with excitement.

"I hope you threw a few of my songs in there." Bobby pinches Aaron's side, tickling him.

"Only almost all of them," his mom says.

"Are you guys coming to the show tonight?" Bobby asks.

"Not this time," Aaron's mom says. "Too many people. And I'm worried about having his oxygen tank in the crowd. They're so expensive, and I don't want it to get damaged."

Bobby's brow furrows, and he sets Aaron down. "Hey Beth, Aaron here is a brave little man who happens to also be my biggest fan. Would you like to interview him?" Bobby asks. He jerks his head to the side, giving me a not-so-subtle hint that he'd like me to distract Aaron for a few minutes.

"Of course," I say, forcing my eyes to stay dry. "This is exactly what I need for my story. What do you think, Aaron? Want to have a quote in Rolling Stone magazine?"

"Sure." Aaron shrugs, and I realize he probably has no idea what that is. My smile breaks into a laugh, and Aaron looks at me like I have two heads.

"I have cancer," he says. "That's why Bobby thinks I'm brave."

"You look *extremely* brave," I say. "And very strong."

"Oh, I am strong," Aaron says. "I can lift up my little sister all the way off the ground."

"That's amazing," I gush.

"I know." Aaron shrugs, but his lips twist into a small smile.

"So how do you know Bobby?" I ask, adding, "And just so you know, he only lets the people he likes most call him that."

Aaron beams. "Bobby comes to my hospital sometimes. He came to my room and brought me a hat. And a lot of my friends there have met him, too. Cancer sucks, but meeting Bobby was really cool."

"I bet," I say, remembering just how great he was with Michael and his friends.

Aaron studies my face as if trying to place me. "I've never seen you with him before. You're pretty. Are you his girlfriend?" he asks.

As if the universe wants to embarrass me, I feel Bobby approach from behind, that familiar energy zipping up my spine.

"If only, little man." He crouches down. "But she used to be, once upon a time."

"What happened?" Aaron asks, either completely forgetting that I'm standing there or just not caring. I brace myself for Bobby's answer, placing a shield of armor around my heart.

"Well, don't tell anyone this," Bobby dips his head and leans close as if sharing a secret, "but she left me for Spider-Man."

Aaron's eyes basically bug out of his head, and Bobby winks at me.

"Okay. I guess that makes sense," he says seriously, nodding.

"Anyway. I'll be seeing you tonight, big guy. We'll have a special place backstage, just for you."

Aaron jumps up and down. "No way! Really mom?"

"Really!" she says, bending down and giving her son a big hug.

"Yep," Bobby says. "And I'll have a new hat for you." He points to his backward ball cap, the one branded for the current tour.

"Thanks, but I don't need a new hat. This one's lucky." He wiggles his head around.

Aaron's mom leans in. "He wore it to his last scan when we found out the cancer shrank, and hasn't taken it off since."

"A t-shirt, then." Bobby nods, his expression turning serious. "We don't mess with luck around here." He pats the pocket where his wallet sits.

Aaron yawns, his little eyes growing heavy.

"Why don't you get some rest? Big night ahead of us, huh?" Bobby says, patting Aaron's shoulder.

"Can we do the interview then?" Aaron asks. "I want to hear more about Spider-Man."

"You got it, buddy," I say, my eyes burning with unshed tears as Aaron walks away with his mom.

Writing this article has just taken on a whole new meaning.

And not just the article, but writing itself.

It's not just a job. Not just a career or a hobby.

It's essential to who I am in my soul. Who I want to be as a human being. It's not just something I love, but a skill I can use to actually make a difference in people's lives.

I can raise awareness for causes I care about, not just donate money at galas. I can explore issues that ignite a fire in my belly, not just discuss them in passing over drinks at the club. I can write poems that capture heartbreak and grief, or love and joy. Stories that make people feel less alone.

And as my angle on the article becomes sharper—Bobby's altruistic side—I realize I don't want to pretend anymore.

I don't want to pretend I don't have the heart of a poet.

I just need to be brave, like Aaron.

"Hey Bobby," I say, stopping him as he heads back to the line of people waiting for him. "You have my permission."

He tilts his head, his eyebrows pulling in. "Permission to what?"

My cheeks heat, but I'm being brave, so I don't look away. "You wanted to put music to my song. So you have my permission. You can have 'Poetry.'"

NOW

September 2024: Atlanta, GA

My love for you is delicate
Like the wings of a butterfly
So I'll hold you gently in my hands
When you can't take to the skies
I'll protect you when you need a rest
Let you stay here by my side
And I'll love you till my dying breath
You. My little butterfly
—A poem certainly not written by Harrison Rouchester, given to Beth Winters
approximately six weeks into dating

The windows of Big Blue are open, and warm morning air floats inside along with the twitter of birds.

Bobby left at nine to make it to a recording session, but I was awake well before then. Tossing and turning as lines of poetry floated through my head.

"Sonnet 18"

"The Good Morrow"

"How Do I love thee?"

Poems all infinitely more passionate than the life I'm currently living. Or…the one I was living.

Because *this* life—with the road soaring by while I write the words that have been scratching the inside of my skull for years—this feels infinitely more passionate. And it has nothing to do with loving another person.

It only has to do with loving myself.

I squeeze my pen between my fingers, turning to a fresh page in my notebook and taking a deep breath. My stomach churns, and tears prick my eyes, threatening to spill over my eyelashes as I drag the pen across the paper with a shaking hand.

I deserve more, I write.

I haven't said the words out loud. I'm not sure I've even fully thought them. Or if I have, I haven't *believed* them.

But writing them feels manageable. Familiar in a way that makes my breath rush from my lungs in one swift whoosh of relief.

I deserve more, I write again, bigger this time.

More than what's waiting for me at home.

More than squeezing myself into the neat, tidy boxes of what Harrison wants for his life and his wife.

I'd rather be alone than with someone who doesn't respect me.

Someone who doesn't believe in me.

I pause, my tears finally spilling over my lashes.

I can't marry Harrison.

There it is.

Black ink tattooed on the page.

Permanent.

Vulnerable and messy, but honest. I wish I could fold up the paper and have that be the end of it. I've made my decision. Confessed my deepest, most terrifying thoughts.

But that's not enough, because I still have to say those words out loud.

And I have to say them to Harrison.

Shame burns in my gut. I should've never let it get this far to begin with. Should've remembered my worth. But I think Harrison broke me down in such small increments that I didn't even notice he was doing it until I was forced out of the situation. Until it was thrown in my face that he wants a perfect wife that reminds him of his mother. He doesn't want *me*, and he's been slowly stealing away pieces of who I am for years.

It's a form of abuse, isn't it? Isolating your partner from the things and people they love until you're all that's left in their life. I'm embarrassed to admit that I didn't even notice it was happening. I'm not sure it was even intentional on his part.

If I'm being completely honest with myself, I'm pretty certain it wasn't. I don't think Harrison planned some elaborate scheme to tear me down, but I think he has such a high sense of self-importance that he doesn't see much further than his own wants and needs. And I was broken enough when I met him to not realize it, grateful for whatever kernel of affection and attention I could get.

I think back on the poems he gave to me at the beginning of our relationship. I don't think he actually wrote most of them, but the ones that were clearly by his hand all have an undercurrent of conceit and possession, dressed up as love and devotion.

I turn my phone over and over in my hands, trying to find words that can make this easier. I don't know what to say to make him understand, but I do know this can't wait until I get home. Right now, I have the conviction and courage to end things, but will I in another couple of weeks?

And even more importantly, would I feel safe enough to break up with him in person?

With a deep breath, I unlock my phone and make the call.

"Harrison," he answers.

"Hey. It's me," I say, my voice shaking.

I hear typing on the other end of the line before he responds. "I called you last night," he says, his voice angry.

Maybe he deserves that anger. I've been distant since I left. But then again, he pushed me in that direction.

"I know. I wasn't ready to talk yet."

"Ready to talk? Seriously? Is this still about when I came to visit—"

"No. I mean, I don't know. It's about all of it." My voice cracks, and I take a deep breath, squeezing my hand into a fist to ground myself. "We want different things, Harrison."

"What are you talking about?" There's no sound of keys in the background anymore. Just a low hum that makes me nauseous.

I take several deep breaths, closing my eyes. "I love you. But I can't marry you."

The silence is louder than the pulse pounding in my ears.

"It's because of him, isn't it?" Harrison's voice is as sharp as a blade, and cuts just as deep. The memory of glass shattering makes my arm sting, and a shiver skates down my spine as I think about what might have happened if I'd done this in person.

I shake my head even though Harrison can't see me, because this *isn't* about Bobby. "No. It's about us. I want to write. To create. We want different things," I repeat, like those are the magic words that will make him understand.

"We didn't until you left to go on this fucking tour!" He's yelling now, but I barely hear him.

"It has nothing to do with the tour, and everything to do with what I need to be happy." I pause. "I'm so sorry," I whisper.

"You're not ending things. This isn't you, Elizabeth." He bites out my name, and my guilt and sadness shift into anger.

"You don't get to tell me who I am anymore!" I shout, standing.

"I'm going to be your husband! I know exactly who you are!"

"You don't, and that's the problem! This would *never* work." My voice breaks, and the sob I've been working to hold back explodes from my chest. "It's over, Harrison."

Harrison's voice drops to a deep rumble. "I'll ruin you before I let you leave me," he says.

"I'll get your ring back to you." I hang up, sobs shaking my body as I drop back onto the couch, covering my face with my hands.

My body feels numb, and so tired, it's as if I've finally dropped the weight I've carried on my shoulders unknowingly for years. I don't know how long I cry before Bobby walks through the bus doors.

"Beth?" He freezes, dropping his guitar case on the floor with a *thud* and immediately pulling me into his arms. "Hey…shhh," he soothes, rocking me gently as he strokes my hair.

He doesn't ask questions. Not until my tears have run dry and my breath has stopped shuddering. "Tell me you're okay," Bobby finally says, tucking my head beneath his chin.

I close my eyes. "I ended things with Harrison," I say, and Bobby stiffens.

He pulls me tighter. "I'm so sorry," he says, and that's all.

No celebration or joy.

No expectations.

He's just here with me, and I'm so grateful, another sob works its way up my throat.

I sniffle, sitting up so I can look him in the eye. "I know I was here for Harrison, but I'd like to stay and finish the article."

"You can stay as long as you want," he says, and I close my eyes as his rumbling voice soothes the wounds in my heart. "Article or not."

THEN

August 2018

Used to have a map
But I burned it in a fire
Trying to thaw this cold I feel
Oh God, I'm tired
—An excerpt from "Prayer of the Lost" by Robert Beckett

The leaves outside have begun to turn brilliant oranges and yellows and reds almost overnight. It's breathtaking, and it pisses me off. The dying leaves are nothing more than hundreds of thousands of reminders that everything ends, and I *hate* it.

I draw every single shade in Big Blue. I can't bear to look.

Not today.

We have less than twenty minutes until we need to leave for Michael's funeral, and I can't find my bracelet anywhere.

I search the kitchen, coming up empty-handed, but I know I took it off here yesterday, so I move to the back and rummage through the bathroom cabinets.

Leaning over the bed, I open Bobby's nightstand, freezing as I push aside his notebook. I suck in a sharp breath, my heart thundering. In the back left corner, tucked away so far back I almost miss it, is a red, velvet ring box.

I shouldn't open it. Ignoring it completely would be the right thing to do. But it doesn't change the fact that my hand keeps moving closer, and I'm powerless to stop it. The velvet is soft against my fingers, and the box is sturdy. I hesitate for a moment, but before I can talk myself out of it, I lift open the top.

My body kicks into overdrive, and my hand comes up to cover the gasp that escapes my lips. Inside the box is a ring.

Not a promise ring, an *engagement* ring. It's simple—a cushion cut stone set into a thin gold band that gets thinner as it gets closer to the diamond. It's understated and elegant, and my fingers shake as I pull it out of the box. As much as I want to, I don't put it on my hand.

It already feels wrong enough that I'm looking at the ring, but sliding it on my finger feels like crossing a line.

Slowly, I turn it over, watching the way it sparkles in the light, but something else catches my eye. Etched into the inside of the band is an infinity symbol, an exact replica of the ones that make up my bracelet.

The hiss of the bus doors opening makes me jump, and my stomach drops. As quickly as possible, I put the ring back in the box and shove it into the corner of the drawer, dropping the notebook on top and rushing into the bathroom. The bedroom opens mere seconds later, Bobby appearing in a black suit.

"Hey, you okay?" Bobby asks. He glances at his nightstand for a brief second, then comes to stand next to me.

"As okay as I can be," I say, leaning into him. "Do you know where my bracelet is?" I ask, and he nods, pulling it out of his pocket.

"I found it by the sink. Thought you'd want to wear it to the service," he says, fastening it around my wrist. His fingers are warm on my skin, and I anchor myself to his steadiness.

I've always known beyond a doubt Bobby loves me. But seeing the ring makes our love feel like a tangible thing. A soft blanket to soothe me and a crutch to lean on, and I wonder if maybe I was meant to see the ring today. If maybe it was fate's way of making sure I know that even on my worst day, I'm not alone.

Not when I have Bobby.

We don't speak on the way to the service. Nor when we walk into the church with Johnny, the cloyingly sweet scent of the funeral arrangements making me feel like I might choke.

Bobby stays by my side as we find our seats in the front row, right by Molly and her family.

He squeezes my hand when the tears fall, his thumb writing words along my skin.

He doesn't leave my side until the tiny coffin is covered in roses, when, with a squeeze of my hand, he walks to the front along with Johnny to where their guitars wait.

Wordlessly, they begin to pick out a melody, slowing the rhythm of Michael's favorite song. Johnny keeps his eyes on Molly's face, but Bobby squeezes his shut, unable to watch as the pallbearers begin their solemn walk up the church aisle.

Anchor me down in the cold dark dirt. Where my roots are tethered deep.

His voice is raw as they carry Michael to where he will rest. I try to focus on Molly, to comfort her. I put my arm around her shoulders, hold her hand as she weeps, but I know it's useless.

There is no sort of comfort that can ease the agony of losing someone you love. The loss of Michael will leave an open wound in all of us. One so deep, I'm certain there will never be a day we don't feel its pain.

NOW

September 2024: Tampa, FL

A melody mine
Notes repeating and circling
Parts of my own bone
Can you tell that you're mine?
Because I feel that I'm yours
Like I've always known
—An excerpt from "Almost There," written and performed by Robert Beckett

When Bobby said I needed a distraction a few days later, I didn't expect him to lead us to a local high school. We're hiding just around the corner from the front doors. Bobby has his hat pulled low over his eyes and his sunglasses blocking his face, and every few minutes he checks his watch, waiting until just before 2:00 to head inside.

Bobby takes my hand, and electricity runs from my fingertips up to my elbow. It's such a casual gesture, but it feels as intimate as sharing secrets under the covers in the dark.

I *should* pull away.

My heart is too tired. Too sore from severing Harrison from the muscle, but Bobby's touch is comforting and I just can't bear to let go.

Bobby leads me confidently down the hallway, pulling two tickets from his pocket and handing them to a student waiting at a fold-out table in front of the door before slipping into the back of the theater. It's almost completely full, but there are two seats in the second to last row.

When we reach our seats and Bobby drops my hand, I feel the loss all the way to my toes. My fingers go cold, and a pang of nostalgia washes over me. Even the lights seem to dim, and I wonder how much brighter my life would have looked if he'd stayed in it.

Wait—it's the theater lights that are dimming. I mentally kick myself for being so foolish. What good is it thinking about what could've been when it's not what happened? When there's a reason it didn't—one that I still haven't allowed Bobby to explain. What good would it do?

The audience applauds politely as a squat, older woman with neon blue glasses and slightly frizzy, white hair takes the stage. She thanks us for coming, then extends an arm as she walks stage left. The curtains open, and my breath catches.

The moment I realize what we're doing, I'm overcome by an intense need to cry. I'm not even sure why. Sure, the play is a tragedy, but I've read it before. It's one of my favorites. Maybe that's why I'm emotional. Because Bobby knows how much I love this play. Or maybe it's because he was thoughtful enough to find something that I would enjoy doing before the show tonight.

Or maybe it's because he's here sitting next to me when Harrison never would, saying plays weren't his *thing*.

I'm just as certain that Shakespearean tragedies aren't Bobby's thing either, and yet, he's *here*.

I force the burning thought down like a shot of whiskey as a waif-like blonde girl who can't be more than sixteen takes the stage. Juliet. She's adorable. Way too young to know what true love is, but then again, how many of us really know true love when we see it?

She trips on the train of her dress as she changes directions on stage, her cheeks reddening, but no one laughs. It's not the only small mess–up that happens, but still, it's magical. I laugh. I hold my breath. And I even cry as the star-crossed lovers take their final breaths.

The entire crowd stands as the cast takes their bows, and I can't help but whistle through my fingers as Juliet takes hers.

"What do you say we make their afternoon a little more special?" Bobby asks, leaning down to speak into my ear so I can hear him over the applause. His breath tickles the little hairs on the back of my neck, making me shiver.

"Let's do it," I say, and as soon as the actors leave the stage, Bobby beelines to the Director, pulling off his cap and asking if he can meet the cast. I don't think the director could be happier if Shakespeare himself was here, and she loops her arm through Bobby's and basically yanks him behind the curtains.

I scramble after them, but Bobby reaches out and grabs my hand, pulling me along so we don't lose each other. I can't help but laugh at the absurdity of what's happening. Of being at a high school production of Shakespeare in a small town in Florida, going backstage to make some teenage girls extremely happy.

Bobby takes at least thirty pictures with different configurations of the cast, signing playbills and notebooks and even a few arms. He's charming and personable throughout it all, but so himself. None of it seems forced or like he's acting. There's no ulterior motive. He simply enjoys making these kids happy.

"I can't believe he's here," I hear as a group of girls giggling with their arms linked together shuffle past me.

"He's gorgeous," one of them says. "And so kind. Even his eyes are kind. Did you see them?"

"Maybe he'll come to our next show."

"Maybe he'll make a big donation so we can afford to have real sets for the spring musical. Do you think Miss Castin will ask him?" Their conversation trails out as they round the corner, and I make a mental note to mention the art department's need for donations, certain he'll want to help.

I turn from where the girls disappeared back to Bobby, who is still talking to a group of students, ones who don't appear to have been in the play. He smiles at me, his dimple making my stomach flip.

Bobby excuses himself, mentioning that he has to get back to get ready for his show, and I don't miss how, on the way back toward me, he slides what appears to be an envelope full of concert tickets into Miss Castin's grasp.

He holds out his hand and I take it, unable to help myself as he leads me back to the car.

"Well?" he asks as he waits for me to buckle my seatbelt. "You always talked about wanting to see that play instead of just reading it. Is it as good when it's performed by teenagers who've probably never been in love?"

"Are you kidding? They're probably right in the middle of their first loves. There's nothing more raw and passionate than that," I say without thinking, my heart beating a little too fast. Bobby pauses, his grip tightening on the steering wheel, and I clear my throat, desperate to move on. "What did you think?" I ask. "Are you a Shakespeare fan now?" I bite the inside of my cheek, ready for him to joke about how boring Shakespeare is, but he surprises me.

"I'm a fan of anything when I'm with you, Beth," he says with a long, loaded look. My face flushes and he looks away, starting the car and pulling out of the parking lot.

I almost say me too.

Almost.

Except at that exact moment, my phone dings. I flip it over to see a text from Harrison along with a blurry tabloid photo of Bobby and me walking hand in hand into the high school.

I see what this is about now.

And then, only a second later.

You're going to regret this.

THEN

OCTOBER 2018

My stomach squeezes as Bobby commands the stage, memories from this afternoon making my skin tingle and my legs feel like jello.

An image of the engagement ring flashed into my mind as he'd slid inside me, my back arching off the bed as he filled me completely. If that was what he had in store for our lives, I was more than ready to say yes.

"Now, before I leave the stage for the night, I have a little something new I'd like to play for you all," Bobby says into the mic. His set is almost over, but he has a surprise for the audience. It's exciting, being one of the few people here who knows what's about to happen. A few weeks ago, Bobby recorded a song with country music's newest star, Kelsey Darling. It was an odd pairing, I'd thought, until I heard the song.

The single hasn't been released yet, but I'm confident it will be all over the radio the second it's dropped. Cheers explode from the crowd and Bobby holds his hands out in front of him.

"Well, all right!" He pretends to be surprised. "I'll take that as a yes! Let's do it, then. I'd like to introduce to you my dear friend, Kelsey Darling." He gestures to the side of the stage, and Kelsey floats out. She's a knockout, with curves that are perfect for those blue jeans country music stars are always singing about, and long, honey-blonde hair that falls to her waist.

She's wearing boots with cut-off shorts and a crop top, one of Bobby's merch shirts with the bottom roughly cut off, and it slides up to show the bottom of her lacy black bra as she reaches Bobby and gives him a big hug.

"Some damn show this man puts on, am I right?" she asks, waving to the crowd, and Bobby's fans scream.

Bobby laughs, but he rubs the back of his neck the way he does when he's uncomfortable, and I clock it as odd. He's *never* uncomfortable on stage.

"We have a new single coming out soon," he says, taking a step back from Kelsey. "It's called, *When Winter Comes.*

"We hope you love it as much as we do," Kelsey adds, looking at Bobby with big, doe eyes, and the way she's staring at him makes me want to rub the back of my neck, too.

I'm not one for jealousy in general, and I've gotten rather accustomed to girls looking at Bobby this way over the past few years. But something about Kelsey's adoring gaze makes my stomach go sour. This is clearly a girl that's used to getting what she wants, and if my gut feeling is right, what she wants is Bobby.

The slow, sad notes of their song begin, and Bobby and Kelsey walk to opposite sides of the stage. He starts them off, singing about being lonely and needing someone when the cold starts to seep in. The first chorus hits, and her voice joins with his. It's undeniably beautiful, and the way their voices meld together is so good it's almost hypnotizing.

Their voices get stronger and louder as the song builds, and they get closer and closer to one another until they're standing only a foot apart and singing directly to each other. I know it's a performance, but it feels so intimate I almost feel the need to turn away.

Don't be ridiculous, I remind myself. *He has a ring. He loves you.* Even watching them sing right now, Kelsey certainly seems more into it than he does. While he closes his eyes for most of it, occasionally looking out over the crowd, Kelsey stares right at him as if she's trying to peer into his soul.

The song ends, and Kelsey leans in to give Bobby a hug. He wraps one arm around her from the side, thanking the audience and waving at them as they exit the stage. Bobby finds my eyes as they walk off, letting Kelsey go the second they're out of sight of the audience, and I don't miss the way her eyes flash with annoyance.

"She's great, right?" he asks me, raising his eyebrows as he takes a swig of his water.

"You both sounded amazing," I say.

Bobby smiles at me as he wipes his face with the hem of his shirt, flashing his abs, and I get the sudden urge to lick them. To pull the shirt off completely and drag him into the ocean and let the salt on his skin mix with the salt in the ocean.

"I think so, too. And guess what? She just signed a contract to come on as my opener for the tour starting in February."

"Oh, really?" I do my best to keep the tone of my voice light and excited, but suddenly, I am *very* glad I haven't accepted that internship overseas. If Kelsey is going to be there with him every night with her giant boobs and doe eyes, so will I. Well, minus the giant boobs part.

"I think the crowd will eat that song up on the road," he continues, so excited about the new song that my jealousy dims.

"I think so, too," I say, wrapping an arm around his waist as we walk side-by-side to his dressing area. "I can't wait to watch you sing it every weekend."

Bobby's silent for a second, looking back at the crowd waiting for the next act to take the stage. His forehead creases as he looks down at me, and I wonder what he's thinking about, but before I can ask, he pulls me closer, kissing the crown of my head.

"What do you say we get out of here?" he finally says.

I smile broadly. I have nothing to worry about. We've always been on the same page.

"It's like you read my mind."

NOW

September 2024: Blacksburg, VA

I won't tie you down to metal wings
Leave you tethered to the phone
While I bare my soul for all to see
And your words stay yours alone
—An excerpt from "Little Bird," written and performed by Robert Beckett

It's only been a week, but the creativity that's unleashed itself since I made my decision is thrilling. When I feel sad, I harness it, pouring it into my words.

When I feel anxious, which, if I'm being honest, is most of the time since Harrison sent that threatening text and then blocked me, I funnel every nerve into productivity.

Even the most amateur poet would think it's cliché to say the world feels brighter now, but it's the truth. It's as if I've been seeing in muted tones, not letting myself experience the full joy and beauty of what life has to offer.

But now I'm seeing everything as a writer again, paying attention to the tiniest details and filing them away to make my prose stronger, and it's working. I'm proud of this manuscript and the progress I've made on it. It feels shiny and new again, the plot stronger, and the love story soaring off the page.

It's taken time to transfer the book from the old stack of papers into a document on my laptop, and only after I changed all my passwords, but I'm glad I did it this way. It's forced me to relive the good memories I have with Bobby. A love story that, until it ended, really was beautiful.

I flip to the last chapter—the one where the rockstar performs his newest single with an upcoming female artist for a roaring crowd—and begin typing it up. I've been avoiding it for days, editing around it, afraid to dive into what was the beginning of the end for Bobby and me.

I try to keep emotion out of it as I slash clunky sentences and change little details, but it's difficult when all I can focus on is the feeling of Bobby's eyes on me—studying me from his end of the couch where he's working on a song.

He's been doing that a lot this week, silently observing, as if I'm a little bird and he's trying to figure out if I have a broken wing, or if I'm going to fly away.

I can't write when he's watching me like this. Especially not *this* part of our story.

Closing my computer, I stretch away the painful memories that inspired this particular chapter—the last one I wrote so many years ago. Even after rereading the entire thing twice, I still don't know how to continue it.

Is it a happy ending?

Or do I go with the truth?

Bobby's eyebrows furrow, and he tilts his head in thought.

"What word are you looking for over there?" I ask.

He shakes his head. "I don't know," he says, tossing down his pen. I don't ask to see what he's writing, and he doesn't offer.

Without a doubt, he's working through his feelings with a pen and paper, just like I am.

"Coffee?" he asks, his voice gruff, and even though we're parked for the night and I really should be going to bed soon, I nod.

"One more won't hurt," I say as he makes his way to the espresso machine. The way he moves is so familiar to me, it's unsettling. I've learned him so thoroughly again the past couple months that I already know he's going to tap the portafilter against his palm four times before inserting it into the machine. That his hands will go straight into his pockets as soon as it starts brewing.

As he does exactly that, I look away, shaking my head. I have no business knowing him so well. Not when I still haven't been able to confront our past. Not when I don't know the entirety of the truth of what broke us.

Bobby's phone rings as the espresso starts to drip, and he answers. "Marissa, what's—" he pauses. "All right. Yeah. Send it to me," he says, hanging up the phone. His shoulders are tight when he turns to face me.

"What's going on?" I ask, nerves buzzing in my stomach.

Bobby crosses his arms. "Before I tell you this, I want you to know that it doesn't matter. I'm not concerned."

"What is it Bobby?" I stand, clenching my hands into fists to keep them from shaking. "What has Harrison done?"

Bobby presses his lips together as if he doesn't want to have to tell me that whatever happened has to do with Harrison, but I already know. His demeanor has completely changed from the calm, comfortable man writing a song next to me to a protector preparing for battle, muscles tense and armor on.

He sighs. "Someone went to the tabloids and sold them a story about me having an affair with my lawyer's fiancée."

Fury seethes in my blood. I knew he'd do everything he could to make *me* look bad and ruin my reputation, but I'd accepted that risk when I chose to end things. What I didn't expect was for him to go after Bobby. Not when signing him to their firm is getting him everything he ever wanted in his career.

"Doesn't that make him look bad? I mean, you're his client! I thought he'd keep you out of it to save his own reputation."

Bobby rubs the back of his neck. "Yeah. About that... I'm not his client. I pulled out of the deal."

My stomach plummets. "Bobby. You didn't." That was his only protection. The only reason I thought Harrison would aim his ire toward me. He *just* had a deal fall through, and look at how that made him behave. If he lost an even bigger one…

I stop myself from finishing that thought, a shiver running down my spine.

Bobby's jaw bunches. "After how he spoke to you? I absolutely did." He lifts his chin as if daring me to argue with him.

I start to pace. "You've just given him all the ammo he needs to ruin your reputation. He'll lie. He'll say *anything* he can to make himself look better," I say, pulling out my phone to look up the story.

Bobby grabs my hands, and electricity surges from his skin into mine. He lowers my phone, then lifts my chin so that I'm looking directly into his eyes.

"I'm not worried about it. People know who I am. Besides, it was only a matter of time before everyone figured out who you were. I'm not concerned about a tabloid rumor."

"But they're saying we're *together*."

Bobby pulls away, putting his hands in his pockets, but doesn't say anything.

"What?" I ask, my voice shaking.

"Would that be the worst thing? For people to think we're together?"

I close my eyes, trying to block out the pain his words pull from my bones.

"Not for me. But if people think you were fooling around with your lawyer's fiancée, it might make your fans question your character." I rub my forehead. "Maybe I should go."

Bobby takes a sudden step forward. "Don't," he says, his voice sounding like he's begging on his knees rather than standing tall in front of me. "Don't go, Beth. I don't care what people think." Bobby opens his arms wide. "Let them think whatever they want. I. Don't. Care." His eyes flick away for a second as he takes a tense breath. When they meet mine again, there's a steady resolve there that wasn't before.

He holds my stare, his shoulders straightening as if he's made a decision. "I only care what you think of me. That's it. Only you."

I swallow, my pulse racing. It feels like we're creeping toward something with no way to slow down—the moment before the rollercoaster tips downward and begins its unstoppable race forward—but do I even want to stop it?

Bobby rubs the back of his neck. "Look, I know you just got out of a relationship. I'm not going to pressure you in any way. We don't have to be anything other than friends. But don't go, Beth." He takes the smallest step forward, but the weight of his yearning crashes into me as if he'd closed the distance and pressed his body against mine. "You know how I feel about you. I don't care about a rumor. None of it matters. Hell, I'd give all this up if it could make you trust me again. All I care about is *you*."

Bobby's chin is high, but there's a vulnerability in his open arms that makes me want to fold myself inside them and stay there forever. To tell him I care about him, too. That I always have, even when I hated him.

But I don't. I sit down, flipping through my manuscript until I come to the last page, the point in the story I never continued, because that's when everything fell apart. I trail my fingers along the paper, my heart thrumming against my ribs.

What do you want Beth? His voice from six years ago circles through my mind.

I don't even have to consider my answer.

I *want* to stay.

Walking away from Bobby now would be like ripping a piece of my heart out and leaving it behind with him. Because he's not the only one who could never fully let go of the other. I might have pushed it down, denied it, and completely avoided it, but it was always there.

Bobby was the love of my life. Even if he shattered my heart. Even if we didn't get our happily ever after because of what happened that night.

The night Bobby swears isn't what I think.

When my eyes meet his again, they're full of questions. Of sorrow and hope and anger and more emotions than I would've thought one person could feel at the same time. But they're all there, unmistakable in the deep blue of his irises.

I *want* to stay.

I *want* to forgive Bobby and maybe find a way to move forward. But first, I *need* to know the whole story. Every painful detail.

"I think…" I swallow, forcing myself to meet Bobby's eyes, anxiety swirling in my stomach. *Be brave,* I tell myself, swallowing. "I think maybe it's time to have that talk now."

Bobby's throat bobs, and he nods, his fists clenching. "I think so, too," he says.

Coffee forgotten, he sits down next to me, our thighs touching, and it sends a shockwave all the way to my toes.

He grabs my hand and squeezes, but I can feel his fingers trembling around mine, and it comforts me to know he's as nervous as I am.

"I know what you think happened that night six years ago. But I didn't at first. Not until a couple weeks later."

My heart kicks up in rhythm, thumping against my ribs. "Kelsey didn't tell you I showed up at your bus?"

He shakes his head. "I had no idea. If I'd known, I would've come and found you, explained everything right away."

I take a deep, steadying breath. "I'm not sure there was much to explain. I know you'd broken up with me, but you didn't even wait a day to be with someone else. I saw her with my own eyes."

"I know you did, but that's where your version of the night starts to fall apart." Bobby runs a hand across his scruff. "Kelsey might've been on my bus that night, but *I* wasn't."

THEN

NOVEMBER 2018

My phone rings as I pull out the key to my dorm, and I grab it, my lips tipping up in a smile when I see it's Bobby.

"Hey. I was just about to head your way," I answer, holding my phone between my ear and my shoulder as I unlock the door.

"Hey, Beth," Bobby says, but his voice doesn't sound right.

"What's wrong?" I ask, freezing. It sounds like he's crying. Not in a tears-streaming-down-his-face way, but he's definitely choked up. He hesitates.

"I wanted to talk to you. Did I catch you before you left?" he asks.

"I was about to leave in a few minutes. Why? What's going on?" My voice is squeaky with panic, but I can't help it. I *feel* panicked. In two years, I've never heard him sound like this.

Bobby clears his throat. "There's no easy way to say this. But I don't think you should come to the show tonight. Or for a while, actually."

The world falls from beneath my feet, and thank God I'm standing near the bed, because I collapse backward onto it.

"I don't understand..." This can't be happening. This is *my* Bobby. We talked yesterday, and he seemed excited for me to meet him tonight.

"I think we need to take some time apart. Just for a little while," he continues.

I'm too shocked to cry. Too taken aback to say much of anything at all. "What's happening? Where is this coming from? I don't—what's happening?" I'm talking in circles, but I don't know what else to ask, because this makes no sense.

"It's just for a while. Really. But I need some time to focus on my career. This tour is going to be a lot harder than I thought, you know? I've never headlined before, and Marissa is adding more dates and radio interviews and talk shows, and I don't want you following me around when I won't even have time to hang out with you. I'll feel too guilty. Plus, you have school to focus on…that internship."

"What?" I truly don't understand. I already told him I'm not taking the study abroad opportunity. My heart splinters, cracks spreading out in every direction.

"It's just not fair to you, Beth." His voice is firm, resolute.

The cracks gape open, and I press my fingers to my chest, trying to push the pain back in. "It's not *fair* to me? We've gone long stretches of time without seeing each other before. Tell me what this is really about, Bobby."

He clears his throat again. "I told you what it's about. This tour is going to be crazy, and I don't want you sitting around waiting for me for a whole year, maybe longer if it gets extended. You deserve more than I'm capable of giving you right now."

"I can decide what's best for me." My words come out sharp and angry, but I *am* angry.

"But you *won't*, and that's the problem. You can't live your life for me. I—hold on a second," he says. There are muffled voices, and I imagine

Bobby covering the phone with his hand so I can't hear what's being said.

"I have to go. I'm really sorry, Beth."

"Are you breaking up with me?" I ask, my voice shaking, because even though I know that's what he's doing, I still can't seem to believe it.

"No. Really." He sighs, and I can hear the exhaustion in his voice. "It's just a break. Just for a little while. I promise. There will be a time for us, but we both have other things we need to focus on right now."

My bleeding heart thunders in my chest, spreading the pain throughout my ribcage. "I can't believe you'd do this over the phone." Maybe it's not Bobby. Maybe it's a clone, or one of those bad scams where they steal your voice and demand money.

"I wanted to talk to you in person, but—"

"You were too much of a coward?" I spit.

Bobby's silent, and I picture him rubbing the back of his neck. "Because I love you too much to let you keep living your life for me," he finally says. "I didn't want you to drive all this way just to turn around again."

"You love me so much you're dumping me?" I cry, big, fat tears filling my eyes. I struggle to breathe, my lungs refusing to cooperate as sobs begin to work their way up my esophagus.

"No! It's just a break, Beth. Listen, I'll call you in a few weeks and we can see how we're doing and reevaluate, okay? Just trust me." Bobby's interrupted again, but this time I recognize the voice.

"They're about to drag you by your hair on stage if you don't get to soundcheck," Kelsey Darling says, and hearing that voice is enough to make my tears turn into anger.

"I really have to go, Beth. Okay? But I'll call you in a few weeks. I promise. I love you. Please believe that," Bobby says, and his voice is so sad it confuses me even more. The phone clicks, and then he's gone.

I'm in absolute, utter shock.

He has a ring. I *saw* it. I touched it and held it and stared at the little infinity sign etched into the back.

What happened? My heart fully shatters as I collapse into bed, crying until my pillow is soaked and my head throbs. Each inhale is a struggle, my body shaking as I search each memory for answers. Our entire relationship runs through my mind. Every single moment.

We never fought.

We didn't disagree on the important things in life.

We both want children.

We're in love. I know that as sure as I know that tides rise and fall in the ocean.

"No," I say out loud as I stand up. If he thinks I'm going to let him end things without a face-to-face conversation, then Bobby doesn't know me at all. I'm not going to torture myself, wondering what went wrong as I wait for him to call me in a few weeks. I'll go insane, waiting and hoping it's him every time my phone vibrates. "No," I repeat, wiping my nose.

I grab my keys and walk on shaky legs to the car, tears flowing freely down my face. It'd be useless to try to stop them. The whole way to the parking lot, people stare at me, but I don't care.

I *have* to see Bobby.

I have to talk to him.

I crank the ignition and pull out my phone. Molly answers on the third ring, but when she says "Hello," I can't speak, afraid that opening my mouth will let all my emotions fly out of my chest and I will truly fall apart, and that will be it.

"What's wrong?" Molly asks. "What happened?"

"Bobby broke up with me," I finally say. I was right. As soon as I speak, I'm hysterical, unable to catch my breath to the point I have to pull the car over on the side of the highway to make sure I don't crash.

"What?" Molly gasps. "I don't believe you."

I wish I didn't believe me either.

"He told me it's just a break, that his tour is too intense, and he needs some time to be able to focus on it. But I know what that means." I don't know how Molly understands me through my shuddering breaths, but she does.

"There has to be something going on," she says. "Bobby's so in love with you. He would do anything for you. Absolutely anything."

"I don't know what else it could be. He said he wanted a break and got off the phone. He said he'd call me in a few weeks." I lay my head against the steering wheel, hoping the cool leather can ease the headache wrapping like a band around my forehead.

"Are you *kidding* me? He expects you to just sit on this for a few weeks?" I hear a car door slam, and I know she's on her way to my dorm.

"Go back inside. I'm driving to talk to him now. He has a show in New Haven."

Molly takes a long breath, and I know she's trying to calm herself down. "What do you need? What can I do?"

I wish I'd thought to bring her with me. That I had pulled up to her house and asked her to drive me, or to just be there while I figured out what to do.

"I don't know. I guess I'll call you after I talk to him," I say, parroting her deep breaths in an attempt to calm myself down.

"I love you," she says. "I'll have my phone all night."

"I love you, too." My voice cracks as I hang up the phone and take several more steadying breaths, slow and deep, until I'm able to drive again.

I need to get to him. I need to understand what's going on. To look him in his eyes and see what could possibly have caused him to make that earth-shattering phone call.

I hardly remember the drive. It feels as if I blinked, and now I'm rushing up to his bus door.

When I try the handle, it's locked, but if I know Bobby at all, he's here. He doesn't go out after shows. Hasn't for as long as I've known him. Pulling out my phone, I look at the time. If anything, he's already showered and in bed.

I bang on the door, hard enough to make sure he'll hear it in the back.

"I know you're in there, Bobby Beckett!" I shout, my open hand turning into a closed fist as I pound on the door. "I'm not leaving until you talk to me."

Through the windows, a light flicks on. *He's coming,* I think, lowering my hand and wiping the tears from my eyes. I straighten my shoulders as the doors swing in, and I open my mouth to demand Bobby tell me what's going on, except it's not Bobby standing in front of me.

It's Kelsey Darling.

My heart stops, and my knees go weak.

This can't be happening.

She's wearing one of Bobby's shirts for his upcoming tour, the hem hanging around her bare legs to mid-thigh, and her hair is messy in a way that makes me want to violently throw up. Kelsey smirks at me, her eyes dragging from my sweatpants and wrinkled shirt to my tear-stained cheeks.

"Can I help you?" she asks, leaning against the door frame and crossing her arms as if barring me entry.

"Where's Bobby?" I ask, my voice coming out far stronger than I'm feeling. "Go get him." I have no interest in talking to this woman.

None.

If Bobby's cheating on me, I want to hear it from his traitorous mouth.

"He's a little busy at the moment. But I'll let him know you dropped by." She winks at me, then starts to turn around.

A sob bursts from my throat—a humiliating, horrible noise that I'm sure Kelsey Darling would never make even in her lowest moments, but it feels as if my soul has been ripped from my body.

As if everything I've ever known has been a complete lie.

My body wants to collapse. To stop functioning entirely. But I force breaths in through my nose and out through my mouth.

The pain in my chest is so sharp now, I wonder if my heart turned to glass when it shattered—if there's somehow shards coursing through my veins that will kill me with a thousand tiny cuts.

How could Bobby do this to me? He said it was a break. Just for now.

So what was it? Had he just wanted to have some time to fuck around? To get Kelsey out of his system without a guilty conscience until he was ready to come back to me?

I would do anything—or, *would have* done anything—for Bobby. But not this. I won't wait for him, pining away and ready to take him back once he's ready to settle down while he lives a rockstar life.

"Give him a message for me," I say, choking on my own voice. "Tell him to never, ever contact me again. Tell him we're done."

"Got it," Kelsey says, as if I told her to tell him it's going to rain tomorrow.

Before she can say anything else, I turn and leave. I don't know what exactly happened with Kelsey on that bus tonight, and I don't want to. I think her being there in his shirt pretty much says everything, and I don't need to know the details.

What I do know, with absolute certainty, is that I will never, ever forgive Bobby for his betrayal.

NOW

SEPTEMBER 2024: BLACKSBURG, VA

It's only just September
But the cold is seeping in
And I know that you don't want me now
But do you think you could again?
—An excerpt from "When Winter Comes," written and performed by Robert
Beckett

The events of that night flash through my mind—the way I had to bang on the door for far too long. Then the lights slowly turning on throughout the bus as Kelsey came from the back to answer.

"What do you mean you weren't there?" My mouth is so dry I can barely get the words out.

"I was a wreck after our phone call. It was the worst show I've ever put on. My heart wasn't in it. All I could think about was you and if I was making the right decision for us to take a break."

I pick up my wine glass. "For the record, it wasn't the right decision."

"I know that now," Bobby says, his eyes haunted. "But back then, I really thought I was doing the right thing."

"But why? Why did you need to make that decision at all? Why did you want to break up?" I ask. "And if you weren't with her, why was Kelsey on your bus?"

"It's… I'm getting ahead of myself." Bobby rubs the back of his neck. "The phone call and Kelsey? Those are two separate stories." He sets his drink down, and it appears untouched. "I told you how my mom regretted giving up her career for my dad."

"I remember," I nod, not sure what this has to do with Kelsey.

"After Michael died, all I could think about was how he would never get the chance to grow up and live out his dreams. Never. And the very same day he died, I found that acceptance letter for the study abroad program, and I *knew* you weren't taking it because of me. It felt like a sign. A reminder that life is so short. I knew if we were together, you wouldn't go. But I also knew you and I would find our way back to one another—that a year was *nothing* in the grand scheme of our lives." Bobby closes his eyes, wincing as if reliving the memories is physically painful. "I felt like I was holding you back."

I want to argue with him, tell him that it was none of his business, what I'd decided. That he was the one who'd told me to not let others make my choices for me. But there's so much regret in his voice, I can't bring myself to make him feel even worse.

"I was young and stupid, but I really thought I was doing the right thing. I thought a year would pass, and we'd be Beth and Bobby again as if it had never happened. I could focus on my tour, and you could go travel Europe and write and read and learn about your favorite poets and authors and before we knew it, we'd be together again."

"I didn't take the spot in the program," I say, keeping my tone gentle.

Bobby's jaw tightens. "I know. All of it was for nothing—the biggest mistake of my life. My biggest regret. And it was for *nothing.*"

"You didn't know," I say, not quite absolving him, but not quite blaming him, either.

"I asked Johnny to take me out that night. All I wanted was to forget. So I slammed beers until I was blackout drunk, crying to the bartender about what a mistake I'd made."

My heart feels like it's breaking as I touch his arm, feeling the need to comfort him somehow. He takes my hand, turning it over and tracing the lines of my palm.

Bobby shifts closer to me. "Kelsey came up to me after the show that night. I think she could tell something was wrong. That something had happened between us. You know, she'd always made me a little uncomfortable, but I couldn't place why. She said she'd had a fight with her band, and asked if she could sleep on my couch. I had no intention of sleeping at all that night unless I was passed out and dead to the world. It didn't matter where I was. I told her she could have my bus and that I'd stay in a hotel with Johnny and the guys somewhere near the bars."

My lungs feel like they're made of stone, and I struggle to get deep enough breaths. Tears prick the back of my eyes, and I have to clench my teeth together to keep from crying. "You mean—" my voice cracks, and I clear my throat, desperate to hold it together. "You mean you really weren't with her that night?"

"No. Of course not, Beth. I would *never* have done that to you. And if I'm being honest, I've had to work through a lot of anger over it, because you believed I would cheat on you so easily. I thought you knew me better than that."

I shake my head, dizzy from his confession. "At first, I think I was in shock. That night, I was so hurt, I couldn't even process it. I cried myself to sleep. But when I woke up, I thought something else had to be going on. I called you that morning, and you didn't answer."

"You called me?" Bobby looks as if his world was just flipped upside down. "Marissa said…" He rubs the back of his neck, his eyebrows lowered as if he can't comprehend what I'm saying. "I had her keep my phone for over a week so I wouldn't call you and take it all back. She said I was doing the right thing. That I was being selfless. But I made her promise she'd tell me if you called."

Anger bubbles in my stomach as Marissa's words run through my mind. *I can't help but feel a bit responsible…*

"Bobby. I called you fifty times. A hundred. I called you over and over for *days*, because after I saw Kelsey, I thought I had to be missing something. I thought if I could just talk to you, you'd clear it all up. But you never answered, and I'd seen Kelsey with my own eyes. I thought you were ignoring me, and after a few days, calling started to hurt too much. I blocked you to keep myself from hanging on when you didn't want me." My heart feels as if it's breaking all over again, that familiar pain spreading through my ribcage.

Bobby cups my face with trembling hands. "Beth, no." His eyes are glistening, his pain so evident, it hurts to look into them. "There has never been a single day of my life that I haven't wanted you. You were *everything* to me." He stops, his Adam's apple bobbing as he swallows.

"I guess Kelsey felt guilty enough after a few weeks to tell me what happened." He winces. "She told me she was wearing my shirt, and nothing else, and that she made no effort to let you know I wasn't there. I fired her from the tour immediately. We had to scramble for a new opening act, and it killed our single. But I didn't care. I'd have quit the damn tour if my contract hadn't been so tight. I knew you were hurt beyond words, and I couldn't find a way to get in touch with you."

"I made it pretty hard," I say. The pain had been so overwhelming, I'd done everything I could to avoid him.

"By the time I realized what you thought happened, I didn't know what to do. I showed up at your house, but your mother turned me away, threatening to call the police for trespassing. She said I'd hurt her daughter, and I would never be welcome in her home again."

My mouth cracks open in surprise. She hadn't told me that, and it made my heart ache to know she'd thrown aside decorum to protect me. I wasn't sure she'd even known Bobby and I had broken up.

"I called your phone, but it went straight to voicemail. My texts went unanswered. I was blocked on all social media. I wrote you letters. I waited at your dorm, but they wouldn't let me in, and then the semester ended, and I didn't know where you were. I went to Molly's, but she wouldn't listen to a single word I said. She sprayed me with a hose when I wouldn't leave her front porch."

Tears are rolling down my face, but I can't help but laugh at the image. At my friend's loyalty. It comes out as a weird, blubbery chortle, and it's just awkward enough to break the tension.

"Honestly, you should have expected that from Molly," I say, wiping my nose on my sleeve.

Bobby smiles. Not big enough for his dimple to appear, but it's a brief break in the sorrow and tension bracketing his mouth. "I should have." He rubs the back of his neck again. "I knew you hated me." Bobby rests his forearms on his knees, sighing. "I would have traveled to Europe to find you, but I had no clue where you were, so I waited the year," he says, subconsciously rubbing the inside of his arm.

I stare at his fingers fiddling with the fabric over his tattoo. The one I'd known was for me the moment I saw it. "Is that when you got the tattoo?" I ask.

Bobby nods. "It was a year of absolute hell. A whole year where I knew you thought I'd betrayed you, and it almost killed me." He pulls up his sleeve, showing me the pink wild rose. "I got this so I could keep you with me while I waited for you to come back home. 'The summer blooms, not heading my one song—'"

A lump forms in my throat at the memory of the last time he quoted the poem to me. "'How can I wait?'" I finish for him, my voice barely a whisper.

"'How can I wait?'" he says with a sad smile. "I prayed every night you were happy. That you were elbow deep in poetry and taking in every moment of being abroad. And then when the year was up, I came to find you."

My breath catches. "You did?"

His lips press into a thin line. "I did. You just didn't see me." He swallows, shifting in his chair. "Your dad had a fundraiser in New York. It was a rare Friday that I didn't have a show, so I went. I had to sneak through a back door to get in. I searched everywhere for you, but for the longest time I couldn't find you. I wondered if maybe you hadn't gone, but it was heavily publicized, and I knew your dad would want the whole family there." He takes another deep breath, but I stay silent, letting him continue.

"I was about to leave, and then I saw you. You were tucked away in a quiet corner, and God, you looked beautiful. My heart stopped. *Actually* stopped." He places his hand on his sternum, gripping his chest like he's reliving the pain of it. "You were with Harrison, your heads bent over your book of poetry, and you were smiling. He leaned in to kiss you, and I couldn't watch. I left before you could see me."

"That was the night I met him," I say breathlessly.

Bobby's eyes squeeze closed as if my admission causes him agony. "I just wanted you to be happy. That's why I'd insisted on the break to begin with. To let you make your own choices without having to think about me or what I wanted. It felt like the same thing. You'd chosen someone else."

"I was dying inside." My throat feels like it's closing, and suddenly I can't catch my breath. "I was in therapy. It took *years*, even after Harrison and I began dating, for me to really feel like I was all in with him."

"I didn't know. All I've ever wanted for you is happiness, Beth."

We sit in silence for a moment, and while I don't know what Bobby's thinking, I'm cursing fate. Why had it tried to keep us apart for so long? Too many coincidences. Too many misunderstandings. That's all that stood in our way.

"There were times I tried to move on," Bobby finally says. "But every girl I've dated has fallen short. Because they weren't *you*." He meets my eyes, and the agony there makes my breath hitch. "I thought about reaching out to you so many times, but I didn't even know where to start. I didn't know where you were, or who you may be with. But I've *never* stopped loving you. Every song I sing, it's about you. I wrote an entire album the year things ended, begging for you to listen to the truth. It's all there, everything I was feeling, every regret I have. I laid it bare for the entire world to hear, all for the almost non-existent chance you'd hear it and know I was sorry. That I was yours, and always would be, even if your heart belonged to someone else."

Tears stream from my eyes as he moves closer, grabbing my hands in his, his thumbs rubbing across my knuckles. "I don't know if it's too late—"

"It's not," I breathe. My bottom lip trembles, but Bobby's touch grounds me—gives me the courage to look him in the eye. "I tried to cut you out of my life completely. But you were always there. Always lingering. I hated you for what happened. I really thought…" I trail off, unable to even say the words.

"I know," he says, so gently it hurts. "I know what you thought. I'm so sorry, Beth. And I know this is the worst possible timing, and that you need to heal from what you've been through and find a way past it, but I just need you to know that I love you."

He swallows as if holding back his own tears. "I love you more than life itself. I always have. More than my life. *This* life." He looks around the bus.

"I was wrong back then about what was important. None of the things I worried about mattered. *You* matter. This thing between us, this love that feels so much bigger than that word can even describe? That's what's important. And if you can forgive me—"

"I forgive you." I shift forward, tilting my face closer to his. "Can you forgive me?" I ask, looking up at him from beneath my lashes, my voice nearly a whisper. It hurts knowing that all this time was wasted. All because of a series of events that should never have happened—Michael's death, Kelsey sleeping on his bus, Bobby going off to get drunk to forget that he'd just chosen to break up with me so I could pursue an opportunity I didn't even want.

"There's nothing to forgive, Beth." Bobby breathes as his hand comes up to cup my cheek. The muscles of his arms ripple as he pulls me closer. "Whenever you're ready, give me another chance. Please."

NOW

September 2024: Blacksburg, VA

I want a love that will go down
Alongside stories long been shared
By the ones with hearts of poets
The words written by the baird
—*An excerpt from "Poetry," written by Beth Winters, performed by Robert*
Beckett

I close the distance between us. Pressing my lips against his.
Softly.
Tentatively.
And it's like a deep breath after being trapped under water, unsure if you'll ever find the surface again.

A rumble leaves Bobby's throat as he deepens the kiss, just for a moment, before he leans back to search my eyes. His chest rises and falls with shallow, rapid breaths. "There's no need to rush. If you need time."

"I just need you," I say, my voice breathy.

It's an echo of the words I'd said that night so many years ago. The most beautiful, meaningful sexual experience of my life, and I lean forward again, reaching up to cup the back of his neck.

His hands slide to my thighs, squeezing as a groan escapes his lips. "You're going to be my undoing, Beth Winters."

"I hope so," I say, pulling him down to meet my mouth again. Bobby doesn't hold back this time, his tongue finding mine, caressing it with long, deep strokes. His hands slide up my back, holding me as if he's afraid I'll disappear. As if his grip can keep me here with him forever.

I climb onto his lap, and the feel of him impossibly hard beneath me is almost *my* undoing.

I break away from the kiss and lift my shirt over my head. My chest is flushed, my breasts rising and falling in my cream lace bra, but I don't feel exposed. I feel beautiful.

Bobby's eyes drink me in, but it's different from the first time we were undressing on this couch. He doesn't look at me like he's discovering a woman's body.

No. He looks at me as if I'm his wildest, most forbidden dream, finally within reach. He lifts me off the couch, carrying me to the back of the bus.

"Where are we going? I like that couch!" I say, twisting back toward it, but Bobby pulls me tighter against him.

"So do I. For the past six years, I've dreamed of you on that couch," his voice is full of need, and so rough, it scrapes against my sensitive skin and makes me shiver. "If you're going to let me back inside you, then I need to know it's not a dream."

He lays me down on his bed, his calloused fingers slipping beneath my waistband and pulling down my pants. It's somehow hurried *and* tender, but there's no awkwardness to his movement. It's just Bobby, older and a bit sharper, more jaded maybe, but kind, and loving, and *good.*

He pulls his shirt over his head, and my mouth goes dry. Bobby at twenty-two was hot, but Bobby at twenty-eight is *unreal.* I count his abs—eight of them—and trace the defined lines that make a V as they disappear below his pants. There's a sprinkling of chest hair between his pecs, and I imagine running my fingers across it, but the thought disappears as Bobby removes his pants.

"You're even more beautiful than you were six years ago," he says, crawling over me. His scruff scratches as he presses kisses from my ankle to my navel, then to the apex of my thighs. He spreads my legs, running a finger along my center before his lips close around the bundle of nerves.

There's no prolonged foreplay, no tentative touches. Bobby claims me in only the way he can. Because even if we lost each other for a bit, I've always been his, and I think we both need to feel that right now.

Bobby sucks and licks like a starving man as he presses a finger inside me, his other hand coming up to tease my breast, his thumb strumming against my nipple like he's playing the sweetest song.

"God, Beth," Bobby breathes. It's the barest whisper, but it makes heat pulse deep in my belly. My name on his lips has always felt life changing, but with his fingers moving inside me, it's earth-shattering. My breaths are shallow and my muscles tight, my body completely out of my control as pleasure builds inside me, but I don't want to come like this. Not for the first time with him again. "Bobby," I pull at his shoulders, and he looks up at me.

"I want to feel you," I say, and he doesn't need more of an explanation. He reaches for his nightstand, but I stop him. I'm protected, and I don't want anything between us tonight.

"You're sure?" he asks, his eyebrows lowering.

"Please," I beg, pulling him back on top of me.

"They're probably expired, anyway," he jokes, settling between my thighs. His thick length presses against my entrance, and once again, Bobby stares at me like he can't believe I'm here.

"I love you, Beth," he says, pressing a kiss to my throat. "And I need you to know that this is it for me. *You're* it for me, and I'm never letting you go again." His words brush against my ear and slip across my skin, warming me.

"I love you, too," I whisper, and with my confession, he pushes inside me, stretching me until I'm once again branded as his.

His body was made for mine, and mine for his, and he thrusts deeper until I don't even know where I end and he begins.

"We've always just fit, haven't we?" he says, his gruff voice echoing my thoughts. His arms shake as he restrains himself, savoring every last moment as he fills me.

And when he finally begins to move, I cry out his name, digging my nails into his back. It's too much and not enough, and I know Bobby feels it too as he loses all control and what was slow and gentle lovemaking quickly becomes frantic and frenzied, years of anger and hurt and love and longing combining as Bobby urges me toward my orgasm.

His hands and lips are everywhere, plucking at my skin like the strings of his guitar, and my eyelashes flutter closed. I try to memorize every sensation, the choreography of his touches.

His hands weave through my hair as he pulls my head back, finding the hollow of my throat with his lips, and the vibration of his groan of pleasure sends me over the edge. I tighten around him, the sensation almost blinding as my body goes tight and wave after wave of ecstasy crashes over me.

And as Bobby finds his own release, spilling himself inside me, I know that even though Bobby was wrong in his decision to take a break, he'd also been right. We might have wasted six years, but there was always going to be a time for us. Because when something is meant to be, even our worst mistakes can't undo what fate has planned.

NOW

September 2024: Charlotte, NC

If you ever were to leave me
I don't know what I'd do
There's nothing that I wouldn't try
To keep from losing you
—*A poem by Harrison Rouchester to Beth Winters, seven months into dating*

A car door slams nearby, and I peer out the window. It's way too early for Bobby to be back from his studio session, and a prickle of unease works its way down my spine. I put my pen down and stand as the bus doors hiss open.

"What are you doing back so…" My voice trails off. "Harrison." I freeze.

His eyes are dark. Wild. And even from several feet away, I can smell the scotch clinging to his breath. His hair is disheveled and the vein in his forehead throbbing, and in his arms is a plastic bag.

Harrison doesn't say a single word as he stands there with his chest heaving and a look of pure vitriol on his face. He dumps the bag on the floor at my feet, the pages floating to the ground with a whoosh.

I don't want to look at the papers, but I can't stop myself, my eyes zeroing in on the black ink.

My heart plummets as I take in the pages of lyrics I keep beneath the false bottom of my jewelry chest.

It stops completely when I notice that mixed among them is my manuscript.

You think I'd give you a new laptop without making sure I have access to everything on it? Harrison's voice slithers through my mind.

He'd warned me he was watching, but I'd changed all my passwords. *How was he still able to get into my files?*

Harrison throws a handful of trinkets on the ground. My infinity bracelet. A guitar pick, also from my jewelry box.

"Care to explain?" The venom in Harrison's voice gives me chills, every word a poison dart. Even at his worst, I've never heard him sound this way—possessed—and I take an involuntary step back. Before I even realize I'm doing it, my eyes are scanning for weapons. Anything I can use to defend myself.

"Explain what? It's just a story, Harrison. Why don't we sit down?" I raise my hands in front of me, trying to placate him, but they're shaking.

"Cut the shit!" Harrison shouts in a rage, throwing a nearby chair to the floor with a crash. I jump, shuffling to the side to try to find a path to escape.

"Want to tell me what you've been hiding?" He stalks forward, his voice so deep and rough it sounds like the growl of a rabid animal.

"I don't—"

The vein in his forehead bulges as his face turns red. "If you lie to me again, Elizabeth, you are going to regret it." He takes a step closer. A slow, deliberate step meant to put me on edge.

I look down at the pile of songs Bobby wrote for me so long ago, racking my brain for how to explain them away. Clearly, he's read them. They're stained with grease and liquor, wrinkled and creased from being folded and unfolded. They're ruined, and if I wasn't so afraid, I'd mourn the loss of them. But there's no room for that in my mind right now. Not when it's flooded with adrenaline and fear.

"Nothing to say? No excuses? No more lies you'd like to tell me?" He slams his hand on the dining table, and I feel the vibration in my chest.

I have to fight to keep breathing, inhaling and exhaling through the panic.

"Let's just sit down, and I'll explain everything—"

"You know," he cuts me off again. "I got a strange feeling the day you met me to have lunch with Bobby. And then you were so hesitant to come on this tour. It didn't make sense. But it wasn't until I visited that I knew you were fucking him," he snarls.

My jaw drops. "What? No! You've got it all wrong. I knew Bobby from when we were teenagers. Just kids. It was a long time ago. But nothing's happened."

"You expect me to believe that? I'm not a damn idiot. I knew something was up with how you two were acting. Imagine my surprise when I started doing some research on the guy. He has a whole fucking album about you! Fourteen songs, and every single one of them is him begging you to listen, professing his love for you, saying that he'll wait for as long as it takes to win you back. The last one is fucking called *Beth*, for God's sake!"

I flinch. "Then it was one-sided, because I haven't spoken to him in six years. I—I never listened to those songs." I'm stammering, but I can't stop. "N—not a single one until he played at our engagement party. I had no idea when I came here—"

"You *humiliated* me!" Spit flies from Harrison's mouth as he screams. He punches the wall, his knuckles coming away bloody, and I back away until my shoulders hit the cabinet doors. "I had your fucking lover sing for all our friends. My clients!"

I raise my hands out in front of me again, hoping it will help keep him from getting any closer. "Listen. You're right. Okay? I should've told you the truth right then and there, but I didn't know what to do. I was afraid, because I loved you so much." The words are slimy as they leave my mouth, but I keep going, scraping the dredges of my feelings for him for anything I can possibly say to calm him down.

Harrison's still for a moment, and I think maybe I've gotten through to him. I slowly lower my arms, reaching toward my back pocket where my phone is.

"Such a good fucking liar." Harrison's on me in a second, shoving me backward. My head hits the cabinet with a *crack*, so hard that my ears ring and I see stars. He grabs my arm, twisting until I'm certain my bones are going to snap.

"Stop! You're hurting me," I beg, but my words don't even touch him.

"This is *your* fault." He twists harder, then even harder when tears flow from my eyes. I try to fight back, but he presses his body against me, pinning me in place as he brings his face to my ear. "You're coming with me, and we're going home. Do you understand? You're gonna be a good little wife, and you will *never* speak to Robert fucking Beckett or embarrass me *ever* again." He hisses his demands, low and violent, and I nod.

With all his strength, Harrison yanks me forward, and absolute terror runs through my blood. I *can't* go with him.

I can't get in the car with him.

He'll kill me.

I dig my heels into the carpet, resisting.

"Of course. Just let me grab my things, and I'll meet you at the car. Then we can go home, and it will all be okay. I'll do better." I try my best to keep my voice calm, but Harrison throws me to the floor. My elbow hits the sharp edge of the coffee table, but I barely notice the sticky blood running down my fingers and staining the carpet.

"Stop lying to me!" Harrison roars, and I swear the bus shakes.

"Stop, please!" I beg, but it only fuels his fury. His face is almost purple as he flips the coffee table. It smashes into pieces on the floor, one of the legs flying through the air and slamming into my eye, and I scream in pain, the agony so severe that my vision blurs around the edges. Harrison approaches me, kicking the destroyed table out of the way so he can get closer.

"Please," I sob.

This is it.

He's going to kill me whether I get in the car with him or not.

Harrison rears back and punches me, hitting my right eye, and the pain is blinding. He grabs my throat, his fingers squeezing as he pushes me down into the floor, but a second later, he's no longer looming over me. Instead, he's on his back on the other side of the room, and Johnny is kneeling over him, slamming his fist into Harrison's face again and again.

"You *fucking* touch her again, and I'll kill you. I will fucking *kill* you!" Johnny screams, hitting him again.

The room spins, and I fight to stay conscious as Patrick reaches my side, helping me to sit. "Let's get you out of here."

"Johnny—" I protest. I don't want to leave him alone with Harrison.

"The police are on their way. We heard screaming, and then the crashes. Come on," Patrick urges.

I have to lean heavily against Patrick to stand, my breaths coming in pants and my head throbbing, but I keep moving. More people rush onto the bus as I struggle to stay upright—Bobby's drummer and his bass player—and a sliver of relief works its way past the pain.

I have to walk past Harrison to get off the bus, but as I approach him, I'm no longer afraid. He's lying on his stomach with his hands behind his back and Johnny's knee between his shoulder blades.

I pause as I pass him.

He's taken too much from me, and I feel a desperate need to take a little bit back.

"I *never* want to see you again," I say. My words are low and forceful, and I'm proud of how I keep the pain out of my voice. "You will *never* touch me again."

"I'll kill you for this," Harrison hisses through bloody teeth, but Johnny shoves his face into the carpet before he can say more.

I move forward, refusing to let his words rattle me, and Patrick pats me on the shoulder.

"You've got some guts, girl," he says, and it's enough encouragement for me to keep my head high until I step foot off the bus. But the moment the door closes behind me, my knees give out.

With shaking hands, I touch my swollen eye, smearing blood across my face. My skin is hot and sticky, and the way it pits under my fingers is so sickening, it makes me dizzy.

Patrick lowers me to the ground, pulling his phone from his pocket and reaching out to hold my hand.

I can barely breathe, the air entering and leaving my lungs in shallow wheezes. A panic attack, I think.

"Bobby," I hear Patrick say through the fog. "You need to get back here. Yes. Right now." I hear Bobby's concerned voice on the other end of the phone, the tone forceful and demanding, but I can't make out what he's saying. I focus on my breathing. In, out. In, out.

"She'll be okay, but listen, son," Patrick says, "I need you to stay calm when you get here."

In the moments before darkness claims me, before I pass out from the agony pounding in my head, I send up a prayer that Harrison's gone by the time Bobby arrives. Not because I care what happens to him, but because I'm certain that if Bobby sees him, he'll kill him with his bare hands.

"Where is she?" Bobby asks, his furious voice floating through the open windows before he even walks through the doors.

Johnny's been waiting for him outside, likely to prepare him for what he's going to see. "She's on the couch. Paramedics have already checked her out and stitched her up. She's fine," he says.

"Wha—she fucking needed *stitches*?" Bobby's voice is as hard as steel. "I'm going to rip his fucking head off—"

"You need to calm down, man," Johnny says, dropping his voice to a soft whisper. "The police arrested him for assault and battery, and the paramedics have cleared Beth. She has a concussion and a pretty wicked black eye. Some stitches in her eyebrow and elbow. But she's going to be fine."

I hear a thump, the sound of something light hitting the ground, and I imagine Bobby throwing his hat in anger and running his hands through his hair.

"Let's get Dr. Meadows here. I want him to check her out, too. Make sure she doesn't need to go to the hospital."

"Already done. He'll be here by three," Johnny says.

There's nothing but tense silence for a moment. "Okay," Bobby finally says.

"Take a breath. Go check on her," Johnny tells him. "I'll wait for Sam to get here."

My stomach drops at the mention of Sam, Bobby's head of security. He's a huge man—an ex-cop who's been with him since the beginning. If Johnny thinks we need him here, he must think Harrison is still a threat.

Footsteps thump on the stairs, and I force a small smile for Bobby, but it doesn't help soften the blow of my injuries. Bobby flinches when he sees me, his breath leaving his body in a whoosh as his eyes widen and his fists clench.

"Jesus, Beth." He's kneeling in front of me in less than a second, his palms gently cupping my cheeks, his thumb caressing my eyebrow.

"I'm fine," I say, despite the throbbing in my head and my completely shattered heart.

"I'll kill him," Bobby says, his eyes darker than I've ever seen them before. His jaw is tight, and his hands are shaking.

"No, you won't." I take his hands in mine, and he stares for a long moment before flipping them over. He grits his teeth, looking at the blood the paramedics missed when wiping off my elbow.

"I'm sorry I wasn't here," he presses a kiss to my palm, and just that small bit of contact makes my heart slow.

"This isn't your fault. This isn't *anyone's* fault but Harrison's."

And maybe a little bit mine, I add silently, biting my lip to keep the tears at bay. My fault for lying for so long.

For letting myself get in this situation in the first place.

"I know what you're thinking," Bobby says, pulling my lip out from between my teeth with his thumb. "And you couldn't be more wrong. *None* of this is your fault. I should have stopped it. I knew what he was the second I met him. I should have seen this coming."

"I wouldn't have listened. You flat out told me what you thought of him, and I *didn't* listen."

"Then I should have tried harder. Men like Harrison get into your head and mess with you, clouding your judgment until you do this. Blame yourself. But I want you to hear me. There is *never* an excuse to lay a hand on a woman. Let alone one you claim to love. Never."

The tears in my eyes spill over my lashes, stinging and burning the swollen skin, but I can't stop them. I *want* to cry. I want to wash away every bit of this day with fat, salty tears.

"I don't know what I'm going to do," I admit.

Bobby wipes beneath my eyes, gentle and tender and so careful of the injured skin. "I can have movers at your house in an hour to get your things in New York. They can take them wherever you want." Relief that all I have to do is agree softens the edges of my pain. I don't think I could bear going back to our brownstone and packing up my things, and it's comforting to know I won't have to.

"Thank you," I croak out.

"Anything for you, Beth. *Anything*. You know that."

I let him hold me as I fall apart, crying until the sun is high in the sky, and the bus gets so stiflingly hot Bobby's forced to let me go to close the windows. He goes to the sink and pours me a glass of water, then sits on the couch next to me, gathering me in his arms and holding me like a child. Careful to avoid my sore spots, he rubs circles on my upper arm with his thumb, presses kisses to my hair and whispers that he loves me. That he's sorry.

I let that love fill me up as I rest my head beneath his chin, my ear against his chest, where the steady thump of his heart beats a rhythm almost like a lullaby, calming my tears.

But I cry again when I realize that even injured and sore and heartbroken, I haven't felt this safe in a long time.

"Knock knock," an unfamiliar voice calls from outside. "It's Dr. Meadows."

Bobby lifts my chin to meet my eyes. "I'd really like for him to check you out," he says as an older gentleman walks in. He's at least seventy, but he has pink cheeks and bright eyes, and vaguely reminds me of Molly's Grandpa Frank.

"I'm guessing this young lady with stitches in her head here is the one in need of my attention?" he raises an eyebrow.

"That would be me," I say, "But really, I'm fine. The paramedics already checked me out."

"Well, I'm already here," Dr. Meadows says kindly. "And I'll be charging Bobby whether I take a quick peek at you or not."

Bobby laughs. "He's right. I have him on retainer. Never know when a sore throat is going to pop up."

"Exactly." Dr. Meadows points at my eye. "That's a nasty bruise there, dear, and I would feel better if I could just take a *quick* once over."

Bobby squeezes my hand. "As would I. Please?"

"Alright." I nod, forcing a tight smile. It's not as if I don't understand where they're coming from. "As long as it's quick."

Dr. Meadows claps his hands together. "Ah, I can agree to that. Let me grab my things."

"How about I start the shower for you while he's checking you out?" Bobby says, his eyes focused on the dried bits of blood in my nails.

"That sounds great, actually," I say, scratching at my arm. Now that a shower has been mentioned, my skin feels itchy and tight.

Bobby pats me on the knee as he stands, his hand lingering as if it's hard for him to let me go. "Take good care of her, Doc," Bobby orders, walking to the back of the bus to give us some privacy.

Dr. Meadows flashes a light in my eyes and inspects my lacerations before grabbing an icepack from the freezer and telling me to apply it to my eye on and off in ten-minute increments. "All things considered," he says, putting his stethoscope back in his bag, "you're in good shape. I know the paramedics warned you about a concussion, but I think your eye there took the brunt of the damage. I wouldn't be surprised if your occipital bone has a nasty bruise." He taps his eye, showing me where he's talking about. "A bit of rest and a hot shower, and I think you'll be just fine."

"Sold," I say, more than ready to wash off this horrible day.

"Beth," Dr. Meadows puts a hand on my arm, stopping me. "You got lucky today that all you have is some surface cuts and bruises. Next time, it could be a lot worse."

I hear the meaning behind his words, and it gives me chills.

He's seen these kinds of injuries before.

Worse, it seems.

"Don't worry. There won't be a next time." I give him a sad smile, partly embarrassed and partly grateful for his concern. He seems satisfied with my answer, so I thank him and walk to the back of the bus.

Bobby jumps to his feet and hands me a towel when I enter, the room slightly foggy from the steam of the hot shower. "Call if you need anything," he says before kissing my forehead and leaving me alone.

I take my time, washing my hair twice and gently cleansing the blood from my eyebrow, careful to avoid the stitches. I let the hot water run over my neck and shoulders, easing the tension that continues to cause my head to ache.

I don't know if it's minutes or hours, but I stay there until the water turns cold before wrapping myself in the fluffy, white towel and grabbing some fresh clothes. I avoid looking at myself until I'm dressed in soft leggings and an oversized sweatshirt and my hair is brushed.

Finally, I stand in front of the mirror, squeezing my eyes shut.

I don't want to look, but I think I need to. To see the physical marks on my body, burn them into my memory so I never allow myself to be put in this position again.

I take a deep, slow breath. Then another. A wave of nausea flips my stomach upside down, but I push it away, then open my eyes.

It's so much worse than I imagined.

Tears sting my eyes, and I shudder, taking a step back. The stitches look like spiders crawling over the swollen blue and purple skin above my eye. There are small cuts across my cheek that I didn't know were there. That I didn't even feel because I was too busy being terrified of losing my life.

My face is pale and gaunt, as if the past few hours have aged me. And in a way, they have. I turn away, disgusted with myself. Not with my appearance, but with the fact that I gave so much of myself away to someone capable of hurting me like this.

NOW

September 2024: Charleston, SC

Little Bird, I can hear you call
Even when you can't say words at all
Little Bird, I can hear you sing
When you lift up your head and spread out your wings
Little bird, will you come back home
If I set you free, If I let you roam
Little Bird, you deserve much more
So I'll wait right here, watching as you soar
—An excerpt from "Little Bird," written and performed by Robert Beckett

It's been four days, but I still jump when Bobby walks through the bus doors, my bruised ribs screaming, and I wince.

"It's just me," Bobby says, sitting down. "You doing okay?"

I nod, but there's no conviction there.

Bobby puts a hand on my arm. "You're safe." He leans down and kisses my forehead, and I breathe him in, letting his warmth calm my racing heart.

"I know. It's just being in here, I think. Right where it all—" I stop, shuddering.

"I think you're right. We just got to Charleston. Why don't we get off the bus for a while, if you're feeling up for it." He tucks my hair behind my ear, so gently, I want to cry.

"I'll go anywhere if it means I can get some fresh air. Let me go change," I say, but Bobby holds tight to my hand as the bus stops.

"You look perfect," he says, standing and holding out a hand. "Ready?"

I take Bobby's hand and let him lead me down the stairs onto a dark sidewalk. "Well…this took an unexpected turn," I say as we approach a wrought-iron fence surrounding an overgrown cemetery.

"You said anywhere," Bobby said, squeezing my hand.

I turn toward the street, trying to place where we are, but it's too dark to make out the street sign.

"I'm shocked you don't know this place," Bobby says. "How is it possible that I know a famous literary spot better than you do?" A self-satisfied smile dimples his cheek when I squint, trying to figure out what he's talking about. "Do you remember when we used to sit at Joe's, and you'd read me poetry?"

My jaw drops open, mostly because the thought of not remembering those days when we first met is complete absurdity. They're etched into my brain like carvings in wood, the memories so visceral that I can still smell the coffee and hear the espresso grinder. I can still feel the warmth of the fireplace on my left side as I lean over a book, my knee pressed against Bobby's thigh.

"Of course I remember," I say, the memory leaving me a little breathless.

He nods. "Back then, I thought you were drawn to the sad stuff. I didn't understand why most of the things you read left me feeling so hollow and empty."

I want to argue with him that the poems I loved weren't sad ones. Or, that maybe they were a little sad, but they were also beautiful. Descriptions of the most intense and universal human emotions in flourishing language that made my heart flutter.

"It wasn't until I got older," he continues, "once I thought you'd moved on and I'd resigned myself to live a life missing my most important piece. You." He brushes a thumb along my jaw, and my mouth cracks open to suck in a breath. "That's when I realized that those poems really weren't sad at all. I'd been given a gift. The greatest gift I could have ever asked for. What we had..." he trails off, his eyes going glassy for just a moment before he blinks the emotion away. "I told myself that I was lucky to have ever had you at all. That there are people who never find their soulmate."

Bobby twists us towards the graves, moving me in front of him and wrapping his arms around me as I lean back against his chest. *"And we loved with a love that was more than love..."*

Suddenly, I know exactly where we are.

The sepulchre by the sea.

"I and my Annabel Lee..." I breathe, my hand coming to rest over my thundering heart.

Bobby's eyes brighten as he watches the realization wash across my features.

"I feel like that poem is tattooed on my bones, I've read it so many times. I can see your face as you watched me read it. It haunts my dreams, sometimes."

"For the moon never beams without bringing me dreams of the beautiful Annabel Lee." My voice is just a whisper, the memory of the day I'd showed him that poem washing over my skin and causing goosebumps to bloom all over my body.

Bobby nods. "That's what we had. A love that made the angels envious. And even though we weren't together, I've always felt like we were luckier than Poe."

I lower my brows, not understanding.

Bobby plays with a piece of hair hanging by my shoulders. "They say Annabel Lee died of yellow fever. She was so young. Even if I'd lost you, you were *alive*. Healthy and happy. At least, I thought you were. To hear after all this time that you weren't..." he trails off, his jaw ticking.

I twist in his arms so that I'm facing him. "You're right," I say. "We're far luckier than Poe."

Bobby looks down at me, his brows lowered as if now he's the one not understanding. "Our story doesn't have a tragic ending. We get a second chance. I think Poe would have done anything for that." Bobby lets out a deep exhale, squeezing me tighter.

"Our story. I like the sound of that," he says. We stand in the quiet for a few moments, the air cooling as the sun fully dips below the horizon. "Do you know the rest of the story? What came after the poem?"

I shake my head. "What happened?"

"The universe didn't want them to be together. Even after she was gone, Poe couldn't be with her. Her father didn't approve, and when she died, he dug several plots so Poe wouldn't know where she'd been laid to rest. He couldn't even visit her body."

My heart sinks, grief heavy in my chest. "I think I'm changing my stance. This poem is very, very sad."

"No." Bobby shakes his head. "Having a love like that is beautiful, no matter how long you get to have it for. But there's one more difference between their story and ours."

"What's that? If I die of yellow fever, you'll make sure to find my grave?" I joke.

"I would. But that's not exactly what I mean," he says, his lips tipping downward. "I know what it's like to be without you. I made that mistake once. The difference is, these aren't just words that rhyme to me. I'll never let us be forced apart again. As long as my heart is beating in my chest, I will always, *always* find a way back to you."

It takes me a moment to answer, swallowing down the lump in my throat and blinking back the tears threatening to spill over my lashes. "You won't have to find your way back to me," I finally say. "I'm not going anywhere."

"Promise me," Bobby says, caressing my cheek with his thumb as he tilts my chin to meet his eyes. There's a vulnerability there that makes me pause, and it makes my heart squeeze painfully to see this strong, confident man so tormented.

"I promise," It comes out as nothing more than a breath of air, my throat too choked up to make a sound. "As long as you promise me the same."

"Until I take my final breath, I'm yours. Even after," he says, leaning down to kiss my forehead before tucking my head beneath his chin.

Warmth spreads through my body as I relax into his embrace, and I do everything I can to commit this moment to memory. The sound of the crickets and the slight whistle of the tall grass as the breeze blows across the cemetery. The way Bobby's breath matches mine as we stand wrapped around each other, enjoying the comfortable silence. The strong, rhythmic beat of his heart tapping out a rhythm that makes me want to write down words to match it.

As long as this heart is beating, this man is mine.

A group of tourists round the corner and Bobby sighs, pulling me back toward the main road to call a cab to take us to where the bus is parking for the night, not wanting to be noticed.

"I'm sorry," I say silently to Annabel as I walked away, silently promising to find a way to get the happy ending that was stolen from her.

As we get out of the taxi and approach the buses with the stars twinkling overhead, my heart feels full—my soul finally at peace. I feel lighter than I have in years. That is, until Sam approaches us with clenched fists and lowered eyebrows.

Instantly, Bobby is on alert, pulling me slightly behind him and tucking me against his back. "What's happened?" Bobby asks, peering over Sam's shoulder toward the bus.

"Everything's clear now," Sam says, "but the bus was vandalized while we were gone."

My stomach sinks. "Vandalized?" I ask. Sam sighs, running a hand through his hair. I've never seen him frazzled before, but whatever happened while we were at the cemetery has definitely unsettled him.

"I kept most of the team with you for your outing," Sam starts. "I thought the buses would be fine. I'm sorry, boss. I thought—"

Bobby holds up a hand, stopping him. "You made the call you thought was right. We're safe. Just tell me what happened," he says, stepping to the side so I'm no longer standing behind him.

"The tires were slashed. All of them," Sam says bluntly. "Violently. And it appears like whoever it was wanted to get into the engine. Looks like they used a crowbar to try to pry open the front panel."

A wave of fear washes through my chest.

"No one's hurt, right?" Bobby asks.

"Everyone's fine. But I'm not comfortable with you staying here until we know more. You, *or* your band."

"Agreed. No one drives the buses until they've been checked and we're sure they're safe." He pulls out his phone, tapping out a message. I peek over his shoulder, reading a message to Johnny telling him to have the band pack bags for at least the night.

"I already have someone working on getting rooms for everyone," Sam says. "You and Beth will stay in a different hotel."

My mind reels, trying to keep up, but Bobby just nods. "Is it safe for us to grab some things?"

Sam leads us toward the bus, and it's like time is moving in jolts. First, I'm numb, standing outside, then all of a sudden I'm climbing the stairs, then in the bedroom.

It couldn't be Harrison, could it?

I want to convince myself it's all a big coincidence, desperately, but no matter how hard I try, I can't. Especially not when I shuffle through the nightstand to grab my computer and notice that right on top of my notepad is the silver bracelet from Harrison.

The one I'd tucked into my jewelry box at home before walking downstairs the morning I'd left for the tour.

Nausea fills my throat, trapping a silent scream inside my chest.

There's only one reason the bracelet with Harrison's initials on it could be in the drawer.

Harrison was here, and he wanted me to know it.

To know that no matter what, I belong to him.

To know that no matter what, I belong to him.

NOW

September 2024: Charleston, SC

If your words stop flowing, I will be your rhyme
And if the clock stops ticking, I'll find you the time
Because I am yours, and you, darling, are mine
And you're safe in the arms of someone who loves you
—An excerpt from "Someone Who Loves You," written and performed by
Robert Beckett

The hotel mattress is heavenly, and for the tenth time in the past few hours, I try to decide if I'm going to drag myself out of it to go to Bobby's show.

"Where will Sam be tonight?" I ask as Bobby puts on his watch. He's freshly showered, and the smell of his soap is oddly calming. I breathe it in, willing it to calm the nausea in my stomach.

"Where do you want him to be?" Bobby asks, coming to sit on the mattress. He puts a hand on my leg, and some of my tension eases. His touch says *I've got you,* and even after the trauma of the past few days, I find that I absolutely believe him.

"I don't know," I say, sighing and rolling to face him. I don't realize my fingers are tracing my stitches until Bobby gently takes my hand and kisses it.

"If you don't want to come because you're tired, or need a break, that's fine. I'll keep Sam here with you. But if it's because you're worried about your injuries, don't be. You're as beautiful today as you are every day. They just show how strong you are." He tucks my hair behind my ears. "And as much as I hate to say it, everyone on tour knows what happened. Staying here won't change that."

I nod, trying to stop the tears burning my eyes. I understand Sam had to tell everyone about Harrison's erratic behavior for their own safety, but it doesn't make it easier to swallow that every one of Bobby's employees knows the details of the worst moment of my life.

I consider burrowing deeper beneath the covers, letting Bobby head to the venue and staying here to talk to Molly, but a sliver of fear sneaks between my ribs and wraps around my lungs at the thought.

I don't want to be alone.

Not with Harrison out there somewhere.

"I'm coming," I say, and suddenly, I can't get dressed quickly enough. I brush my hair and teeth, and am just finishing changing my clothes when Sam knocks on the door.

"Car's here, boss," he says through the door.

Bobby takes my hand and doesn't let go. Not while we walk through the parking garage or as we slide into the car. Not on the short drive there, or when we sneak into the back of the venue, the sound of his opening act vibrating through my body.

It's a familiar sensation, a comforting one, and by the time Bobby needs to put in his in-ears, I feel strong enough for him to let go.

The crowd is as wild as ever as Bobby takes the stage, and I pull out my notebook, ready to jot down anything that pops into my brain for my article. Thinking about work gives me something to focus on besides Harrison's threat and the injuries marking my body, and I savor it, focusing on the performance like I haven't seen it over a dozen times in the past month.

About halfway through Bobby's set, Sam appears behind me. I feel his presence before I see him, and the feeling of his eyes on my back makes my palms go sweaty and my stomach flip.

I want to ask what's wrong. What happened to cause the sudden shift in his posture and position, but I don't. The words are stuck in my throat, held down by a layer of ignorance and denial I can't, or won't, break through.

He doesn't say anything as he hovers behind me for the remainder of the show, only stepping away to pull Bobby aside as he exits the stage before his encore. They share a brief exchange, Bobby's eyes flashing to mine, his brows lowering in concern, and my lungs constrict. He points at me, saying something to Sam emphatically before walking back out on stage.

Seeing Bobby's reaction sets my entire body on edge. "What is it?" I say when Sam resumes his spot just behind me, my voice coming out thin and shaky. Sam looks off to the side, then clears his throat.

"I'm not sure I should—"

"Sam. Tell me what's going on," I demand.

With a deep exhale, Sam lifts his gaze and turns to face me. "Venue security caught Harrison trying to get in tonight. At least, they think it was him. He purchased VIP tickets off a resale website."

My blood runs cold.

He's here.

My mouth cracks open, but in shock or horror, I'm not sure. Showing up at the venue—one filled with security— is calculated. Unhinged. It shows planning and foresight, and even worse, a lack of fear. And that absolutely terrifies me.

"They initially stopped him because he was drunk," Sam continues, "and when they asked to verify his identity, he ran." Bubbles of nausea form in my stomach. Once again, I feel stupid. Foolish. But after everything that's happened, I can't be surprised by Harrison's actions anymore.

"I've made arrangements for you and Bobby to stay in a different hotel under new aliases. I've been doing this a long time, ma'am, and I don't have a good feeling about this," Sam says, shaking his head.

"Okay," Panic creeps deeper into my chest, and I force myself to take slow, even breaths. "Okay. Do you think someone could get my things? Just a change of clothes?"

"Already done. I think it's best you leave immediately once Bobby finishes. It will minimize Harrison's chances of figuring out where you are."

Normally I'd argue, but something doesn't feel right. There's an uneasiness in my stomach that tells me we need to get away from here before something terrible happens, so I nod, confirming that I'll be ready to leave once Bobby's done. Sam takes a step back and dips his head to speak into his earpiece again.

Bobby only plays one song for his encore tonight, and even that feels a little forced. It's obvious he wants to get off the stage and get me somewhere safer, and I don't disagree. Knowing that Harrison was here somewhere trying to find either Bobby, or myself, makes my blood run cold.

I don't have to tell Bobby that Sam suggested we leave immediately.

"Let's go," he says as soon as he walks off stage, handing his guitar over and putting a protective arm around my shoulders.

Sam hands Bobby a bag. "Take the west exit. A car is waiting for you. There's a disturbance at the east concord I'm going to go check out. With any luck, we'll catch him there, and I'll meet you at the hotel."

My stomach swirls with nerves as we hurry through the back halls of the venue, stopping when we come upon a nondescript door, and Bobby pushes it open, peeking his head through before pulling us outside.

A black SUV is waiting for us, and I breathe a little easier. The driver gets out and opens my door, and I slide in quickly, keeping my head down. "I'll take it from here," Bobby says, and the driver pauses. He looks nervous, his brow glistening with sweat and his eyes darting around. "But Sam said—"

"I know what Sam told you. But if someone's after Beth, then no one will be driving her but me. Tell Sam I insisted. I'll take the blame."

The driver looks like he wants to argue, but Bobby clears his throat, holding his hand out for the keys.

"Yes, sir," the driver hands them over and slips inside the door to the venue, likely to tell Sam exactly where Bobby is and that it's not his fault he's not the one driving us to the hotel.

Bobby locks the doors as soon as we get in, then looks in the rearview and side mirrors, making sure we're alone.

"This feels a little dramatic, doesn't it?" I joke, trying to lighten the mood. But really, his nerves seem appropriate, and the reminders of why are all over my body. Maybe we're worrying for nothing.

But maybe we're not.

I'll kill you, for this.

His parting threat circles through my mind, and I shiver.

"Let's go, please," I say, buckling my seatbelt. I slide the shoulder strap around my back as I lean down to grab my phone from my purse.

Bobby checks the mirrors once more, then puts the car into drive. The relief I feel once we're moving is almost instant.

Bobby's jaw stays clenched tight. He squeezes the steering wheel, his eyes darting around nervously.

As Bobby pulls the car onto the interstate, I shuffle through the stations on the radio, trying to find something calm and serene to help slow my heart rate, but nothing helps. I don't think I'll feel safe until we're behind a locked door at the hotel.

Bobby changes lanes a few times, shifting in his seat as he glances in his rearview mirror repeatedly.

"Bobby, it's fine—" I start, but as I look up at him and his white-knuckle grip, I pause.

"Someone's following us." Bobby says quietly, as if trying to keep whoever it is from hearing him.

"What?" I twist in my seat to look, but Bobby pushes me back down.

"Stay down," he orders as he presses the accelerator, so instead, I lean over to look in the side mirror. Bobby changes lanes, and sure enough, the car behind us does as well.

"What do we do?" my voice comes out high pitched, hysterical, and I take a deep breath. The car appears to be black, but it's impossible to see through the windshield, though I can make out a vague outline behind the driver's side. Whoever it is swerves back and forth, and is driving so close, I can't even see the car's headlights. A lump of fear works its way up my throat.

Bobby pulls the shoulder strap from where I'd moved it behind me back across my chest, using one hand to make sure the belt is tight. He looks at me out of the corner of his eye. "Get Sam on speakerphone," he says, unwilling to take his hands off the steering wheel again as he maneuvers around a minivan in front of us.

I do exactly as he says, my hands shaking as I grab his phone and press Sam's name in his contact list. Sam answers on the first ring. "Bobby, why the hell didn't you let Phil drive you?"

Bobby ignores him. "There's a black sedan following us. Did you get Harrison?"

"It was a false alarm. Someone discharged a fire extinguisher, but they were gone when I got there. What do you mean someone's following you?" Sam's voice is sharp, and I picture him pacing. A car door slams on the other end of the phone.

Bobby's knuckles go impossibly whiter on the steering wheel. "I noticed them when I pulled onto the main street from the venue. They followed me on the interstate and every move since. He's driving erratically. Right on my tail."

The car behind us swerves to the right, but I can't tell if he's trying to pass us on the shoulder or simply losing control of the vehicle. The sound of metal on metal crunches from behind us as our car lurches forward, and I cling desperately to the armrest, my fingernails making imprints in the leather.

"Shit! He's ramming us from behind," Bobby tells Sam as the car jerks violently to the right. I let out a hiss of pain as my injured elbow slams against the side of the door.

"Shit!" Bobby yells again, looking in the rearview. "Sam, he's trying to run us off the road." The car slams into us again, and I hold in a scream. Bobby presses his foot to the accelerator, speeding up and merging between cars to change lanes, but there aren't enough people on the road to put space between us and the car trying to kill us. He's behind us again in a second, and Bobby slams his hands on the steering wheel. "Sam!"

"Phil followed after you left. He's coming up behind you, and the police are on their way," Sam says with forced calm.

"They'll be too late," Bobby snaps, "He's going to ram us off the damn road!"

Bobby's terror is palpable, and it amplifies my own. It's hard to breathe. Hard to even think.

"Take the first exit you see," Sam orders. "If he seems like he's trying to make you crash, you need to be going at a slower speed. You're more likely to lose him on back roads than the highway."

By some miracle, an exit appears in front of us and a sob of relief bursts from my throat. Bobby gets in the left lane to speed up, then cuts across both lanes to take the exit ramp. He waits until the last second, so long it's almost too late to clear the guardrail, but it doesn't matter. The black sedan follows, its tires squealing as the back of the car fishtails.

"Dammit," Bobby hisses under his breath. The sedan speeds up, moving onto the shoulder again.

Bobby hits the gas, but the sedan is faster, flying forward and cutting in front of us. Bobby hits the breaks and swerves to the left, our tires squealing as they try to find purchase on the road.

It's too late. We crash head on into the sedan, the horrible groan of metal collapsing in on itself and the clang of glass shattering making my ears bleed.

It's said by those who survive that time slows when you think you're going to die.

That's only partly true.

As our tires squeal and the metal frame of the car crunches in a deafening roar, I process *everything*.

Each second feels like thirty as pieces of glass fly around my head like glittering, lethal diamonds. I'm thrown back into my seat, all too aware of the searing agony of the bones in my nose snapping beneath the airbag. The sharp bite of pain when my seat belt catches, cutting into my skin as it tightens across my chest and collarbone.

My stomach lurches, and suddenly we're upside down, then upright again, then upside down. Rolling and rolling, orange and yellow sparks exploding brighter than fireworks on New Year's Eve as the top of the car is ripped apart by the asphalt.

The smell of gasoline and burning rubber makes my head swim, and the metallic tang of blood dripping from my nose into my mouth almost makes me vomit.

My whole life flashes before my eyes. My parents' disappointment. Molly's grief. Birthdays and graduations and late nights writing poetry beneath my covers. The sloping lines of the words gifted to me—the ones I've kept tucked close to my heart.

Harrison's poems.

Bobby's lyrics.

Someone cries out my name—a deep, desperate prayer.

An anguished, broken plea.

I'm aware of every miniscule detail as time slows to a nearly stagnant pace. And yet, I don't even have time to scream as my head smashes into the side window, and the world goes dark.

NOW

September 2024: Charleston, SC

I'm visiting Michael.

The distinctive scent of hospital disinfectant fills my nostrils, and I hear the steady beeping of monitors. I've been to see him hundreds of times, except—I wince, my head suddenly throbbing. I squint against a bright light behind my eyelids, but my eyes won't open.

My head swims, and I feel the sudden urge to vomit. But... that doesn't make sense, I'm just visiting Michael.

"Beth?" someone says. A voice I don't recognize. A warm hand touches my shoulder. "Wake up, honey."

I try to move, and the monitors beep faster. The uncomfortable bed creaks beneath me as I shift. Something's wrong. I'm not visiting Michael. Michael died years ago. I remember now.

Before Harrison hurt me.

Before he tried to run Bobby and me off the road.

Bobby. I start to panic, and now the monitors are alarming.

"Give her a dose of morphine," the same voice orders. "Beth. Open your eyes for me."

Bobby. The memory of him shouting my name as the car flipped and rolled gives me the strength I need to pry my eyelids open. I try to speak, but my voice comes out as a croak. My throat is horribly dry and scratchy, and it hurts to swallow.

Someone puts a straw into my mouth, a doctor, based on her white coat. "Small sips," she says, then pulls the cup away when I don't listen.

"Is he okay?" I whisper. It's all I can think about as the memory of the crash repeats like a loop in my mind. We were rolling and rolling, and glass was shattering, and the airbags…

"Let's talk about you first, okay? I'm Dr. Mulder. I was the one who did your surgery," the doctor says. She looks too young to be a surgeon, with unruly, curly blonde hair tied in a high ponytail. The only lines on her face are ones of exhaustion, and I wonder how old she is.

"Surgery?" I ask, my throat only feeling slightly better.

"You fractured your femur in the accident. We had to put in a metal rod, as well as an external fixator." She peels the bedding back to reveal a giant metal cage around my upper leg with screws going through my skin. "Your nerve block hasn't worn off yet, but you'll be sore later. You fractured a few ribs and had a pretty nasty contusion on your head, but by all accounts, you're lucky you survived."

I shake my head, trying to get past the fuzziness in my brain from the anesthesia and morphine. "Can I see him?"

Dr. Mulder's lips tip down, and the room suddenly feels so much smaller. "Your nurse can take you to his room in a few hours, once we're sure your pain is under control, and you've gotten some rest."

My relief is so strong, it rips the air from my lungs. "He's alive?"

Dr. Mulder and the nurse share a look. "He's alive. But Beth, your husband sustained significant injuries in the crash."

Husband? The word registers, but I move past it. If the only way I can get information is to let them think Bobby and I are married, I'm not going to correct them. "I don't understand." I shake my head. "Is he going to be okay?"

Dr. Mulder sighs, and she takes my hand. "We're not sure. We're still in the early stages of testing, but our preliminary findings weren't reassuring. I'm so sorry."

My heart is racing, and my vision goes black at the edges, my breaths coming in short gasps. I can't speak, even though I want to scream and sob and argue. Maybe I'm in shock. Or dreaming. I *have* to be dreaming. Because this isn't possible. I refuse to believe Bobby and I found each other again only for him to be taken away so soon.

"Try to breathe in through your nose and out through your mouth. We're doing everything we can for him," Dr. Mulder says. "I need to ask you a few questions about your other injuries. It appears you already had a black eye and stitches upon arrival. The man you were in the car with, is he responsible?"

"What? No, of course not." I struggle to sit up, hoping it will give my lungs more room to expand, but the pain is too severe. "It was the other driver. Harrison."

"Your husband did this to you?" she asks, her eyebrows lowering.

"Fiancé. Well…ex-fiancé, but yes."

"I'm sorry. Your driver's licenses had the same address, and you're listed as Harrison Rouchester's emergency contact in his advanced care directive. We assumed he was your husband."

"He has an advanced care directive?" My head is swimming, my brain moving too slowly to keep up.

"It's not uncommon for lawyers. Paramedics found his business card in his wallet, and his firm sent it over to us. So you are no longer in a relationship with Mr. Rouchester. Is that what you're saying?"

"No, I'm not. But that doesn't mean… You're saying he could die?" I ask, my forehead throbbing so badly I wince, and my nurse switches off the overhead lights for me.

"It's possible, but we don't have enough information to know yet. You're his health care proxy, so unless you say otherwise, we will follow the directive. Per his advanced care directive, he wants all possible treatments."

I nod my head absently, overwhelmed. "That sounds like him," I say, almost numb. Dr. Mulder places a hand over mine, her gaze flicking to my stitched brow.

"Would you still like to see him?" Dr. Mulder's eyes are clear, but I see the humanity there. I don't sense that I will get any judgment regardless of my answer.

"I don't know." I shake my head, still feeling fuzzy. "I—I shouldn't be his proxy. Not with what happened. Can it be changed? To his parents?"

Dr. Mulder assesses me, evaluating the older, already yellowing bruises *not* from the car accident. "I'll need it in writing. But yes, you can refuse."

I nod, swallowing down the lump of grief in my throat threatening to choke me, and a small wave of relief soothes the rising panic enough to allow my mind to kick back into focus. "What about Bobby? Can you tell me how he is?"

Dr. Mulder gives me a sad, regretful smile. "I'm afraid I can't. I can only give information on his condition to immediate family. But his mother is here. I'll let her know you're asking after him."

His mother is here. Does that mean he's alive? Or did they call her because someone has to make the same decisions for him as I'm supposed to for Harrison?

The shock wears off all at once, like ripping off a bandage. Suddenly, I can't stop shaking, and sobs pour out of me in violent waves.

"Please, get her for me. Please," I beg, but my tears are so thick in my throat I'm not sure she understands me.

"You *will* be okay, Beth." Dr. Mulder sounds more like a friend than a surgeon. "You survived this accident. Maybe even worse." She pats my hand. "I'll let your friend's mother know you'd like her to visit, and I'll be back tomorrow to check your incisions. In the meantime, is there anyone we can call for you? Your parents, maybe?"

I shake my head through my tears. "No. Um… My friend. Molly," I say, grateful I won't have to be the one to tell her about the accident.

I'm not sure I could handle the worry I'd hear in her voice, and I'm all too close to falling apart completely as it is.

I give the nurse, who introduces herself as Crystal, Molly's number. "Please, ask her to hurry," I say, my eyes growing heavy as I fade back into the darkness.

NOW

September 2024: Charleston SC

I want adventure to be remembered
Hold onto truths instead of lies
And a love that makes the angels weep
I want to feel that, before I die
—An excerpt from "Poetry," written by Beth Winters, performed by Robert
Beckett

"Let me in that room right now. Or I'll call my lawyer. She's my *sister*. Legally, I can see her." Molly's voice wakes me up from a restless sleep.

Crystal is standing in front of my door, her arms crossed in front of her. "Miss. Winters is resting. I suggest you let her, or I *will* call security."

I clear my throat, still so thirsty. "It's okay. I'm awake," I croak.

"Hmmph," Crystal says, turning to check on me. She strides over to the bed and pulls out her stethoscope, listening to my heart and lungs as Molly rushes in.

"Thank God you're okay. What the hell happened?" Molly says, wasting no time getting straight to the point.

"Have you seen Bobby? Is he okay?" I ask, scrambling to try and sit. I cry out in pain as agony sears through my ribs and the external fixator on my leg snags on the sheets.

"Slow down," Crystal scolds. "Your friend's mother came to talk to you, but you were asleep. Probably the morphine."

Crystal helps me into a sitting position, then adjusts my blood pressure cuff. Molly presses her lips together, waiting for Crystal to finish.

"I want to be very clear." Crystal turns to Molly, her tight, black ponytail accentuating her severe features, making her look especially stern. "Beth is my patient, and her well-being is my responsibility. I will be watching that monitor," she points to the screen where my heart rate and oxygen readings track across the screen, "and if I see any indication you're working her up, I'll withdraw visitation rights. Got it?"

"Yes ma'am." Molly salutes her. She moves to sit on the edge of my bed but stops when Crystal scowls. "I won't upset her. I promise. We'll just pray and watch cartoons. No. Not cartoons. That coyote is stressful. We'll meditate instead." Molly smiles broadly, and I almost laugh. But my ribs hurt too much, and I'm too worried about Bobby. And even though I hate to admit it, I'm sad about Harrison.

Crystal gives her a look that makes me think she'll be kicking her out in a few minutes, regardless of what that monitor shows.

"Thank you," I say.

"Press that call light if you need anything," she reminds me before narrowing her eyes at Molly and leaving the room.

"Bobby's okay? You spoke with his mom?" I say, wasting no time once Crystal is gone.

Molly grabs my hand. "He's in and out. How are you feeling?"

"I'm fine. Molly, what do you mean?" Usually, I can read her easily, but she's not quite looking me in the eye. It makes my lungs constrict, panic fluttering through my blood with every heartbeat.

She pulls out her phone. "I took notes, but I still don't quite understand what the doctor was saying." Once she has her notes app open, she grabs my hand, finally meeting my eyes. "Are you sure you can handle this? It's not good news, Beth…"

A sob tries to break free from my throat, but I hold it in, taking deep breaths. I'll be damned if I let that monitor go off before I know what's happening.

"Okay," Molly tilts her head, studying me for a second before continuing with a reassuring squeeze. "The paramedics said Bobby was partially ejected from the car. His sternum was crushed, and a shard from the windshield penetrated his chest into his heart."

I gasp, nausea surging up my throat, and the monitor's beeping picks up in rhythm. In less than a second, Crystal is there, standing in the doorway. "I told you—"

"Please," I say, my voice breaking. "I have to know."

Crystal takes a deep breath, but when she looks at me, her eyes are soft and kind. "Five minutes. If your heart rate doesn't slow in five minutes, I'm going to insist you rest."

"I'll hurry," Molly says, and suddenly, they seem to be on the same page.

I nod at Molly to continue, expecting Crystal to leave. But instead, she steps just inside the room and leans against the wall.

"Umm…" Molly says, flustered. "He was hemorrhaging into his chest wall and pericardial sac?"

"Bleeding into the tissues that protect the heart," Crystal says, nodding for Molly to continue.

Molly gives her a small smile of thanks. "It caused a cardiac tamponade…"

"The heart was compressed by the blood in the sac," Crystal clarifies.

"Yes, and he went into cardiogenic shock. Which is abrupt heart failure? Right?" Molly asks.

"Right," Crystal says. "It causes cardiac arrest."

Molly nods. "I have that right here. He went into cardiac arrest and was taken directly to the OR where the blood was drained from around his heart, and he had a massive transfusion protocol."

Crystal nods but doesn't add anything.

"He was unstable when he got to the ICU, and shortly after arriving, went into cardiac arrest again, and his heart completely failed despite max vasopressor therapy."

Crystal is nodding, confirming without saying so that Molly's notes are correct. "Vasopressors raise blood pressure to get blood to your organs."

"Surgeons were consulted immediately for ECMO cannulation and placed Bobby on the transplant list as status one."

Crystal walks forward to sit on my bed, and suddenly, it's like she and Molly are on the same team. "It's the most urgent designation for transplants. ECMO essentially pumps the blood through the body through a big machine, oxygenating it. It's not a long-term solution."

I'm still breathing slowly, in through my nose and out through my mouth. Everything feels fuzzy, and I consider pinching myself to see if I can wake up. "So, he needs a heart transplant."

Molly nods, her lower lip trembling. "I'm sorry, Beth."

"Can I see him?" I ask Crystal, letting her see the full extent of my pain. It's a mistake. The second I let my guard down, I can't pull it back up. I start to sob, then sob even harder because the way my chest heaves makes my ribs burn with agony. My head hurts, and my heart hurts, and then my oxygen drops, the monitor beeping so loud it makes my headache grow.

"Off the bed," Crystal orders Molly, who jumps up without hesitation. "You need to breathe, Beth. You can see him. But not until you calm down. I can't take you off the monitor, even just for a visit, until you're stable."

But I can't stop the panic. My head swims, my vision blurring.

"You're going to be okay," she says, pulling a syringe and vial from her cart. "This will help with anxiety. Let you sleep a little. Okay?"

I nod, because I'm desperate for an escape from this agony I'm feeling, both physical and emotional. A shard of glass punctured Bobby's heart. He coded more than once. He died, and was brought back, and could die again if he doesn't get a new heart.

Whatever medicine she puts into my IV is cold, but its calming effect is immediate.

"I'll be right here," Molly says as my eyelids grow heavy. "I won't leave you."

But I wouldn't know if she did. The world fades until there's nothing but darkness, and I let it cover me like a blanket until there is nothing at all.

NOW

September 2024: Charleston, SC

"She's going to be okay."

It takes me a second to place the voice in my pain medicine and sleep haze. It's Johnny, but I've never heard him sound like this. So broken and small and vulnerable. I crack open my eyes, trying to keep still so I don't interrupt their conversation.

"Not if Bobby doesn't make it through this," Molly says, her voice just as tiny and broken. "She won't survive losing him a second time. You didn't see her when they broke up. It took years before she was even a shell of herself again."

Johnny's head has been resting in his hands, but he looks up at Molly's words. "Are you joking? Bobby *never* recovered. I haven't seen him anywhere near happy until the last couple of months. If she'd just answered the damn phone. If *you'd* just answered the damn phone, we wouldn't be in this situation."

"I'm not going to have this argument with you again," Molly rubs her forehead, sighing.

Again? Have they had this conversation before?

I wonder if I'm still sleeping. If maybe this is a dream, because as far as I know, Johnny and Molly have always just been casual acquaintances.

Johnny runs a hand down his face, collapsing backward in the chair. "You're right. I'm sorry. It's just—" he presses his lips together, but his expression is hidden in the darkness. "What's the point of it all? Life is so senseless and cruel."

Molly stays silent. I know she's thinking of Michael, and I wish I could get up and go to her, wrap her in my arms and make sure she knows she's not alone. I hear her sniffle, and I almost speak up, but I stop when Johnny kneels in front of her and does what I wish I could as he pulls her into a tight hug. His hand smoothes her hair as she starts to sob, and tears gather in my own eyes, but still, I don't move. Whatever this is, they need it.

"I'm sorry. I should be the one comforting you. What you've been through is so much worse—"

"Stop that," he interrupts her. "There's no *worse* when it comes to grief. Losing someone changes you. It doesn't matter who it is."

Molly nods into his shoulder. "I still think about him every day. And when I got the call that Beth was in the hospital…"

"Shhhh," Johnny soothes. "They're both going to be okay."

"Do you really think so? That Bobby can survive this?" Molly pulls back, searching Johnny's eyes, and the moment is so intimate, I have to look away.

The door to my room cracks open, my CNA Hannah knocking gently as she pulls the blood pressure machine in. "Sorry," she whispers. "It's time for vitals, then I'll let you get back to sleep."

Molly narrows her eyes at me as I pretend to wake up, yawning exaggeratedly and feigning confusion. "What? What time is it?" I ask, continuing to play dumb, but Molly's guarded posture tells me I'm not fooling her.

"A little past midnight," Hannah says, wrapping the cuff snugly around my bicep. "I'll be out of your hair in just a moment, promise."

Johnny stands, brushing off his pants. "I'm going to head back to the bus. Just wanted to check on you, Bethy." He leans over my bed and presses a kiss to my cheek, something he used to do to annoy Bobby, and it makes my heart swell and shatter all at once.

"Get some rest, and make that one rest, too," he says in my ear. "She won't admit it, but she's exhausted."

Hannah finishes with my vitals and Johnny follows her out of the room, leaving Molly and me alone. I don't miss the way her eyes linger on the doorway once he's gone.

"Here. Help me scoot over," I say, shuffling to the side of my bed toward the rail. Molly hops up, moving the pillow supporting my leg. I pat the bed beside me, and she climbs in, curling up against my side.

"You're a terrible liar," she says, but there's no anger in her voice. "I can't believe you were eavesdropping."

"I would never do such a thing," I say. "But if I *did* hear, I might be wondering what you guys were talking about."

Molly grabs my hand. "It was nothing. I'm just worried about you. And I can't help but feel responsible."

"What?" I try to twist toward her, sending a stab of pain through my thigh.

Molly's lip trembles, and she takes a deep breath. "I hate Harrison. I've never liked him."

"It's not your fault. You told me—"

"I know I said you could do better. That you shouldn't marry him. But I should have made you hear me."

I shake my head. "I should have known on my own. I should have been stronger."

Molly exhales deeply. "If you're not going to let me blame myself, I'm not letting you, either. Harrison did this." We sit in silence for a bit, the mood heavy. I long for sleep, for the escape it gives me from my grief and terror.

"I can't lose him, Molly," I whisper, breaking the silence. "He can't die." Tears prick my eyes, my lungs struggling to fully expand.

"He's your soulmate, Beth. I just have to believe that the universe isn't so cruel it would take him away again so soon," Molly says, pushing the button to recline the bed a little more, as if sensing my need for rest.

I say a silent prayer that she's right and tag one on that she'll find her own happiness, too. I think after everything we've gone through, we deserve a bit of peace.

"You're wrong you know," I say, my eyelids growing heavier, and I lean my head against Molly's, letting them close. "Bobby is the love of my life. But *you* are my soulmate."

NOW

September 2024: Charleston, SC

I thought I was prepared to see Bobby. Hoped that by some miracle, I'd look at him and realize it was all a dream, or maybe that Molly and Crystal had been wrong. That he was just broken and bruised like me.

But nothing could have prepared me for what I see when they wheel me into Bobby's room. He's sedated, a tube down his throat and several IV poles with what feels like dozens of different medications and lines attached to them. At the head of the bed is an enormous machine with two thick tubes, each about the diameter of a quarter, and they're full of blood.

"Ten minutes, Beth," Crystal says. "I could get in a lot of trouble for letting you in here," she says. Technically, it's not visiting hours, and as Bobby's in the ICU, and I'm not family, I'm not supposed to be in here.

But the accident was two days ago, and my surgeon finally gave me the okay to transfer to a wheelchair and leave my room. It had been hell getting upright with my broken ribs and fixator. Even worse, when the physical therapist came to teach me how to transfer safely with a walker to my wheelchair. I'd needed a lot of help, and there were a lot of tears, but it didn't matter.

Nothing was going to stop me from seeing Bobby.

He looks like he's in pain, his forehead creased and his lips tipped into a frown, and I take several deep breaths to keep myself from breaking down. He's in there. And I won't make things harder for him by falling apart.

His face is pale and covered in bruises. He looks so big lying in the bed, but so helpless. It's alarming how much he doesn't look like himself, and I try to ignore the tubes and tape and wires. The way his sheet is pulled up to cover his chest.

When I'm as close to the bed as possible, Crystal locks the brakes on my wheelchair. "I'll step out and give you some privacy. But I mean what I said. You have ten minutes, and then I have to bring you back to your room."

I nod, my eyes prickling with tears. I never want to leave. "I understand. Thank you, Crystal," I say, reaching forward and grabbing Bobby's hand. His fingers are cold, startlingly so, and I squeeze tighter, hoping some of my warmth will seep into his skin.

"I'm here," I say as Crystal slides the door closed. The click of the ventilator and beeping of the monitors become background noise as I rub circles on the back of his hand with my thumb. "Listen to me. You need to hold on. You need to fight. Because you promised we would have our time, and we haven't yet. I want forever with you, Bobby Beckett."

I choke on a sob, forcing it down as I lay my forehead on his hand. I wish I didn't have this cage on my leg so I could climb next to him and curl into his side. I'd stay there until his new heart was beating in his chest and he opened his eyes, searching for me.

"He wants that with you, too," someone says from the doorway, and I sniffle, trying to hide my tears as I wipe my eyes with the back of my hand. I turn around as a woman from my past walks to the other side of Bobby's bed, grabbing his other hand.

Bobby's mom doesn't look like she's aged a day, and just like the first time I saw her, I'm taken aback by her striking resemblance to Bobby. They have the same blue eyes, clear and bright and deep. Their hair is a similar shade of brown, and when she gives me a sad smile, the sight of the dimple in her right cheek takes my breath away.

"I'm glad you're back, Beth." Her eyes are warm, but nerves still flutter in my stomach. Surely, she knows the truth about our past.

Does she hate me for my part in it all?

"Me too." I look back at Bobby, squeezing his hand. I only have a few minutes left.

The door slides open, and an unfamiliar nurse walks in, her eyes narrowing in suspicion as she looks me up and down. "I'm sorry, it's immediate family, only."

Kimberly straightens. "Absolutely not. She stays as long as she wants to," she says, walking around the bed.

"Ma'am, I'm sorry, but it's hospital policy. Immediate family only in the ICU."

Kimberly's eyes are tired as she reaches down and pushes the hair from Bobby's eyes. "It isn't blood that makes someone family. If my son is clinging to life, if he's going to make it through this horrible, painful ordeal, it's only so he can make his way back to *her*." She lifts her chin, daring the nurse to argue.

The nurse's nostrils flare as she takes a deep breath, but she nods, leaving without another word.

I can't see Kimberly through the tears in my eyes. "Thank you," I whisper, my voice breaking.

She looks back at Bobby. "He'd kill me if I let them kick you out. You should be here just as much as I should. You're the love of his life." She smiles softly, her dimple softening the pain clinging to the lines of her face.

What I wouldn't do to see that dimple appear in Bobby's cheek.

My throat feels tight and scratchy, choked with tears and things I wish I could say, and I cough, trying to clear it. "He's mine, too. We just lost each other for a while."

She sighs, her dimple disappearing. Kimberly finally pulls her gaze away from Bobby and meets my eyes. "I know Bobby thinks I regret giving up my career for his father. But I don't. I should've done a better job reminding him that I would've given up anything for my husband. *Anything*."

There's a fervor to her voice that causes chill bumps to break out on my arms. "It was a choice I made freely and happily. Choosing him was the best decision of my life. Because it gave me *years* of true love and happiness, and it brought me Bobby." She looks back to her son, placing a hand on his cheek. "But that's hindsight, right? We all just do the best we can, and one day we look back and realize the choices we made changed the entire trajectory of our lives. For better or worse."

"Maybe it was supposed to happen the way it did. Maybe Bobby would've never achieved what he has if he'd been tied down to me. I'd like to say I believe in fate. But this?" I squeeze Bobby's hand. "*This* wasn't supposed to happen. We're supposed to have more time."

The sad smile Kimberly gives me tells me she knows exactly what I'm feeling. She lost her husband, the love of *her* life.

"The doctors have assured me they're doing all they can to find him a heart. He has a common blood type. That should help, and—"

It happens in less than an instant. Bobby's monitors start beeping wildly, the line for his heart rate going flat. Several nurses I don't know rush in, followed by Crystal. They lower the head of his bed all the way, and he disappears behind a wall of people.

Crystal wheels me toward the door as another nurse urges Kimberly behind me. "Bobby!" I scream, twisting in my chair to try to see him. "Please take me back," I beg. Even knowing there's nothing I can do, I need to be with him. I don't want him to be afraid. Alone.

Crystal doesn't even flinch. "We have to let them do their job. And to do that, they need us out of the way." She parks me at the end of the hallway, urging me to take deep breaths, but I barely hear her.

Bobby's heart may be the one that stopped beating, but I feel like mine is giving out as pain erupts behind my sternum. "He can't die," I beg. "Please," I pray. To God. To the universe. To whoever will listen. "Please don't let him die."

I was discharged this morning, but I haven't left the hospital. I can't when Bobby's heart actually stopped just one day ago.

Two and a half minutes. That's how long Bobby's heart stopped beating before they were able to get it working again. Two and a half minutes that felt like two and a half hours, holding my breath and praying until Crystal told me they had a heart rhythm.

A weak one, but it was there.

I try to stay strong when the doctors tell us they don't know if Bobby's body can handle another event, but all that does is make it harder to breathe. It feels like I finally woke up after years of living a monotonous half-life just to have it ripped away moments later, like the universe is playing a cruel joke on me for the sins of my past.

Exhaustion pulls at my skin, but it's not enough to convince me to rest. Not when Bobby's life hangs in the balance.

But it's not just my body that can't rest. My mind is restless, too. I want to close that chapter of my life with Harrison completely, but I don't think I can without seeing him at least once.

It's a strange feeling, having him in the same hospital as me, lying in a bed two floors up, still unconscious, according to Crystal. Even stranger that my heart can't seem to sort out how it feels.

I have so much anger toward him over what he did to me, for causing the accident and putting Bobby's life in danger. But I also feel a little sad. I desperately wish it wasn't the case, but part of me still mourns for the person I once thought Harrison was. The man I thought I loved. That I was going to marry.

We spent years together, and most of those years were filled with good memories. It doesn't excuse his violence, but it does make it hard to leave the hospital without saying goodbye.

Which is why I find myself being wheeled to his room before Molly takes me to the Airbnb she rented for us while I recover, with the promise that she'll stay with me as long as I need.

Seeing Harrison is no less shocking than it was seeing Bobby, but in a different way. There's only a ventilator connected to a tube down his throat, his IV, and a few small bandages on his face and arm. A larger one wraps around his head.

Molly wheels me next to the head of his bed with ease, the area completely empty compared to the ECMO and dozens of tubes and wires that make getting close to Bobby so difficult.

Harrison's parents aren't here when I arrive, and I'm grateful. I don't need to see them or argue over whose fault this is. I don't need to discuss what happened.

I'm here to say goodbye to Harrison.

And I'm here to say goodbye to that chapter of my life.

Regardless of what he did to me, I really did love him once. Before he wore me down. Before work became everything to him.

Even if loving him had been misguided.

Even if our love had just been some sort of life raft to save me from drowning after Bobby and I broke up.

Even if loving him had nearly killed me, it didn't change the fact that I *had* loved him.

And it doesn't change the fact that I hope he doesn't die.

I lock my wheelchair in place, but I can't bring myself to grab Harrison's hand.

"If you're in there or if you know what's going on, um… It's Beth," I say. It's awkward talking to him, but I have words that need to be released from my body, so I continue. "Honestly, I'm not sure *you* even know what you did. I don't understand it. I'm sorry I wasn't honest with you," I say, needing to get the apology off my chest for my own healing.

Nothing could absolve him of what he did to me, but I don't want to be the kind of person who hides the truth from the people they love, either.

I pause, my chin trembling as I fight back tears. "I needed to say that this is goodbye for me. And that no matter what happens, I hope you can find peace. And. Well… That I forgive you."

I'm not sure if what I'm saying is true—if forgiving him is even possible, or if he could ever deserve it—but I also know that a healthy, happy man doesn't beat his fiancée or try to run her off the road. Maybe Harrison was fighting demons I never knew about.

Once again, it's not an excuse.

Just reality.

I may never forgive him for his violence, for not being able to control his anger. But for my own closure, I need him to hear that I do, in case someday, it somehow becomes the truth.

I'm done with leaving things unsaid.

"Goodbye, Harrison." My voice cracks. "Maybe you'll get another chance. I hope you do," I say, looking at him one last time before wheeling myself out of his room and closing that chapter of my life forever.

NOW

September 2024: Charleston, SC

I want a tale that the choirs will sing
Epics to be read again and again
I want a love like the ones written and spoken and sung
A love like in poetry written by the dead
—An excerpt from "Poetry," written by Beth Winters, performed by Robert Beckett

As I sit at Bobby's bedside this afternoon, I don't stop working on my novel.

I *can't*.

I know it's irrational, but the need to finish it, to get our happy ending down on paper, is as hot and fervent as a wildfire.

Maybe I can write it into existence—Bobby getting a heart, him and I living happily ever after.

I shift, switching hands as I shake out my tingling arm. I've been typing with one hand, refusing to let go of Bobby. Both Kimberly and I snap upright at a sudden commotion in the hallway. The door to Bobby's room slides open, and my heart pounds in my throat as a nurse walks in, maneuvering around me to listen to his lungs.

"Your friend here is about to get very popular," the nurse says, switching the stethoscope to the other side of his chest.

The nurse's words don't have time to register before an entire team of people file in, immediately pulling down the sheet and disconnecting lines.

I roll myself back to let them do their job. "What's happening?" I ask, my voice shaking, terrified to ask the question desperately trying to escape my lips. The only time I've seen this amount of activity in Bobby's room was when he coded, but the line on the monitor remains jagged, peaks and valleys beeping every so often to remind us that his heart is still beating.

"Wait. Does this mean…" I can't even think it.

"We have a heart," the surgeon says as he strides in, pulling out his own stethoscope and listening to Bobby's lungs.

"We have a heart?" Kimberly's voice cracks, and she walks over to me, clasping my hands in hers. We cling to each other, desperately waiting to hear those words again. The surgeon is silent for a moment as he moves the stethoscope around Bobby's chest.

"We have a heart," the surgeon confirms as he stands back up, grabbing Bobby's chart.

For the entirety of this week, I've done my best to hold it together. For Bobby's sake. Just in case he could hear me. But hearing that Bobby will get his transplant in time shatters me completely. A sob breaks free from my chest, and my head falls into my shaking hands.

Bobby's getting a heart.

It's a miracle, and I promise myself that if Bobby makes it through this surgery, I will never let a misunderstanding break us again. I will spend the rest of my life earning his love, just as I know he will do the same. Because a love this big is a precious gift, one we've almost lost twice now.

"We need to prep him," the surgeon says, speaking to Kimberly. "The sooner we can do the transplant, the better the outcome will be. We're not out of the woods yet," he reminds us. "His body has suffered quite a bit of damage. We'll be bringing him back to pre-op in just a moment. Say your goodbyes." The doctor turns to a woman in scrubs and a white coat and begins discussing medications.

"You're going to be okay," I say to Bobby through my tears. "You *have* to be okay. I'll be right here. I'm not leaving. I'll be right here when you wake up." Kimberly helps me stand from my wheelchair and I lean forward to give Bobby a kiss on his forehead, my lip shaking and my hands trembling as I cup his face. "I love you," I whisper against his skin. "I love you, Bobby Beckett. Please come back to me."

It takes every bit of control I have to sit back down and move my wheelchair back, allowing Bobby's mother a chance to say goodbye. We're ushered from the room and into the waiting area, and Kimberly's given a phone, which she passes off to me. "They'll call you with updates," a nurse says before disappearing back in the direction of Bobby's room.

Molly jumps up from her chair the second she sees my red nose and tear-streaked face. "What's happening?" she asks, kneeling next to me.

"We have a heart," I say, smiling and crying at the same time. It's an odd feeling, the mixture of complete, overwhelming joy and utter terror, but somehow they coexist within me, making my pulse leap and my stomach twist.

Molly's eyes widen as she sucks in a breath. She grabs my hands, squeezing, her eyes welling with tears.

"Okay. Coffee, I think. Yes?" she asks, fidgeting as she stands to brush off her perfectly clean pants and pull her hair into a ponytail.

I nod, knowing I won't drink it. Just the thought of putting anything in my stomach is enough to make it roll with nausea, but Molly needs to feel useful, and I need a moment. A moment for what, I'm not exactly sure, but suddenly, this room feels too small. Too full of other people and their worries and hopes and grief.

Once Molly clears the doorway, I excuse myself. Kimberly asks if I need help, but I wave her off with a small smile, telling her I'll be right back.

I wheel around the hospital, and for some reason, the movement is therapeutic.

My heart rate slows as I push and glide.

Push, glide.

Push, glide.

A rhythm I force my breaths to match until my pulse has lowered, and I'm lost. The phone in my lap remains silent, and I wonder if Bobby's chest has been opened yet. If they've removed his heart and allowed a machine to take over. If maybe he's dreaming of me, of us. If he's fighting and clawing his way back. If he knows just how dangerous a procedure like this is.

My stomach rolls, and the hallway spins, forcing me to close my eyes. I take several deep breaths. He has to be okay.

Push, glide.

In, out.

Minutes pass. Maybe hours. I've lost all sense of time. It's not until I'm rolling past a familiar doorway that I realize where I am.

Room 824.

Harrison's room.

Except, it's not Harrison I see inside, but a small woman with a mop. The bed is gone, as are the ventilator and IV pole.

There are moments in our lives that will forever stand out like a snapshot.

Events that change our very being, marked by questions we wish we'd never had to ask.

Before I can process the many emotions making my hands shake and my stomach churn—foolishness that I hadn't considered this possibility before, guilt that I begged the universe for a heart for Bobby, gratitude that he's getting another chance at life—I wheel myself inside the room, glancing at the whiteboard where the date and nurse's name are written just below the space for patient's name: Harrison Rouchester.

"Excuse me?" I ask, my voice choked. "The man who was in this room. Do you know where he went?"

The woman cleaning turns, pulling an earbud out of her ear. "I'm sorry?"

I repeat myself, the nausea in my stomach growing with every word.

"I don't get that information. Sometimes it's a room transfer. Sometimes they're discharged," she says, shrugging.

I focus on breathing in and out, on calming my racing heart as I consider what she didn't say.

A third option. The most likely option.

Sometimes the room is empty because the person who'd been occupying it is gone.

I turn around, suddenly wishing I wasn't alone.

That I'd never left Molly's side.

It doesn't mean anything, I tell myself as I push my way out of the hallway and toward the elevators. The donor might not have even been from this hospital. It's far more likely they're not. The surgeon said any heart within a three-hour helicopter ride would be diverted here. Not to mention I don't even know if Harrison is an organ donor.

Was an organ donor.

It's all too coincidental, too overwhelming, so I force the possibilities buzzing through my mind down, burying it deep beneath layers and layers of excuses and reasons it can't be him.

I press the down button on the elevator, desperate to get back to the waiting room. A large group of people make their way down the hall as I wait for the doors to open. A family, it looks like.

A happy one.

I wonder why they're here as I take in their smiles and soft laughs. It's certainly not the death of their abusive ex-fiancé, or the potentially life-saving heart transplant for the love of their life. Maybe the birth of a baby. Or maybe, someone they love was just saved. A small white card flutters to the ground behind them as they turn a corner.

"Hey! You dropped this!" I say, but they're moving too fast, too caught up in their joy to hear me.

The elevator dings, and the door slides open, but I don't enter it. For some reason, my body won't move. Instead, I wheel to the card, picking it up.

A Prayer to St. Jude: Patron saint of lost causes, it reads above a picture of a peaceful-looking man in a white shroud. There's a prayer below it, one I recognize. *St. Jude, I entrust my petitions to you...*

I heard that line a thousand times from Molly's mom's mouth as she sat next to her dying son.

It didn't work for her.

I tuck the card in my pocket, unable to bring myself to throw it away. *Maybe this time*, I think, just as the phone in my lap begins to ring.

NOW

September 2024: Charleston, SC

Will you wait forever by the water's edge
Like Edgar and Annabell Lee?
Or smell a red, red rose and for me yearn
Like Robert beneath spring trees?
Will someone ever crave to kiss my lips
The way the moonbeams kiss the sea?
And through your thoughts, and passions, and delights
Will you count the ways you love me?
—An excerpt from "Poetry," written by Beth Winters, performed by Robert
Beckett

The steady beep of the monitor almost lulls me to sleep. Almost. Except it's been six hours since Bobby was brought from the recovery room, and he still isn't awake. Now that he's no longer sedated, they were able to extubate him, and it brings me comfort to see his chest rising and falling on its own, no ECMO machine in sight.

I squeeze his hand, reassured that his skin feels warmer since surgery, and while I don't know much about the heart, I'm hoping it's because his new one is pumping blood throughout his body efficiently enough to warm even his fingers and toes.

Beep. Beep. Beep. The monitor continues, but it never fades into background noise. It's almost like a poem in and of itself, or maybe a song—melodic and rhythmic and saying so much more than words ever could.

Beep—I'm working.

Beep—I'm beating.

Beep—I'm alive.

Now if he would just wake up.

Bobby's surgeon, Dr. Lasley, clears his throat as he enters the room. He's checked in every hour since surgery, assuring us nothing's wrong and that Bobby's body is just resting. The surgery went perfectly, he'd said. Actually, his exact words were, "If they were to film the perfect heart transplant to show aspiring doctors in medical school, it would be this one."

Dr. Lasley pulls out his flashlight, quickly flashing it in Bobby's eyes before moving on to listen to his heart and lungs. I hold my breath, and I wonder if I'll ever feel normal again, or if I'll always be waiting for the other shoe to drop.

"He sounds great," the doctor says, turning around. "I promise, I have no current concerns. He should wake up any time now."

I exhale slowly, trying to calm my nerves. "Is there a time we should worry? If he doesn't wake up, I mean?"

The doctor jots something down on his notepad, taking a moment to answer. "If he's not awake by tomorrow, I'll be reevaluating why. Otherwise, you're looking at a completely normal part of the recovery process."

I wring my hands in my lap, nodding my head. "Got it. Stop worrying." I say, and Dr. Lasley laughs.

"At least try. He's in good hands." He turns to leave. "I'll be back in another couple hours. Try to get some rest. You're still recovering yourself," he says.

"Dr. Lasley?" I blurt out before he can leave. Every time the doctor has come to check on Bobby, I've tried to work up the courage to ask him about the donor. At the end of the day, it really doesn't matter.

Either way, Harrison is gone, and Bobby has a new heart. Knowing where it came from changes nothing, but not knowing somehow feels *wrong*.

"Yes?" He turns back around, raising his eyebrows.

"I'm sorry. I know you're busy. But I was wondering about the donor," I say.

He holds his hands up. "I'm afraid that's protected health information. I'm not able to divulge any details about the donor, other than they had AB+ blood and were a perfect match for Mr. Beckett."

I press my lips together, my heart sinking. "I see. Thank you," I say, not wanting to hold him up anymore.

I shift in my seat, wondering when Kimberly will be back with our coffees. Neither of us have slept in days, and seeing as I can't propel myself with my hands full, she offered to get them for us. She said she needed caffeine, but really, I think she wanted to give me a moment alone with my thoughts.

With Bobby.

I'd told her the whole story over the past few hours—of who Harrison was and what happened between us. How Bobby became involved.

She'd listened intently, nodding and patting my hand when the tears made it hard to speak. "It's all just fate, Beth. We have so little control over our lives. We can do everything right, and still, everything can end in a second. None of this is your fault. None of it." She'd said as I fell apart, crying until my breaths came in hiccups and my eyes were out of tears.

I snap out of the memory, jumping when the monitor starts to beep a little faster. My heart stutters and my stomach drops. *Something's wrong.*

I reach for the call button, but Bobby's fingers twitch in mine. He groans, and I cry out in relief.

"Bobby? Hey. I'm here," I say, squeezing his hand tight.

Bobby squeezes back, his eyes opening a crack. "Where am I? What—" his hand comes up to his sternum, his fingers weakly tracing the bandage wrapping around his chest.

"You're okay." I gently grab his hand and lower it, worried he'll somehow hurt himself. "There was an accident. But you're okay."

Bobby nods groggily, his eyes finally opening enough for me to look into their deep blue depths, and it almost makes my own heart stop. "You said you'd be here," Bobby says, his voice hoarse. "I heard you. Everything was dark, but I heard you. All I wanted was to get back to you." His eyes trail over my bruises, then fixate on my leg.

"I'm fine," I say before he can work himself up. "I've been discharged already. I just need a little time to heal."

Bobby squeezes my hand, his calloused fingers tracing along my thumb. "Tell me what happened," he asks. So with a deep, steadying breath, I do. I tell him about the accident, about waking up and thinking he was dead, then finding out that it was Harrison who had suffered the head injury. I tell him how he'd coded, and that he'd been almost out of time. By the time I finish, my tears are so thick I can hardly speak at all.

Bobby's quiet for a while, his hand still warm in mine as his thumb continues sweeping against my skin. His voice is raspy when he speaks again. "The heart." He swallows deeply. "It's Harrison's, isn't it?" Bobby asks, his brows coming together and his grip tightening around my fingers.

"I don't know," I whisper, breathless.

Bobby nods as if confirming it. "I saw him. In my dreams. During surgery, or when I was coding, maybe? I don't know." He shakes his head. "I saw him, and then I woke up here."

I can't speak, can hardly breathe.

"He told me he didn't deserve your forgiveness." Bobby looks down at my empty ring finger.

I suck in a sharp breath, goosebumps blooming along my arms. The room suddenly feels warmer, but I shiver.

Was it possible Harrison had actually heard me when I'd said goodbye to him? When I'd forgiven him and told him I hoped he got a second chance?

"Do you have any paper? And something to write with?" Bobby interrupts my thoughts.

"What? You need to write a song? Now?" I ask, my jaw dropping.

He nods. "Just something I don't want to forget," he says, looking around for a way to jot down what's running through his head. I want to tell him to worry about it later. That he needs to rest, but there's an urgency in his eyes that makes me pause.

"Okay, hold on. Let me look." I scramble for my purse, where I find a black pen and a coffee receipt.

"Here," I say, and Bobby gives me a tired smile as he looks at the charges. "Non-fat latte, add lavender." His voice is raspy. "Glad to have you back, Beth."

My heart squeezes as I watch him scribble something on the paper with a weak, messy hand. Tears fill my eyes. He's alive.

"I could say the same to you, Bobby Beckett."

ONE YEAR LATER

2025, New York City, NY

Will you sing along with me,
A second chance melody?
—An excerpt from "Second Chance Melody," written and performed by
Robert Beckett

An usher escorts me to the front row of Madison Square Garden, where an empty seat waits for me. It's completely ridiculous. This is Bobby's first performance since his transplant, and I've told him a hundred times I want to watch from the side stage, but he wouldn't hear of it.

"Your leg might get tired," he'd said again and again, as if I haven't been walking on it for nine months and going to physical therapy three times a week for a good portion of that. I still have a slight limp, but aside from a little soreness at the end of the day, I've made a full recovery.

Today is a big day. Bobby and I closed on an apartment. A penthouse, actually, with views of New York that inspire me to write in ways I never have before. But that's not the only reason it feels so monumental. No—the other reason is that I turned in the final copy of my manuscript this morning.

Mine and Bobby's love story.

Filled with poems inspired by love and loss, of missed time, and finding it again.

While Bobby recovered, I wrote an ending. A clean, uncomplicated one, where Bobby received a stranger's heart, and we lived happily ever after.

It took some time, and a lot of therapy, to finally get to a place where I wanted to replace my fictional ending with what feels like the truth.

We still don't know if Bobby's new heart used to beat in Harrison's chest, and we've made peace with that.

It's one of the many things I've had to make peace with. Getting past the guilt has been an equally hard challenge. There was a time when self-blame followed me like a shadow. Maybe if I hadn't lied to Harrison, he wouldn't have snapped. Maybe if I'd recognized that something was going on at work, or I'd been better at communicating, things would have been different. But I've learned to let that mindset go.

No matter what my mind tries to tell me, I know now that it's not my fault. We all make choices, and they are ours alone to own.

Years ago, Bobby chose to set me free to pursue my dreams. I chose not to go to Europe and study abroad. I chose to ignore all of Bobby's attempts to reach out to me. Harrison chose to try to love me, and then he chose violence.

None of it changes the end result.

We're here.

We're alive.

And as I watch Bobby walk confidently on stage, I've never been more in love.

He looks healthy, vibrant. His blue eyes are bright as they fall directly on me, and my skin heats.

I stand up and cup my mouth with my hands, shouting like his number one fan.

He smiles, but points at me, then the chair, raising his eyebrows. I roll my eyes but oblige him. Just for tonight. We've both been through a lot, and if I'm honest, it's nice to have someone care about me enough to over-worry about my needs.

I sit for the majority of the show, mostly so Bobby will be able to focus on his performance.

Johnny starts playing, and the crowd loses their minds, screaming for so long, he has to loop through the intro to The Application three times before they quiet down enough to let him start singing.

Every moment is magical, but when Bobby sings the last note of "Someone Who Loves You," patting his pocket where my poem still acts as his good luck charm, my heart feels so full, it's like the sun is shining directly into it.

It's not just me wiping away tears. I don't think there's a dry eye in the house. Thanks to the *Rolling Stone* article and the excessive news coverage about the crash, everyone knows the story of Beth and Bobby, and while it's taken some adjusting to get used to the cameras and the tabloids, I think most people are genuinely happy for us.

The house lights come up, and Bobby hands over his guitar. "Thank you, everyone," he says, taking a seat on the stool behind him.

I'm confused, and I strain my neck to peek at the floor where Bobby's set list is taped to the stage. I thought he was going straight into "Roots" next, which is far too up-tempo to sit down to perform, but maybe there was a last-minute change.

"As all of you know," Bobby says, "This has been a difficult year for me. But even though it's had its challenges, it's also been the best year of my life." The crowd cheers, but Bobby holds up his hand to silence them.

"There's someone very special to me here in the audience tonight." A spotlight moves from the stage to where I sit, and I squint against the brightness.

"There was a moment after the accident where I didn't think I'd ever see her again. I don't know if it was God, or a dream, but when I woke up from surgery, there was a lyric that kept running through my head. I even asked Beth to give me something to write it down on from my hospital bed."

Tears fill my eyes, but I don't bother trying to blink them away. Bobby picks his guitar back up. "I had them bring me this once I was cleared to hold it, and I wrote this song in just a few hours. I've been sitting on it all this time, waiting for the right opportunity to share it. And I think tonight is that night."

I feel like I can hardly breathe as Johnny walks out, carrying his guitar and a stool. The arena grows quiet as the rest of the band exits the stage, and all the lights go out except for the spotlights on Bobby and me.

He strums a chord, and the audience goes completely silent.

There's a melody inside my head
It came to me as I roamed
Through the listless dark, your voice called to me
My soul listened, and I came home

It's a melody I've sung before
But it always came out wrong
Now the jumbled notes suddenly make sense
So will you let me sing my song?

Bobby continues to sing, dropping down on one knee, and the crowd explodes in cheers, but I barely hear them. It's just me and Bobby, the boy I fell in love with at eighteen years old. The boy I would have married if he'd asked me in a McDonald's parking lot with a french fry ring.

Will you sing along with me
A second chance melody?
A chance to fix what has been broken
To take a breath and finally
Let the hurt that went unspoken
Fade away into a memory
So God, if you're giving second chances
I'm gonna ask that girl to marry me

Bobby jumps off the stage, kneeling again in front of me and leaning close. "I told myself the day I woke up that if I made it to a year after the transplant, I'd ask you to be my wife. I'm done wasting time. Marry me, Beth."

I nod through my tears, my hands shaking as he slides a ring on my finger—a cushion cut stone on a thin gold band—the same one I found on his bus so many years ago.

"I love you. Forever," he says, pulling me close and kissing me like there aren't thousands of fans watching. He pulls away and presses a scrap of paper into my hands, then stands again to take the stage. Johnny continues to play as Bobby looks back out at the crowd. "There's not going to be an encore tonight, folks. I hope you can understand." The crowd roars as Bobby jumps back up on stage, settling back on his stool to finish the song.

Will you sing along with me,
A second chance melody.
Let me fix what has been broken
I think it's time to finally
Let the hurt that went unspoken
Fade into nothing but a memory
So here's to second chances
And the girl who's gonna marry me

The world associates hearts with love. We buy giant pink boxes filled with chocolates for Valentine's day, or draw little hearts above our signature. People tell you to speak from the heart. And we've all had our hearts broken. But I don't think those things are what love is about at all. Love is in the choices we make every day. In the fragments of ourselves we give away for someone else to keep safe and hold close, and the shiny new pieces we find inside us because of it.

Love is the words we choose to say
It's the poems we write every day

Whether they're intentional or just words strung together
Gone in a moment or immortalized forever
Whether they rhyme
Or not

I've studied them my whole life—the words of those who understood love best of all. But as I look down at the lyrics Bobby wrote on my coffee receipt a year ago, I can't help but think that this just might be my favorite poem of all.

Love fantasy romance? Click HERE to read Megan's Completed Magic of the Wildflowers Trilogy, available on Kindle Unlimited!

Want more of Beth and Bobby and to stay up to date on new releases by Megan Shade? Sign up **HERE** for my newsletter and get an exclusive bonus chapter from Bobby's POV!

ACKNOWLEDGEMENTS

I hope you enjoyed Beth and Bobby's story. Please follow me on socials (@meganshadeauthor of TikTok and Instagram) and sign up for my newsletter **HERE** for updates on new releases, giveaways, and more!

To everyone who read this book, THANK YOU. This project has been so special to me, and has taken up so much of my heart for years, and I feel so grateful you gave it a chance.

As always, my first thank you has to go to my husband, who, even though he can't write a song, is my Bobby Beckett. His unwavering, unconditional support and belief in me is life changing, and it's something every woman deserves.

To my editor, Sara, I love you. You make my work shine and understand what I'm trying to say when I can't figure out how to say it. Thank you for reading and re-reading and re-re-reading—for answering so many questions, for brainstorming, for correcting my frequent misuse of all things grammar, and for your friendship. This book belongs to you as much as me, and without you, Poetry by Dead Men wouldn't be what it is. Book Sara at https://saracoombescom.wordpress.com/.

Most authors say this, but I truly think I have the best friends and beta readers out there. Thank you for reading (and re-reading, and re-re-reading) and giving me your invaluable input. I love and appreciate all of you, and truly and honestly could not have done this without you! In no particular order, Shannon, Taylor, Deborah, Kerry, Tiffany, Katie, Brett, and Anna and Helen (EVERYONE CHECK OUT THEIR BROKEN PROPHECY SERIES **HERE**). Enormous shout out to my friend Janelle for always encouraging me, loving me, and for all the free marketing advice.

Special shout out to Steph, Sam, Kate, and Marissa for reading and just being amazing friends, and for all being characters in this book in one way or another.

I want to specifically thank Hannah Teachout for her help. If you're a querying author and need any assistance with your query letter, pages, or synopsis (among other editing needs), definitely check her out at https://www.hannahmteachout.com/. You unlocked something in me that made this book (and my writing) so much better, and I'm so very grateful!

A big thank you to Sam (Ink and Laurel) for a GORGEOUS cover. Check out her work at inkandlaurel.com.

As always, thank you to Sarah McFarland for your proofreading expertise.

And last but not least, thank you to my family for always supporting me.

DISCUSSION QUESTIONS

1. Throughout the book, Beth struggles with what she wants for herself vs. other's expectations of her. Have you ever been torn between your heart and the opinions of those you love? What did you end up choosing and why?

2. Molly and Beth are sisters just as much as they are friends. Do you think you get to choose your family? Why or why not?

3. Beth's journey is one of tragedy, pain, and heartache, but also of hope, redemption, and self-discovery. If you could only choose one word to describe how her story made you feel, what would it be?

4. Much of the reason Beth is with Harrison is because after losing Bobby, she fell into the life that was expected of her by her parents and society. How much do you think her upbringing factored into staying with Harrison for so long, even after he showed his controlling and violent tendencies?

5. Beth struggles with walking away from an established relationship with Harrison, knowing it would completely upend her life. How did you feel about this? Were you frustrated with her decisions or empathetic toward her situation? Did your view of her change as you read the book?

6. Beth kept secrets from Harrison, not only about her past with Bobby, but also who she really was at her core. Do you think it was wrong of Beth to agree to marry Harrison when she had a past he didn't know about, or do you think we all deserve our secrets?

7. Discuss the title of the book. Did you recognize the meaning after reading the prologue and chapter headers, or were you surprised at the end to find out one of them would not survive?

8. Johnny expresses some frustration toward Beth for cutting him out of her life after her relationship with Bobby ended. Do you think his frustration is justified? Why or why not?

9. Do you think Harrison actually wrote the poems he gave to Beth? Which ones do you think he wrote, and which do you think he stole and/or hired someone to write?

10. Do you think Bobby received Harrison's heart? Why or why not? If so, and you were in Beth's shoes, how would that make you feel? Would you be able to be at peace with it?

11. Bobby wakes up from surgery with a memory of seeing Harrison. Do you think they actually spoke? Harrison stated during their interaction that he didn't deserve Beth's forgiveness. If it really was Harrison, do you think he was genuinely remorseful?

OTHER BOOKS BY MEGAN SHADE

<u>THE MAGIC OF THE WILDFLOWERS TRILOGY:</u>
A WILDFLOWER IN THE WIND
A SUN SCORCHED BLOOM
A PETAL IN THE CROWN

www.ingramcontent.com/pod-product-compliance
Lightning Source LLC
Chambersburg PA
CBHW032342310726
48973CB00007B/1819